Nicola

Second Hearts

by G.J. Walker-Smith

Second Hearts

Print Edition

Cover by Scarlett Rugers, http://scarlettrugers.com

Other Books by G.J. Walker-Smith
Saving Wishes (Book One, The Wishes Series)
Storm Shells (Book Three, The Wishes Series)

Contact the author:
https://www.facebook.com/gjwalkersmith
gjwalkersmith@gmail.com
gjwalkersmith.com

Dedication

For mum, wish you were here.

1. Sober Words

It was shaping up to be a bad day.

We'd been in the tiny south-western African town of Kaimte for almost three months, the longest we'd stayed anywhere since leaving Australia over a year earlier. Kaimte was a haven for backpackers over the summer months. Constant sunny weather and brilliant surf were a huge drawcard. Casual work was easy to find and short-term rental properties were in abundance, thanks mainly to a local landlord called Leroy Van Der Walt. He owned a long row of decrepit old shacks along the beach, affectionately known as the cardboard village. The minuscule rent he charged made them perfect abodes for non-discerning tenants like us.

Mitchell maintained that one big winter storm would be all it took to send the huts toppling like a deck of cards. On days when the wind shifted the loose roof tiles and we could see sunlight bleeding through the cracks in the ceiling, I believed him. Not surprisingly, our plan was to be long gone before winter.

Leroy was a great landlord - unless you owed him money or needed something repaired. It wasn't unusual for residents to pack up and skip town in the middle of the night rather than face him over a couple of hundred dollars in owed rent. Defaulters often came home to find their possessions scattered along the beach in front of their house. He was by far the most intimidating man I'd ever met. And that was partly the reason it was shaping up to be a very bad day.

Our rent was due.

Mitchell and I had secured jobs within days of hitting town. I waitressed at a local café and Mitchell laboured for a local building company. The money wasn't great, but we were managing. Every Friday afternoon Mitchell would walk to Leroy's office in town to deliver the rent. It was a routine that had gone off without a hitch for weeks - until today.

Taking a short cut through an industrial estate didn't work out so well. Mitchell was a big guy, over six feet tall and brawny, but he was powerless against the three men who knocked him to the ground and emptied his pockets. Sore and shaken, he made his way home sporting a nasty cut above his eye.

"I think it needs stitching," I said, working hard to keep the worry out of my voice.

"We don't have money for rent, Charli. We definitely don't have money for a doctor," he grumbled.

Gingerly removing the cloth from his forehead, I held it out to him. I didn't need to speak. Mitchell grabbed my wrist and pulled it back to his face, catching the trickle of blood as it ran down his cheek. "I'll go to Zoe," he said shakily.

We'd met a lot of travellers during our time in Kaimte. Mitchell had fallen head over heels for an English nurse called Zoe. I don't think it was quite love - just major like. She was a female version of him. Blonde, tanned and good looking.

Twenty-four year-old Zoe and her best friend Rose lived a few houses down from ours, at number sixty-three - a curious number considering the shacks totalled eighteen. Maybe the other forty-five had succumbed to the weather or a rampaging Leroy.

By the time we'd made the short trek down the beach to their house, I was exhausted. Mitchell's arm was slung over my shoulder and I did my best to prop him up, but it was hopeless. Woozy and weak, he was dead weight.

Zoe appeared on the balcony as soon as I called her name. "What on earth happened?"

"He was mugged," I explained, staggering to the side as Mitchell did. "I think he needs stitches."

"Oh, dear." She sounded nowhere near as horrified as I thought she should. "I'd better take a look then." She walked out the door a minute later, armed with a small toiletry bag filled with medical supplies. Mitchell sat on the edge of the veranda and she knelt in front of him, humming a tune as she stitched him back together.

"It could have happened anywhere," she reasoned. "I once had my handbag snatched in Knightsbridge. Any place can be rough."

I wasn't used to rough. I was used to Pipers Cove. The only crimes to happen there were crimes against fashion. And as strong and tough as Mitchell was, he was clearly traumatised by the ordeal. His hands were shaking.

"There. All done," Zoe announced, quickly kissing his lips before leaning back to admire her work. Mitchell snaked his arm around her waist and pulled her in close again. That was my cue to leave. He could thank her in private. I needed time alone to think.

Hanging out at our shack wasn't exactly inspiring, so it wasn't something I did often. It was tiny and tragically underfurnished. Our beds, two beanbags and an old tea chest were just about all we had, and unless I could come up with a way of paying the rent, we were about to lose it all.

Daylight had long since faded by the time Mitchell arrived home. He looked a mess. A jagged line of sharp black sutures ran horizontally across his brow, and in the few hours since I'd seen him his eye had blackened.

He smiled. "No real harm done, Charli."

"It doesn't look that way."

He flopped down beside me on the beanbag, pushing me aside. "What are you doing?"

I shoved back with all my might, and didn't shift him an inch. "Trying to work out how we're going to make up the rent."

"What did you come up with?"

"I think we should move on," I suggested. "We can fly north to Dakar and go just about anywhere from there."

He half-frowned, then brought his hand to his head. The expression must have hurt. "I like it here. I thought you did too. What happened to our plan of staying until the end of summer?"

"I want to leave, Mitch."

"Look, if it's about the rent –"

I shook my head. "It's not about the rent. Didn't today frighten you?"

Mitchell drew in a deep breath, exhaling slowly. "I'm sure it was a one-off. I shouldn't have been anywhere near that area."

"What if I had been with you?"

"I would never have taken you down there," he scoffed.

I changed tack, trying to talk him around. "We've been here a long time. There are other places to see."

Levering himself off the beanbag, he reached for my hand, pulling me to my feet. "I like it here, Charli."

I had no right to argue with him. Mitchell had made so many concessions for me over the past year that pushing the issue would have been criminal.

Whether I liked it or not, our partnership was never going to be equal. Throughout our trip he had protected me, watched out for me and sometimes carried me, never once complaining. I don't know what I did for him, other than provide company. And judging by the string of broken romances he'd left along the way, companionship was not something Mitchell Tate ever lacked.

We never argued. It wasn't something he was good at. When we disagreed, he'd walk away before I had a chance to kick up. He didn't respond to being given the silent treatment, either. If anything, he seemed to enjoy it. That meant I had no choice but to let the subject drop – for now.

It took three days for Kaimte's very own dictator to catch up with us. Leroy was sitting on our porch when we arrived home from our morning surf. We'd had fair warning that he was there. His paisley shirt could be seen half a mile down the beach.

The aging man with wiry long grey hair walked with a wooden cane. It was an unnecessary prop. There was nothing frail about him. It was more likely a big walloping stick for his delinquent tenants.

I approached the shack with my arm hooked tightly around Mitchell's.

"I'll deal with it," he promised, leaning down to whisper the words. I nodded stiffly.

"I've been waiting for you two," roared Leroy, levering himself off the deckchair with his cane.

"We just need a few more days," explained Mitchell.

"Impossible!" he boomed, smashing the cane down on the concrete floor. "You're out!"

"We just need a couple more days, Leroy," pleaded Mitchell.

Pointing his cane, Leroy stared straight at me, narrowing his already beady eyes. My grip on Mitchell's hand tightened.

"I've been more than patient with you two. You have twenty-four hours."

It didn't sound like much but coming from Leroy, it was a remarkably generous gesture.

"We'll have it for you tomorrow," promised Mitchell, relieved.

I said absolutely nothing during the exchange. Leroy hung around much longer than necessary, raving about how irresponsible we were, occasionally whacking his cane on the floor for effect. By the time he left, I was a wreck.

I followed Mitchell into the house and paced around the small room, trying to calm myself. Mitchell didn't look anxious at all. He flopped on the beanbag, leaned back and closed his eyes. I hoped he was hatching a plan and not sleeping.

"What are we going to do?"

"We're going to pay him," he replied flatly.

"With what? Good intentions?"

He opened his eyes, tilted his head and grinned craftily. "Since when have I been full of good intentions? We'll just have to dip into the travel money."

His lax solution infuriated me. Keeping money aside for plane tickets was the most sensible thing we'd done. Neither of us had saved a cent during our time in Kaimte, so our travel kitty was the only hope we had of being able to move on.

"If we use that money, we'll never save it up again. We're never going to get out of here."

"Charli, have I ever let you down?" I glared at him and he laughed. "Okay, let me rephrase my question. Have I ever let you down since we left home?"

"No," I mumbled.

"So trust me."

I trusted Mitchell implicitly, but that was beside the point. My desire to leave was growing stronger. Unfortunately, he didn't feel the same way.

"I'm not going to be able to talk you around, am I?"

"I like it here, Charli," he repeated for the umpteenth time. "I just want to see the summer out."

I shook my head, defeated. I walked out of the room giving him the false impression that the subject was closed.

I was less than thrilled with the idea of using our travel money to pay the back rent, but we had no choice. Mitchell retrieved it from our hiding spot under the floorboards in my bedroom and took it to Leroy the next day. We were square. The monkey was off our back. I took every extra shift at work that was going over the next week, to build up our savings again. Being a grown up was beginning to suck.

Free time was usually spent at the beach or hanging out with our friends. Any precious free time I had lately was spent sleeping, which is why seeing a group of people partying on the beach in front of our shack when I got home made me groan out loud.

"Charli!" Mitchell called, rushing toward me. He lifted me off my feet as he hugged me much too tightly. "I'm glad you're home."

I wondered if that was because his party was already out of hand and he needed me to tell them all off and send them home. It had happened before.

"Why are we having a party, Mitch?"

He slung his arm around my shoulder. "I only invited Zoe and Rose for a few drinks, but you know how word travels."

He wasn't kidding. All our fellow cardboard villagers seemed to be there. A huge bonfire roared. The sun was setting, slipping behind the line where the ocean met the sky. The air was still and warm. It was the perfect night for a party.

Rose and Zoe sat on the front step talking to Melito and Vincent. Mitchell had nicknamed them the sleek Greeks because of their Casanova-type personalities. They lived in the shack next to ours and were forever bringing us trays of pastries and other homemade treats. "From our motherland," Melito would proudly announce. Mitchell would tease me, insisting it was their way of wooing me. Mitchell was missing the bigger picture. I was certain that middle-aged sleek Greeks had eyes only for each other. The residents of number four were a Lebanese couple, Rashid and Sabah. Their English was poor, so conversing with them was difficult. Our friendship was based purely on smiles and hand gestures. Bernie and William, two twenty-something Brits taking a year long sabbatical from their jobs in advertising, found their way to Kaimte after reading a travel brochure at a bus stop in Tanzania. Our new friends were the most eclectic bunch of people imaginable.

It was Vincent who called to me first, raising his glass in my direction and speaking loudly. "Welcome, Charli!"

Before I'd even stepped up on to the porch, I had a glass of cheap wine in one hand and a plate of food in the other.

The last of our guests left at three in the morning, relocating to Melito and Vincent's shack, lured there by the promise of ouzo and Greek pastries. I collared Mitchell at the door. The last thing he needed was more alcohol. "Stay here with me."

I tugged on his shirt and he staggered back as if I'd tripped him. It was impossible to think I could save him if he'd fallen. I stepped aside to stop him squashing me on the way down. He remained upright by leaning against the wall. "You're my best friend," he slurred.

"You're my best friend too."

"Leaving the Cove was a good decision. We have fun, don't we?"

Mitchell was very reflective when soused. It made a nice change. He wasn't renowned for deep conversation when sober.

"We do. Are you ready for bed?"

"That wouldn't be a good idea for three reasons," he said, holding four fingers in the air.

"What reasons?"

"One, I'm scared of your dad." He took a heavy step toward me. "And two, I'm very afraid of your dad."

I had to laugh. Alex was scary where Mitchell was concerned, even from half a world away.

My dad Alex and his girlfriend Gabrielle had packed up and left Pipers Cove a couple of months after us, arriving in Marseille in time to spend Christmas with her family. That was supposed to be their happy ever after. But the best laid plans of mice and men often go awry. Through no fault of Alex's, they were back in Pipers Cove six weeks later, in time for Gabrielle to resume her teaching position at beginning of the school term. She had got homesick, and small town gossip and her little cottage on the cliff trumped Marseillaise castles and baguettes. I doubt Alex tried hard to talk her out of returning to the Cove, nor would he have needed to. He was never thrilled about leaving in the first place. He was, however, still thrilled by anything to do with the Parisienne.

Mitchell took another step forward, so unsteadily that it couldn't possibly have been intentional. Both of my arms shot out. Luckily, he managed to steady himself.

"What's the third reason?" I asked.

Mitchell turned and staggered toward the beanbag. He fell into it so hard that I was worried it might explode. "The third reason doesn't matter. Reasons one and two cancel out the need for reason three."

"Tell me reason three," I demanded.

He looked at me through lazy eyes, probably seeing little more than a blurred form in front of him. "Reason number three. Never sleep with a girl who's in love with someone else."

"Yeah, okay. You got me. I'm madly in love with Vincent."

He groaned. "I'm not an idiot, Charli. It's written all over your face… and your diary. You still love Adam, and no matter how far away you go it's not far enough."

"You read my journal?" I was appalled and embarrassed. It was the first diary I'd ever kept. I'd always maintained that pouring your heart out via pen and paper was asking for trouble, and Mitchell's snooping confirmed it. My journal had nothing to do with documenting our trip or my day-to-day life, that was taken care of by the thousands of pictures I'd taken. I wrote about things that were too hard to explain, and too private to tell anyone. Mainly, I wrote about him.

Even in my head, I referred to Adam as *him*.

I had travelled thousands of miles from home but hadn't moved an inch. A year apart had changed nothing. I loved him. I had always loved him. And my decision to end our relationship had grown into the most painful regret of my life.

"I didn't mean to read it," he said, unconvincingly. "I didn't even know you kept a diary."

"You weren't supposed to know," I barked. "It was private."

"I read the whole thing. Every word."

"Ugh! Shut up!"

"It was actually pretty good. March was pretty dull but it picked up again in April."

"Shut up, Mitchell!"

I wanted to clout him but it wouldn't have been a fair fight. He was clearly disadvantaged by the alcohol he'd consumed. It was acting as a truth serum and it also seemed to make him keep talking. "You should find a better hiding spot if you don't want me to read it." He shifted to the side, producing my journal from under the beanbag. "Ta-daa!"

I snatched it. "There's something seriously wrong with you."

"I know," he agreed. "But there's nothing wrong with you."

I shook my head, scowling. "What are you talking about?"

He made a half-hearted swipe for the book, but was too uncoordinated to take it from me. "I read it. Have you ever read what you've written? If you did, you'd see that there's nothing wrong with you. You're just scared. You were scared when we left home and you're scared now."

He'd hit my rawest nerve, dead on. "And you're drunk."

"Of course I'm drunk. Do you think we'd be having this conversation otherwise? Get brave, Charli. Toughen up and go after what you want."

Within days of leaving Australia I'd made my decision. I planned to spend a few weeks travelling with Mitchell before jumping on a plane to New York.

But time was my enemy.

After three amazing weeks of surfing in Mauritius we found our way to Madagascar. By the time we arrived in Johannesburg six weeks after that I was second-guessing my decision. What if Adam had moved on? What if he'd met someone else? Or worse, what if he'd forgotten all about me? The longer I spent without him, the more I'd convinced myself that Adam Décarie was doing just fine without me.

Writing down my fears had preserved my sanity. I was on the trip of a lifetime, visiting some of the most beautiful places on earth, and yet I couldn't shake the hopelessness of being completely in love with a boy I'd known for only two months – a very long time ago.

"It's not that simple," I mumbled.

The beans crunched beneath him as he struggled to lean forward. Grabbing his hand, I helped him to his feet. Once upright he fell forward, pushing me backwards. I lay flat on the floor, struggling under his weight.

"It's totally simple," he said, ignoring the fact that I was gasping for breath beneath him. "What's the worst that could happen?"

Answering him required air in my lungs. With both hands on his chest, I managed to heave him off. "What if I go all the way to New York and he doesn't want me?"

"Then you put it to bed. But at least you'll know you've given it your best shot."

I turned my head to look at him, marvelling at the fact that Mitchell Tate managed to become smarter when intoxicated. "What would you do without me?"

"I'd manage. I've matured a lot lately," he insisted. A huge burst of laughter escaped me but his tone remained serious. "It's been a long time since I did anything dumb like try to cook popcorn in a frying pan."

"Mitch, that was just a week ago," I reminded him, between giggles.

He reached across for my hand. "I'd be fine, Charli. And you would be too."

***

I dragged myself out of bed at ten the next morning. Mitchell was already up, sitting on the front veranda soaking up the morning sun and eating something that looked like one of Melito's filo pastry creations from the night before.

"Is your stomach made of cast iron?" I asked, appalled. He turned to face me, grinned and stuffed the whole thing in his mouth.

We sat on the raised veranda, dangling our legs over the edge and gazing at the uninterrupted view of the ocean ahead. The veranda was the only redeeming feature of the shack. Some days, when the ocean was a millpond and we weren't working, we'd waste the entire morning out there.

"You just missed Bernie and Will," he said. "They were on their way home from the sleek Greeks. It turns out that the party got a whole lot rowdier once we left."

"What did they have to say for themselves?"

He shrugged. "Not much. They said they're thinking of heading up the coast next weekend. I wouldn't mind a weekend up north. Too bad we're broke and trapped like rats."

He bumped my shoulder and I looked across at him. I couldn't help smiling at his goofy expression. Mitchell was back to being carefree, content and sober. Nothing fazed him – not even the prospect of being a broke, trapped, rat.

That's where we differed. I was beginning to feel as though I was failing, and it was starting to weigh me down. The whole purpose of this journey was to find my place in the world. We'd travelled thousands of miles. How far was I supposed to go, for crying out loud?

I had to consider that I'd been wrong all along. What if happiness wasn't a place? What if it was enough just to be with the person who made you happy? Surely then I'd be content wherever I was – even if it was New York City.

I looked at the bigger picture. There was a possibility that I had thrown away the best love I would ever know. And going through the daily grind of surfing, working and sleeping was doing nothing to get it back.

"Mitch, do you remember our conversation last night?"

A smile crept across his face. "Refresh my memory."

I rolled my eyes. "We talked about me going to New York. I think I'm going to do it."

"It's about time," he teased. "I was beginning to think I'd be stuck with you forever."

I nudged his shoulder, faking annoyance. "Don't get too excited. It's going to take months to save up."

"Why don't you just call Alex? He'd send you money if you needed it."

The mere suggestion bordered on lunacy. As far as Alex knew, I was comfortably living on the proceeds from the sale of Adam's boat. If he ever got wind that we were broke he'd have a coronary.

"I'm going to work it out for myself."

"I'll find extra work, Charli. I'll do what I can."

"You don't need to do that. I only need one thing from you."

"Name it."

"Don't let me talk myself out of going. No matter how long it takes."

Mitchell slung an arm around my shoulders. "You got it, sister."

2. Crazy Brave

The midweek markets in Kaimte had to be seen to be believed: vendors selling everything from local crafts to fresh fish and vegetables crowded into a row of tin humpies lining the main street. I loved the atmosphere.

I roped Zoe and Rose into coming with me. I usually went with Mitchell, but true to his word he'd found extra work that week, labouring for a landscaper.

"It's so grotty," whispered Zoe, much too loudly.

Rose shushed her, grabbed her elbow and quickened her pace.

"It's all really fresh," I told her.

"Of course it is," she agreed. "It's all still covered in dirt."

Zoe was a mixed bag. I'd always suspected that backpacking was more Rose's bliss than hers. She was a girly girl who liked her creature comforts far too much to be completely content living in the cardboard village. On the other hand, carrying out a torrid affair with a beach bum surfer like Mitchell showed that she wasn't totally averse to slumming it once in a while.

Mitchell's attraction to Zoe was much easier to define. She was part Beautiful, just like his sisters. She was prissy, although her penchant for tiny bikinis and matching sarongs bordered on trashy. But Zoe would never graduate to full Beautiful status. She was far too smart and too kind-hearted, even if scrubbing dirt off vegetables was beneath her.

"Can we sit for a while? It's hot," she complained.

I looked around, trying to see somewhere suitable to dump her for a few minutes while I finished browsing.

"There," suggested Rose, pointing to a small shed over the road. The makeshift café only traded on market days. Patrons sat outside on dirty plastic chairs, drinking lukewarm cans of Coke.

"Will you be okay here for a minute?" I asked hopefully. "I just want to check out the stalls over there." I pointed further down the street, but she paid no attention.

"We'll wait here for you," promised Rose.

I had walked only a few metres before the crowd swamped me. I couldn't even see the café when I turned around. All I could do was keep pace with the flow of traffic. Some days I hated being short. I walked for a few minutes, seeing nothing but people's backs before finally breaking off to the side. I had no idea where I was. I didn't seem to be in the markets anymore. The buildings were permanent structures but still ramshackle and dilapidated.

To my left was a fabric store, overflowing with bolts of brightly coloured cloth. A heavyset African woman stood in the doorway calling me inside with a flick of her head. "Come and see, little girl," she coaxed.

"No, thank you."

I began walking again but got no further than the shop next door. A man tugged my backpack as I passed his doorway, yanking me inside. "Little girl," he purred. "Come inside."

It was hardly an invitation. I was already inside. The relative safety of the road might have been miles away.

To regain control, I turned around, pretending to browse. Crooked wooden shelves lined the corrugated tin walls, displaying dodgy-looking electrical items and bric-a-brac. The man followed closely behind me as I walked, but he wasn't the scariest one in the shop. Another two men sat near the back wall, leering at me.

Playing it cool was not an option. I was terrified. No one knew where I was. *I* didn't even know where I was.

"You have a nice shop," I complimented shakily.

He looked past me to the other men, speaking in a language I didn't understand. Unnervingly, they all laughed.

I didn't dare look at the thugs behind me. All my attention was on the one blocking my exit.

"Find what you like," he instructed. "We buy and we sell."

I nodded, unable to swallow the lump in my throat so I could speak.

They weren't typical villagers. Their clothes were western style. The ringleader wore jeans and a long-sleeved shirt – totally inappropriate, considering the hot weather. Around his neck was the thickest gold chain I'd ever seen. The necklace looked authentic, but the huge kitschy gold Rolex he wore looked like a prize out of a gumball machine.

"We have phones. Do you need a phone?" he asked.

His question reminded me that my phone was in my bag – albeit useless. Who was I going to call? Mitchell's phone had been stolen during the mugging. I could call Alex. If he hurried, he could catch the next flight out and come to my rescue in about three days.

Quickly, I hatched a plan. Mitchell needed a phone. I'd buy one, thank the scary men, and hopefully be on my way in one piece.

"I will buy a phone," I told him, trying to sound strong.

Rolex man clicked his fingers twice. "Get the box," he ordered. I heard the goons behind me shuffle to their feet.

Please don't let it be a Charli size box, I prayed.

I contemplated making a run for the bright light of the outside street but wasn't sure I'd make it out before he grabbed me again. When he called me over to the counter, I went.

The smaller of the henchmen upended a cardboard box on the counter sending at least fifty phones tumbling in all directions.

"I'll give you a good price," he assured. "Choose one."

They all looked the same to me – with one exception. Mitchell's phone had a distinctive bright orange cover, just like one of the phones in front of me.

I picked it up, moving quickly to hide the fact that my hand was shaking.

"I like this one."

"A very good choice," praised Rolex man. "It's only just come in."

I was certain it was Mitchell's phone. My potential murderers were also thieves. Fear quickly gave way to anger. Standing in front of me were the men who'd knocked the stuffing out of Mitchell and left him bleeding in an alley. Convinced that my fate would soon be the same (or worse) I realised I had nothing to lose. "I have something to sell," I announced, shrugging my off my backpack.

The men watched silently as I took out my camera and unscrewed the lens. If there was a chance I might live to continue my trip, I didn't want to do it without my beloved camera. Parting with one lens was bearable.

Rolex man studied it closely. "This is no good without the camera. I will take both."

I shook my head. "No. Just the lens."

"No." He handed it back to me.

I actually felt deflated. For a second, I'd been hopeful of solving all of our money problems. I saw no point in haggling with him. He was calling the shots and I'd just revealed all my cards. The thieving would-be murderers now knew I had a valuable camera in my possession.

"What else do you have?"

I tried to think quickly but came up blank.

"The stone," he said, pointing to my necklace.

I brought my hand to my throat, clutching my black opal pendant.

"No." My rough tone made them laugh.

"Black opal is rare and valuable," said Rolex man, amazing me with his knowledge of gemmology. "Give it to me."

I wanted to put up a good fight. He was probably about to rip it off my neck at any second anyway. "I want five thousand for it. U.S. dollars," I declared.

A huge grin swept his face and I could hear the other men snickering. "You are a very funny girl." Funny was good. Funny meant they might not kill me.

"Five thousand," I repeated.

Rolex man paced around, rubbing his chin while he deliberated. "I will give you three thousand."

It was actually a pretty fair offer - much less than what it was worth but not altogether unreasonable. I had to consider it. Three thousand dollars was a ticket to New York and back again if I needed it. I tried to focus more on the bigger picture and less on the heartbreak of parting with the opal Adam had gifted me.

"Fine. Three thousand… and the orange phone," I agreed. "And I want U.S. dollars."

"I do not keep that amount of money here. There are many thieves around." I almost laughed out loud but thought better of it. "I will have to go and get it."

"I'll wait." I truly was an idiot.

More than an hour and a half passed before Rolex man returned. I had no choice but to wait for him. I got the distinct feeling I wasn't free to leave. He strolled in as if he'd been gone only minutes and dropped a tattered manila envelope down on the counter in front of me. "Count it," he instructed.

I thumbed through the notes, counting silently in my head. I was glad I counted silently. Unbelievably, there was an extra four hundred dollars in the pile.

"Three thousand dollars, right?" I asked, confused.

"That is what we agreed."

I quickly tucked the envelope under my arm, hoping that the smugness wasn't evident in my expression. With a heavy heart, I undid the clasp on my necklace and handed it to Rolex man.

"Come back any time," he said, focusing all his attention on the necklace in his hand.

I didn't bother answering. I turned and walked as fast as I could, straight out into the safety of the crowded street. It had been almost two hours since I'd left Rose and Zoe at the café. Knowing they'd be long gone, I began walking home, oblivious to how frantic Mitchell would be.

"Where the hell have you been?" he yelled, running down the beach toward me. "The girls said they lost you. I've been looking everywhere."

I stopped dead in my tracks, bracing myself as he threw his arms around me. It wasn't a tight hug, just badly executed. Perhaps he forgot that he was a foot taller than me and that's why he hugged my head.

He looked me up and down, inspecting for damage.

"I'm fine," I insisted.

"Where have you been?"

I was excited to tell him. Doing business with gangsters wasn't an every day event for me. Mitchell didn't seem to share my enthusiasm, but to his credit, he let me finish the tale before berating me. "You sold your necklace to thugs? Are you out of your freaking mind?"

"You're the one who told me to get brave."

He wrinkled his nose at the reminder of his drunken remark. "You weren't meant to take it so literally! What if something had happened to you? Imagine that phone call to Alex." He groaned in absolute disgust.

"I'm sorry."

"I'm done. Don't talk to me." He quickened his pace, knowing there was no way I could keep up with his long strides.

Mitchell didn't go home. He trudged through the sand to Zoe and Rose's hut, disappearing through the front door as soon as it opened. I didn't really care. I was still flying high, exhilarated by my rare rush of courage. The feeling remained long after I arrived home. I sat on the floor, counting out the hundred dollar bills and stacking them in a neat pile, elated to confirm there was indeed an extra four hundred dollars in my bounty.

I, Charli Blake, had successfully crossed into the big leagues. I'd ripped off my very first gangsters.

The money was safely tucked away under the loose floorboard when Mitchell arrived home. He thumped down beside me on the beanbag, throwing me aside like a rag doll. I waited for him to speak first, unsure if he was still angry.

"I'm sorry I yelled at you. You deserved it but I'm sorry. I'm not your keeper. It's not my job to look after you." His speech was obviously well rehearsed. He spoke slowly and precisely.

"But you do look after me. I would never have made it this far without you. Today turned out to be good for me. It's my turn to look after you."

Mitchell tilted his head, staring at me like I was crazy. "How do you figure that?"

I reached in to my bra, retrieved his orange phone and held it out to him.

"I think this belongs to you."

He snatched it from me, shaking his head in disbelief. The colour literally drained from his face. He realised what I already knew. I'd spent the afternoon in the company of the men who put six stitches in his forehead.

"Did you see what they did to me to get this phone?" he asked, gritting his teeth. "If they'd cut you up in to tiny little pieces and chucked you in a dumpster, you would have deserved it. And you think today was a good day for you?"

Seeing Mitchell angry was completely foreign territory. I had no idea how to handle him. "The end justified the means, Mitch. I've got enough money to go to New York now."

He wasn't the least bit impressed by my sketchy reasoning. "You're never going to see sense, are you? I can't let you go off on your own, Charli. It's not going to end well."

"You can't stop me." I regretted the childish comment instantly. I'd just made him more furious.

Mitchell quickly stood. "I don't want to stop you. It's not up to me to stop you. You get yourself in to the worst scrapes purely because you don't think." He tapped his temple with his index finger. "How much thought have you put in to your trip to New York?"

"Enough," I uttered.

"Great. So you've contacted Adam to tell him you're on your way."

"No," I admitted. But where was the romance in that?

Mitchell leaned down close. "You know why you haven't called him, Charli?" He didn't pause long enough to let me answer. "Because you're winging it, just like you always do. Leaving things up to the universe isn't always going to work in your favour."

I didn't feel as though there was an alternative. If I put any real thought into it, I'd talk myself out of going. I desperately wanted Adam back in my life. I craved the happy ending I'd been dreaming of for over a year. But in the back of my mind was one constant thought: he might not want me any more. No amount of planning would prepare me for that. I had no choice but to throw it out to the universe. Whatever would be would be.

It was that philosophy that got me through my encounter with Rolex man and his henchmen. Explaining to Mitchell was impossible. I saw no point even trying. "I think we should agree to disagree."

"Fine, crazy weirdo."

I'd heard him call his sisters a mountain of names far worse than that. Crazy weirdo I could live with.

3. Lessons

New York in November was not a place I wanted to be without winter clothing. There wasn't much call for winter coats in Kaimte – or anywhere else we'd been in the past year. One phone call to Gabrielle solved that problem, and another one I hadn't even considered.

Within days of speaking to her, Mitchell and I borrowed Melito's jeep and drove down to the parcel depot at the small airport. Waiting for me was a huge suitcase filled with enough winter clothes to see me through several New York winters.

"She was supposed to just pack up my stuff," I grumbled, pawing through the mass of clothes on the floor in front of me.

"Beggars can't be choosers, Charli," teased Mitchell, pulling on a very chic grey wool cap.

I didn't recognise a single item. I couldn't even consider them hand-me-downs. Everything was brand new, including the shiny brass key that tumbled out of an envelope I'd just found.

Mitchell waited until I'd read through the accompanying letter before asking me what it was for.

"This," I said, waving the key in front of him, "is a key to an apartment Gabrielle owns in Manhattan."

Of course the Parisienne owned real estate in New York. Nothing about the idea was shocking to me.

"You really do have a way of falling on your feet, don't you?" he asked, donning a scarf that matched his hat.

"I have connections," I replied, snatching the hat off his head. It was almost embarrassing. I was hardly able to claim independence when I'd been gifted a roof over my head and a complete new wardrobe to boot.

"Can I ask you a question?" Mitchell's tone matched his suddenly serious expression.

"Sure."

"What are you going to do if it doesn't work out with Adam? A lot can change in a year."

I paused only momentarily. "I'll be sad."

Truthfully, I'd be devastated. I'd probably just curl up and let the despair have me. At least I'd look good, courtesy of my new designer wardrobe. But all Mitchell needed to know was that I had enough smarts about me to be able to survive. Alex had demanded the same reassurance. He'd never understood my need to have Adam in my life. Needing him was never a term he was comfortable with.

"He might not feel the same way, Charli," he'd said gently.

When it came down to it, it didn't matter. I wanted to see his face – even if it was to be for the last time. I had thought of nothing past that point.

Once all loose ends had been tied, there was no point in staying in Kaimte any longer. Letting go of Mitchell was going to be hard, so I drew it out as long as I could. We made a weekend of it, borrowing Melito's jeep again and driving south to Cape Town. Two days passed quickly and before I knew it, we were saying our goodbyes at the airport.

"If it doesn't work out, you come back," he instructed.

"I will."

Excitement bubbled within me, preventing me from standing still. Mitchell grabbed my hand to keep me stationary while he rattled off his list of rules. "Don't let anyone near your bag, make sure you keep some money in your pocket, call me as soon as you get there and don't forget to wind your clock back."

"Anything else?"

"Yes." He released my hand and slung his arm around my shoulder. "Don't talk to strangers."

"Mitch, everyone will be a stranger."

"Okay, don't talk to strange-looking strangers," he amended.

There were a million things I wanted to tell him, none of which I could articulate well enough.

Mitchell Tate had saved me. At the lowest of the low, after my best friend Nicole had betrayed and deserted me, he'd picked me up and dusted me off. We hadn't spent longer than a few hours apart in over a year. Mitchell had never needed me. I, however, wouldn't have survived the first week away from home without him.

There was something very cathartic about leaving him behind. Mitchell was free to make his own way without having to worry about me.

He wouldn't have to worry about the rent for a while either. I'd used some of my gangster loot to pay his rent up until the end of summer. It's not something he would have approved of, so I held off telling him until the last minute.

"You're going to need that money," he scolded.

"You can't miss what you don't have."

"I know for a fact that's not true. I'm going to miss you, crazy weirdo." He grabbed my face in his hands and kissed me hard on the lips. "Now go. You've got a plane to catch."

I fought against turning back to look at him as I made my way through to the departure lounge. The only way from here was forward.

***

The long flights and brutal change in climate were exhausting. By the time I'd cleared customs, collected my luggage, and hailed a cab, I was dead on my feet. I slept through most of the taxi ride, waking only when the driver whistled to rouse me. "This is the place."

I staggered toward the front door of the building, dragging my mammoth suitcase behind me. I paused when I got there, fearing the cab driver had misunderstood the handwritten address I'd thrust at him when I got in his taxi. I looked up at the red brick building in front of me. It looked to be about ten stories tall and had a canopied entrance. *It must be a hotel,* I thought, unable to fathom the idea of anyone living there permanently.

The doorman greeted me at the door, granting me the widest smile I'd ever seen. "Good morning, Miss." His cheeriness was a little unnerving considering I'd been functioning for nearly twenty-four hours without sleep.

"Hi there." I smiled. "I wonder if you could help me."

"I'll do what I can."

I handed him the scrap piece of paper I'd jotted the address on.

"You're here, Miss," he said.

I glanced around the foyer. The taupe marble floor was so shiny that I wanted to take my shoes off and skate across it in my socks. The mere fact that I considered it suggested I didn't belong there.

"My name is Charli," I told him.

The doorman tilted his head and tipped his black hat with his white gloved hand. "It's a pleasure to meet you, Miss Charli. My name is Marvin."

Something told me Marvin wasn't as prim and proper as his job commanded him to be. There was warmth in his dark brown eyes that I found comforting.

"Can I call you Marv?" I asked, cheekily.

He chuckled. "All of my friends do."

"How long have you worked here, Marv?"

He rocked back on his heels, flicking his wide lapels proudly. "Fifteen years now, Miss Charli."

"Do you remember Gabrielle Décarie? She used to live here."

"Indeed," he replied. "Miss Gabrielle hasn't been here in some time, though."

I rushed through my story quickly, explaining that I would be squatting in her apartment for a while.

"It will be a pleasure having you here," he said kindly.

I felt relieved. A friendly face was exactly what I needed on my first day in a strange city. Marvin fit the bill perfectly.

***

Gabrielle's apartment was on the eighth floor. I stepped out of the elevator into a small foyer that housed a sofa that didn't look like it had ever been sat on. Twisting my key in the lock of the door, I bumped it open with my shoulder and dragged my luggage inside.

The picture I'd built in my head of what the apartment would look like was spot on. It had big windows, hardwood floors throughout, white walls and high ceilings. The granite kitchen looked brand new, and the bathroom was more luxurious than any hotel I'd stayed in. Gabrielle had warned me that it was unfurnished, but I couldn't have cared less. I was more than used to making do with whatever I had.

The only stick of furniture was in the bedroom, a huge bed that looked as new as the kitchen. I tore the plastic cover off the mattress, lay down and slept like a baby for the next fifteen hours.

Marvin quickly became my go-to man. I wouldn't have survived the first few days without him.

My very tight budget didn't quite match the part of town I lived in, and even without mentioning it Marvin seemed to know. He'd overheard me in the lobby asking one of my neighbours, Oliver, for directions to a local supermarket. Oliver's recommendation was a gourmet deli on the corner. "It's called Hammerstein's Gourmet," he announced in his trademark camp tone. "They do fabulous antipasto platters. You must check it out. Such wonderful produce."

"Miss Charli," whispered Marvin, stopping me at the door.

"Yes?"

"Tell me what you're looking for." His broad grin was contagious.

"Bread, milk and tea," I replied. "Nothing too fancy."

He took a small notebook out of his pocket and drew me a very basic map. "Everything you need is here."

I looked at the page in my hand, studying the directions to Easybeats grocery store. "You're a lifesaver, Marv."

For some reason, Marvin read me perfectly. Charli Blake was definitely more Easybeats than Hammerstein's.

***

Marvin sketched me quite a few maps over the next couple of days. With his help, I managed to navigate my way around a little bit of my new city. So far I loved New York, which left me wondering what might have been if I'd been courageous enough to stick to my original plan of following Adam a year ago.

On day four, I pulled Marvin aside and asked him for directions to the most important address of all; the Décaries' building. It wasn't until I saw the map that I realised it was just a half hour walk away.

I had to strike while the iron was hot and before I lost my nerve. Braving the bleak winter chill, I said goodbye to Marvin and headed off to reclaim my bliss. I had no idea how to follow through with my heart's desire. I had no clue what I'd say to him. What if Adam told me to go away? Or worse, what if he stared at me blankly and asked me who I was? Being forgotten would be worse than being rejected.

Adam's building was even grander than the one I was staying in. Each floor boasted a curved wrought iron balcony and huge black framed arched windows. There was a grace about the stately old building that Gabrielle's didn't have. My posture seemed to straighten just because I was standing near it.

I mulled over my choices. I could approach the doorman and ask to be let in. He'd call upstairs and tell Adam that Charli Blake was there to see him. My heart started to race as I played out the conversation in my head.

"Charli, who?" Adam would say.

"Charlotte, tell him it's Charlotte," I'd plead.

The doorman would push me out the door, shaking his head. "I'm sorry. He says he doesn't know you."

I shuddered, warding off the make-believe rebuff.

Taking a step back, I looked up at the tall building and considered option two. I could just wait for him to come out. It was only eight in the morning. Sooner or later he'd have to appear. That plan unravelled quickly too.

The Décaries' doorman looked seriously hardcore. Perhaps he knew how ridiculous he looked in the military-style hat with coordinating gold trim.

I crossed the street to get out of his view, feeling a little foolish. I was completely alone in one of the biggest cities in the world, hinging my entire happiness on a boy who'd possibly changed his mind about me long ago. I decided to stay put anyway and was rewarded early. Adam walked out the door after just a few minutes.

I stood blatantly staring at him. If he'd glanced up for even a second, the jig would've been up. But he didn't, giving me ample opportunity to ogle him some more.

Adam Décarie remained perfect. He was still insanely good-looking, even from a distance. He chatted with the doorman for a while, actually managing to raise a smile out of him, and then strolled out on to the footpath.

My heart stopped. I didn't have time to think about what would happen next. Adam looked straight ahead - and smiled at me. It was the same perfect, bright grin that coloured most of my memories of him. I wanted to run and leap into his arms. I wanted to kiss him in a way that made up for a year of missed kisses. But something held me back. It could have been nerves. I could have been a little stunned by him. But most likely, I held back because I realised he wasn't smiling at me.

Focusing only on him, I hadn't noticed the brunette girl cut across the street a few metres down from me. Stealing my next move, she bounded into his embrace and hugged him tightly. Adam's reaction was gut wrenchingly familiar. He kissed her.

And that was the moment that I was overtaken by pure grief.

Everything seemed to slow down, including my thought processes. I'd reached a dead end. All hope, anticipation and goodness about the best love I'd ever known left my body in an instant. My only saving grace was the realisation that he hadn't seen me at all. There would be no awkward confrontation, no moment when he'd have to let me down gently. For Adam and me, there would be no more moments at all.

Pulling myself together as best I could, I slipped into the stream of pedestrian traffic, making the short journey back to my apartment with a heavy heart, an empty head and a weightless soul.

Marvin was a sharp guy. Hiding my devastation from him was impossible. He was waving a white handkerchief at me before I'd even reached the door. I smiled through my tears, graciously taking it from him as soon as I was within reach.

"Miss Charli," he cooed. "Why so sad? Was there a problem with the map I drew you?"

A preschooler would have understood his directions and Marvin knew it.

"No, no problem. Some things just don't work out, that's all."

"Ah, but Miss Charli." He flicked his wide lapels with his fingertips. "You're in New York. Anything is possible."

For some reason I laughed. I couldn't help it. And then I cried again, a loud embarrassing sob. I'd remembered Adam once telling me the same thing as he waltzed me around the boatshed. "We can do anything, Charlotte," he'd told me.

Poor Marvin looked stricken, like he wanted to comfort me but had no idea how.

I sucked in a long breath, trying to compose myself. "I love your city, Marv. I'm just not sure it's going to work out for me. I'm pretty sure it's time for me to go home."

He put his gloved hand to his heart, nodded his head and stepped aside to usher me through the door.

If there was a level of emotion below the pit of despair, I was there.

I sat on the floor in the kitchen, tearing sheets of paper towel off the roll to stem my endless flow of tears. My whole body ached, but my thoughts were surprisingly clear. I'd decided to leave New York, relieved by the knowledge that the process would be simple. All I had to do was book my ticket. I hadn't even made it as far as unpacking my suitcase properly. The trickiest decision I had to make was where to go.

I cast my mind back to the three options Alex had given me before I left home: revisit a safe place I'd been, find my way to Adam or go home to him. None of the places I'd visited could be considered remotely safe without Mitchell by my side. And finding my way to Adam hadn't worked out too well. That left option three, and the idea wasn't as awful as I expected it to be. I was tired, lonely and a little bit fragile. It seemed like the perfect time to go home to my father.

An hour passed before I felt calm enough to call him with the news. Talking to Alex required preparation. Any hint of sadness or uneasiness resulted in a volley of questions that I usually had no answer for, followed by threats of jumping on a plane to come and get me.

Today I was given a reprieve. Gabrielle answered.

"Charli." She punched out my name as if she'd been hanging by the phone, waiting for my call.

I tried to hold it together but failed dismally, blubbering to her as if my world was ending. And at that point, I was pretty sure it was. "I saw him," I snivelled.

She sighed. "Oh, dear. Tell me what happened."

I explained the whole sorry saga in six messy sentences.

There was a time when Gabrielle could have forewarned me that Adam had met someone else. They used to be extremely close, but Gabi and Adam no longer spoke at all. Years of exchanging long handwritten letters had ended. I'd never asked why, fearing it had something to do with me. Adam deserved a clean break. If cutting Gabrielle off was part of that break, then so be it.

"I want to come home," I whimpered pathetically.

She groaned. "Why would you want to do that?"

"It's my home, Gabrielle," I snapped at her, totally distraught.

Going home would definitely cramp her style. Maybe that's why she offered up her swank New York apartment.

"Charli, if things had worked out with Adam, would you even be considering coming home right now?" But it hadn't worked out. Not one thing had worked out the way I'd planned and hoped it would. "Your adventure had nothing to do with Adam," she continued. "You wanted to see the world. Open your eyes and look around. You've arrived."

"I can't stay." My protest came out sounding like a growl. "I don't know anyone, I don't know my way around and I'm running out of money."

"And what does any of that have to do with Adam? Do you like New York?"

I had to concede that my predicament did have nothing to do with Adam. He had no idea I was even in his city. I'd stood twenty metres away from him and he still didn't know.

"I do like it here."

"*Très bien,*" she soothed. "Calm yourself and look at the bigger picture." She spoke in her best French teacher voice. I hadn't missed it one bit. "You're living in a gorgeous part of the city, in a perfectly secure building. Do you like the apartment?"

What wasn't to like? It was a palace. I'd spent a year hopping from one hovel to another. I would've considered any abode with running water and a roof that didn't leak palatial.

"It's great. The apartment's not the problem."

"Look, give New York a chance. Go and get a job. Get out and meet people. You won't regret it."

Coming from anyone else it would have been difficult to believe, but Gabrielle was speaking from experience. She'd landed in New York at the same age as me, managed to make a go of it and stayed for four years. But there were differences. She had family here, a zillion dollars at her disposal and a green card allowing her to work legally. I had none of these things.

"Charli, if you come back here, you're going to want to leave again in a few months. Leaving the second time is going to be much harder than it was the first time."

I knew she was right but refused to tell her so. "I'll give it a week and see what happens."

"Good girl." I could tell by her tone of voice that she was smiling. I wondered if she could tell that I was mocking her by pulling a face. "Is Alex there?"

"No, he's still at the café." It didn't matter where in the world I was; I was always oblivious to the time difference. "I'll get him to call you when he gets in."

"No, leave it a few days," I said. "I want to have better news to tell him."

"You'll be fine, Charli. I have every faith in you."

4. Elvis

Finding a job was paramount. If I could secure a job, there was a fair chance I'd find a brand new life along the way. Chic restaurants and cafés were in abundance near my apartment so I decided to try my luck, approaching most of them in search of work.

I got knocked back every single time.

Perhaps I was approaching this job thing the wrong way. Everyone I'd spoken to that morning had been on the receiving end of my best sell ever. When asked about my qualifications, I pumped my experience up to stellar levels. According to my fake mental résumé, I'd worked everywhere from Michelin star restaurants to high-end boutiques – no mean feat considering I'd spent the past year in African countries. The closest I'd come to a high-end boutique was the market stall in Kaimte that sold bogus Prada handbags.

If I could just find an employer needing the services of a slightly scattered would-be photographer with a degree in fairyology and a penchant for magic moments, I'd be a shoo-in. So far, that particular employer had eluded me and the minute I walked into Nellie's Restaurant, I knew I wasn't going to find him there either.

The restaurant was bigger than most, boasting a split-level dining area and a mezzanine level above to cater for large functions. It was busy. Hectic to the point of bedlam. Servers rushed around carrying huge plates of food and a long line of people stood waiting to be seated.

A very frazzled woman flicked through the reservations book, making promises I was fairly sure she couldn't keep. "We should have a table for you in another ten minutes, sir," she told the man who was first in line.

"We'll wait," he replied gruffly.

The food must have been really good. Either that or I'd stumbled into another Manhattan restaurant where you qualified as awesome just because you were seen there. Seizing the first opportunity I had, I excused myself and pushed my way to the head of the line. The frazzled girl behind the podium frowned at me.

I frowned back.

"You're going to be waiting at least an hour," she warned, furiously thumbing through pages again.

"No, no. I'm here about the job."

"What job?"

"Err, the waitressing job," I lied.

"Is Paolo expecting you?"

I quickly glanced at my watch. "Yes, ten minutes ago."

She smirked, and I sensed she knew something I didn't. "Be my guest," she said, pointing toward the door to the kitchen.

I was still trying to psyche myself into entering the kitchen when the door violently swung open. I stepped aside quickly, making way for a waiter precariously balancing three plates of food in his arms. I jumped into the kitchen before the door swung shut – straight in to the sights of the restaurateur from hell, Paolo.

"You!" He pointed straight at me.

"Me?" I asked in a tiny voice, turning my head to see if anyone was standing behind me.

"What do you want?"

For such a short man, Paolo was terrifying. He wasn't much taller than me. If it had come to blows between us, I was fairly certain I could take him – unless he sat on me. He was as wide as he was tall.

I was about to answer when his attention switched to a girl who'd just leaned across him to pick up a plate of food.

"Gretchen!" he yelled, making the girl jump. "What do you think you're doing?"

"This is the order for table six," she uttered, recoiling as if he'd just slapped her.

"Not unless there's a rabbit seated at table six. Do you see any meat on that plate?"

I studied the plate as closely as Gretchen did, hoping to see a fillet mignon hiding under the mass of salad, just to prove him wrong.

"Get out of my sight," he hissed, waving his arms like he was shooing a fly. Gretchen sprang to life. She reached behind her back, whipped off her little apron and threw it at him.

"You can stick your job, Paolo! I've put up with this for months. I don't need your stupid job."

She'd made it almost to the door by the time her angry rant was over. Paolo liked to get the last word in. "Gretchen," he snarled.

I expected to hear him tell her she'd never work in this town again. New York seemed like the perfect place to hear someone scream those words.

"I want your name badge."

The look she gave him while she unpinned it from her blouse was blistering. He held out his hand and she slapped the badge in his open palm.

Quickly glancing around the kitchen, I noticed that not one person had paused to watch the fireworks. Perhaps it was an everyday occurrence they were all used to. Did I really want to work in a place like this? Of course I did. I was desperate.

"What do you want?" he asked, turning back to me. It was as if the last minute had happened only in my head. He didn't miss a beat.

"I wanted to talk to you about a job."

"There are no vacancies. We're not hiring."

"Yes, you are," I insisted, following him as he walked through the kitchen to a small adjoining office. Paolo sat at the desk. I went no further than the doorway.

"You're pushy. I like that."

I breathed a sigh of relief. "Thank you."

"You're also annoying. I don't like that."

"Please, Paolo. I really need this job," I begged. "I'll work just for tips."

Paolo leaned back in his chair, so far that I thought it might tip backwards, and wondered if I'd laugh if it did.

"There is no job."

"I want Gretchen's job," I replied, thinking on my feet. "In case you misunderstood her intentions, she just quit."

He leaned forward again, resting his elbows on the desk. "Do you think you're going to enjoy working for me?"

I shook my head. "No. I think I'm going to absolutely hate it."

He laughed, a light chuckle at first before throwing his head back in a roar of guffaws straight out of a horror movie. "Fine," he said finally composing himself enough to speak. "You start tomorrow. You've got the breakfast shift."

I grinned. "Thank you. My name is Charli, by the way."

"Not anymore, it's not."

"Excuse me?" As much as I hated my name, I wasn't planning on changing it any time soon.

Paolo pulled open a drawer, took out a container filled to the brim with name badges and thumped it on the desk, dropping Gretchen's badge into the mix. No wonder the kitchen staff hadn't reacted to her meltdown. They'd seen it many times before. My mouth fell open as I watched him rifling through the pile.

"You're now known as Priscilla," he announced, sliding the badge toward me. "I want to see how you work out before I spend two dollars on a new name badge."

I stepped forward and picked it up, studying it closely for bloodstains or other signs of trauma. "Priscilla? Really?"

"It's Priscilla or Walter." He waved the Walter badge at me. "You don't look much like a Walter. Take it or leave it, kid."

"Fine," I grumbled. "I'll see you tomorrow."

"Don't be late," he warned, shooing me out the door.

I didn't care that he was a monster. He'd given me a job. There was a skip in my step as I walked back to my apartment. I was hopeful that Paolo was the gateway to my new brilliant life.

***

Working for Paolo was every bit as horrendous as I expected it to be. It was as if his sole purpose in life was to make his staff miserable. But his constant criticism, screaming and shouting bounced right off me. I just didn't care. Slowly but surely, a whole new world was opening up to me and I was running with it.

It was easier to get to know the regular patrons than the people I worked with. Other than retrieving plates off the servery, the kitchen was a no-go zone. It was mayhem in there, and if Paolo was lurking, it was worse. The dining area had a much more pleasant atmosphere.

A lot of the patrons were regulars and I had my favourites. Merle and Betty Swanston were a sweet old couple who came in every morning for brunch. Betty loved regaling me with stories of their life together. They'd been married for over fifty years. I knew that because she'd made a point of telling me every day in the week since I'd first met them.

Phoebe was another interesting character. She was the most elegant woman I'd ever seen, easily capable of giving Gabrielle a run for her money. Her jet-black hair was always styled in victory rolls and her lips were ruby red, reminding me of a movie star from a bygone era. Phoebe had her quirks. She never cared which table she was seated at, but was pedantic about how it was set. From a distance I'd watch her rearrange the cutlery, refold her napkin and buff her glass with a cloth she kept in her handbag.

"Get back to work, kid. This is not a freak show," Paolo would hiss, every time I slowed down to watch her.

"Oh, but it is, Paolo. I love this city."

And I did. If I couldn't put the pieces of my life back together and start afresh in New York, it couldn't be done.

Not all the customers were sweet like the Swanstons or glamorous like Phoebe. Some were just jerks. A repeat offender was an investment banker called Bryce. When he dined alone he was tolerable. But when he was sharing a meal with a couple of work colleagues, he was a pig.

My heart sank when he walked through the door at the beginning of my shift that morning. It practically fell through the bottom of my feet when I saw two of his friends trailing behind him. Being polite to customers, regardless of how gross they were to you, was one of Paolo's many rules. I doubt being chatted up was something he had to deal with very often.

"You're so beautiful," Bryce told me, leering as I approached his table to take their orders. "Let me take you out for a drink."

"No," I hissed, with forced restraint.

"Burned, Bryce," quipped one of his friends, making the other laugh.

Bryce tried harder. "Okay, cutie, how about you ask me out?"

As repulsed as I was, I managed to look him straight in the eye as I pointed to the door. "Sure. Get out."

The table erupted into laughter. I asked them one final time if they were ready to order.

"Not yet," replied Bryce, leering at me.

I walked away muttering obscenities under my breath. Paolo was standing near the kitchen door as I approached, and by the look on his face I was almost certain he'd seen what had just gone down at table nine.

"Pay attention," he grumbled, pointing to something behind me.

I turned around to see a man at table three trying to catch my eye by waving. I'd seen him a few times that week but hadn't been the one to serve him. Tables for one were quick to turn, so other waitresses tended to claim them quickly.

I drew in a calming breath and walked toward him, smiling so artificially that my cheeks hurt. "May I help you?"

"I hope so, I'm hungry," he replied.

I smiled more genuinely. "Would you like to hear the specials?"

"Why don't you sit down and tell me? You look like you could take a load off."

Here we go again, I thought. But I had to admit this guy was nowhere near as repulsive as Bryce and his chums. He was very good looking – in a snobby, holier-than-thou kind of way. He wasn't boyishly handsome. He was kind of dark and broody, but his brown eyes were warm and bright.

"I don't need to sit down. I've only been at work for half an hour," I said, icily.

He stared blankly at me for a second, making me uncomfortable enough to look away. "You think I'm hitting on you," he finally exclaimed, looking as if the notion was ridiculous. "Look, if it makes you feel any better, I'm waiting for my date to arrive."

It didn't make me feel any better. I was even more humiliated.

"Would you like to hear the specials?" I repeated.

He ignored me. "What's your name?" He leaned forward, peering at the badge pinned to my chest.

"Priscilla," I announced.

A bright grin swept his face. "Well that's a huge coincidence, because my name is Elvis."

Elvis was clearly lying.

"It's nice to meet you, Elvis," I said dryly.

He nodded politely. "You too, Priscilla." I picked a menu off the table and thrust it at him. He pretended to read it for a moment, snapped it shut and hit me with his next question. "Where are you from?"

He didn't recognise my accent. It was licence to give Priscilla a whole new ancestry. "Africa. I arrived two weeks ago." It was only half a lie and I felt no unease in telling it.

Elvis didn't get a chance to ask me anything else. His date arrived. A pretty blonde rushed over to the table, apologised for being late and crushed her lips to his the second he stood up.

I didn't need an excuse to leave. Bryce whistled from across the room.

"We're ready to order," he yelled.

Fan-bloody-tastic.

5. Smash Cake

Winter was starting to get to me. I hated having to bundle up like an Eskimo just to go outside. It reminded me of being back in Pipers Cove. The weather was the only thing that reminded me of home. New York City was about as far removed as I could get from the tiny town I'd grown up in. It was fast paced, busy and exciting. I left my apartment every morning just to walk, making sure I ventured one street farther than I had the day before. My confidence was building, my knowledge was expanding and most importantly, my grief was subsiding.

To say I never thought of Adam any more would be a lie. I thought of him all the time. Many things in New York reminded me of him. This was his place. But I was no glutton for punishment. Since my disastrous stakeout at his building, I'd never been back. New York was a huge city - plenty big enough for the both of us.

As hard a taskmaster as Paolo was, going to work was still the highlight of my day. I walked to the cloakroom, hung my coat and spent the next minute or so covertly scanning the dining room from the kitchen side of the mirrored window in the door.

Betty and Merle sat at their favourite table, all loved up and tucking in to their eggs. Phoebe was polishing her glass in preparation for her breakfast and thankfully, mercifully, Bryce was nowhere to be seen. The rest of the dining room was relatively quiet. All the tables near the windows were taken, but the centre section and mezzanine level were empty, lifting my mood instantly. I hated carrying food up the stairs. I had enough trouble doing it on level ground.

Betty called out to me the minute I walked out of the kitchen, waving her napkin as if I was hard of hearing.

"Good morning," I beamed.

"Do you know how long we've been married, Priscilla?" asked Betty, for the millionth time.

"Fifty years?" I asked, hoping I sounded unsure.

Merle covered his mouth with his napkin and chuckled. It was a rumbly sound that no one under the age of eighty could replicate.

"No," she said, confusing me. "We've been married fifty-one years today."

I leaned down and gently hugged her frail, diminutive frame. "Congratulations to you both. I hope you're doing something nice today."

Merle answered, waving his shaky finger at me. "When you get to be our age, every day is nice."

I agreed, smiling.

I wanted to do something special for the Swanstons. When I saw them standing to leave, I rushed to the counter near the door so I could be the one to take care of their bill. Rushing was unnecessary. It took them ages to walk across the room, arm in arm to steady each other.

Merle reached for his wallet. "Not today, Merle," I told him, glancing around for any sign of Paolo. "Your breakfast today is on the house. Happy anniversary."

A certain amount of guilt must have accompanied the gesture because when someone called my name - well, Priscilla's name - I almost jumped out of my skin.

"Oh, it's only you," I said, spinning to see Elvis at the tiniest table we had, nestled near the door.

He smirked roguishly. "You could get fired for that, you know. Comping meals is considered stealing."

I strolled toward his table. "Are you going to dob on me, Elvis?"

His dark laugh led me to think he was contemplating it. "If I knew what dob meant, I might."

"What are you doing here, anyway? I haven't seen you in a while."

"What do most people do here, Priscilla?"

I cringed. Having a pseudonym bothered me only when he said it.

"They eat. Would you like to hear the specials?"

He laughed. "No. The specials are always the same."

"Yeah, but today they're *really* special."

"Sit for a minute," he ordered, pointing to the chair opposite him.

I glanced around the room to see Paolo standing at the podium near the front door, watching me like a short, fat hawk.

"I can't." I discreetly moved my head in an upward nod, gesturing toward Paolo.

Discretion wasn't Elvis's forte. He twisted in his seat and stared straight at him. Realising he'd been caught, Paolo started thumbing through the reservation book. "Pretend you're reading me the specials," said Elvis, giving me a wink.

I pulled out a chair and sat down.

I enjoyed stealing a few minutes with Elvis now and then. He was funny, smart and handsome. He also knew he was funny, smart and handsome so he was cocky too. In the few weeks since I'd first met him, he'd dined at Nellie's with at least four different women, showering each one of them with enough attention to make them think they were the only one. Elvis was clearly trouble, but I took heart in the fact that I was at least clued up enough to realise it.

***

Waiting tables is not for the fainthearted. That morning I dealt with a screaming baby who threw her food around, two adult babies screaming at me because their orders were wrong… and Bryce and his pals.

"What's a smash cake?" he asked, pointing to the item on the menu.

"It's a favourite of all the little children who come in here," I said acidly.

I wasn't lying. The white cake piled high with sickly sweet frosting was a must-have for any toddler who dined at Nellie's. Little ones who weren't coordinated enough to eat it with a fork would pick it up and smash it against their mouths.

"We'll take three of those."

Something about Bryce made his friends think he was hilarious and witty. I'd tried to figure out what it was but come up blank each time. To me he was one of the most repugnant people I'd ever met.

"Would you like sprinkles on your smash cakes?" I spoke in the same slow tone that I used when asking two year-olds that question.

"Sure, why not?"

I turned to walk away but Bryce grabbed my elbow. "Don't touch me," I snapped, shrugging free.

"You're not very friendly today, beautiful."

"I'm never friendly to you."

His friends began to snigger, spurring him on to be even more offensive. But he didn't get a chance to say anything else cringe-worthy.

Elvis walked in.

"Can I sit here?" he asked, pointing to the table next to Bryce's.

"Yes, of course," I replied.

The party of chubby investment bankers didn't seem to appreciate company. The table fell silent.

I walked the short distance to Elvis's table. "Good morning, Elvis," I crooned.

He looked up at me and smiled. "Hey."

"I haven't seen you in a while."

"Did you miss me?"

"Not one bit," I quipped, handing him a menu.

He laughed. "I didn't think so."

It had been nearly a week since Elvis had been to the restaurant. I had missed him but would never admit it. Pathetically, besides Marvin, Elvis was the closest thing I had to a friend in New York.

Once I'd served the fat bankers their cake and coffee, I didn't expect to have to deal with them again that day. When Bryce called me over to complain about his food, I was furious.

"Is there a problem?"

"There might be," he hinted, turning the plate in a full circle. "I'm trying to figure out where the smash is. I see the cake and you remembered the sprinkles but there's no smash."

His horrid friends snickered into their closed fists. I was a hundred percent certain I was about to lose my job because of them, and at that moment I wasn't concerned in the slightest.

"It's just called a smash cake, moron."

"I know that, honey. I'm just wondering what the smash looks like, just so I can keep an eye out for it. I wouldn't want to break my teeth on a hard piece of smash."

His friends chortled louder and I was totally at a loss why. Schoolboys wouldn't have found him the slightest bit amusing.

"Are you planning to eat it or shall I take it back to the kitchen?" I asked, giving him one last chance to be a normal human being.

Bryce leaned so close to me that I was forced to take a step back. "Just show me the smash," he whispered, making my skin crawl.

At the very end of my rope, I balled up my fist and thumped it down on the cupcake, sending chunks of cake and frosting splattering all over the three of them. "There. Your smash is served."

I heard chuckling again but a quick glance around the table showed it wasn't coming from the bankers. Their cake-spattered faces were all frozen in stunned silence. Elvis was the one chuckling.

I grabbed a napkin, wiped the cake off my hand and strolled back to the kitchen as if nothing had happened. As usual, no one in the kitchen took any notice of me, but Paolo wasn't as oblivious. I knew he'd fire me the instant he heard about it. I spied through the window in the kitchen door, trying to see which part of the dining room he was lurking in. To my surprise, he was nowhere to be seen.

What I did see was Elvis standing beside the table of smash cake victims, talking to Bryce. I didn't want him pleading my case. There wasn't any point. Paolo was not a man renowned for his forgiving nature. As soon as Bryce demanded to see the manager to explain what I had done, I'd be cactus.

I went about the rest of my shift as if nothing had happened. The fat bankers were gone by the time I ventured back to the dining room, and so was Elvis. I crossed paths with Paolo a few times but he mentioned nothing to do with my cupcake assault that day, or the next… or the day after that. For some reason, I'd got off scot-free. Not only had I escaped the wrath of Paolo but also no longer had to deal with Bryce and his goons either. They never set foot in Nellie's again.

***

When I was growing up, we ate sandwiches for dinner for weeks on end. Alex was a woeful cook. As long as he was sure all major food groups were covered, he saw no problem with it.

Since I'd been in New York I'd reverted to old habits, living on cereal and sandwiches. The kitchen in Gabrielle's apartment was beautiful. The off-white cabinets and glossy black granite bench top were a chef's dream. But it was all for show. I'd moved into an apartment that hadn't been lived in for nearly six years. It was a beautiful, stylish, empty shell.

The lack of furniture didn't concern me in the slightest. I had a huge comfortable bed, and when I was in it I felt like the queen of everything. At first I thought Gabrielle had left it behind, naïvely thinking a king-size bed was too big to pack up and ship out with the rest of her belongings. Marvin let slip one day that it had been delivered just days before my arrival – along with a mass of very expensive bedding that I found in the linen closet in the hallway. I'd made a point of thanking her during one of my weekly check-in phone calls home.

"I couldn't have you sleeping on the floor," she'd told me. "Please don't tell your father that there's no other furniture there. He worries enough as it is."

That was the beauty of Gabrielle. If there was a line between a hand up and a hand out, she never crossed it.

Living without furniture was bearable, but living without decent food was not. I craved home-cooked meals. After cereal for dinner the second night in a row, I decided that a home-cooked meal would be my mission for the week. In order to do that, I was going to have to come up with a way of equipping the kitchen.

No one noticed the empty backpack I was carrying when I arrived at work that morning. The people I worked with barely noticed me at all half the time – except Paolo, who took great delight in berating me at the front door for being three minutes late for my shift.

Offloading my bag in the cloakroom, I headed into the dining room to start work, grabbing Phoebe's egg white omelette off the servery on my way past.

I chatted to her for a short minute before heading to the Swanstons' table to greet them. We were in the midst of the fifty-one-years-of-marriage conversation when from the corner of my eye I saw Elvis walk in.

I rushed over to him, steering him away from Paolo by linking my arm through his. "There's a table for you near the window."

I didn't dare look back at Paolo. Stealing his moment of glory by denying him his meet-and-greet was huge no-no.

"You're very keen this morning," noted Elvis.

"I take my job very seriously."

He chuckled darkly. "No, you don't."

Releasing my grip, I pointed to the table I'd reserved for him and handed him a menu. I couldn't have cared less about his order that morning. I had a plan, and Elvis was my unwitting accomplice.

"I need your help." I sounded desperate, like I was about to ask him for a kidney. I rushed through the plan I'd hatched on the short walk in to work. Elvis didn't say anything for a long time, giving me a look I'd seen a million times before but never from him. He thought I was as unhinged as my plan.

"You're going to steal pots and pans?"

"Not steal, borrow," I clarified. "And I need you to keep Paolo distracted while I do it."

"Priscilla, I'll lend you some money. Go and buy some new pans."

He reached for his wallet and I grabbed his arm to stop him. Elvis glanced across at Paolo, put his wallet back in his pocket and straightened up.

"No, I don't want to buy them. I just want to borrow them and then I'll return them when I'm done. Will you help me?"

"You're never going to make employee of the month. You know that, right?"

I had more chance of winning a Nobel Prize than making employee of the month. My record was less than exemplary, and Elvis had been privy to every one of my indiscretions thus far.

"Please, Elvis?" I pouted a little.

"Who else have you mentioned this absurd scheme to?"

I shrugged. "Just Marvin, my doorman."

"Let me get this straight. You're a poor, struggling waitress and yet you live in a building with a doorman?"

"Look, will you help me or not?"

He sighed. "Fine. Go, do your thing. I'll keep your manager busy."

He raised his hand, looked at Paolo and clicked his fingers. Paolo scuttled across the floor, weaving in and out of tables like a plump penguin.

"Go," whispered Elvis.

I slipped away, confident that my partner in crime could buy me the time I needed. I'd gambled a lot by implicating Elvis. He could have thrown me to the wolves at any moment, but for some reason I trusted him.

I was like a ghost in the kitchen. No one raised an eyebrow when I retrieved my bag from the cloakroom and snuck into the adjacent storeroom.

It was a treasure-trove of goodies. I took a small skillet and the only saucepan small enough to fit into my bag. Glancing around the dimly lit, windowless room, I sighed wistfully. There was any amount of food in there. I could have made a hundred meals just from the groceries I could source from the storeroom. But I took nothing else. I wasn't a thief. I had no intention of taking anything I couldn't return later.

Back in the cloakroom, I hid my bag under my coat, hoping that nobody would discover my loot before I could escape with it later that morning.

I didn't speak with Elvis again that day. Paolo had made it his personal mission to serve him himself. I glanced at him as I walked over to serve the table next to his, and he winked at me and smiled.

I mouthed two words. *Thank you*. And later that night, when I sat on the floor in the kitchen eating the meal I'd cooked myself, I silently thanked him again.

6. Devil's Advocate

Arriving late to work was never a good idea. On days when Paolo was on the warpath, the only thing I could do was duck for cover.

"Where the hell have you been?" he bellowed, the second he laid eyes on me.

"I'm sorry I'm late."

"Not as sorry as you're going to be," ribbed Taylor.

I'd met Taylor only once before. She was the girl standing at the podium near the door on the day I'd weaselled my way in to the job. And she looked just as frazzled and run off her feet as she had that day.

"Why?" I asked, following her through the kitchen door.

Paolo called after her. "Taylor, make sure she gets her costume."

What costume? Surely the drab black pants and white blouse we wore were punishment enough.

I followed Taylor into the staff cloakroom and closed the door behind us. I said nothing as she rummaged through the large plastic bag hanging on one of the hooks. I still said nothing when she threw a stiff white tunic at me. But when she dumped a white fluffy marabou halo on my head, I couldn't hold my tongue any longer.

"What is this about?" I asked.

"'Tis the season and all that junk," she quipped. "Paolo makes us dress up every year at Christmas."

I'm not sure what was more disturbing: the fact that Paolo wanted us in costume or that Taylor had worked at Nellie's long enough to know it was an annual event.

"No way," I protested, thrusting the musty-smelling dress at her. "Christmas is three weeks away."

"You're getting off lightly. You're the angel this year. I'm one of Santa's gnomes." She dipped in to the bag again, dragging out a pair of red and white striped tights, making me laugh.

"An elf, Taylor. I don't think Santa had gnomes."

"Whatever." She shrugged. "You're the angel. Be happy."

"Do I have a choice?"

"Nope." She pulled open the door and breezed out as quickly as she'd come in, leaving me holding the angel dress and halo.

We managed to stay costume-free for most of the morning. Paolo started rushing around, ordering everybody to suit up before the lunchtime rush. I held out.

"Right now!" he ordered, clapping his hands as he approached me. "I want to see a Christmas angel, right now!"

"I'm allergic to taffeta," I protested.

"And I'm allergic to insubordinates. Wear it or walk out the door."

"I'll make a deal with you, Paolo."

Instantly he stopped walking and turned back to face me. I knew I'd piqued his curiosity.

"I'll wear your dumb costume under one condition. You get me a new name badge… with my real name on it."

Paolo deliberated for a moment before throwing his head back in a quick bray of laughter. "Fine. Whatever. It's a deal." He waved his hands in the air as he walked away.

"Do you even know my real name?" I asked, as he got to the door.

"Email it to me," he replied, disappearing into the kitchen.

I couldn't help laughing. Taylor the Christmas gnome jingled her way past me a few seconds later and I laughed even harder. It was going to be a long day.

I didn't usually work the lunchtime shift. Working just a few hours in the morning suited me perfectly. It left the rest of the day free for exploring my adopted city.

Breakfast at Nellie's was usually busy, but nothing compared to lunch. The build-up of people at the door was growing and tables were turning over much slower than usual.

Since my morning shift the day before, Nellie's restaurant had undergone changes. Every spare surface had been decorated. A huge pine wreath hung from the balustrade; a herd of gold papier mache reindeers took pride of place near the foot of the stairs and pine garlands hung from the ceiling. The crisp white table linen had been replaced with bottle green tablecloths and red napkins.

I had to admit it looked festive. It just meant nothing to me. I was too far from home and the people I loved to even consider getting into the Christmas spirit.

Waitressing was a lot like being a fly on the wall. Moseying around the dining room allowed me to catch snippets of all sorts of conversations. Travelling under the radar and eavesdropping wasn't going to happen today. I was expected to go about my work looking like an obese Kewpie doll with a drinking problem. The taffeta dress was far too big and I had to keep hitching it back onto my shoulders. Adding to my troubles was the halo. I just couldn't keep it on straight – proving something I'd known for years. I was never meant to wear a halo.

"You look wonderful," praised Paolo, clapping his hands together loudly.

"Err, thanks."

Grabbing a fistful of my puffy sleeve, he pulled me to one side. "I'm giving you one table. It's a party of six. Do you think you can handle it?"

"I'll manage," I told him, shrugging free. "What do you want me to do until then?"

His wily grin made me uncomfortable. "Mingle. It's Christmas."

I had no intention of mingling. My table wasn't due until two. I had an hour to kill and no desire to be seen in my angel suit, so I retreated up to the mezzanine floor to hide. Every now and then I'd peek over the balustrade. It was busier than I'd ever seen it.

I was still spying from the top floor when Taylor, the Christmas gnome, started seating people at my table. A well-dressed woman and an elderly lady took their seats and Paolo rushed over to them. I could tell by his over-the-top gestures that he was going out of his way to welcome them. That should have been the moment that I headed down the stairs to tend to them. I could see Paolo swinging his head from left to right, looking for me. He gave up searching when his focus shifted to another couple coming through the door. My heart began thumping. The couple on the receiving end of Paolo's royal welcome were Adam and the brunette. I hadn't seen him since the disastrous day outside his apartment building weeks ago. And that was how it was supposed to be.

The decision to stay put came quickly. Self-preservation was more important than keeping my job. I pulled out a chair and sat down.

I couldn't help staring at them, studying their every move. Adam politely pulled out a chair and brunette girl swept down the back of her black knee-length dress before sitting down.

I thought brunette girl was pretty. Not outstandingly beautiful like Phoebe or Gabrielle, but pretty nonetheless. She clearly adored Adam. She was constantly glancing across and smiling at him. Part of me was glad that he was happy. Another part of me wanted to pick up a saltshaker and drill it at brunette girl's head.

Another woman soon joined the table, but from the get-go she seemed on the outer. After greeting her, no one seemed to pay her any more attention. The out-of-place woman with short platinum blonde hair spent the next few minutes talking into her phone.

The sight of Elvis walking through the door was a welcome distraction. I wondered why he was in for lunch rather than breakfast. It became painfully clear a few seconds later when he walked to Adam's table, kissed the platinum blonde on the cheek and sat down.

My head exploded with information. No wonder I'd felt such a kinship to Elvis. There had always been a familiarity about him. The reason why was now screaming at me. He was a darker, broodier, older version of Adam – his brother.

Elvis was Ryan Décarie.

Putting two and two together, I quickly identified the rest of the party. The smartly dressed lady was their mother – whom I should have recognised from the pictures Adam had once shown me. I wondered where their father was. It seemed unfair that I didn't get to scope him out too. I couldn't place the older woman, but the platinum blonde was Elvis's girlfriend of the day.

I contemplated making a run for it, convinced that I could make it down the stairs and out the door so quickly that the only thing they'd see would be a blur of white taffeta and marabou. But that wasn't to be.

Elvis… Ryan looked up and spotted me, nodded his head to the side, and motioned for me to come down. I shook my head and he frowned quizzically. The silent standoff continued for a few seconds before he excused himself from the table and climbed the stairs. I pushed my chair back from the edge of the balustrade, out of the view of the ground floor.

"Why are you hiding up here?" he asked, pulling a chair over. "I wanted you to meet my family. They're excellent tippers." He winked at me.

"I'd rather stay up here, thanks all the same."

He leaned forward to catch a glimpse of his family below. "Can't say I blame you. I'd rather hang out up here too."

"Don't you get along with them?"

"We get along fine."

"Who's the blonde?" I nodded my head in her direction.

Ryan pulled a face at me and I couldn't help smiling. "Her name is Aubrey."

"Why do you have so many women, Elvis? Can't you just find one you like and stick with her?"

He groaned as if the idea was absurd. "I get so bored. And I can't stand whining. 'You're late picking me up. Blah, blah, blah. Do I look fat in this dress? Blah, blah, blah. You slept with my sister. Blah, blah, blah.' It gets old very quickly."

I laughed. "So why did you choose Aubrey today?"

"Because my mother can't stand her. It spices things up."

"Don't you want more than that? Don't you think there's a girl out there who has a sister you don't want to sleep with?"

"And end up as dull as them?" He pointed down to Adam and the brunette. "I don't think so."

"Maybe they're good together." I had no idea why I felt the need to defend brunette girl.

"They're a train wreck," he scoffed. "Her name is Whitney. Her friends call her Whit, which is ironic considering she has none."

Of course her name was Whitney. I would've also accepted Britney and Courtney as suitable names for the girl who'd stolen my happy ever after.

"How long have they been together?"

He shrugged. "Three or four years - give or take."

Ryan had unwittingly just driven the final nail in to my coffin of good Adam memories. His words burned to my very core as I drew a horrible conclusion. None of it had been real. I'd fallen in love with a boy who'd never belonged to me in the first place.

"That's a long time," I croaked.

Ryan squinted at me suspiciously. "Why are you so interested in my brother? I can take you down there and introduce you if you'd like. I'd love to see dim Whit squirm a little."

I vehemently shook my head. "No, I'm just curious. Why don't you like her?"

"Well, she's a dimwit. He almost came to his senses and cut her loose a couple of summers ago. We have a cousin that lives in some backwater town in Tasmania, of all places." He screwed up his nose as if Pipers Cove was the worst place on earth. There was a time that I might have agreed with him. "Adam decided he'd visit her at the last minute. He and Whitney were supposed to be spending the summer in Europe with a group of their friends."

"But Adam backed out?" I guessed, trying to piece the story together to match up with the version I already knew.

"Yeah, at the very last minute. They were waiting for their connection at Heathrow when he bailed and jumped on the next plane to Australia."

"Why did he do that?"

Cross-examining Adam's brother weighed on my conscience a little but I figured none of it mattered any more.

"Who knows? It was a spur of the moment thing. I can't imagine why anyone would want to hang out with cousin Gabrielle for two months. She's the stuff of nightmares." He shuddered, feigning horror, and I smiled. Anyone would think he was referring to a demon. There was a time I would have agreed with him.

"He ended up meeting some small-town hick girl and it was all downhill from there. He fell in love with her and she stole his soul," he said, theatrically. "The Adam who left New York bound for Spain was nothing like the Adam who returned from Australia two months later."

"Why?"

Ryan frowned at me again. Embarrassed, I looked away.

"What's with the twenty questions, Priscilla? Seriously."

"I'm just buying time. I'd much rather hear your story than go downstairs and wait tables."

"Fine." He continued his tale. "She ended up cutting him loose and he came home sad and empty, which probably explained why he went straight back to dim Whit. She's void as well."

"Did Whitney ever find out about the other girl?"

He shook his head. "She has no clue. I told you, she's dim. To this day, Adam is pathetically in love with small-town-hick-girl and Whitney doesn't even know it. They'll probably marry eventually and rear dull little children. It's dismal really. So I'm going to stick with the Aubreys of this world. It allows a much happier frame of mind."

"You might be right," I falsely agreed.

"Well," he said, lightening the conversation by slapping his hands on his knees. "Now that you know some of my family dynamics, can we go downstairs?"

I shook my head. "I'm not going down there. Paolo can fire me."

"Paolo won't fire you." He spoke with absolute certainty.

"You don't know Paolo."

"Priscilla, not waiting on your table is a drop in the ocean compared to other things you've done. You haven't been fired so far."

The sinking feeling that overtook me when things weren't quite adding up set in. "Yes. Why is that?"

A grin swept his face and his eyes drifted. "See that gorgeous old lady sitting down there?" he asked proudly, pointing at his family's table. "That's my grandmother, Nellie. I named the restaurant after her."

"Oh my God." I buried my face in my hands.

It was going from bad to worse. No wonder he ate there almost every morning. He *owned* the restaurant. And it was a sheer miracle that I was seeing Adam there for the first time. It also explained the rock star welcome from Paolo. What it didn't explain was why Ryan hadn't fired me in the first week. He knew every one of my criminal misdeeds. He'd even been my accomplice in a few.

I lifted my head, peeking at him through the gap in my fingers. "Why haven't you fired me?"

"I like you, Priscilla."

"You know my name's not, Priscilla, right?"

He reached across, pulling my hands free of my face. "From the second I met you. Your *faux nom* doesn't suit you well."

I winced at the blatant reminder of who this man was. Fluency in the French language was not something the Décarie brothers had to practise. It was the primary language spoken in their home, even by their mother who was English.

"Elvis doesn't suit you either. As far as I'm aware, Elvises aren't French."

"How do you know I'm French?"

"I know a lot of things about you," I grumbled.

Smiling slightly, he launched in to a long, foreign monologue. I remained completely stone-faced.

"Well?" he asked, awaiting my verdict.

"You can take the boy out of Marseille, but you can't take Marseille out of the boy," I muttered.

"How do you know I'm from Marseille?"

I shrugged, adding to my illusion of apathy. "Lucky guess."

"A hell of a guess."

"Translate what you said," I demanded.

"I said you look absolutely ridiculous in that costume and your halo's not straight." Ryan leaned across and attempted to straighten my headband, smiling as crookedly as my halo.

"I know who you are, Ryan," I said gravely.

He abruptly withdrew his hands and leaned away from me.

I couldn't expect him to have any clue what was going on. I took in a deep breath, having no choice but to try explaining it to him.

It was the longest story I'd ever told anyone and I kept my eyes locked on his the whole time. Ryan's expression didn't waver as he tried to process the information.

"So you're small-town-hick-girl?" he asked finally.

"The one and only," I confirmed.

"You're Charlotte?"

"Charli, yes," I corrected, unwilling to give him licence to use my full spidery name.

"And you came all the way to New York for him?" I nodded. "And Gabrielle ponied up her apartment so you could stay?" I continued nodding as he whittled down the story I'd just told him. "And seeing dim Whit with him changed your mind?"

"Adam is doing just fine without me. He's moved on."

"Is that what you think?" he asked.

"Yes. What do you think?"

Ryan laughed hard, once. "I think I'm glad I didn't sleep with you."

"Be serious, please," I whined.

"I'm totally serious. That could've been really awkward."

I shot him a poisonous glare. "I'm not talking to you about this any more."

"Look, if it's sensitivity you're after, you're talking to the wrong brother. Go down and talk to the right one," he suggested, pointing to the ground floor.

I refused to give him the satisfaction of looking at Adam. "It won't change anything."

"Don't you think you should let Adam decide that, Charlotte?" He said my name painfully slowly as if it was a difficult word to pronounce. "You could be the girl who saves me from having to endure dull little nieces and nephews in the future. If you stick with him, I could eventually be the uncle to a small pack of criminal masterminds. They'd be cute little weapons of mass destruction."

"Are you done?"

He grabbed my hand. "Not quite," he replied, thrusting me forward to the balustrade.

I tried to step back, but Ryan stood behind me, mercilessly blocking my path. Not content with having me on show, he called his brother's name. Adam tilted his head upward, chasing Ryan's voice. From that moment on, I focused only on his face.

Even from a distance, I swear I saw the colour blanch from his cheeks. Adam rose as if I was pulling him by an invisible string. He began weaving between other tables to get to the stairs, and I was thankful the restaurant was packed to capacity. It hindered him long enough for me to deal with the self-appointed devil's advocate standing behind me.

"You have no idea what you've just done," I said bitterly.

A tiny hint of remorse flashed across Ryan's face. "He'd want to know you're here."

"That wasn't for you to decide."

For some reason, Ryan suddenly had a change of heart. He stepped away, allowing me to move. "There are service stairs at the back, if you want to leave."

I didn't waste a second, bundling my dress in my hands and making a run for it like a cracked-out Cinderella.

The back stairs on the mezzanine led to the kitchen. Paolo collared me before I'd even made the bottom. "Your table has been seated for half an hour!"

"I know," I replied, pulling the ridiculous dress over my head. "I'm sorry, Paolo. I know the timing's not great, but I quit. Tell Ryan I quit." I threw the dress at him, grabbed my coat from the cloakroom and bolted.

7. Ebbs and Flows

It was going to take a lot longer than the twenty-minute walk home to wrap my head around what had just happened. Working out my next move was going to take even longer. Making sense of why I had run was probably never going to happen.

"Miss Charli," greeted Marvin, tipping his hat.

"Hi, Marv." I smiled because Marvin deserved the best from me. "How are you?"

"Fine and dandy. Thank you for asking."

"Marv, can I ask you a question?"

"Of course."

"Do you ever run, when you really should stay?"

"I'm sixty-three years-old, child. I'm too old to run. Are you on the run, Miss Charli?" he asked, pulling the door open for me. His smile voided the serious tone in his voice.

"Only from myself, Marv," I replied, stepping through the door.

If Marvin was worried that I was on the run from someone, he should have been vetting my visitors better. I'd only been home a short while when there was a loud, frantic knock at my door. No one had ever knocked on my door before.

As absurd as it sounds, I wasn't expecting to see *him* standing there when I opened it. Adam looked like he'd had a bad shock and was trying to recover. "Flee-itis, Charlotte?" He didn't say it jokingly. His tone was deadly serious.

"How did you know I was here?"

"It's not rocket science," he replied. "Gabrielle's apartment was the first place I thought of." His hands flew up in a stay-put-and-shut-up-for-a-minute motion. "Don't speak. Just hear me out." I braced myself, waiting to be told to get out of town and leave him and dim Whit in peace.

"It took me a long time to learn how to live without you, but I did it. Life goes on, right?" He didn't pause to let me answer. "You promised that you'd become nothing more than a girl I used to know."

The reminder crushed me. At the time I would have told him just about anything to make him leave. Barely a word out of my mouth that day had been truthful. And the fact that he was reminding me of it showed that of everything we'd shared, the ending is what he remembered most.

"Forgetting you was never going to happen. There's just no getting around it – or over it, apparently. That's why I'm here, right? You ran and I chased you." He sounded annoyed with himself, as if following me home proved a lack of willpower on his part.

"Adam, I don't know why you're here," I mumbled.

He grimaced, clearly conflicted. "There's so much I want to tell you. The problem is, I have two different conversations playing out in my head."

"Pick one."

"Would you prefer the heart wrenching tale of misery or the speech packed with magic and romance?"

I shrugged. "You know me, Adam. I'll take magic over misery any day."

He drew in a breath but didn't seem to exhale, making his words come out in a rush. "I want to tell you that if you let me through the door, there's a fair chance I'm never going to let you go again."

They were words I'd longed to hear, but it was somehow wrong. His pained expression soured everything he'd said. It was as if I'd put an invisible gun to his head and made him confess to his deepest, darkest secret.

"Tell me the miserable part." Hearing it would be nothing more than a formality. Misery had a name. Whitney.

"I'm a realist, Charli." The small smile he gave was nowhere near as bright as I remembered it being. Ryan was right. There was an emptiness about him. "I wouldn't cope if I had to endure an ending all over again. The pieces would be too small to pick up a second time."

Dim Whit hadn't rated a mention. That would have thrilled me if he weren't shutting down my fairy-tale ending in the same speech.

"So where do we go from here?" I asked, trying to hold myself together.

He smiled again, more genuinely this time. I held my breath, awaiting his answer but the elevator doors opened, silencing him instantly.

My neighbour, Oliver, stepped out into the tiny foyer we shared, cradling his little white dog like a baby. The spoiled rotten Maltese terrier – aptly named Fluffin – didn't protest.

Adam turned around and politely said hello.

Oliver shamelessly looked him up and down. "Well, good afternoon," he crooned. "Don't mind me," he said, fumbling in the pockets of his orange and green striped happy pants for his keys. "I'll be out of your hair in just one sec."

Nothing was said until Fluffin and Oliver disappeared into their apartment.

"Look, do you want to come inside?" I motioned toward the door behind me.

"I warned you what would happen if you let me in."

"Having you hold on to me forever doesn't seem like the worst kind of fate, Adam."

"You're impossible to hold," he said grimly. "That's always been the problem."

"You'd be surprised. I'm not so restless anymore."

He dropped his head. "It's good to see you, Charli."

"Well, look at me then!"

Obeying my obnoxious demand, his eyes drifted up to mine. "How long are you planning to stay in New York?"

"I don't know." He wasn't giving me a reason to stay.

"That's the tragedy," he said, slightly smugly. "You're a wanderer." He turned and punched the button on the elevator.

I knew I had him for only a few more seconds. "Where are you going?"

"Back to my real life, Charli. The one you insisted you didn't belong in."

The elevator doors slid open.

Last chance, I thought, punching out a quick question. "Why didn't you ask me why I'm here?"

"Because it doesn't matter. Ryan said you've been in town over a month. That, and the fact that you hightailed it out of the restaurant as soon as you saw me prove that your reasons for being here have nothing to do with me."

Furiously I shook my head. "You're so wrong. I came here for you. I went to your apartment to see you." The elevator doors closed behind him but he stood statuesque, missing the opportunity to leave. "It took me a year to work up to that moment, Adam."

"So what happened?"

"Whitney happened."

In fairness, I shouldn't have said her name so bitterly. According to Ryan, I'd been the other woman, not her.

"I'm so sorry, Charli."

I wondered why. Maybe he felt bad that I'd found out about her that way, or maybe his regret was more ancient. The simple truth was that Whitney had been on the scene long before I fell in love with him.

"Do you love her?"

He shook his head, telling me no. He punched the button on the elevator again, harder this time. "I've got to go. Let's just leave it at that."

"Do you think you're the only one who has something to say? What about the things I need to say?"

"What else is there to say?"

"Look at me," I ordered. He turned around. I had his complete attention – at least until the elevator arrived again. Of everything I'd planned to tell him, only one sentence came to mind. "I love you."

It hardly blew him away. Adam stood so still I could see his chest move as he breathed. At least it was proof of life. I could have gone back into the apartment and brewed a pot of tea in the time it took him to react.

"Say it again," he said at last.

I couldn't blame him for thinking he'd misheard me. Those three words had never crossed my lips before – even when I thought he was actually mine and I had the right to say it. Perhaps I'd said it wrong. Sucking in a long breath, I tried again, enunciating every word.

I didn't even sound sincere. It sounded like I was trying to coax him away from the elevator doors that had just opened again.

His frown softened only slightly. The flash of hope that surged through me was brief. He stepped into the elevator and turned back to face me one last time.

"Stay," I begged.

His dark blue eyes screamed the saddest apology I'd ever seen. "It would never work, Charli. I'm so sorry."

The elevator doors closed and Adam Décarie disappeared from my life for a second time.

Picking up and dusting myself off was getting harder to do.

All self-control eluded me. I picked up a scatter cushion off the never-been-sat-on couch and hurled it at the already closed doors. My aim was terrible. It thudded against the picture hanging on the wall by the elevator. It crashed to the floor making enough noise for Oliver to come running out of his apartment, Fluffin in arms.

"You're probably going to have to pay for that," he said, trading glances and his pointed finger between the mess on the floor and me.

I stared at him blankly, dumbstruck by the sight of a grown man with curlers in his hair. The sight of Fluffin wearing two curlers in the long fur on top of her head was even more disturbing.

I nodded and slunk backwards through my apartment door.

***

My father's uncanny knack of calling me the second I entered dire straits was just plain spooky. I had no intention of explaining the afternoon's events to him but found myself doing it anyway. Alex was so quiet that I had to ask him if he was listening to me.

"Of course I'm listening. Why was the dog wearing curlers?"

"Alex, that's not the important part. It doesn't matter why the dog was wearing curlers."

"No, you're right. I'm sorry. Are you okay?"

It was too late for fatherly concern. The moment was lost thanks to a pampered Maltese terrier called Fluffin. "I'm fine. Everything is fine."

"I worry about you."

"Don't worry about me. At least I know where I stand."

Alone and fed-up was where I stood, but that was the kind of information that would've driven him out to the yard to spend the day chopping wood.

"When are you coming home, Charli?"

"Despite everything, I'm going to stick it out a while longer."

To Alex, it was a perfectly acceptable answer. It meant I was coping. It showed that I hadn't hinged everything on Adam and I was capable of moving forward without him. All I had to do now was convince myself.

The reality was that nothing had changed. It had been weeks since I'd discovered that Adam had moved on without me. I'd left it alone and begun to heal. Seeing him again was like ripping a scab off an old wound. Being told he wasn't going to stay was like having a limb amputated with a rusty blade. Every dealing I'd had with him since arriving in New York had left me more injured. If I were to survive, I had to take Mitchell's advice, cut all ties and put it to bed.

***

I was woken the next morning by a knock at the door. The longer I ignored it, the more urgent the loud rapping became. Unable to stand the persistent noise any longer, I got dressed, dragged a brush through my hair and made my way to the door.

I hadn't put any thought in to who it might be - probably because I knew who it wouldn't be. Standing at my door was an elderly woman I recognised as one of my neighbours. I'd passed her in the main foyer a few times. The light brown shirt - which she wore tucked in to her beige elastic waisted slacks - matched the colour of her teeth perfectly. The only spark of colour was coming from the flashing Santa badge pinned to her chest. I hoped she wasn't going to ask if she could borrow a cup of sugar. I didn't have any. I didn't even have a cup to put the imaginary sugar in.

"Good morning," she greeted. "My name is Mrs Edwin. I live in apartment thirteen."

I smiled politely. "Hello."

She cleared her throat before continuing her well-rehearsed speech. "It's come to the attention of the board that there was an incident in this foyer yesterday afternoon." She pointed to the empty hook on the wall near the elevator. "Some artwork was damaged during a dispute."

Her choice of words was laughable. A one-sided tantrum could hardly be considered a dispute. And I'd recognised Gabrielle's signature on the bottom of the fallen picture. Talented yes. Picasso, no.

"I'll replace it," I offered, wondering how long it would take for Gabrielle to send me another one.

"I was hoping you'd be a reasonable young lady." She grinned, exposing her horsey teeth and handed me a folded piece of paper. "I trust you'll rectify it quickly."

Probably not as quickly as Oliver had ratted me out, I thought.

The paper she'd handed me was an invoice.

I gasped. "Four hundred dollars? That's highway robbery! I know the artist. She'll replace the picture."

Mrs Edwin shook her head. "The concern is not with the picture. The replacement value of the frame is four hundred dollars." I refolded the paper and tried handing it back to her. She pushed it away, refusing to take it. "Perhaps next time you'll keep your temper in check."

"I can't pay this right now," I complained.

She dropped her head and looked at me from above her gold-rimmed glasses. "We're a close community in this building. It's important to remain in good standing. Wouldn't you agree?"

Defeated, I sighed. "Wait here, please," I instructed, retreating back into my apartment.

It nearly killed me to dip in to my precious travel money but the last thing I wanted was to make enemies of my neighbours. I returned to the door and handed Mrs Edwin the wad of cash.

She thanked me and counted it - out loud. "You've been most reasonable, Miss Blake. It's greatly appreciated. If there are any further expenses, I shall let you know."

"Thanks so much," I replied sardonically.

She began to wish me a Merry Christmas but I stepped back inside and closed the door in her face before she got the words out.

Seven hundred and twelve dollars was the sum total of my wealth after I'd paid for my criminal damage. On the plus side, it meant there was no time to hide away and dwell on my train-wreck love life. I was back on the job hunt.

Landing a job took no time at all. I was a bit savvier this time around. I embellished nothing and didn't even have to lie. Thanks to my short stint at Nellie's, I was an experienced server.

I was now waitressing at a midtown restaurant called Mama Sicily's. I had no idea who Mama was. I was interviewed by a man called Roger who didn't look Italian at all. I cornered him outside while he was having a cigarette break. He agreed to hire me, told me I could start the next day and dissolved into a vile coughing fit.

***

My life in New York was rollercoaster of ebbs and flows.

I returned to my apartment full of the hope that had all but disappeared the day before. My lone celebration consisted of a bunch of fresh flowers bought from the newsstand at the end of my block. I was still arranging them in my makeshift vase (a water bottle I'd cut in half) when someone knocked on my door, bringing on the next ebb.

"Go away," I called from the kitchen. "I've got no more money."

"Priscilla, open the door."

Dealing with Ryan seemed slightly less grating than Mrs Edwin, but I was still annoyed with him. The whole saga of the day before was essentially his fault.

"What do you want?" I asked, opening the door just wide enough to see him.

Ryan flashed the trademark, knee-weakening Décarie grin. I was *so* over that grin. "I'm here to apologise." He produced a huge bouquet that put mine to shame. "Are you going to invite me in?"

Relenting, I took the flowers. "Be my guest," I muttered, stepping aside.

Ryan stood in the centre of the barren lounge room and turned around in a full circle. "I love what you've done with the place."

"Very funny."

"No, I'm serious. It looks great now Gabrielle's not in it."

"Ryan, why are you here?" Perhaps he wanted his frying pan back.

"Like I said, I came to apologise. What I did yesterday was pretty low, even for me."

"It ended badly," I told him, standing in the kitchen, butchering another water bottle to house my new flower arrangement.

"Don't you have a vase?" he asked, wincing as I hacked through the plastic.

"Yes, but I only use it on special occasions."

His laugh echoed in the empty apartment, and as hard as I fought against doing it, I laughed too. He walked to the lounge room window, pushed the sheer curtains aside and studied the unimpressive view of the building next door.

"Adam will come round, Charli."

"No. We're done. And I'm fine with it."

Ryan turned back to me, and wisely decided against questioning my change of heart. "I have a gift for you." He reached into his pocket. "I want to make peace."

"You don't need to make peace. I forgive you."

He placed a small white box on the kitchen counter and slid it to me. "Open it, please."

"You should know I'm not good with presents. Adam once gave me a very expensive necklace," I explained, refusing to touch the box.

"Did you lose it?"

"No, I sold it to some African gangsters."

Ryan chuckled darkly. "I'm not shocked by that at all." He tapped the lid of the box with his finger. "This gift is practically worthless."

I'd heard that lie before, but ignoring my reservations I picked up the box and peered inside. Amongst the tissue paper lay a plastic name badge.

"Adam told me you preferred Charli over Charlotte."

"Adam was right."

"So you'll withdraw your resignation?" He frowned as I shook my head.

"I've already taken another job."

"But you were the most devious, crooked, underhanded waitress I've ever had. It's worth keeping you around just for entertainment purposes."

I should have been insulted, but it was a fair description of my career at Nellie's.

"Yeah, well, I'm trying to change my ways," I muttered. "What did Paolo say when you ran it by him?"

"He cried a little bit," he teased. "Taylor didn't have a problem with me rehiring you. I asked everyone else's opinion but no one in the kitchen seemed to know who you were."

I couldn't be sure that he was joking. It all sounded completely plausible.

"Well, I'm Mama Sicily's problem now. I start tomorrow." I picked up the water bottle vase and carried it to the corner of the room, setting it down on the floor. I took a step back to admire it. The glorious display looked like a glimpse of spring in middle of winter.

"Who do you owe money to?" asked Ryan recalling my hostile greeting at the door.

I explained my run-in with Mrs Edwin, and the reason behind it - omitting Fluffin and Oliver's hairdos. Alex had had trouble focusing on the main story once I'd filled his head with that mental image. I didn't want to make the same mistake with Ryan.

"You've settled the debt," he told me. "She can't come back for more."

"Huh?"

Straightening his pose, he brushed his hands together as if he was dusting them off. "*Fait accompli,* Charli."

"You sound like a French lawyer," I accused, scrunching up my nose.

"I am a French lawyer."

I choked. "Why are you running a restaurant then?"

"Everyone needs a hobby."

"That's your hobby?"

He smiled but didn't look at me. "No. It's what I do. I liked the idea of picking up a failing business and making it successful. We turn over a lot of money."

I spoke without thinking. "You don't need the money."

"You're right, we don't," he agreed, miffed. "But when money is no object, how do you measure success, Charli?"

I had no answer for him. It wasn't a predicament someone with seven hundred dollars to their name ever was ever likely to face.

"Adam is studying law." It was a stupid thing to say. It wasn't as if he didn't already know.

"Like a trooper," he jibed.

"It's not a very creative choice of career, is it?"

One of my favourite things about Ryan was his sense of humour. If it were possible to push him over the edge, I hadn't yet managed to do it. "What can I say? It makes our mother happy."

Ryan didn't strike me as the type who'd undertake a law degree to make his mother happy. He'd invited a girl his mother detested to a family lunch, sheerly to rattle her cage.

"Trite."

"It's the truth, Charli. She's shallow." His wily expression made it impossible for me to tell whether he was joking.

"Is Adam studying law to make his mother happy?" I cringed as I said his name. I'd mentioned him far too many times for someone claiming to be over him.

"Adam has a tendency to toe the line rather than break the rules and go after what he really wants. That's why you're here alone, right?"

"He doesn't want me," I snapped. "That's why I'm here alone."

"Is that what he told you?" I played right into his hands by saying nothing. "Exactly. He never told you that. Adam never told you a lot of things."

"You're right," I said sourly. "He never told me about dim Whit."

It wasn't my finest moment. In my heart of hearts I knew that prior knowledge of Whitney wouldn't have changed a thing. I loved him because I couldn't help myself.

"Dim Whit won't be an issue anymore." He said it darkly, like he'd done away with her himself.

"Why?"

"Because he dumped her, yesterday. Right before he took off after you. He pulled her aside and told her it was over. It was like a bloodbath, Charli." Very inappropriately, he smiled. "Adam left and Whitney started howling like a banshee."

"Oh, that's awful. The poor girl."

Appalled by the sympathy I was throwing her way, Ryan groaned, confirming what I already knew. If the Décarie brothers had been twins, Ryan would have been the evil one. "There's nothing poor about her. She's an idiot," he insisted. "He's wasted more than enough time with Whitney Vaughn."

"Are you really that callous, Ryan? He dumped her in front of an audience."

"I guess he just got caught up in the moment. I've been waiting years for it to happen."

I didn't know what to make of Adam's actions. I'd only ever known him to be warm and sweet. Those were the traits I loved. I wondered if they were the qualities Whitney loved too – before he smashed her heart to pieces in a crowded restaurant.

"It was a brutal thing to do," I insisted. Peeved, I walked back over to the kitchen bench to continue work on my first bouquet. I showed none of the care I had with the other arrangement, viciously snipping the stems and jamming them into the plastic bottle. It was hard not to think selfishly. As badly as I felt for dim Whit, the sole source of my ire was the realisation that by the time Adam had knocked on my door, he was free and easy – and still didn't choose me.

Perhaps sensing I was a menace with the scissors, Ryan announced he was leaving. He glanced around the stark apartment one last time. "Are you going to be alright here?"

I glared at him. "Of course I am. I live here."

"Look, Charli, if you ever need anything, anything at all, I want you to call me." He took out his wallet and handed me his business card. "Or Adam. If you can't reach me, call Adam."

Like that was ever going to happen. If I were lying in a heap, bleeding to death, I wouldn't call Adam. I thanked him and dropped the card on the bench. It was nice to know I had options outside the three Alex had given me.

8. Humble In Victory

Mama Sicily's was nothing like Nellie's. The only thing it had going for it was the fact that Paolo didn't work there. It was a tiny, pokey place decorated with dark red walls and a brown tiled floor that felt sticky under my feet. The restaurant was packed with so many tables and chairs that it was hard to move. It was wishful thinking on Mama's part. In the two days I'd been working there, I'd never served more than three tables at a time.

Working only for tips meant that slow shifts were not very profitable. It left plenty of time for idle chatting, which is exactly what my only front of house co-worker, Sophia, liked to do.

"Where do you go tanning?" she asked, munching on a handful of peanuts she'd swiped from the bar.

"The beach, usually."

She guffawed like I'd told the world's funniest joke. Sophia turned my stomach. She had to be related to Mama Sicily - there was no way the girl could have held the job otherwise. She was lazy, impolite and unkempt. For the second day in a row, she wore a tight-fitting white shirt with sweat stains under the armpits. Her skin-tight black jeans were at least a size too small. She was Just plain horrid.

Apart from Sophia, the food, the atmosphere and the lack of patrons, something else bothered me. Roger, the manager, insisted we pool our tips and split them evenly at the end of the week.

The tip jar was kept under the counter. Several times a day, Sophia would bring it out and count the money. I wanted to believe that she didn't pocket it. Her clothing was stretched to the point of splitting. There was nowhere for her to conceal the cash.

"Where do you get your hair done?" She yelled the question across the empty restaurant while I tried to dust the tacky plastic flower arrangements on the tables.

It was the first time I'd smiled since I began working there. "Chateau de Tate."

Mitchell had been my most recent hairstylist - under sufferance. After one disastrous attempt by my own hand, he had no choice. I'd cut it so crookedly that he had to lop four inches off it just to even it up and stop me bawling.

"Is that in Manhattan?"

"No, Sophia," I muttered.

"I went blonde once." I looked across the room at her, trying to imagine her lanky black hair ten shades lighter. "It took three years to grow all the way out. I couldn't be bothered changing it."

It was incomprehensible. Sophia had spent three years looking like a skunk because she was too lazy to do anything about it.

I decided on the long walk home that it was time to quit my ghastly job. I couldn't find a single reason to stick it out. Even Marvin agreed with me when I sought his opinion at the door.

"Leave it in the past, Miss Charli. Blue skies tomorrow."

As far as I was concerned, Marvin was the king of the good advice.

I forced myself to work one more day. The plan was to finish my shift, collect my half of the tips and kiss Mama Sicily's good riddance forever.

Roger wasn't taken aback when I told him I'd quit. "You lasted longer than I thought you would," he grumbled, in between hacking coughs that made me queasy.

Sophia wasn't exactly forlorn either. "You're not cut out for this job."

"No, it's too fast paced for me." My patronising tone was wasted on her.

She nodded in agreement.

With an hour to go before the end of my Mama Sicily's experience, I suggested that Sophia split the tips. I only kept half an eye on her as she counted it out, which was a mistake. She called me up to the bar to hand me my share - a measly twenty-eight dollars. There had been at least twice that in the jar the day before.

"That's not right," I said, calmly.

"I just counted it. That's half." She thrust the money at me and I snatched it from her.

"Call Roger in here," I demanded. "That's wrong."

Sophia tipped her head back and boomed out Roger's name. He skulked through the kitchen door.

"Charli thinks I'm ripping her off."

"Well, are you?" He didn't sound like he cared one way or the other.

"No. I gave her half," she lied.

He looked at me and shrugged his grubby shoulders. "There you have it. She gave you half."

A revolted groan escaped me and I walked outside to get my temper in check. I wanted to rant, rave and throw things but my last tantrum was fresh in my thoughts. I couldn't afford to pay for any more damages.

It took only seconds to come up with a plan. Sneaking further down the street, out of Sophia's sight, I called Ryan.

"What do you need, Charli?"

"I need you to come down here and help me with something."

"Something illegal?" I could hear the amusement in his voice.

"Yes, yes, yes. Illegal, immoral, unethical, all of those things." I rushed out the words, ticking all boxes, not wanting to waste a single second.

I let Ryan finish laughing before rattling off my short but particular shopping list and giving him directions. He didn't question it, promising to get to Mama's as quickly as he could.

Ryan didn't disappoint, calling me half an hour later to tell me he was waiting outside. I walked out the door on the pretence of needing some air, leaving Sophia folding napkins at the bar.

"What are you up to, Charli?" he asked, handing me a tiny bag.

In it was a cheap pair of diamante earrings pierced through a piece of cardboard.

"Oh, perfect," I cooed.

"They're junk," he scoffed. "They cost me five bucks on the corner."

"Trust me, they're perfect."

Ryan shook his head. His quizzical smile broadened as I laid out my plan.

"Are you sure about this?"

I pulled one of the earrings off the piece of card and handed it to him. "I'm only trying to get what's fair."

"What's fair, Charli?"

I thought for a long moment. "A hundred dollars."

"All of this for a hundred dollars? I'll give you a hundred bucks, right now."

"No. I earned that money, fair and square," I growled, slapping his arm as he reached for his wallet.

"I get it, Charli. Let's go."

Sophia barely cast a glance in my direction as I walked back inside. When Ryan walked in a second later, she sparked back to life, leaning forward to give him a perfect view of her cleavage. "Can I help you?"

"I hope so," replied Ryan, smoothly. "I was in here last night with my girlfriend. I can't remember the name of the gorgeous girl who served us."

Sophia stared at him, stunned. "That would have been Fatima."

"Yes!" He clicked his fingers loudly. "That was her name."

"Fatima's not gorgeous," she scoffed. "She's two hundred and sixty pounds and has a moustache."

I was pretending to straighten the table settings while I listened to my brilliant plan unravel. It wasn't Ryan's fault. I'd never had the pleasure of meeting gorgeous Fatima either. I couldn't have warned him that for the first time ever his sweet-talking would backfire.

"Anyway, my girlfriend lost an earring while she was here," he said, getting back to the story.

"What does it look like?" she asked, dubiously.

Ryan handed the junky gem earring to Sophia. "It was the same as this one."

We both watched in silence as she examined it with the precision of a gem dealer. "How much is it worth?"

"Practically nothing. The value is purely sentimental."

Predictably, Sophia quickly lost interest, dropping the fake bling into his palm. "Well, we haven't found it here."

"I'll tell you what," he said, returning the earring to his pocket. "Let me write down my number."

Sophia reached into the bowl of peanuts on the bar, and shovelled a handful into her mouth. "You're cute and all but I don't date customers." Her chomped-out rebuff made Ryan retreat as if she'd just whacked him. "I'm not giving you my number. I'm leaving my number here in case you find the earring."

I could tell he was in danger of losing his patience - and his lunch - so I intervened in the hope of wrapping it up quickly. "Are you offering a reward?" I asked, stepping toward the bar.

"Why, yes. Yes I am." His overacting was terrible but for some reason, Sophia didn't notice.

"How much?" she asked.

"Two hundred dollars," Ryan announced, sticking to the plan.

Sophia reached for the notepad she kept under the counter.

"Write down your number. If we find it, I'll call you."

Ryan wrote down his phone number, thanked her and got out as quickly as he could without running. As soon as he was gone, Sophia tore the page off the pad and stuffed it into her bra.

"Sophia, I have to tell you something," I began.

"I don't think he was interested in you, Charli. I'm not giving you his number."

"No, I wanted to tell you that I found this while I was setting the tables this morning." I reached into the pocket of my apron and pulled out the 'missing' earring.

Sophia's greedy eyes lit up and she lurched across the counter to snatch it from me.

A quick step back was all it took to ward her off. "Uh-uh," I scolded, wagging my finger at her. "Finders, keepers."

"Fine. We'll go halves," she spat. "When he gives me the money, I'll give you half."

"Like you gave me half of the tip jar? I don't think so."

I was almost at the front door when she called me back. "Okay, okay, listen. I'll give you half right now."

She squeezed between the tables to get to me, waving a hundred dollar bill.

"That's fair," I agreed, snatching it from her grip.

"The earring," she demanded, holding out her pudgy hand. Keeping my end of the bargain, I handed it to her.

I stood long enough to see Sophia scuttle back to the bar, groping herself to retrieve Ryan's number. I walked out of Mama Sicily's for the last time, triumphant. By the time I met my accomplice at the corner, the skip in my step had transitioned into a happy dance.

"I think you're supposed to be humble in victory, Charlotte," Ryan chided.

"Impossible! I'm never gracious in defeat, either."

"I doubt you've ever been defeated." Ryan grabbed my coat from my arms and held it for me. "What do you have planned for the next hour or so?"

I almost laughed at his question. I had nothing planned for the next six months or so. "Nothing important."

"Good. I want to show you something." His arm was outstretched, hailing an approaching cab, before he finished his sentence.

I didn't ask him where we were going. I spent the fifteen-minute cab ride staring out the car window, soaking in my surroundings. Being in New York never grew tiresome.

"Just here will be fine," instructed Ryan, thrusting some money at the driver as the cab pulled to a stop. He practically yanked me out of the car.

"Are we in a hurry?" I asked, struggling to keep pace as he strode down the street.

"I'm supposed to be meeting someone at four."

"Who?"

He didn't answer me.

For a horrible second I thought he was dragging me along on one of his dates. When we finally stopped walking, I glanced to my left and right, breathing a little easier when I was unable to spot any beautiful, irate-looking blonde women.

"Well? What do you think?" he asked.

"About what?"

Ryan pointed to a two-storeyed building across the street. Scaffolding framed the entire outside - not an uncommon sight in New York.

"We've been working on it since last summer," he said proudly. "It's nearly finished."

"What will it be when it's done?"

He frowned as he stared across at it, leading me to wonder if the answer should have been obvious. The maze of steel framework hid the building well.

"It's another restaurant. Not as big as Nellie's, more intimate and upmarket."

I wanted to ask him more, but was distracted by a man rushing across the street toward us. The orange hardhat on his head and the rolled up blueprints under his arm made it apparent he was working on the building.

I took a step back while the meeting took place on the pavement. Ryan pored over the plans while hardhat man discussed the very boring subject of travertine floor tiles. Apparently, they were going to take longer to lay than first anticipated.

Hardhat man had a habit of nodding incessantly whenever Ryan spoke. Perhaps he was scared of him. I wouldn't have blamed him if he were. Ryan sounded scary. He was abrasive and uncompromising, demanding they stick to the deadline and fulfil their contractual agreements. For a man who didn't work in his trained profession, he sure sounded like a lawyer.

Ryan waited until hardhat man had scurried back across the street. "Do you want to go inside?"

I nodded eagerly. We waited for a break in the traffic and I followed Ryan down a side alley to a big blue construction door that looked out of place against the old building. He pushed it open and ushered me in ahead of him.

"Wow!" It was all I could manage to say.

The interior of the building had been gutted. All that remained was one large ground floor with a mezzanine level above. Obviously Ryan had a thing for mezzanines.

A group of men were working on the ground floor, laying huge square tiles. Hardhat man looked even more nervous now that Ryan was in the building.

"Look up."

I looked up at the very high ceiling and saw the biggest chandelier I had ever seen in my life. When he flicked a switch, it lit up like an upside-down tree of diamonds.

"Wow!" I'd gotten away with it the first time. Now I just sounded foolish.

"Does that mean you like it?" he asked, walking back toward me.

Tiny flickers of light danced around the room. For a girl who grew up chasing fairies, gemstones and anything glittery, there was nothing not to like.

"It's amazing."

"I think so too. It's the first time I've seen it lit." He took out his phone and snapped a quick picture.

"That won't cut it," I scoffed.

"Fine," he said, trying to hand his phone to me. "You do better."

"You're never going to do it justice with a picture taken on a phone. You've just wasted a moment in time you're never going to get back."

Returning his phone to his pocket, he stared at me like I'd just lost my mind. He was part of the ninety-nine percent of the population who just didn't get it. It was an unwanted reminder that Adam was in the one percent who understood perfectly.

"You're quite possibly the strangest person I know," he said. I got the distinct impression he was telling me the truth.

"Can I come back here with my camera?" I asked.

"Sure, any time. I wouldn't want any of those little moments to escape uncaptured."

"Sarcasm is the lowest form of wit, Ryan."

"No, Charlotte, dim is the lowest form of wit."

"Smooth, Ryan," I muttered, trying not to smile. "Real smooth."

9. Trespass

Two days after quitting my job, I decided to make good on my threat to return to the restaurant with my camera. I wasn't expecting it to be so quiet. When I had been there with Ryan, it was noisy with workers, loud power tools and music blaring from a communal stereo. Today it was deathly quiet.

"Hello?" I tentatively called, making my way through the unlocked blue door. I got no response.

Ignoring my unease, I walked across the wide-open space, flicked on the light switch and peered up at the chandelier.

I quickly determined that the best vantage point was from the mezzanine level. The only access was via a rickety-looking ladder propped against the edge of the open top level. It was worth the climb. From the top, the beautiful light fitting looked twice as big, and even more out of place in the construction zone surrounding it.

The trouble with magic is that it's usually an ephemeral moment. My moment disappeared the second the blue door opened. Two men walked in, and I recognised one as the nervous man Ryan had dealt with when we were there a few days earlier. He didn't seem so fidgety this time round. His composure was ironclad when he spotted me upstairs, accused me of being a thief and threatened to call the police. I wondered if he was expecting me to pocket the chandelier. It was the only thing I could see worth stealing.

"I'm just here taking pictures," I explained.

Hardhat man was unconvinced. He marched to the ladder and lowered it to the floor, stranding me. "You've no business being here. You're trespassing."

"So you're just going to keep me prisoner?"

He nodded. "Until the police get here."

All sorts of horrible thoughts flashed through my mind as he reached for his phone - mainly about being rounded up by the NYPD and deported. Arriving back in Australia wearing an orange jumpsuit and handcuffs wasn't appealing, so I fought a bit harder for my freedom.

"Call Ryan Décarie, the guy I was here with on Wednesday." I wanted to see him cower at the mention of his name but he didn't. "He'll vouch for me."

He shook his head. "No dice. I don't deal with that man unless I absolutely have to."

Mercifully, the other man chimed in with another suggestion. "You could call the other one. What's his name? Aaron?"

It took me a second to work it out. Ryan often referred to a business partner but had never once mentioned that it was his younger brother. "Adam," I corrected. "Yes, call him."

I could see hardhat man was at least considering it. "Does he know you?"

"Yes. You should call him. He'll go much easier on you than his brother. If Ryan finds out you're holding me here he's going to flip out."

It was a completely hollow threat. For all I knew, Ryan would wash his hands of me and tell them to call the police anyway. The bigger fear was that Adam would do the same thing.

It was still a relief that he called him. I cringed hearing him telling Adam that he'd cornered some foreign girl stealing from the building site. There was no way it was going to end well.

"He's on his way. Stay put until he gets here." It wasn't like I had a choice. The ladder lay on the floor many metres below me and as far as I knew, I hadn't yet learned to fly.

It was a long half hour. I used the time to take the pictures I'd come for in the first place, but by the time Adam walked through the door I was ready to call the police and surrender.

Both men jumped to attention when the blue door opened. Adam marched over to them, looking every bit as annoyed as I expected him to.

"Where is she?"

Hardhat man pointed up. "She's probably here for the copper wire."

Adam looked up and stiffly threw out his arms. "Trust me," he said dryly. "If she were here to steal copper wire it would only be to make a charm bracelet."

Both workmen laughed, albeit uneasily. Adam shook their hands, praised them for their vigilance and suggested they take the rest of the afternoon off. The men didn't argue, quickly packing their tools and disappearing out the door.

"What are you doing here, Charli?" Adam asked, pacing around and looking anywhere but up.

"Taking pictures."

He stopped pacing. "Trouble just finds you, doesn't it?"

"Yes, Adam. Like magic," I replied, matching his snippy tone. "Just put the ladder back for me so I can get down, please."

He reinstated my escape route and I backed down the wobbly ladder. Adam reached up, taking the camera from me as I neared the bottom rung.

"Just so you know, I didn't break in," I said, stepping safely back on the floor. "Ryan knew I was coming to take pictures."

"Your new BFF should have had more sense." He hooked my bag over my shoulder. "You could have fallen and broken your neck."

I stared at him for a long moment, trying to work out whether he was angry or concerned. I decided it didn't matter either way. Ryan had been my saving grace more than once since I'd arrived in New York. I wasn't going to apologise for that.

"I'm fine," I told him, stating the obvious.

"Are you heading home?" he asked, changing the subject. "We could share a cab."

"No, thank you. I'm going to walk. I haven't found a café that makes a decent cup of tea yet. Today might be my lucky day."

"You've just spent an hour being held hostage and you think today might be your lucky day?" I nodded, returning his small smile. "Look, there's a tea house not far from here. It's supposed to be pretty good. I'll take you there."

Perhaps I wasn't as immune to the Décarie effect as I claimed to be. I agreed to go.

10. Five Minute Rule

In all my travels, I'd never once been to a tea house. I expected it to be eccentric and hippy, with burning incense and panpipe music. I couldn't have been more wrong. The Pink Rose Tea House was English themed, and understandably, Adam was out of his element from the get-go. If the lacy tablecloths, bone china cups and my company hadn't already unnerved him, the menu certainly would have. He was strictly a coffee drinking New Yorker.

"You'll have to help me out here, Charli," he whispered, peeking over the top the menu. When the waitress appeared at our table I let him off the hook by ordering for him. Fidgeting with the edge of the tablecloth while we waited for our order to arrive compensated for the lack of conversation. It also reduced the risk of me doing the airhead hair twirl thing.

"Do you wish you hadn't come here?" he asked, finally breaking the lull.

I shook my head, glancing only briefly at him. "No. I like tea."

"You know that's not what I meant," he replied, huffing out a hard breath that almost sounded like a laugh.

"I'm glad I came to New York," I relented. "I wish I hadn't come looking for you, though. I wish I'd kept you up here instead." I tapped the side of my head with my finger. "In my mind, the reunion was much better."

Adam leaned back in his chair, staring at me for too long for it to be anything other than strategic. He had a few more seconds to consider my words while the waitress delivered our tea. We both straightened up as she set the table.

"Enjoy," she said, smiling brightly before walking away.

There was no way Adam was going to enjoy it. Most men would struggle when it came to sipping tea out of a delicate china cup - except perhaps my neighbour Oliver. I'd once seen him wearing a shirt with a pink floral pattern very similar to the one on the teacups.

"I love you, Charlotte," Adam declared, pushing his cup to the centre of the table. It was an unfair thing to say. "But things change."

"Because of the horrible way I ended it?"

He shook his head. "I knew you were lying."

"You lied to me too. You never told me about dim Whit."

Playing the Whitney card was the only thing I could think of to even up the score sheet. My moral compass was askew, but I wasn't the only liar at the table.

"I wanted to," he insisted, softening his expression only slightly, "a hundred times. I just couldn't figure out how."

"I. Have. A. Girlfriend." I ticked the words off on my fingers. "Not so tricky."

"I wish I had been the one to tell you about her. I hate that you heard it from Ryan."

"What makes you think I've been speaking to Ryan about it?"

He smirked at my attempt to play innocent. "He's the only person who refers to her as dim Whit - besides you, apparently."

"You should have told me about her, Adam. From the beginning." I drummed my finger on the table with each word. My annoyance was false, designed purely to mask the chagrin of being caught grilling Ryan for information. "It wouldn't have changed how I felt."

"What does it matter, Charli? What's done is done."

Hearing him sound so defeated wasn't something I was used to, and for the first time I wondered if the damage we'd done to each other was permanent.

"Why are we here then, pretending to drink tea?"

He almost smiled. "Because I'm having trouble staying away from you."

"That's because you love me."

"Yes," he conceded. "But I'd rather do it from a distance."

"Why?"

Hearing the answer would feel like emotional suicide but I needed to know. I promised myself that I'd consider it closure. If I had answers, perhaps I'd no longer think about him.

Adam exhaled a long, unsteady breath. "I don't know how it would work out long term. I couldn't endure another ending, Charli. I'm not brave enough."

I sat mindlessly stirring my tea as I mulled over his words. As much as I hated to admit it, his answer was perfectly understandable. It just wasn't what I wanted to hear.

"I get it, Adam. I do." I wished I'd sounded stronger but the lump in my throat made me sound as if I was about to burst into tears at any second. "But for the record, I would've risked it."

He smiled. "You always were braver than me."

"You and I were guaranteed a happy ending. I've known that from the very beginning. I'm sorry I made you forget that."

I placed my teaspoon down on the saucer and reached for my bag from under the table, preparing to make a quick exit.

Adam didn't protest.

"Thanks for the tea," I said, smiling as normally as I could.

He nodded stiffly. "Any time."

Ever polite, Adam stood up as I did. I put on my coat, thanked him again for the tea that neither of us drank, and slipped out the door into the freezing December afternoon.

I took my time getting home, stopping along the way to window-shop and check out the over-the-top Christmas decorations. It was after six by the time I finally moseyed though the front door of my apartment building.

Marvin had already left for the day and the night doorman, whose name I didn't know, stood in his place. A quick hello was the only conversation I'd ever been able to drag out of him. Today, I was perfectly happy with that. I was done talking.

I stepped out of the elevator into my tiny foyer to find Adam sitting on the sofa that could no longer be referred to as never-been-sat-in.

"I was beginning to worry that you weren't coming back," he said.

"I live here. Why are you here?"

He stepped in front of me as I opened the door, blocking the doorway.

"Because I'm having trouble staying away from you." He spoke slowly, as if it was a hard question to answer.

I leaned forward, whispering my words as if we weren't alone. "It's because you love me."

I brushed past him, leaving him to close the door.

He followed me to the kitchen. "What if you're wrong about the happy ending, Charlotte?"

I dumped my bag on the counter. "It's still worth the risk. I'm playing by the five minute rule."

"Which is?"

I rushed the words, expecting him to make a bolt for the door at any second. "Give every opportunity five minutes. If that's all it's good for, so be it. But I'm not going to miss out on something amazing because I was too scared to take a chance."

He smiled but it was tinged with sadness. "I can't begin to tell you how much I've missed hanging out in La La land."

I couldn't pinpoint the moment his arm slipped around my waist, nor did I try to fight it. I was too focused on making sense of his turnaround. I put my hands on his chest to keep him at bay while I steadied myself. I'd become so used to emptiness that the rush of warmth was overwhelming.

"You're welcome back any time."

Whether he'd planned it or not, his hold on me was the only thing keeping me upright.

"You revoked my membership, remember?"

"A girl can change her mind."

Brushing my hair off my shoulder with his free hand, he smiled, brighter than before. "That's what I'm afraid of."

"I've never changed my mind about you, Adam. That's why I'm here. Why are you here?"

I still wasn't entirely sure which direction we were headed. Two hours earlier he was cutting me loose. I was done chasing the impossible.

"Because I love you."

I avoided his eyes, but felt his warm gaze. My focus was solely on his mouth. I could feel his kiss before it happened. And when he crushed his lips against mine and I could finally be sure that his touch was real, I was cast back to a time that just a few hours earlier, I thought was gone forever. Nothing had changed. Not his touch, nor his taste. Even his annoying knack for breaking our embrace just before my heart thumped out of my chest remained the same.

"What happens now, Charlotte?" he breathed, resting his forehead on mine. "Tell me what you want."

Oh, where to begin? If I'd had more time to think, I could probably have come up with something maudlin and sweet. "I just want to feel you in my bones again."

Despite my lack of refinement, the power of my words was huge. And when he lifted me off my feet and carried me out of the kitchen, I wondered why I'd waited so long to say it.

A few steps into the next room, he lowered me to the ground, distracted by something other than my bones.

"Charli," he said ominously. "There's no furniture."

I giggled. "I have a bed."

He turned back to me. "That's it?"

"I have a frying pan, too." He looked appalled. He probably would have been even more outraged if he knew I'd stolen it from his restaurant. "And a laundry basket," I added, proudly.

"Some things never change."

He leaned forward, kissing a long line down my neck as he unbuttoned my coat.

"Some things have changed but I'll save them for another day," I murmured.

I couldn't claim to be the same girl he knew a year ago. My life had altered hugely. I wanted to tell him everything, and I wanted to know everything – just not at that very minute.

"Do you still believe in magic, Charlotte?" he asked, pushing my coat off my shoulders. It fell to the floor in a heavy heap.

"Of course." In a million lifetimes, that would never change. "Do you?"

"Absolutely." He murmured the word against my mouth. "I look for magic every day."

On the brink of giving in, I pulled myself together enough to ask one last question. "Do you ever find it?"

"Today I did," he told me, sliding his warm hand up the back of my shirt. "And she's still beautiful."

11. Set In Stone

Waking up alone wasn't exactly how I pictured our first morning together.

I sat up, wrapping myself in the sheet. Through the doorway, I could see Adam in the empty lounge, clad only in a pair of jeans, talking on his phone. If it was supposed to be a private conversation, he had no chance. The acoustics in the small, empty apartment rivalled any good concert hall.

Love is inherently selfish. I didn't want him to talk to anyone. As far as I was concerned, we should have been left alone to live out the rest of our days in my tiny apartment. For me, it was an obtainable goal. Thanks to my inability to maintain employment, I had nowhere else to be. Adam, however, would fail miserably as a recluse. It was just after seven in the morning and someone was already trying to track him down. After eavesdropping for a minute, I realised it was Whitney.

"No, Whit. There's nothing to work out."

She obviously didn't agree. It was at least ten seconds before he got another word in. "Look, I'm not discussing this right now."

There was another long pause, presumably to accommodate more ranting. That was the only concession he made for her. His tone was granitic and curt and it summed up exactly why eavesdropping was a very bad idea.

I didn't even pretend that I hadn't been listening when Adam returned to the room. I tried to keep my voice casual. "How is Whitney?"

He pushed me back on to the bed with his whole body, burying his head in the crook of my neck. "It's not a problem, Charli."

"Ryan told me that you dumped her at Nellie's, the day you saw me."

Adam rolled to one side. "She doesn't even know about you," he mumbled, staring at the ceiling. "It had nothing to do with you."

I believed him – to a point. Adam hadn't ended their relationship to be with me. A short while after, I'd stood in front of him, begging him to stay with me to no avail. I had no idea what his reasons were – then wondered if Whitney did.

"Why did you break up with her?"

He turned to catch my eye, frowning. "Because I don't love her."

"Why string her along for four years then?"

"Ryan really did give you the scoop didn't he?" he asked. "I stayed with her because it was convenient – for both of us. We have the same circle of friends. We hang out at the same places. My parents like her." He rattled of the reasons as if he was reading from a list. "It worked for a while."

"I wonder how Whitney would feel about being used like that. She's probably heartbroken."

"Not over the loss of me," he said bitterly. "It was a two way arrangement."

I didn't ask him to elaborate. I didn't want to hear another word about it. Ignorance was bliss, and that ignorance was going to save me from rethinking my opinion on which of the Décarie brothers was the evil one.

"We have so much to figure out, Adam."

His hand slipped under the covers, sweeping a long trail down my body that scorched my skin. "It'll work out. I promise."

As distracting as his wandering hands were, I needed to know how. In the cold light of day, the transition into Adam's New York life seemed a little tricky. "You have to listen to me for a second," I demanded, squeezing his fingers to stop them creeping.

He heaved a long sigh. "I'm listening."

"I don't need anything set in stone. I just need to know we're on the same page." I would've been content knowing that we were reading the same book.

"I have no problem setting things in stone, Charli. I'll do it right now." He practically leapt off the bed. I wrapped myself in the sheet, bundled the excess in my arms and followed him to the kitchen.

"What are you looking for?" I asked, watching as he rummaged around in a kitchen drawer.

"This," he said triumphantly, holding a black marker pen in the air.

I'd always found it strange that although I lived without furniture, I still managed to fill a drawer in the kitchen with junk.

Reaching for my hand, he led me through to the lounge room, took the lid off the pen and scrawled a number one on the pristine white wall.

"What are you doing?" I asked, aghast.

"Setting our future in stone." He sounded much too proud of himself. The Parisienne would kill him for a lot less.

"Gabrielle will skin you alive."

"Gabrielle will never know. She doesn't stop by often."

He dotted his pen on the wall. "What's first on the list?"

"I don't know."

"Where are we going to live?" he prompted.

"You want us to live together?"

He looked at me. "I think we've wasted enough time apart, don't you?"

Words failed me. I wanted to lurch forward, drop him to the floor and have my way with him, but my legs wouldn't work. I nodded instead.

"Okay. Well, we can either stay here or you can move in with me."

"I'm sure your parents would be thrilled."

"I'm sure they wouldn't be, but I'm grown. They don't actually get a say when it comes to who I live with."

"They might notice me there, Adam."

"I don't live with my parents, Charli. I share an apartment with Ryan."

"But I saw you there," I accused, "the day I came looking for you."

Adam shrugged. "It must have been a Friday. Ryan and I have breakfast there every Friday morning. It stops our mother from coming to our place to check up on us."

It was by sheer luck that I'd seen him that day. There wasn't an ounce of magic involved. If it were magical intervention, Whitney wouldn't have been there to sour the memory.

"Make a decision, Charlotte." He tapped the pen on the wall, snapping my thoughts back to the task. "The list is long."

"I couldn't stand living with Ryan," I muttered, staring at the vandalised wall.

"Fine." He turned to the wall and began writing. "I'll move in here."

He didn't need my input for number two. Furniture.

"Things get a little more complex at number three, Coccinelle," he warned, calling me by the nickname I feared I'd never hear again. "I have another two years of law school left. Do you think you could be happy here for that long?"

"I like New York."

"Well, isn't that ironic?" he drawled. "Makes you wonder why you fought against it for so long, doesn't it?"

He slipped his arm around my waist. We stood admiring his vandalism.

"Should repainting the wall be on the list?"

"No. It can stay there forever. Our children can scrub it off," he mumbled, brushing my hair aside as he leaned in to kiss my shoulder.

Twisting in his arms, I studied him closely. "The list will be very long by then."

"I hope so," he whispered.

Convincing Adam to return to the bedroom was easy. All I had to do was abandon my grip on the sheet.

"We should never leave this bed," I insisted, breathing the words into his ear.

He groaned in agreement, sending a hot rush right through my body that he felt. He responded by sending me to a place I was happy to revisit – the point of no return.

12. Little Elephant

Adam and Ryan's apartment was only a few blocks away, on a street I'd never explored. "I haven't been down here before."

"Good," replied Adam, tightening his grip on my hand. "It's a very seedy part of town."

It didn't look seedy. The street was lined with trees that winter had stripped of leaves. The stately pre-war buildings were elegant and grand. The cold, crisp air smelled clean and traffic was at a minimum.

Adam was adaptable. I'd seen him spend hours scraping and sanding a grotty old boat, dressed in paint-spattered jeans with flecks of wood in his hair. The thought of Ryan residing in a less than prestigious area seemed impossible.

"You're lying, aren't you?" I accused.

He chuckled. "Yes, I'm lying."

He was *really* lying. The inside of the apartment was every bit as modish as I anticipated. The front door opened on to an open plan living room. The floor was syrup coloured timber, and the walls were rustic, exposed red brick. It was masculine, industrial and stylish. The only seedy thing in the apartment was Aubrey, Ryan's date from the fateful lunch at Nellie's. She was sitting on the couch, touching up her makeup.

Ryan was there too, standing at the granite island bench, thumbing through a newspaper. "I was wondering how long it would be before you two surfaced," he mocked.

"Hello to you too," said Adam. He turned his attention to dodgy Barbie. "Good morning, Aubrey. I haven't seen you here for a while."

Aubrey snapped her compact shut and stood, smoothing her night-before dress and her bedroom hair. "Well, they do say absence makes the heart grow fonder."

"You're assuming Ryan has a heart. That's charitable."

Aubrey muttered an insult I didn't quite catch and walked to Ryan. She whispered something in his ear that made him simper and breezed past us to the door.

Ryan was the second seediest thing in the room. I couldn't help noticing his eyes following her the whole way. Once she was gone, he turned his attention to me, dropping the sordid stare and smiling sweetly. "How are you, Charlotte?"

"Fine, thank you."

"Staying out of trouble?"

"Leave her alone," warned Adam. "Pay no attention to him, Charli."

"Have you found another job yet, Charli?" asked Ryan.

"Not yet."

"You can come back to Nellie's, you know."

"You wouldn't want her back," said Adam, searching through the kitchen cupboards. "Where's the tea?"

"We don't have any tea," claimed Ryan. "No one of sound mind drinks tea. Why don't I want her back?"

"Charli drinks tea. You don't want her back because she doesn't have a green card."

Ryan glared at me, appalled. "Oh, joy. Why am I not surprised?"

I didn't answer him.

Adam gave up looking for tea and tried to tempt me with a mug of coffee, promising it was the best in New York.

"This is how it starts, Charli," Ryan foreboded. "Before you know it, he'll have you hooked on the harder stuff. Espressos, Turkish coffee…."

I walked in to the kitchen and took the mug from Adam, totally buckling under peer pressure.

"It's Saturday. Why are you dressed like you're going to a funeral?" asked Adam, absently stirring his coffee while he looked his brother up and down.

The Décarie boys were tragically good looking. Ryan's biggest problem was that he was well aware of it. He straightened his grey silk tie and brushed the shoulder of his dark grey suit like he was dusting it off. "I've been summoned to breakfast with the queen," he announced in a faultless British accent.

"Why?" asked Adam.

"Because you haven't been taking her calls all week. I assume she wants the lowdown on dim Whit. She's not happy with you. I thought I'd take her somewhere classy so she can't raise hell in public."

Instantly I knew that the queen was their mother. I began to feel incredibly nervous but had no clue why.

"Thanks," Adam said, seemingly unconcerned by his mother's fury. "I owe you one."

Ryan fidgeted with his tie again. "You already owe me many. You shouldn't have told her Charli was in town. She thinks you've dumped Whitney and run off with the little minx." Ryan pointed at me and I scowled. "Her words, not mine, sorry," he whispered, expressing badly acted pity.

"Ridiculous," uttered Adam.

"How does she know about me?" I asked. More importantly, why had she formed such a low opinion so soon?

"We've always known about Adam's little summer romance," said Ryan. "He just wasn't expected to bring her home."

***

Adam's bedroom was at the end of a short hallway. It shared the same rustic brick walls as the rest of the apartment but the large window on the far side of the room made the space bright.

I followed him in and sat on the edge of the bed, scanning the room without moving my head.

Adam slid open the wardrobe, dragged two suitcases from the top shelf and dropped them beside me.

Alex had often accused me of being a mini cyclone. Seeing the boy I love dragging clothes out of his wardrobe and dumping them into suitcases proved that I was. In a few short days, I'd completely upturned his life.

"Are you sure you want to do this, Adam?" I asked, giving him a chance to renege on our set-in-stone futures. "I can repaint the wall."

He punched out a quick laugh. "I don't want to spend another minute without you. The wall stays."

"I've turned your life upside down," I said gravely.

"You did that the day I first met you, Coccinelle."

"Even your mother hates me."

"My mother hates the idea of you."

I wanted to ask him what he meant, but Ryan's appearance way halted the conversation. A confused frown swept his face. "Are you leaving?"

Adam answered his question by zipping one of the suitcases closed.

Ryan turned his attention to me, still frowning quizzically. "What is it about you?"

I had no idea how to answer him. His phone rang and I had an instant reprieve. He read the number on the screen and rolled his eyes. "It's for you," he said, holding the phone to Adam. "It's your mother."

"She's your mother, too. And she's calling your phone."

"Answer it," he demanded.

Adam shook his head.

"Fine, we'll all answer it." Ryan hit the speaker button and Fiona Décarie's urgent voice filled the air.

The family was a hodgepodge of accents. Now a new one was thrown into the mix. Fiona Décarie was undoubtedly English, and spoke with a plum in her mouth to prove it.

"Hey, Ma," Ryan drawled, holding the phone in the air. "Are we still on for breakfast?"

"Of course. Darling, have you heard from Adam? Is he home yet?"

Adam swiped his hand across his throat.

"No, he's not here," fibbed Ryan.

Something in his expression told me he was not to be trusted. I expected him to force the phone upon Adam at any second. But he didn't, leaving their mother free to launch into a diatribe.

"Well, where is he? I know he's with that dreadful girl but, where? He's not answering his phone."

Adam winced as she called me dreadful. I sat perfectly still, trying to appear unaffected.

"He's moving in with her, Ma. I think it's pretty serious."

"What? Is he out of his mind? Poor Whitney will be devastated. Try talking some sense in to him, Ryan. I won't have him throwing his whole life away on some two-bit trollop."

"The trollop's actually quite sweet." He looked at me as he said it. Perhaps I was supposed to be flattered.

Adam walked back to the wardrobe, dragging clothes off hangers less carefully than before.

"She hails from a country of convicts!" she screeched.

Ryan laughed and I heard Adam groan. I couldn't bring myself to look at him.

"As far as I know, Charlotte is a law-abiding citizen - for the most part."

The evil Décarie brother was taking far too much pleasure in the exchange. I wanted to snatch the phone and hang up on her. Speaking up and defending myself didn't enter my thoughts. Fiona Décarie was playing on a level far above anything I was capable of.

"I won't stand for it," she snarled.

"You might not have a choice."

"No little vagrant pauper is going to ruin my son!"

At least she'd done her homework. Vagrant pauper I could deal with. It was a fair description. The sting of being referred to as a minx and a trollop was harder to deflect.

"Will you calm down, please?" asked Ryan. "You're blowing things a little out of proportion."

The wild woman let loose again, mainly about her irresponsible, reckless sons. Ryan found the humour, but Adam's face reminded me of someone chewing tinfoil. Unable to listen any more, he lurched forward and snatched the phone before walking out of the room talking a mile a minute in French.

The second he was gone, the air felt calmer.

"Shall I translate?" teased Ryan.

"Is she always like this?"

"No. When she meets you, she's going to be sweeter than candy. If she had any idea you were privy to that conversation, she'd never have said a word."

"Why does your mother hate me so much?" I asked bleakly. "I haven't even had a chance to upset her yet."

I shouldn't have looked at him. The wily grin on his face was less than supportive. "You're always going to be the little elephant in the room, Charli."

"Explain it to me," I ordered.

Ryan sat on the bed beside me, heaving a loud sigh as if talking to me had suddenly become a chore. "It's complicated."

"Dumb it down then," I said dryly.

"Fine, I'll do my best. Because of Adam, you've just stumbled into a most exclusive club." He spoke using the same posh accent he'd adopted when referring to his mother as the queen.

"Cool. Who's in it?"

Welcoming the sarcasm, he laughed. "Some of the most spoiled, entitled trust fund scions in the country."

If that was Ryan's idea of dumbing it down, he clearly thought I was smarter. Unashamedly, I took my phone out of my pocket and Googled the definition. "Scion. A descendant, heir or young member of a family. Couldn't you have just said that?"

Ryan smirked. "I could have, but I love your naïvety."

I wanted to grab him by his silk tie and throttle him. "I am not naïve," I snapped.

"Thinking you can run with that crowd makes you naïve. Adam and Whitney have been together since prep school. A few days ago, he dumped her without warning or reason. All their friends have been rallying around, trying to console dim Whit. They'd probably be doing the same for Adam except he's fallen off the radar."

"None of that has anything to do with me!"

Perhaps sensing I was close to garrotting him, Ryan stood. "Don't you see?" he asked gently. "You're always going to be the girl who took him from her. That pack of lions are going to eat you alive." He sounded like he truly felt sorry for me. "They're a hundred percent Team Dim Whit."

"Well, thank you for the vote of confidence," I grumbled, folding my arms. "Don't underestimate me."

"I have never underestimated you, but feeding you to the lions would be an act of cruelty. How are you planning to deal with that?"

I didn't hesitate. "I'm going to learn to speak lion."

Ryan shook his head. "It's not possible, Charli – which brings me back to your original question. You wanted to know why my mother dislikes you so much."

"Yes."

He leaned forward, speaking in a slow whisper. "Even if it offends you?"

"You've done nothing to preserve my feelings so far."

He smiled as if I'd given him permission to let loose on me. "Your pedigree doesn't cut it. Whitney Vaughn, however, comes from good stock. Her family are hoteliers. There's no way Fiona Décarie is going to sit back and watch the wheels fall off. She's Team Dim Whit all the way too."

It was impossible to feel ill will toward Ryan for spelling it out so harshly. I just didn't want to be affected by anything he'd told me. None of it seemed fair. Every new place I travelled to, I arrived with a clean slate. My New York slate was supposed to be sparkling.

"All I care about is being with him, Ryan."

"Then I suggest you carve your own path while you're here. Make your own friends, because there's going to be no warm welcome from Adam's camp."

It pained me to admit it, but he was right. I couldn't put myself in the position of relying on Adam to do anything other than love me. Meshing our lives together could go no further than him and me. I didn't need the complication of trying to seek his family's approval, or convincing his friends that I wasn't the crux of the Adam and Whitney breakup.

"I want my job back," I blurted.

"Seriously?"

"Yes, starting Monday."

***

Adam reappeared soon after, not looking near as traumatised as I expected him to. The way he thrust Ryan's phone at him, thumping him in the chest with it as he passed, was his only hint of anger. Leaning hard on the second suitcase, Adam zipped it closed.

"That's it?" I asked. "Two suitcases?"

He nodded. "I'll call someone to pick them up."

"You can call someone to do that?"

"So naïve," muttered Ryan.

Adam's scalding glance was wasted on Ryan; he was already on his way out the door. I appreciated the privacy.

Reaching for my hands, Adam pulled me to my feet and into a strong hug. I wanted to know what had transpired with his mother, but bit hard on my bottom lip to stop myself from asking. There was only so much torment I could take in one day. He leaned back to look at me, sweeping my hair from my face and tucking it behind my ear. "Let's get out of here," he whispered.

I followed him out, loosely holding his hand. The evil brother was standing in the kitchen, using the reflection of the glass in the oven door to check himself out.

"We should try and sort some furniture out this afternoon," suggested Adam.

"Or we could do it tomorrow." Nothing about shopping for furniture appealed to me.

He leaned down close. "We've got to do it today."

Ryan chimed in from the kitchen. "Call a decorator."

"We don't need to," said Adam, still looking at me. "We just need to go shopping."

"The only hope for that place is professional intervention," insisted Ryan. "You definitely need a decorator."

Mitchell and I had resided in some downright fleapits during our travels. Considering Gabrielle's apartment anything short of luxurious was laughable.

"Spoiled scion of the rich," I muttered, loud enough for him to hear.

Adam stared. "What did you call him?"

I knew he'd heard me perfectly well the first time. "Nothing." An innocent smile had never been an easy look for me to pull off, but I tried anyway.

"Well played, Charlotte," praised Ryan. "But no amount of wit will make up for your lack of style."

"I have plenty of style."

"I'm sure you do," he agreed. "And when you've furnished the apartment, I'll be glad to come over and admire the striped banana lounges and beaded curtains."

I tried to catch Adam's eyes but he was grinning at the floor. Clearly his memories of La La land still burned brightly. I'd shown him enough crazy to make him believe that banana lounges weren't out of the realm of possibility.

"Don't you have somewhere to be?" I asked.

Ryan checked his watch. "Yes, I do." He picked his keys off the counter. "See you Monday, Charli. Don't be late." The door slammed and the evil brother was gone – but his last comment lingered, just as he'd planned.

"What was that about?" Adam asked, hooking his finger through the belt loop on my jeans and pulling me in close.

I slipped my arms around his neck, trying to predict how he'd take the news that I was once again, his newest employee. "I'm working at Nellie's."

"You don't have to do that." His low tone and the way he murmured the words against my mouth stole my ability to argue the point. "In fact, you really shouldn't do that. Wait until we get your visa sorted and you can work legally, if you want to." He lifted me off my feet and lowered me on to the couch, blanketing my body with his.

"Can we talk about something else, please?"

His voice dropped a tone lower. "I don't want to talk at all."

"We shouldn't get banana lounges, Adam. I don't think they're practical." I ran my free hand down the black suede cushion beneath me. "We should get something like this."

"Easy," he murmured. "We'll just take this one. Ryan will go berserk. That might be fun."

I couldn't help laughing. Nor could I help exacerbating the situation. "I like the coffee table too."

"Consider it done," he breathed. "We'll take that too."

13. Intelligence Gathering

Ryan's job offer came with some stipulations. My coveted breakfast shift had been snapped up as soon as I'd quit, so I was relegated to working evenings. Real life is the ultimate romance thief.

I stood in the doorway of the bathroom, watching Adam through the mirror. I could've let myself drift with thoughts of how incredible he looked, bare-chested and sleepy, leaning against the sink while he shaved. But it was just an unwelcome reminder that he had somewhere else to be.

"What are you doing today?" I asked casually.

Adam rattled off his schedule of classes, pausing briefly while he glided the razor down his soapy cheek. Procedures, torts and contract law followed by a few hours of study.

"Well, assuming torts have nothing to do with cake, what does it mean?"

Rinsing the razor under the flow of water, he chuckled. "Nothing to do with cake. It means a wrongful act done wilfully," he explained, "for which the injured party can sue."

"I see," I replied, drawing out the words. "Kind of like us stealing your brother's furniture?"

Adam dragged a towel off the rail. Burying his face in it did nothing to dull his laugh. "Technically it belongs to both of us," he replied. "Which reminds me, it's being delivered this afternoon. Will you be here?"

I nodded. "I start work at four. I won't see you until late."

He sprayed a quick burst of cologne at his throat. A divine woody chypre scent filled the air. "I'll come to Nellie's for dinner," he suggested.

"By yourself?"

"I can bring a date if you'd prefer." I rolled my eyes. "This is New York, Charli. People dine alone all the time."

"Yeah, weird, lonely people. Waitresses like me make fun of the weird, lonely people."

I cast my mind back to my first few weeks alone in the big bad world without Mitchell. Of all the things I managed to achieve solo, dining alone in a restaurant wasn't one of them. The whole concept was just too depressing.

"Waitresses at Nellie's have to be nice to me, Charlotte," he pointed out. "I'm the boss."

"Yes you are. How did that happen, exactly? How does a boy like you end up as a part-time restaurateur?"

"Depends on who you ask. Ryan will tell you he graciously let me in on the deal of a lifetime."

"What's the real reason?"

"We're the third proprietors in five years. The other two went bust. He was a little nervous going it alone. A fifty-fifty partnership with me means that his risk is halved."

"That was generous of him," I teased. "Weren't you nervous too?"

He shook his head. "We inherited the money we used to buy it. It's not like it was hard-earned. Besides, Ryan runs a tight ship. If anyone can make it successful, he can."

"So he runs it alone?"

"Pretty much. I do eat there a lot, though."

"What a shame," I said wistfully. "I was kind of hoping you had some pull there."

"I have major pull, Charlotte," he purred. "I can walk in there and get your morning shift back just like that." He snapped his fingers, making me jump. "There are benefits to sleeping with the boss, you know."

As tempting as his offer was, having him pull strings was hardly carving my own path. Besides, the tips would be better in the evenings and Paolo, the tyrant day manager, wouldn't be there.

"I'll manage," I told him, sighing heavily for effect. "All I have to do is play it cool and stay out of trouble."

"I'm not sure that's possible," he said quietly. "All things considered."

"What does that mean?"

The sheepish look on his face told me I wasn't going to enjoy his answer. "You're probably going to meet a lot of people there, Charli. A lot of my friends go there, usually for dinner."

Finally I got it. "You mean Whitney."

His perfect face contorted into a frown. "We haven't discussed how we're going to handle that."

It made no difference. Thanks to the heads up from Ryan, I was more than prepared for a run-in with dim Whit and the rest of his purple circle.

"You said it yourself, Adam. She knows nothing about me. I think we should keep it that way. She doesn't need to know I even exist. If I see her, I'll pretend I don't know her."

"You've got nothing to hide," he said, annoyed. "And nor do I."

"It's the right thing to do," I insisted. "In time she'll move on and won't give a damn who you're seeing."

"It won't work, Charli. We've been down that road before."

I stepped forward and pressed my hands against his chest. "It's for my benefit, not yours. Ryan told me all about your friends. You know how they're going to react to me."

"Ryan needs to learn to shut his mouth."

"I get to pick my own friends, Adam. I don't need to try fitting in with yours."

***

Having Paolo berate me at the door for being three minutes late was not something I'd missed, which is why seeing him there when I arrived for my first shift back was devastating. The man never slept. Killing him with kindness was my plan.

"Good evening, Paolo," I greeted him, sashaying past on my way to the cloakroom.

"Stop right there!" he barked.

Fearing he might have a coronary if I didn't, I stopped and turned to face him. "Is there a problem?"

He clicked his fingers, beckoning someone behind me. "Thankfully, you are no longer my problem. Meet your new manager."

I turned around preparing to see someone as scary as him, but the girl in front of me was hardly frightening. Not much older than me, she had a great smile and an air of quirkiness that I warmed to instantly.

"You must be Charli." She held out her hand, revealing a little heart tattoo on the inside of her wrist. "Paolo told me all about you. My name is Bente."

I shook her hand. "Ben-ta?" I asked, unsure of my pronunciation.

"Yeah, I know." She rolled her eyes. "Sucks to be me, huh? It's Dutch."

The imbecilic nod I gave continued for too long, undoubtedly giving the impression I was a little slow.

Paolo's phone ringing broke the awkward pause. "I know nothing about a lost earring and I don't owe you any money! Stop calling me!"

"He's been getting those calls for days," whispered Bente. "He's going to blow a gasket sooner or later." I stifled a giggle, hoping I didn't look too guilty.

Paolo left soon after, presumably at the end of his shift, turning control of the restaurant over to Bente. "Come," she said, linking her arm through mine. "I'll show you the ropes."

The ropes Bente wanted to show me had little to do with actual work. She led me over to a quiet corner of the restaurant, under the stairs leading up to the mezzanine.

"I call this the information station," she whispered, patting her hands on the wooden buffet. "If you're quiet, you can hear any conversation going on at tables nine, four and seven. It comes in very handy at times."

"For what?"

"Intelligence gathering. It makes it easier to deal with dicks. If you know what you're up against, it kind of kills the need to smash cake in their faces."

My heart sunk. I'd never stood a chance. Paolo really had told her all about me. "Look, Bente –"

"Relax, Charli," she said, grinning wryly. "I appreciate fine work when I see it. Just don't let the princes find out."

"The princes?"

"Yeah, the owners. You'll meet them sooner or later."

My thoughts quickly spun in a different direction. Paolo had obviously filled her in on the fact that I was hopeless at my job, but not about my affiliation with Adam and Ryan.

"Why do you call them that?" Perhaps she knew they both referred to their mother as the queen.

"Because there are two of them. They can't both be king." Something about my expression must have looked seriously off because she instantly tried downplaying her last comment. "Look, relax, they're okay. Ryan, the older one, is a bit of a control freak. He's a dick, actually, but easy enough if you handle him right."

Anything Bente said about Ryan I could handle, probably even agree with, but something about hearing dirt on Adam made me feel queasy, which is why asking her about him made me nothing short of idiotic. "And the other one?"

"Adam. He doesn't have much to do with running the place but he eats here a lot – usually at table seven." She winked at me.

"Intelligence gathering?" I asked, in a tiny voice.

"Now you're getting it," she praised, patting my shoulder.

"Because he's a dick?"

"Sometimes."

"Great," I said, drawing out the word as long as I could.

"Cheer up, Kemosabe," she teased, pretend punching me in the arm. "Welcome aboard."

With nearly two hours to kill before Nellie's opened for dinner, we had the run of the place. The first task was setting the tables.

"Is this really what you want to do forever?" I asked, wondering how someone as sassy and bright as Bente ended up waiting tables for a living.

"Of course not, but it's a job, right? I'm almost through my journalism degree. Serving tables pays my way. We weren't all born with silver spoons in our mouths like the princes."

Abandoning the napkin folding, I turned to face her. "Why are you so rough on them?"

"Look, let me give you a little advice. You're a very pretty girl. Adam and Ryan like pretty things. Sooner or later one or both of them is going to try taking advantage of that. Never break the cardinal rule of working here."

"Which is?"

Bente handed me a tray of cutlery. I followed her to the closest table. "Don't sleep with them," she said, waving a fork in the air like a wand. "They treat women like dirt." Something told me that her opinion was an educated one. She was speaking from experience.

"So, which one did you sleep with?" I tried to sound as if I didn't care either way.

"Ryan. A long time ago. No big deal."

Her cavalier reply didn't wash. "I think it was. That's probably why you can't stand him."

The cutlery chinked loudly as she placed the tray on the table.

"Very perceptive, Charli," she praised. "Look, guys like that don't go for girls like us. Not long term, anyway. It was nothing more than a one night grope in the cloakroom."

I would never be able to think of the humble cloakroom in the same way again.

"Okay, so that explains your feelings toward Ryan; but what's your gripe with Adam?"

"Ah, Adam," she said wistfully, turning her focus back to the table setting. "I had such high hopes for him, but ultimately he's just as much of a dick as his brother."

"Did you find that out in the cloakroom?"

Bente threw her head back in a bray of laughter. I braced for her answer. "No, I've never touched him, I swear." Perhaps alarmed by my expression, her hand flew across her heart. "He's just ice cold. He's been dating a girl called Whitney for years. No idea why. I doubt he even likes her most of the time. Anyway, he dumped her a few days ago and like a true coward, he's been laying low since. Whitney's been in here a few times this week looking for him, pining like a little bitch."

"So, you don't like her either?"

"No. She's a whiny, needy try-hard. Whitney needs to have Adam around. Within their group there's a hierarchy," she explained. "Some are more important than others. I don't know what it's based on, maybe money or looks or popularity, but some are higher up the ladder than others. Whitney needs Adam so she can stay in the fold. Adam never needed Whitney. He just let her hang around like a puppy. That makes him a dick."

"I'm sure he never meant to hurt her," I defended.

Bente stared across the table at me, shaking her head. "Stop defending him. I've heard a whisper that he's already got a new girlfriend. He should have had the decency to make things right with Whitney before moving on to the next victim."

I wasn't feeling much like a victim. I felt like the wicked instigator of the whole mess. I wondered if that made *me* a dick.

"So why did he stay with Whitney for so long?"

"I have a theory," she replied, waving cutlery at me again. "All their friends are paired off. They're all couples. By staying with Whitney, he had a constant date at the ready. Every time they attended a party or fashion show or whatever the hell it is that preppy brats do for fun, she was conveniently waiting in the wings, only too happy to oblige."

"You know a lot about this. Your investigative journalism skills are supreme," I teased.

"I love studying them. They're like my pets."

"Do you think Whitney wants Adam back?"

"Of course – because she wants to retain her position at the top. I don't think she'll do it without Adam. It might be the end of her reign."

Bente spoke of Adam and his friends as if they were pawns in a chess game. Just thinking about it made me feel like I needed to shower. Trying to keep my distance from them was absolutely the right decision.

"I can't wait to meet the new girl," she said gleefully. "It's going to shake them all silly."

It was time to fess up, fearing that if I didn't, I'd hear something I really didn't want to. "Bente, I have a confession to make." I winced as I said it. "I'm the new girl."

She placed the bunch of cutlery on the table and stared at me for so long I felt uncomfortable. Her hand flew up. "Wait! We need pie." She scarpered across the restaurant, disappearing through the kitchen doors.

A more conscientious employee would have continued setting the tables. I pulled out the nearest chair and sat down instead. The doors burst open a short while later and Bente rushed out, plates in hand.

"Is this really necessary?"

"Of course it is." Paolo would have flipped his lid if he'd seen the way she dumped the plates on the table. "It's pecan pie. Every good story begins and ends with pecan pie."

The slab of pie in front of me was more food than I usually consume in a day. She obviously expected the story to be long.

"What do you want to know?"

Like a true journalist, Bente wanted to know everything, starting from the beginning. For the most part, it was a story I enjoyed telling. It only became arduous once I got to the lost-my-mind-and-let-him-go part.

"That explains so much," she mused, between mouthfuls of the sickly sweet dessert.

"Like what?"

"Like why you keep defending him, for one."

I stabbed at my pie with a fork, avoiding her inquisitive stare. "I love him."

She shook her head. "I've only ever known your prince charming to be a frog, Charli. I can't imagine Adam being in love with anyone other than himself. Are you sure we're talking about the same guy?"

I nodded. I loved him unconditionally. He was my frog. And regardless what was thrown at me, I planned to keep it that way.

Our banter could have continued for hours if the madman barrelling in to the restaurant hadn't interrupted us. Bente jumped as he crashed through the front door, but I barely reacted. I knew Ryan was there for me.

"You!" he yelled, pointing at me. "Little Miss Larcenist. Where's Adam?"

"Not here. Why would he be here?" I spoke as casually as my thumping criminal heart would allow. He looked truly angry.

Ryan grabbed me by the elbow, leading me away from the journalism student, who sat in wide-eyed stunned silence.

"We could have sorted this out amicably, you know," he hissed. "Adam could've told me he wanted to take the furniture, I would have said no. He would have seen things my way and left empty handed."

I snatched my arm free. "That's your idea of an amicable resolution?"

"I don't have time to go shopping for furniture, Charli," he whined. "IKEA would be a very nice day out for the two of you."

His patronising approach riled me. "Can't you call someone, Ryan? Hire an interior decorator?"

He pointed his finger at me. "Oh, you're good," he crooned. "But I'm not under your spell, Charlotte. I want my couches back."

"So why are you telling me? Go and ask your brother."

Ryan shook his head at me, still wagging his finger. It seemed an eternity before he unlocked eyes and stormed out of the restaurant. He saved his parting words for Bente. "Watch her," he ordered. "Count all the silverware before she leaves."

Ryan had been gone for at least a minute before Bente finally spoke. "Frog or no frog, it's going to be a lot of fun having you around, Charli."

***

I wasn't expecting the furniture to still be there when I arrived home. Not only was it there, it was perfectly positioned in the room. Gabrielle's little apartment had taken on a whole new feel.

The two black suede couches and low glass table took up most of the room, but the biggest presence in the apartment was Adam, who stood in the kitchen smiling like he was truly pleased to see me.

I kicked off my shoes and took off my coat, instantly feeling lighter and less tired.

Adam seized my face in his hands and kissed me intently. It took a few seconds for me to realise that the ringing I heard was not in my head; it was coming from the pocket of my coat.

"Let it go," he urged, unsteadily.

I couldn't let it go for a good reason: I knew who it would be. Alex was the only person who called me that late at night. Calculating time differences wasn't something he excelled at either.

Breaking free of Adam's hold was relatively easy. Keeping my composure while I spoke to my father was a little trickier. I had other things on my mind, namely the gorgeous French American being held back only by my hand on his chest.

It should have been a pivotal phone call. For the first time in a long time, I had important news. I wanted to blurt the whole story out and get it over with. I wanted to tell him that I'd come full circle and was back in the arms of the boy I belonged with. But I didn't. We spoke about the weather. And when that subject ran cold we moved on to our plans for Christmas.

"What do you have planned?" he asked me.

I repeated the question out loud, purely for Adam's benefit. He pointed to himself, coaching me through my answer. "Err, I'm going to spend Christmas with Adam… and his family," I replied, frowning at Adam. I'd only added the word family after he'd mouthed it to me. Nothing about the idea appealed to me.

"I don't understand. Explain it to me, Charli." Alex sounded calm but something in his tone suggested he was going to spend the rest of the day chopping wood, his favourite pastime when frustrated by his wayward child.

"I belong with him and you know that," I said strongly.

"How does Boy Wonder's girlfriend feel about that?"

I should have known Gabrielle had been keeping him in the loop. I was purposely selective about the things I told Alex, but Gabrielle knew everything. Confiding in her was coming back to bite me, hard. It was just another reason for Alex to find fault.

"Alex, I have to go."

Cutting the conversation short seemed like a good idea. I could tell that no good was going to come of it the second he referred to Adam as Boy Wonder.

"Is he there with you now?"

"No," I lied.

Adam held out his hand, motioning for me to give him the phone, but I backed away. No good could come of that, either. Alex didn't intimidate Adam in the least, and the ten thousand miles between them would make no difference to the tension between them. I managed to end the call after promising to be careful, not to do anything stupid, and behave myself. Only then did I let my hand drop. Adam took immediate advantage, stepping forward to close the gap between us. "I take it he's not happy?"

"He's concerned about me."

"He has no reason to worry about you. You're in very good hands."

I put both hands on his face, holding his eyes in mine. "He's always going to worry about me. I need him to do that."

"I know you do." I didn't quite believe him. "Charli, I have no problem with Alex. I'm glad he stepped back from the tree, but I know he'll never leave the forest."

"What about Gabrielle? I know you have problems with Gabi. You haven't spoken to her in months."

"That's entirely my fault, not hers. Once I finally decided to pick up the pieces without you, it made sense to distance myself from Gabrielle."

At first it seemed like a selfish thing to do. Then I realised it was more about self-preservation. Losing Adam had pushed me to the very brink, and time hadn't healed any of my wounds. Perhaps losing me had had the same effect on him.

"We've done some serious damage along the way, Adam," I said sadly.

"Not to each other." His lips lightly touched mine while his hands wandered. "We're together and we're fine."

***

I didn't mention Ryan and the couches until the next morning. Adam didn't seem concerned.

"Don't you feel a little bit bad about it?"

"Not one bit," he replied, grinning mischievously at me from across the kitchen. "Quite the contrary actually."

I didn't find it funny. I thought they were both acting like the spoiled brats that they were. I sidled up to him, wrapping my arms around his middle. "Maybe you should apologise."

"I have a better idea," he said. "I think we need to equip our kitchen. I'm already tired of eating cereal out of plastic bowls."

"We have a frying pan," I pointed out.

"And an awesome frying pan it is," he said, stifling a smile. "But we can do better."

"How?" I was a little afraid of hearing the answer.

"A little one-stop-shop that I know of."

His attempt at being cagy failed miserably. Instantly I knew he was about to burglarise his brother's apartment again.

"Adam, no. We'll go shopping."

"You hate shopping."

"Not enough to be your accomplice," I grumbled.

His hands rested heavily on my shoulders, as did the knowledge that our romance might be even shorter lived the second time around. If Adam were to raid Ryan's apartment again, he'd be a dead man. I wanted no part of it, and refused to hear the devious plan he'd probably spent hours concocting.

"Go to school," I ordered, pointing toward the door.

He leaned down to kiss me. "Not yet. I still have half an hour to kill."

14. Social Butterflies

Scanning the restaurant the second I walked through the door was a ritual for me. I could usually tell in an instant what sort of night I was in for.

Tonight was going to be rough. Whitney was there. I had no idea who the girl dining with her was, but the wink Bente gave me as she bustled past led me to think they weren't seated at an Intel table by coincidence.

I didn't know quite how to handle it. Whitney had no idea that the girl about to serve her table was the same one who'd carried out a near perfect snatch-and-grab manoeuvre on her boyfriend. She looked sad. Her shoulders were slumped and she looked like she needed a good night's sleep.

Bente handed me two menus and a few words of encouragement. "You should go over there and introduce yourself to Whitney. Extend an olive branch." Her intentions were less than honourable. She'd have been just as content to see me walk over to Whitney and knock the stuffing out of her with said olive branch.

"Who's the other girl?" I asked.

"Kinsey Ballantyne, bitch extraordinaire. Whitney's best friend."

It was important not to give too much credence to Bente's opinion. As far as she was concerned, anyone associated with Adam was spoiled and rich, and had a blown-out sense of entitlement. Except me, for obvious reasons.

"I'm sure she's not that bad."

"Yeah." Bente gave me a push. "Keep telling yourself that."

I marched over to table seven, menus in hand and a smile plastered on my face. "Hi there," I greeted cheerily.

"About time," muttered Kinsey, snatching a menu from me.

I turned back to Bente. She stood with her arms folded, looking smug.

Kinsey clicked her fingers, snapping me back to attention. "Would you like to hear the specials?" I asked, determined to play nice.

"Can you focus long enough to recite them?"

Nothing about Kinsey Ballantyne was intimidating, least of all the way she spoke to me. I didn't think the rude blonde was as pretty as Whitney. Her features were hard; I put that down to the fact she was so skinny. She looked downright hungry. Maybe that's why she was so mean.

"Just let me know when you're ready to order," I suggested. I hightailed it back to Bente, finally letting go of my fake smile.

"Pleasant, aren't they?" she taunted.

"I think they know who I am." I couldn't think of any other reason why she would have been so rude to me.

"They're clueless. Don't take it personally, Charli. You're just a lowly server."

"With a short attention span apparently," I snarled.

"Oh well, you've set the bar low then, haven't you?"

I should have left it alone, but I couldn't. Insulting my intelligence was practically an invitation to mess with them. I made sure Whitney got exactly as she ordered, seafood penne, which she politely thanked me for. Kinsey wasn't impressed with the massive fillet steak I dumped in her place.

"What the hell is this?" she barked. "I ordered a romaine salad."

"Yes, you did," I agreed. "But I thought you'd like this better."

Kinsey's glare didn't match her gentle tone. "You're new here aren't you? First day?"

"No; first week, though." I almost sounded proud.

"Do you realise it's your last?"

I tried my hand at looking shocked and surprised by her words. "You're going to get me fired?"

"I could have your job in a second," she said, clicking her fingers to strengthen her claim.

"You don't need to take my job. They'd probably hire you too," I said dumbly. "We keep application forms out the back. I can get you one if you'd like."

Whitney reacted before Kinsey, bringing her napkin to her mouth to stifle her giggle.

Kinsey stood up, scanning the room for someone important enough to complain to. "I know the owners," she warned. "You're finished here."

"Wow? Really?" I tried to sound perturbed. "Lucky for me, the bosses aren't here."

"Bente's here," said Whitney, throwing me under the bus. Kinsey caught Bente's attention by waving at her like someone hailing a cab. She sailed over and winked at me.

"Can I help you?"

"This girl is useless. She needs to go."

"I can't make that decision, Kinsey. And neither can you. You'll have to call Ryan."

Whitney groaned at the mention of Ryan's name. Obviously the dislike was mutual.

"No," replied Kinsey, glancing at Whitney. "I'll call Adam."

Whitney's face lit up at the mention of his name.

I listened to the one-sided phone conversation as Kinsey stated her case, wondering how many times she'd done it before - and how many times the princes had accommodated her demands.

Finally, she handed the phone to me, sneering.

"Hello," I said, in a deliberately shaky voice.

"Firing you would definitely be to my advantage, Charlotte." I could hear the innuendo in his voice, and his low tone was as sexy as hell.

I stared straight at Kinsey as I spoke. "No, please don't fire me," I begged, much to her delight. I held the phone closer to my ear, not wanting Kinsey or Whitney to hear the very descriptive ways he came up with to kill the rest of the evening if he were to fire me. "I'll keep it in mind," I said, before ending the call and handing the phone back.

"I told you," said Kinsey victoriously. "Hit the road."

I leaned down a little closer to her and spoke quietly, trying my hand at being a menace. "I'm not going anywhere. I guess you don't have as much pull as you thought you did. Eat your steak, love. You look like you could do with the calories." I walked away leaving Bente to deal with the aftermath.

Then things turned bad.

I'd been so caught up torturing Kinsey that I hadn't noticed Ryan walk in. He stood by the podium at the door, flicking through the reservations book. He glanced up briefly as I approached. "Charli," he purred ominously.

I cut straight to the chase. "Look, I've had a really sucky night so far so if you're planning to haul me over to coals, do it now, please."

"Why would I do that?" he asked, still studying the reservation book.

I might have jumped the gun. Perhaps he hadn't yet discovered that his apartment had been looted again. And it had been. I was home when Colin the delivery guy dropped off six boxes. I'd left it for Adam to unpack when he got home, certain I'd be struck by lightning or hit by a bus if I dared touch it.

Keeping quiet was only delaying the inevitable so I told him all about his brother's crime spree.

"I know."

"And you're not upset?"

"No. He did me a favour actually. Out with the old and in with the new." He glanced over at Whitney's table. "Adam can relate to that concept, I'm sure."

"That was below the belt."

"You're right. I apologise," he said, not very sincerely. "What I meant to say was that I used it as an opportunity to redecorate."

"I thought you said you didn't have the time."

"I don't, which is why I employed the services of a designer - and she's working out beautifully."

I knew there was more to it. His whole demeanour had taken on the dark edge he adopted whenever he was being an ass.

"Is she working on you or the apartment?"

He leaned down to whisper. "Her name is Yolanda. She's blonde and gorgeous and we're meeting up later for a drink - to discuss my design options, of course."

"Of course, design options," I repeated, making no secret of my disgust. "So Adam gets a reprieve because you've somehow managed to twist it to your advantage?"

His wry smile left me with no doubts. No matter how hard Adam tried to be devious and underhanded, he was never going to match his older brother.

"Would you rather I hold a grudge and destroy him slowly?"

"No. I wouldn't."

"Good, because he doesn't need the extra pressure. He warned me not to introduce you to dim Whit if your paths crossed. How's that working out for you, Charli?"

I cocked one eyebrow. "She's still sitting there, isn't she? Perfectly unharmed."

He looked past me. "Kinsey looks a little distressed."

"Kinsey tried throwing her weight around. I guess she forgot that's only about eighty pounds."

Ryan chuckled blackly. "Don't get too cocky. She's not your only competitor this evening." He flipped a few pages of the reservation book and held it up to me.

"Décarie." He tapped his finger on the page. "Table for two at eight o'clock."

My eyes widened in horror. "Your parents?"

"What's it going to be, Charli?" he quizzed. "Fight or flight?"

I didn't even need time to think about it. "Fight, Ryan. It's what I've been doing since I got here."

Bente couldn't understand my nervousness. "You have to meet his parents some time," she enthused. "They're decent people. They've always been very nice to me."

"How nice do you think they'd be if *you* were seeing one of their princes?"

"Good point," she admitted, looking to the floor.

"I'm screwed."

Bente leaned forward and patted my shoulder. "Well, it was nice knowing you, Charli."

Clearly she wasn't going to be much in the way of moral support. Nor was Ryan. He left early to meet up with Yolanda, his new plaything. Thankfully, Kinsey and Whitney left too. Introducing myself to Adam's parents while they were still there would have blown my charade to pieces - not that I expected to escape the evening unscathed.

I was painfully aware of Fiona Décarie's feelings toward me. I was her vagrant-pauper-trollop-minx nightmare. I had no idea what her husband's take on it was. Jean-Luc had hardly rated a mention.

I was standing near the information station when they arrived. Taylor showed them to their seats. Both of them thanked her, giving me slight hope that they weren't completely tyrannical.

Bente sidled up, handed me two menus and mercilessly told me to get on with it. "What are you, Charli?" she whispered. "A man or a mouse?" I was about to claim mouse status when she pushed me in the back, sending me stumbling forward.

I smoothed my hair, drew in a long breath and approached their table. "Hello." My mouth was so dry it felt like I was chewing on sand. "My name is... Charli. You're Adam's parents?" I wanted to slap myself for asking such an obtuse question.

"Charli?" asked Jean-Luc, frowning slightly. I nodded, too worried about what I might say if I answered out loud. Jean-Luc stood up, leaned forward and kissed both of my cheeks. "It's lovely to finally meet you."

Utter relief washed over me. Perhaps I was going to live through it after all.

"Please, sit down for a moment," said Fiona, smiling. "It would be lovely to chat for a while."

I did as she asked because I was too scared not to. Ryan had warned me about the sweet façade she'd display in my presence. It was a front she maintained to a T.

Adam's parents knew rather a lot about me. I had been under the impression that I was some dirty little secret, an indiscretion of Adam's that wasn't supposed to last longer than his Australian vacation. "Isn't it remarkable how people find their way back to those they love?" asked Fiona, making me sound like a lost puppy.

I nodded but didn't answer, fearful of saying something sarcastic and rude.

Jean-Luc asked what our plans were. I had no answer for him either. We hadn't discussed the finer details. "Don't put her on the spot, darling," said Fiona, placing her hand on his. "She's only just arrived."

I was thankful for the reprieve. Jean-Luc flashed the very familiar Décarie grin and I smiled back, not sure what my expression was exposing. My verbal skills weren't exposing much at all – except that I was socially inept.

It was a terrible impression to make on a New York social butterfly. I could see it in Fiona's flawlessly made-up sapphire eyes. She thought I was little more than a moth from Pipers Cove.

Jean-Luc was a little more forgiving. He asked many questions about my travels, seeming genuinely interested. Anything to do with my time away from home was easy to talk about. Conversation flowed freely, until his phone rang and he excused himself from the table.

I had trouble maintaining eye contact with the queen once he'd gone. She obviously didn't. She glared at me.

"It's a frightful situation when the so-called love of my son's life is waiting tables in his restaurant." Her tone was ice-cold.

"It's important to me that I pay my own way," I told her.

"You understand that my sons lead very privileged lives, don't you?" I nodded. "It's a life we enjoy. If Adam chooses to lower his standards and slum it for a while I'm prepared to humour him. But you must understand something, Charli…."

"And what might that be?" I asked, matching her refined vernacular – just to prove that I could.

"You're a temporary fixture in his life."

I forced myself to look at her. "You're going to make sure of that, aren't you?"

She sneered, but spoke gently, the way Kinsey had when she thought she had the upper hand. "If it's the last thing I do."

Jean-Luc returned to the table, unaware of the nasty turn to the conversation. "Sorry about that. Where were we?"

I stood up. "I was just leaving," I said, smiling as normally as I could. "I have to get back to work."

"I must say, Charli, I find it admirable that you've taken a job. Being self reliant is a remarkable attribute," praised Jean-Luc.

"Thank you. It was lovely meeting you both." I darted my eyes between the two of them, hoping Jean-Luc wouldn't see through me and Fiona wouldn't have the chutzpah to call me on my obvious lie. "I hope to see you again soon."

"Of course," beamed Fiona, so artificially that I wanted to gag. "Adam has invited you to dinner on Christmas Day, hasn't he?"

"Yes. I'm looking forward to it," I lied, backing away from the table.

Bente jumped me the second I was out of earshot. "Well?" she demanded.

I let go of my rigid expression. "Kill me now," I whispered, dangerously close to tears.

I didn't object when Bente suggested I take an early mark. I doubt it had anything to do with feeling sorry for me. I was a subpar waitress at the best of times. When I was hiding out in the cloakroom I was positively useless.

"Look, just go out the kitchen door," she urged. "You won't even have to face them."

I took her advice, ghosting out the back door without raising the attention of a single person in the kitchen.

Adam didn't ask me why I was home early. He just took it as a windfall. I didn't feel the need to fill him in on the night's events at that moment. Just being in the same room as him somehow dulled the horror.

He kissed the top of my head. "Hungry?"

"Starving," I replied, shrugging off my coat.

He began patting himself down, searching for the pocket that held his phone. "I'll order pizza."

I used the time to remove all traces of Nellie's. I unclipped my hair, untucked my shirt and kicked off my shoes. Our new black couches were almost as comfortable as our bed. Sinking into the soft suede cushions made staying awake difficult.

"Dinner should be here soon," said Adam, snatching me from the brink of sleep. He lifted my feet and sat beside me, repositioning my legs across his lap. "Are you tired?"

I couldn't really claim to be tired. My hard night had nothing to do with being run off my feet; my exhaustion was more to do with the emotional beating I'd taken at the hands of his mother.

"No, I'm fine."

"I heard you had a busy night." His expression remained flat but I could hear the amusement in his voice.

"You heard wrong."

"I thought meeting Whitney, Kinsey and my parents would have made for a very busy night."

I lifted my head, trying to gauge his expression, but his face gave nothing away. "How did you know?"

"Mom called me."

Perfect. I should have known she'd get in first. Thinking of all the horrible things she could have said was more torturous than playing the actual conversation back in my head.

"What did she say?"

"She apologised. She told me you were an absolute delight and she was sorry that she'd jumped to conclusions before meeting you."

Nothing about him was dishonest. I had to believe that he was telling me the truth as he knew it.

"That was very sporting of her," I muttered.

Adam leaned across, stroking his hand down the length of my hair. "She wasn't too proud to admit she was wrong, Charli. I think you should give her the benefit of the doubt."

I wanted to slate him for his gullibility. But I didn't. I smiled, giving the impression that all was forgiven. "I can do that, for you," I assured. "But you should probably know something...."

He looked worried. "What?"

"Kinsey Ballantyne is always going to be fair game. She gets nothing but the benefit of my bitchiness."

He threw his head back in a rush of relieved laughter.

"Silly preppy girls," I grumbled. "They're so easy to spot."

"Really? How?"

"I have a theory. It's all in the name. A name ending with *ee* automatically lowers your intelligence. Whit-ney, Kinsey – "

"Char-*li*," he volunteered.

"I didn't say it was a perfect theory."

Anything he was about to tease me with next was halted by a knock at the door. Adam jumped off the couch to answer it while I headed in to the kitchen to get some plates.

Colin, the delivery guy, had undoubtedly made a killing during the Décarie brothers' game of furniture ping-pong. A quick search through my now full kitchen cupboards led me to think he'd earned every cent. Along with cutlery, crockery and appliances, he'd managed to box up napkins, dishwashing soap and some matchboxes from a downtown club. I spent a long moment taking it all in, wondering which item Ryan would miss the most. I decided it would be the matchbox from The Renoir Club. On the back was a girl's name and phone number. I sniggered when I read it. Her name was Kat-*ie*.

***

I was more than content with pizza for dinner, but Adam felt the need to apologise. We sat on the floor side by side, our backs against the couch, using the coffee table as a makeshift dining table.

"If I'd known you'd be home for dinner, I would have attempted something more complicated than pizza," he told me, brushing crumbs off his hands.

I bumped my shoulder against his arm. "Don't sell yourself short, Adam. Pizza is a very complex meal."

He twisted his upper body to look at me. "How do you figure that?"

I dropped my half-eaten slice back in the box. "Well, it's a round meal, cut into triangles and served in a square box. You'd need to be a Columbia law student to understand that level of complexity."

A slow smile crept across his gorgeous face. "Do you think it's possible to be in love with someone's mind?"

I shrugged. "I guess so."

"I'm in love with your mind, Charlotte." He announced it grimly, as if it was a terrible affliction.

"Damn," I sighed. "I was kind of hoping it was my body you were in love with."

Dinner was effectively over.

15. The Purple Circle

Kinsey Ballantyne was turning into a major thorn in my side.

After our run-in the night before, I wasn't expecting to see her at Nellie's again any time soon. Any normal person would have been embarrassed by her failed attempt at getting me fired. But Kinsey wasn't normal. She was resourceful. Rather than staying away, she brought reinforcements.

As usual, I relied on Bente for the lowdown. They were her pets, after all.

"Well, you know Whitney and Kinsey," she said, pointing at them with a limp wrist.

"Who's the other girl?"

The willowy brunette would probably have been quite attractive if she smiled. In the ten minutes since they'd been seated, I hadn't seen her sullen expression change.

"Seraphina Sawyer," she announced poshly. "They call her Sera. She's seriously rich."

"Aren't they all?"

"Yes, I suppose that is a prerequisite. But Sera's harmless. She's very quiet." We busied ourselves folding napkins, giving us an excuse to linger at the information station. "The guy next to her is Jeremy, her boyfriend - again, quiet and non-venomous."

"And the other guy is Kinsey's boyfriend," I guessed.

"Parker. He's a mixed bag - super polite, huge tipper." She winked at me. "But he's Kinsey's boyfriend. That makes him a tool."

I had to agree with her. He had to be somehow lacking. No one in his right mind would voluntarily pair up with Kinsey.

Bente told me his full name was Harvey Parker. Dropping his given name in favour of a one-word-rock-star title made sense. If anyone knew the frustration of having an antiquated, ill-fitting name, it was me. And Harvey was a million times worse than Charlotte.

I studied Parker a little more closely. Bente was putting faces to names for me: Adam had very vaguely broken down his group of friends while we were discussing my run-in with Kinsey.

Like Adam, Parker was a disgustingly wealthy second-year law student at Columbia. The similarities ended there. He was fairly average looking – neither attractive nor ugly. His dark brown hair was short and neat. His khaki chinos were pressed and neat. His navy blue V-necked pullover was preppy and neat.

Parker was neat. That was the only conclusion I could draw by looking at him. Finding out whether he was as void as his girlfriend would involve talking to him.

"I've got Kinsey's table," I told Bente.

Instantly, she giggled. "So you're up for round two already?"

"It keeps things interesting."

"Well, things are about to get a whole lot more interesting, Charli." My eyes followed as she pointed toward the door. "Your frog just walked in."

I wasn't expecting Adam at the restaurant that night. Apparently his friends weren't either. Kinsey spotted him first. She stood and called out his name, waving him over. He motioned to her with one hand, telling her to wait a minute.

Adam hadn't spent enough time at Nellie's to become acquainted with the information station. It seemed a long moment before he finally spotted me.

"Charli," he said smoothly as he approached.

"Adam," I replied, muting my smile to avoid prying eyes. "I'm working. I get off at eleven."

He leaned forward, whispering his words. "Bail. Come home with me."

"I get off at eleven," I repeated, looking past him as I spoke.

"Fine, I'll wait."

I gave him a half smile that I knew would've looked odd. It was the best I could do considering five pairs of eyes were boring into me and Bente was hanging on every word.

Adam walked over to his friends and sat down at the only spare place at the table – next to Whitney.

"Yup, very interesting," Bente whispered before dissolving into a fit of maniacal giggles.

The purple circle welcomed Adam back to the fold as if he were some long-lost friend they hadn't seen in years. Maybe a week felt like a year in New York time. Kinsey demanded to know where he'd been and what he'd been up to. Adam ignored her.

"Nice of you to show up," said Parker.

He probably had good reason to sound miffed. I can remember Nicole adopting the same standoffish demeanour when I deserted her for Adam. Of course, she got her own back when she deserted me permanently a few months later.

Adam smiled. "It hasn't been that long."

"You don't have to avoid me, Adam," griped Whitney. "We're grown-ups."

Bente giggled and I purposely stepped on her toe. She swiped at me and knocked the stack of napkins we'd folded on to the floor.

"Great," I whispered. "Now we're going to have to fold them again."

She scooped them into a messy heap and dumped them on the buffet. "Exactly. It gives us an excuse to stand here. I wouldn't miss this for the world."

Bente was right – the conversation at table four was going to make a great show. It was the first time Adam and dim Whit had been in the same room since he'd dumped her.

"I'm not avoiding you, Whit," insisted Adam, barely casting a glance in her direction.

"Of course he's not," soothed Kinsey, reaching across to pat Whitney's hand. "He probably just needed time to think."

Adam cut her down instantly. "There's nothing wrong with my thought processes. I've just been busy."

Whitney's head dropped and I prayed she wasn't about to cry. That would have been tragic. Perhaps Jeremy sensed an impending meltdown too, because he jumped in. "Well, wherever you've been, it's good to have you back, man."

"Yes," added Sera charging her glass. "We've missed you."

"Not as much as dim Whit has," mumbled Bente, quickly stepping to the side to avoid another toe stomping.

Unlike Adam, Ryan was acquainted with the information station. He sidled up behind us. "Don't you get tired of all the cloak and dagger, Charlotte?" he whispered from behind. "Why don't you just go over there and introduce yourself to your predecessor?"

I spun around. "How would finding out about me do anything other than make things worse?"

"Why are you worried about her feelings? He got tired of her long before you arrived. He has a right to move on."

"And Ryan should know," teased Bente. "He just described his whole relationship philosophy."

He pulled a face at her and she matched it with one of her own.

"Stop it, children." I walked away. Offering to wait on Adam's table was completely self-serving. Not wanting them to know anything about me didn't stop me being curious about them.

A disgusted groan escaped Kinsey before I'd even made it to their table. "This is the girl I was telling you about," she huffed to no one in particular. I took it to mean she'd told everyone at the table about our run-in. I stood clutching my notebook against my chest like a shield as her minions studied me.

"How are you this evening?" asked Parker, stealing my best waitress greeting.

"In fine form, thank you for asking," I replied.

Parker shot a smirk at Jeremy and Adam. Both of them looked to the table, unsuccessfully hiding their amusement.

The only venom seemed to be coming from Kinsey. Sera and Whitney stared blankly at me, but Kinsey looked as if she was about to scratch my eyes out. "I want someone else to serve us," she demanded.

I turned my head from left to right, pretending to search for someone to accommodate her. "Nope. Not tonight. It's looks like you're stuck with me."

Jeremy laughed out loud and Sera nudged him in the side to shut him up.

"Adam," Kinsey began. "She's hopeless. I can't believe you're putting up with this."

Adam shrugged but said nothing.

I tapped my pen on my notebook. "Look, I'm pretty busy, so if you want to order something, now would be the time."

"See what I mean?" Kinsey spoke as if I was invisible. "She's rude."

"And you're rather mind-numbing, but you don't see me complaining," I replied.

If I thought there was a chance of having my eyes scratched out before, it was practically a given now. Kinsey attempted to stand up but Parker pulled her back down.

"Okay, okay," soothed Adam, playing peacemaker. "Look, perhaps there's someone else who could serve us?"

I doubted my bad attitude toward Kinsey came as a surprise to Adam. I'd forewarned him that she was fair game.

I heaved out a long sigh as if it was all too hard. Kinsey's glare remained as she tried to make sense of why he was cutting me so much slack. I didn't get a chance to say anything. Ryan – privy to the whole conversation from the information station – appeared at my side. "Is there a problem?" he asked, like he didn't know.

"They don't like me." My choice of words made both Décaries chuckle. It was the first time I noticed how similar their laughs were.

"I like her," volunteered Parker, looking at me like he was stuck in some sort of trance.

"Ugh!" Kinsey groaned, folding her arms tightly and leaning back in her chair.

"Oh, Kinsey," said Ryan wistfully. "How are you, darling? You're looking as toxic as ever."

"Go to hell, Ryan," she snapped.

"Don't hate Charlotte because she's rude," he taunted, slipping his arm around my waist and pulling me close. "Hate her because Parker thinks she's beautiful."

Parker threw both hands in the air defensively, speaking to Kinsey. "I never said that!"

"You didn't have to," baited Ryan, lowering his voice and winking at him.

"Okay, enough now," said Adam, finally drawing the line. "Let's just order."

Ignoring Adam, Ryan turned his attention to Whitney. "What about you, dim Whit? What are your thoughts on our new waitress?" Whitney didn't answer, prompting him to continue torturing her. "I'll bet Adam thinks she's pretty, don't you Adam?"

The whole table was deathly silent and all eyes were on Adam - except mine. My baleful glare was directed squarely at Ryan. I contemplated stabbing him with my pen. It wouldn't have stopped him talking about me like a piece of meat, but it might have freed me from his clutches.

"I'm sure he finds her attractive," said Whitney, finally finding her voice. "All of the women you bang when you fall out of the whore tree are beautiful, Ryan. That's usually all they have going for them. Clearly you didn't hire her for her good manners."

"Bravo, Whitney," praised Sera, grinning at her.

I wanted to pat her on the back and congratulate her too. It didn't even bother me that she'd mistaken me for one of Ryan's blondes. It was the first time I'd ever heard anyone put him in his place.

I knew there had to be more to Whitney than the meek shell of a girl I'd seen up to that point. Adam didn't suffer fools easily. There's no way he would have invested so much time in her if she were as shallow and empty as Kinsey.

It was a bittersweet moment. Whitney Vaughn wasn't timid and dull. She was just heartbroken. And little did she know, I was partly to blame.

I knew the second Ryan opened his mouth he would have come out fighting, blowing our charade to pieces whether he meant to or not. It would have been the quickest way to destroy Whitney.

I dragged him away from the table, back to the information station. "Not one more word," I ordered, wagging my finger at him.

Ryan grinned wickedly. "Oh Charli, what a tangled web we weave when first we practice to deceive."

He wasn't entirely wrong. My webs were becoming more tangled by the day. And it was entirely my own doing.

16. The Right Question

"Charlotte, you have to wake up." That was my Saturday morning wake-up call. Nothing about his smooth voice sounded urgent so it was hard to take him seriously. "I have something to show you." I groaned and snuggled in closer to his warm body. I slowly ran my hand down the length of his arm, tangling my fingers around his. He leaned in and kissed me, doing nothing to convince me that getting out of bed was a good idea. "You have to come outside to see it."

The minute Adam got up and started getting dressed, the bed held no interest for me. "Why are we going outside, exactly?" I asked, dragging on my jeans.

"It wouldn't be a surprise if I told you. Come and see."

Spending time in New York City had presented me with a cache of new experiences. I now had one more to add to the mix.

Snow.

I was so excited to see it, I could hardly breathe. I wanted to run across the marble foyer and out the front door the second I saw the sheet of white on the pavement outside. The only thing holding me back was the firm grip Adam had on my hand. Not even Marvin's conversation could engage me for very long. Adam stood talking to him at the door while I stepped into a foreign world.

I stood completely still, gloved palms outstretched, catching the small white flakes as they drifted through the frigid air. Cold weather wasn't exactly new to me but I'd never seen snow. And after the events of the night before, the simplicity of a new experience breathed new life into me.

"Can we go for a walk?" I asked, impolitely interrupting Adam and Marvin's conversation.

"How far do you want to go, Charli?" teased Adam.

"Miles and miles."

Marvin chuckled heartily. "You have a long day ahead then, Miss Charli." He pointed to the sea of white lightly blanketing the street.

I had no idea what to expect. I'd woken up in an alien universe. Luckily for me, I was with someone who was willing to show it to me.

Central Park was where we ended up, in front of the picturesque Bethesda Angel fountain. I trudged through the powdery fresh snow like an unsteady toddler. Adam patiently stood watching.

"She's beautiful, don't you think?" I asked, staring across at the angel, blanketed in white.

"Exquisite," he replied, sounding totally uninterested.

I looked back at him, grinning. "I get the impression you're not enjoying this as much as I am, Adam."

"*Tu va attraper la mort,* Charlotte." He translated before I had a chance to speak. "You're going to catch your death of cold."

I stomped back to him. "Saying it in French doesn't make it true, monsieur. It's a total myth."

"How can you be sure?"

I hooked my arm through his as we wandered over to the steps. "Because a Czechoslovakian fairy once tested that theory."

"More theories?"

"It's true, Adam. Her name was Maruska and she was hopelessly in love with a boy called Bedrich. But he cruelly rejected her so she vowed to get even, determined to make him catch his death of cold," I explained. "Every night for years and years she'd wait until he was sleeping and hide lumps of snow under his pillow."

"Classy. Did it work?"

My grip on his arm tightened. "No. He remained perfectly well, found the love of his life and lived happily ever after. Eventually Maruska died alone and miserable, which proves only that a broken heart can kill you. Cold weather can give you frost bite or hypothermia, but not a deathly flu."

Adam stopped walking, halting both of us. He took a step forward and turned to face me. He looked at me so intently, I began to fear what he was going to say.

He grabbed my hands. "Let's get married."

I was sure he'd left off half the sentence, and attempted to correct it. "Let's get married *some day*? When we're grown up, sensible and know what we're doing?"

He dropped his head but kept the hold on my hands. It seemed an eternity before his eyes drifted back up to mine. "No Charlotte, right now."

Nothing about him seemed unsure. I couldn't pass it off as a joke or something said in the heat of the moment. We were standing in the snow, for crying out loud. The moment was freezing.

"Cold weather brings on delirium."

His hands slipped around my waist, drawing me close. "I'm not delirious. I'm playing by your five-minute rule. I'm loved and I love. What more could I possibly want?"

"Longer than five minutes, hopefully," I teased.

"Five minutes or five lifetimes, Charli. I don't care. I'll take what I can get."

I sometimes feared that Adam was unfairly enchanted by my fairy tales. I'd never forgotten the stories Alex had regaled me with throughout my childhood. As I grew I began to realise that he'd invented most of them to win whatever war was being waged with me at the time. It would be fair to assume that the Jamaican fairy, Ezola, didn't really fade and wither away because she refused to eat vegetables – taking all of the sunlight with her and plunging her kingdom into darkness for eternity. But some tales were too brilliant not to be true. And those were the stories I carried with me. I'd grown up saving wishes, believing that fairies made beds for their babies in tulip blooms and chasing kisses from fairies on windy days.

My father had a lot to answer for.

To everyone else on earth, these were strange flaws. But Adam loved my craziness. We'd spent over a year apart. The dynamics between us had hardly changed. He loved me just as he always had. I loved him more, and made a point of telling him so every chance I got.

There was love and absurd amounts of desire and affection. But curiosity was noticeably absent. There was a time when I couldn't answer Adam's questions quick enough.

Since I'd been back in his arms, he'd never once asked me about my year away from home. It was as if he was happy to strip it from history and pretend we'd never been apart. I couldn't do that. My year of travelling had altered me just as much as Alex's fairy stories, and if Adam didn't know all about it, he'd never truly know me.

"You haven't asked me the right questions yet," I told him.

Adam tried again. "Charlotte Blake, will you please marry me?" He spoke very slowly, enunciating every word. "That's not the right question?"

I shook my head and his confused frown became more concentrated.

"Did you ever wonder about me, Adam? While I was away, did you ever think about where I was or what I was doing?"

"Every single day." He spoke grimly as if I'd reminded him of something horrible.

"You've never asked me about it."

His arm moved up my back and he hugged me tightly, whispering his answer in my ear. "Because none of it matters to me."

I wedged my arms between us, breaking our embrace. "I wasn't out robbing banks! I was doing exactly what I'd dreamed of my whole life."

"At what cost, Charli?" he asked quietly.

I spent a long time trying to make sense of his question, but couldn't. I had no clue what he was talking about, and demanded he explain it to me.

"About a month after I got home, Nicole called me, distraught."

He looked straight at me, no doubt trying to gauge my reaction at the mention of her name. If he were successful, he would have picked the moment that my heart fell through the bottom of my feet. Any mention of Nicole Lawson was bound to mean trouble.

"What did she have to say for herself?" I asked, fighting the urge to yell the question.

"She told me that you'd changed plans and decided to travel with Mitchell instead of her." He sounded so disappointed in me that I wanted to apologise – until I remembered that I'd done nothing wrong.

Nicole left town without even calling her mother. It was abominable to think she'd found the time to call Adam and fill his head with lies after doing her vanishing act. It crushed me to think she'd been so intent on destroying me.

"Why did she feel the need to keep you in the loop, Adam?" I asked, perfectly calmly.

He shrugged. "Misery loves company, right? I guess she thought I'd understand what she was going through."

"I see. You can't really blame me, though. I had thousands of dollars from the sale of the boat burning a hole in my pocket." Adam's expression remained totally blank. If he was outraged by my alleged wickedness, it didn't show. "Dumping Nicole in favour of Mitchell made total sense. Because of him, I got to see Africa."

"I don't need to know this, Charli," he grumbled.

"It's not even true, Adam," I snapped, finally coming clean. "And if you'd stayed in contact with Gabrielle, you'd probably know that by now."

His eyes never left mine as I set him straight. It was important that he knew everything. Adam dug a groove in the snow with his boot as he listened to the story of how my lifelong best friend had stolen the money he'd gifted me, skipped out of town and smashed my already broken heart. "The lie she made up about me leaving with Mitchell was just good guess work. She probably knew he was my last hope of getting out of town. If Mitch hadn't taken me with him, I'd still be stuck in the Cove."

"And all of this happened within a month of me leaving town?"

I nodded. "Everything fell apart once you left."

His blue eyes bored into mine with an intensity I hadn't seen in a long time. It was the look that always left me wondering what he was truly seeing. Finally he leaned forward, pressing his cold lips hard against mine, scaling back to a light touch as he murmured two tiny words against my mouth. "Marry me."

To keep my mind clear and my body upright, I broke his hold. I wasn't against the idea of marrying him. There was something remarkable about knowing I had something most people spend their lifetimes searching for. Nothing would ever change my mind about him. And apparently nothing I ever did seemed to perturb him either.

"Are you sure you want to marry me?" I asked. "We've spent far more time apart than together."

"It makes no difference. I have loved you the whole time. My heart gave me no choice." He smiled at me and I was suddenly in real danger of being swept away in the moment. "It's not that I can't live without you, Charli. I've proved that I can. It's just that I don't want to, ever again."

I grinned at him. "I can see why having me around frightens your mother so much. You used to be so sensible."

I could almost hear Fiona's voice in my head, screaming at me to leave her boy alone.

"Eventually, she'll recover," he insisted, reaching for my hands, squeezing them hard as if he was trying to reassure me.

"Alex won't. He'll kill you."

"I'm not afraid of your father."

"You should be."

He smiled, totally unruffled. "If you're searching for a reason not to marry me, you needn't try so hard, Charli. Just say no. I'll wait."

His cockiness made me laugh. "How long?"

"For you? Forever. How long would you like me to wait?"

I studied his bright eyes for a long moment, deliberating. "Five days," I said finally.

He dropped my hands and folded his arms. "Wednesday?"

"Yes. Monday for wealth, Tuesday for health, Wednesday the best day of all." I ticked the days off on my gloved fingers. "Thursday for losses, Friday for crosses and Saturday, no luck at all."

"What about Sunday?" he asked, chuckling.

"No mention of Sunday," I replied. "But Wednesday's a great day for a wedding."

***

Even the simplest of weddings requires a certain amount of preparation.

First thing Monday morning we were at the office of the City Clerk applying for a marriage licence. It didn't seem that complicated to me. We filled out the necessary paperwork, forked out thirty-five dollars and were handed a licence.

Adam's frown intensified as the process went on. I waited until we were out the door before questioning him. "Are you having second thoughts?"

"No. I'm learning to go with the first." He slipped the paperwork into his pocket, freeing his hand to reach for mine. "You're looking a little anxious."

Adam held my hand as we manoeuvred our way down the icy steps. "I think we should consult with an immigration lawyer, Charli. We need to change the status of your visa."

I groaned. "Not today."

"Ignoring it won't make it go away. We've got to get all of our ducks in a row."

"Lining up ducks is your forte, not mine."

"How about I take care of the ducks and you concentrate on the more important details?" he suggested, sounding much calmer.

I could think of a hundred details more important than my immigration status. I wanted everything to be perfect. Getting married would be the last big secret we could share. And it would probably last only as long as the day.

Forewarning his mother would've been horrendous. Adam had spelled out two scenarios. The first was that if by some miracle she decided to give her blessing, it would turn into a New York high society event that neither of us would take any delight in. The second scenario seemed much more likely. She'd rant, rave and destroy me bit by bit, ensuring there would be nothing left for her youngest son to tie the knot with. Of course, Adam put it much more diplomatically. "She'll be displeased," he'd told me.

I decided not to tell my father either. Adam bravely volunteered to call him - even offering to ask for Alex's permission. I shuddered at the thought. I knew I was meant to be with Adam. My soul commanded it. After all we'd been through, promising to love each other forever just wasn't a big leap. Such powerful declarations usually sounded desperate and off kilter when said out loud, especially to my father, so telling Alex after the deed was done made total sense to me. The only family member who would be privy to our news prior to the event was Ryan. Both of us knew that convincing him to bear witness for us would be a hard sell. He was the most cynical person I knew when it came to matters of the heart.

Our journey to his apartment was spent coming up with a game plan. "Don't let him talk you out of anything - or into anything for that matter," warned Adam, extending his hand to help me out of the cab.

I was careful not to mention Ryan's new furniture when we walked in. The fire we were about to start needed no extra fuel. Two new black leather couches took up the space left by the lounge suite we'd pilfered. Yolanda had obviously been a worthwhile investment. They suited the room better than the others had - not that I'd ever tell him.

Ryan sat on one taboo couch and I sat beside Adam on the other, tangling my fingers through his as I braced myself for the conversation ahead. I left all the talking to him, and as expected, Ryan was appalled by the whole idea.

"Why on earth would you want to do something like that?" I wasn't exactly sure which one of us he was talking to. His eyes darted between us. "What are you thinking? You're both crazy."

"If I'd wanted a lecture, I would have told Mom and Dad," said Adam. "We want you there. All I need from you is a simple yes or no."

Ryan slapped both hands on his knees, breathing as if he needed more oxygen. "When is this debacle taking place?"

"Wednesday."

"Christmas Eve? Why Christmas Eve?"

I hadn't realised we were planning to marry on Christmas Eve. Judging by the glance Adam gave me, he hadn't either. But he ignored the question. "Will you do it or not?'

Ryan turned his attention to me. "Is he making you do this, Charli? Blink once for no, twice for yes."

"Idiot," mumbled Adam.

I shifted in my seat, concentrating on not blinking at all.

"Are you after his money? He'd probably just cut you a cheque if you asked. You don't need to betroth yourself to him."

"I love him. That is all."

My input meant nothing. The speculation continued. "Is it about a green card? Is that why you're doing this?"

My temper was finally beginning to creak and give way. "Does it look like I care whether I have a green card or not? Working illegally – in *your* restaurant – suits me just fine."

"Touché, Charlotte," drawled Ryan, getting on my last nerve. "So, when are you planning to tell the family about this ridiculous turn of events?"

"I believe Christmas Day is traditionally a day of family joy and togetherness," stated Adam, smirking at his brother.

Ryan's laugh was positively sinister. "The queen is going to lose the plot. You realise that, don't you?"

"I know, and I don't care. I believe in this," said Adam, smiling as he glanced at me.

"I know you do," conceded Ryan. "And I support your stupidity."

"So you'll do it?"

Ryan sighed heavily, making way for the ridiculously convoluted Décarie phrasing. "I would be honoured to bear witness for my besotted little brother and his enchanting bride."

I jumped out of my seat and lurched forward, throwing my arms around his neck. "The rumours about you being a selfish pig are not true."

He broke my grip and pushed me away. "Of course not. Who started that rumour?"

"I did."

Ryan looked at Adam. "And this is the girl you want to spend the rest of your life with?"

Adam flashed me a devilish grin. "Absolutely."

17. Star Splinters

Being at work that night was dreadful. Even Bente was at the end of her rope with me.

"Charli," she hissed, grabbing my elbow and pulling me aside. "Table two are complaining that they've been sitting twenty minutes and haven't even seen a menu."

I cocked my head, leaning past her to peek at the party in question.

"I'm sorry. I'm a little off my game tonight."

Bente's expression softened the instant she smiled. "Honey, I don't think you have a game. But I'm between a rock and a hard place here. You're screwing the boss, so I can't fire you. I'm just trying to work with what I have."

I couldn't argue with the truth.

"I need to tell you something," I said gravely.

"Will baring your soul make you more productive?"

"It's worth a shot."

Bente groaned wearily. "Okay, shoot."

"I'm getting married." I didn't say it like a giddy bride. I spoke as if I was about to be dragged to the altar kicking and screaming.

Grabbing my elbow again, she practically dragged me through the kitchen and into Paolo's office. As usual, no one in the kitchen batted an eyelid.

"Are you freaking kidding me?"

"I love him, Bente."

Bente sat on Paolo's chair and buried her face in her hands. "You know something?" she asked, looking up at me. "I actually believe you when you say that. But I think you're both mad - especially you."

"Why?"

"A society wedding is a fierce animal. It's going to take on a life of it's own, Charli."

"We're not having a big wedding. We're not even planning to tell anyone."

Her eyes widened. "You're eloping? His mother will lynch you."

I shrugged. "His mother hates me anyway."

"She does," she agreed. "What are your plans? Tell me everything."

Clearly, Bente had forgotten about the restaurant she was supposed to be running. Not even the banging and clanging coming from the kitchen alerted her.

"We're getting married on Christmas Eve." I said it with meaning, as if we'd chosen the day rather than stumbled upon it by accident. "That's everything."

"That's the day after tomorrow!" she exclaimed. "Charli, how are you going to pull this together in a day and a half?"

"You're going to help me." I spoke with absolute certainty.

"I am?"

"Please, Bente. I want it to be perfect."

She slouched down in the chair, looking up at the ceiling. "You know what I love about you, Charli?"

"My fantastic waitressing skills and sunny disposition?"

"Besides that," she replied, grinning. "I love your optimism. It hasn't even entered your head things with your frog might not work out, has it?"

I shook my head. "Nope. I love him with my whole heart."

"And soul?" she teased. "The transition isn't complete unless your soul is jacked too."

"He *is* my soul. Sometimes I think I only breathe because he does. What do you suppose that means?"

Bente wrinkled her nose. "I guess it means the frog is a keeper."

I could afford to be smug now. "I should marry him then."

"And I should help you organise it," she conceded, albeit begrudgingly. "What do you need?"

"A dress. I need the perfect dress."

"Fine," she replied. "Tomorrow, we'll hit the shops."

***

Shopping for a wedding dress was an absolute ordeal.

Bente was surprised to learn that I had very specific ideas on what I wanted to wear when I got married. "I thought this would be over in an hour," she grumbled, raking through yet another rack of dresses. "You're supposed to be whimsical and spontaneous."

"Not about this. My dress has to be just right."

It wasn't about vanity or fairy tales. It was about covering all bases. Not only was I notoriously whimsical and spontaneous, I was incredibly superstitious. And it was those superstitions that made finding a near perfect dress a few minutes later bittersweet.

I took the dress and held it up, studying it closely.

"Is that the one?" asked Bente, hopefully. "It's gorgeous."

It really was. The simple floor length satin gown was strapless. The sash around the waist was tied in a bow at the back that trailed to the floor. No lace. No beads. No diamantes. It was simple and exquisite.

"It's almost the one," I said sadly.

Bente sat on a nearby chair and groaned, loud enough to gain the attention of the snippy sales assistant. The woman approached us – for the third time – and asked if she could help us with something.

"Well, Charlotte?" asked Bente, matching her haughty tone. "Can she help us?"

I held the dress out to her. "Do you have this in any other fabric?"

The woman squinted at me over the top of her glasses.

"Special orders can be arranged on request."

"Great. Can it be ready by tomorrow morning?" Bente asked.

The woman let out a strange guffaw. "We're not magicians." I wanted to call her out on her false advertising. According to the sign out the front, Elspeth's Bridal Boutique guaranteed a magical wedding day. By rights, she should have been a magician.

I left the shop feeling dejected. Bente wasted no time in questioning me. "What was wrong with the fabric?"

"It's satin. You can't have a satin wedding dress. It's extremely bad luck."

She hooked her arm around mine as we wandered out on to the street.

"Oh, good grief," she uttered. "Ninety percent of wedding dresses are satin."

"Not mine. It's bad mojo."

Bente began to laugh. "Charli, I hate to break it to you but you're running out of time. Isn't that bad mojo?"

I stopped walking, yanking her to a stop too. She'd raised a valid point. There might have been some ancient superstition that considered disorganisation to be a bad omen.

"We need to fix this," I said, sounding alarmingly desperate. "Do you know a dressmaker?"

"That can knock out a designer gown in a few hours? I'm not a magician either."

"Think, Bente," I urged, shaking her as if that made a difference.

She stared at me for a long time, trying to come up with a solution. "I might know someone," she said at last. "My sister Ivy's pretty handy with a needle and thread. We'll go to her."

"Excellent," I replied, breathing a little easier. "Lead the way."

***

I loved getting out of the Manhattan bubble for a minute, especially with Bente. My first ever subway trip was the short journey to Ivy's house in Astoria. The modest two story home on a busy street was a world away from the doorman-attended buildings I was becoming embarrassingly used to.

The tiny front yard was decorated with cheesy Christmas ornaments, including a half deflated snowman that Bente kicked on the way up to the porch.

"Bente!"

She shrugged. "The damned thing has been there since last Christmas."

We stepped on to the porch. Bente pounded on the door, yelling her sister's name. After a long minute, the door opened and my eyes drifted down to the tiny girl standing there. Bente sweetened her tone. "Hello, princess. Are you going to let Aunt Bente in?"

The little girl stood on the warm side of the screen door, defiantly shaking her head.

"Now, Fabergé," growled Bente, abandoning the gentle voice.

"Fabergé?" I whispered. "Like the eggs?"

"Yes, absurd isn't it?" She rattled the handle on the screen door. "Ivy!"

Fabergé was unperturbed. Her chubby hand dug into the bag of chips she was holding and stuffed a handful into her mouth.

Finally, her mother appeared and unlocked the door "Scoot, Fabergé." She turned her daughter by the shoulders and nudged her away.

"About time," grumbled Bente. "We're freezing out here."

"Well, hurry up and get inside then. You're letting all the heat out."

Ivy looked like a grown-up version of little Fabergé. She was a plump brunette woman in her mid-twenties with a cherubic face that didn't quite match her stern disposition. Once the introductions were out of the way, Ivy got straight down to business, asking me what sort of dress I was looking for and chastising me for leaving it until the last minute.

"Look, can you do it or not?" asked Bente impatiently.

Ivy glared, as if the question was absurd. "Of course I can. Go down to the sewing room. I'll put Fabergé down for a nap and be right there."

Hearing that there was a room purely dedicated to sewing made me hopeful that Ivy could come through for me. Seeing the room made me nervous all over again. It looked like the backstage area of a burlesque theatre. Everywhere I looked there were glitzy miniature gowns encrusted with rhinestones, beads, feathers or all three. None of the fairies from my childhood imaginings would have ever been caught wearing dresses like that - except the ones hooked on acid.

"I'm not sure this is going to work out," I said, making Bente giggle.

"Relax, Kemosabe. These are all Fabergé's. Ivy handmade every one of these creepy dresses." She waved her arms around. "Every few months she dolls Fabergé up with fake eyelashes and a spray tan, dresses her in one of these creations and enters her in a pageant."

It was unfathomable. The little girl couldn't have been more than four years-old. "Who would do that?" I whispered in disbelief.

"Look, you have to at least appreciate the talent. Some of these dresses take her weeks to make."

I turned my attention to the iridescent lime green creation hanging on the wall behind me. The jewel-encrusted bodice looked like it weighed more than Fabergé did.

"Does she ever win?" Bente led me across the hall to the lounge. The cluttered room was crammed full of two-foot tall trophies, sashes and shelves of princess crowns. "Promise me something, Bente?" I grabbed the cuff of her sleeve. "Don't let your sister anywhere near my dress with a glue gun."

"I promise," she replied, dissolving into a fit of giggles.

"Although I would kill to have a tiara," I said, eyeing off the display of crowns. "Maybe I'll borrow one of these."

"Take your pick," encouraged Bente, waving her hands around the room.

"I was joking."

"Go ahead and pick one. Ivy won't mind." She cocked her head back and yelled upstairs. "Ivy! Can Charli borrow one of Fabergé's tiaras for her wedding?" I cringed, more at the screeching than the request. Ivy's affirmative reply came quickly, and equally as loudly. "See, I told you," Bente said smugly. She picked up a huge over-the-top crown and placed it on my head. It was so big I had to hold it with both hands to keep it steady.

"I had something a little less showy in mind." I handed the crown back and reached for a small pavé crystal tiara. "What about this one?" I asked, securing it in my hair with the combed edges.

Bente turned around to read the accompanying sash. "You look beautiful, Little Miss Pork Belly."

"Pardon?"

"That was her title. First place at the Little Miss Pork Belly Pageant." I read the sash. Sure enough, she was telling the truth.

A quick glance around the room showed that Fabergé had won many other dubious titles. Miss Top Pup was my laugh-out-loud favourite.

"Are you sure this is appropriate?" I asked, readjusting my small crown.

"Of course it is. It only becomes questionable if you decide to wear the sash too."

I needn't have wasted so much energy doubting Ivy's talent. Bente had had the good sense to snap a picture of the almost-right dress with her phone while the sales assistant had her back turned. Using that as a guide, Ivy created a flawless replica – in ivory silk. The whole process took less than five hours, including the trip to buy the fabric. By four o'clock, I was trying it on for the final time.

"I think it's prettier than the one in the store," beamed Bente.

"It's too plain," volunteered Ivy. "I can glitz it up."

"No!" Bente and I said in unison.

"To each her own," Ivy muttered, fussing with the bow at the back.

"I can't thank you enough for this," I told her. "I can't wait for Adam to see it."

"Let's hope he's easier to impress than his brother." Bente scolded her sister, telling her to shut up. "What? I'm just saying that I hope he's a nice guy."

"He's lovely. Ryan's not a bad guy either, once you get to know him," I added.

Ivy tugged so hard on the hem of my dress that I nearly tumbled off the chair I was standing on. "Ryan's not nice. He strung Bente along for weeks. I don't know why she tortured herself by keeping her job. I would have told him to shove it."

I looked across at Bente, seeing a mix of embarrassment and awkwardness in her expression. I realised that she'd seriously downplayed the story of the romp in the cloakroom with Ryan.

"Well, Adam is the best person I know. I can't wait to marry him." My comment wasn't an honest declaration of love; I was attempting to steer the discussion away from the subject of his brother. That conversation could wait.

"Well, you have the perfect dress to do it in," announced Bente, stepping aside so I could see my reflection in the full-length mirror behind her.

I had to agree. It was exactly what I wanted.

Finding a dress had been my only mission for the day. Adam's task was to organise the rings. The look on his face when I arrived home suggested it hadn't been a simple one.

I draped my dress bag over the couch and fell into his welcoming arms. He kissed my forehead and I lifted my head to look at him. "Are you alright?"

"It's been a long day," he admitted. "I've spent the entire afternoon shopping for a ring."

"Can I see it?"

"I'm not sure."

His response made me nervous. I'd never told Adam about the fate of the black opal necklace he'd given me. But I *had* told Ryan. I wondered if he'd sold me out.

"I promise I'll never sell my wedding ring to African gangsters, no matter how desperate I am," I blurted, holding my hand to my heart.

"Charlotte, what are you talking about?"

"Nothing," I replied, cursing my big mouth. "I'll tell you another day. Please, can I see it?"

"I want to tell you about it first," he said, rather glumly.

"Are you going to give me a lesson in gemmology, Adam?" I asked, delighted.

"I should at least try."

I snuggled in close to him, listening attentively. Poor Adam, so desperate to make the right decision had become overwhelmed by the endless options on offer. "I knew I couldn't just buy a big fat diamond. It wouldn't hold any meaning, would it?"

"Sure it would. It would mean I married well. I'd probably be able to swing a country club membership with a rock on my finger."

"Probably," he agreed, almost smiling. "I spent the best part of the day researching. The problem is, just about every stone signifies something."

I was amused that he'd overanalysed it to the point of confusion.

"So what did you finally settle on?"

Displacing me, he reached in his pocket. "If you don't like it, just say the word," he said, placing a ring box on my lap.

He'd talked it down so much, I wasn't sure if I should open it. "Before I look at it, tell me what it means."

Adam looked as if the conversation was causing him unbearable pain. "Well, I made a few mistakes today. Looking for a meaningful ring after telling the sales assistant that you'll pay whatever it takes to get the right one isn't such a bright idea. They kept showing me huge solitaires. On your hand, they would look like a baseball." He placed his hand against mine, palm to palm. "After looking at ten million rings I ended up in a place on Fifth Avenue. I changed my approach and told the sales assistant that I wanted a ring with a legend behind it weightier than the stone in it."

"And how did that work out for you?"

"Better, I think. She told me a few clichéd stories that didn't mean much, but one sounded interesting. She told me that the Romans believed that diamonds were the splinters of stars."

My eyes drifted down to the small velvet box sitting in my lap. "I didn't know that."

"Have I just given you a lesson in stars, Charlotte?"

"Oh, trust me, Boy Wonder. I know about stars."

His smile broadened. "Educate me."

"You'd already be educated if you'd read *Peter Pan*."

Adam leaned over and picked his iPad up off the floor. "I'll download it and read it now," he said, tapping the screen. "Maybe I'll download the French version and read it out loud to you. Who knows, if I put a seductive spin on the accent, I might get lucky tonight."

I giggled, more at his Machiavellian expression than his silly words.

"I am a sure thing, Monsieur Décarie," I declared, still sniggering. "I am the surest thing you've ever had."

The download finished and he and placed the iPad on my lap.

"Tell me about stars, Charlotte," he ordered.

I swiped through the pages of the book, quickly finding the quote I was looking for. I cleared my throat. "Stars are beautiful, but they may not take an active part in anything, they must just look on forever. It is a punishment put on them for something they did so long ago that no star now knows what it is."

He lunged toward me. "You are so lovely," he moaned.

I put my free hand on his chest, holding him at bay while I continued reading. "So the older ones have become glassy-eyed and seldom speak, winking is the star language. But the little ones still wonder. They are not very friendly to Peter, who had a mischievous way of stealing up behind them and trying to blow them out."

I placed the iPad down on my lap and dropped my hand. Adam didn't seem to notice that I'd stopped reading. He didn't move.

"How much of your childhood was spent trying to blow out the stars, Charli?" he asked.

I dropped my head, a little embarrassed by the admission I was about to make. "I used to try all the time. When I was little, Alex used to put me on his shoulders, telling me I'd have a better chance if I were closer to the sky. When there were no stars on overcast nights, he'd tell me that was because he'd already blown them out."

Adam frowned slightly. "Do you wish you'd known the truth back then?"

"About stars on cloudy nights?"

"No, that Alex is your dad."

I barely had to think about my answer. "Alex was always my dad, even before I knew it. Nothing changed once I found out the truth."

His hand moved to the side of my face, cradling my cheek. "Are you sure you don't want me to call him and confess that I'm about to permanently steal his only daughter away?"

As brave as his offer was, it bordered on insanity. Alex wouldn't give us his blessing in a million years.

"No. In my experience, confessing to crimes is better done after the event. He'll try and talk me out of it."

Adam leaned across, pressing me into the cushion, ignoring the fact that the ring box and iPad had fallen to the floor.

"Do you think he could?" He sounded worried.

"No." I quickly kissed him. "I never have second thoughts. I always go with the first. Can I see my ring now?"

He groaned a long sigh into my shoulder. "Yes, of course." I wriggled beneath him, making a grab for the box. "If you don't like them, I'll take them back."

"*Them*?"

He sat up, releasing me. "There are two rings," he murmured. "If I'm going to give you stars, I'm going to give you as many as I can."

I'd never worn a ring in my life. The prospect of wearing two on one finger was a little daunting.

I flipped open the lid of the box and stared.

"Do you like them?"

He took them out and slipped them on my finger. In a terribly clichéd pose, I held my hand out, wiggling my fingers to enhance the twinkling.

There was nothing not to like. Pieced together, the rings looked like a delicate string of jewels wound around my finger over and over. When separated, they looked like little diamond curly fries. They'd match my Miss Pork Belly tiara perfectly.

"I adore them," I told him, grabbing a fistful of his shirt and pulling him back to me.

***

Adam wasn't thrilled by the idea of spending the night before our wedding apart. He was even less thrilled when I told him Ryan had agreed to put him up for the night – providing he promised not to steal anything while he was there.

I had it all worked out. Ryan would pick me up from our apartment in the morning, and Bente would make sure Adam was at the marriage bureau by ten.

The plan was flawless but hard to execute. The gorgeous boy with the cerulean eyes just didn't want to go. I gripped both of his hands, keeping him at a distance while I pushed him toward the door.

"I can't just leave you here," he complained, dipping his head to murmur the words so close to my mouth that his lips brushed mine.

"I managed just fine for a month before you got here."

"It's not the same."

"Of course it's not." I waved behind me. "I have furniture now."

"Let me stay."

His voice was so smooth and persuasive that it took effort to say no, but I managed to hold my ground. "The day after tomorrow, when you wake up, I'm going to be right beside you."

He took my face in his hands for the final time that night. "Yes, Charlotte," he breathed. "And you'll be legally obligated to be there."

My ensuing laugh was cut short. It was the most divine of kisses – desperate, deep and expectant. He was the one who ended it, as if leaving me gasping for air was revenge for making him leave.

I stood at the doorway, waiting until he reached the elevator before calling out to him. He turned, granting me a knee-weakening half-dimpled smile.

"I'll see you tomorrow," I said.

Ignoring the fact that the elevator doors had just opened, he stalked back toward me. Claiming the win, I stepped inside and quickly closed the door.

Seconds later, a note appeared by my feet.

For a boy who'd mastered three languages, his note was remarkably simple. There weren't even any words. The little hand-drawn love heart was the most precious message I'd ever received.

18. Promises

Ryan arrived early the next morning. I was happy to see him for a few reasons. Firstly, he was a distraction. My conscience was getting the better of me that morning. I'd actually considered calling Alex to confess that I was about to tie myself to Boy Wonder forever. Secondly, I was having trouble reaching the zipper at the back of my dress.

As soon as I opened the door, I turned around, holding the front of my dress against my chest. He didn't need instruction, just stepped forward and zipped it up.

"Thank you."

"You're welcome."

I turned to face him, nervously smoothing the front of my dress. "What do you think?"

"At the risk of sounding highly inappropriate, you look stunningly beautiful."

I rolled my eyes at his convoluted compliment. "Can't you just be normal?"

He smiled. "Fine. You look hot, Charli."

"Better," I praised. "See how easy that was?"

"You're ridiculous," he uttered, grinning again.

He closed the door, and for a few seconds an awkward silence filled the air. I wondered if that was the moment I was supposed to tell him he looked hot too. It would have been an unnecessary compliment. Ryan always looked handsome. Today was no exception but I could tell a little more effort than usual went in to his outfit. His navy blue suit and matching tie were so impeccably pieced together, he looked crisp enough to snap at any moment.

"Can we go now?" I asked.

He glanced at his watch. "Now? We'll be early."

"I'm all dressed up and it's wasted on you," I said, grabbing the skirt of my dress and fanning it out. "I should be out there showing off."

Ordinarily he might have protested, but that day was mine. Perhaps he knew that. Ryan was good at picking his battles. He helped me put on my coat and followed me to the door, saying nothing until we were in the elevator. "You know, Gabi will freak out when she sees your artistic efforts on the wall in there," he said irrelevantly.

"Do you care?" Ryan and Gabrielle weren't close, and that was putting it mildly. He called her worse names than I did. "I thought you didn't get along with your cousin."

He shrugged his shoulders. "I don't. Never did. Never will."

"Yes. Why is that?"

Through the mirrored wall of the elevator he flashed me a lazy grin. "What do you want me to tell you? Are you waiting on some scandalous story?"

"I might be. I'd love to hear a scandalous story involving Gabrielle."

"It probably won't happen," he said, sounding disappointed. "She's too clean-cut for that. That's basically why we don't get along. She's probably shacked up in Tasmania with a goat farmer."

"No. She's shacked up in Tasmania with my father." I said it a little acidly.

Ryan picked up on it immediately. I knew there was no way to go back and convince him that I actually approved of their relationship. His loud laugh bounced around the confined space we were in. "The princess and an old man? I didn't see that one coming."

I cringed at the mental picture he was probably conjuring up in his mind.

"He's hardly old. My dad just turned thirty-six."

I watched the mental maths through the mirror. "So how old are you? Twelve?"

The doors slid open. I called him a name and walked across the foyer to the door. I was good at picking my battles too.

***

If Ryan was upset at being over an hour early, he didn't let on. There's no way he could have been bored. Hanging out at the Manhattan Marriage Bureau reminded me of sitting in the lounge of a busy airport, only a lot more stylish.

The waiting hall was a long narrow art deco room with stylish long green couches, shiny marble columns, and chandeliers hanging from the ornate ceiling. Couples and their posses loomed everywhere. And like airport travellers, I couldn't help wondering what brought them there.

It was a first-come-first-served process, and I could progress no further without my groom – who wasn't due to meet us there for another hour. Ryan and I sat down on a couch, waited and watched. Some brides were dressed to the nines. I considered myself to be dressed to the sevens (the fives if I'd taken my tiara off). A handful of extremely casual brides were in jeans and tired winter coats. There was a token knocked-up bride, a nervous groom who looked to be there against his will and a sweet-looking old couple who reminded me of the Swanstons from my breakfast shift days at Nellie's.

"I wonder what their stories are," I whispered to Ryan.

"I imagine there are many levels of stupidity in this room," he replied flatly.

I scolded him with a harsh look. "Do you think *I'm* stupid?"

"I think you're too young. I don't think you know anything about life."

"I don't need to know everything. I just need to know what makes me happy. Your brother is it."

Ryan huffed out a sarcastic grunt. "I hope you hold that thought, Charli. Being part of my family is a tough gig."

"You're in it. It can't be all bad."

Ryan leaned back in the couch, resting his head as he looked to the ceiling.

"You know, when I was a kid, I always dreamed of having a sister," he mused. "But I wanted her to be older, with really gorgeous friends."

The majority of Ryan's snide attitude was false, a front he maintained for reasons unknown. One of my favourite pastimes was calling him out on it. "Eventually Ryan, you're going to be a really nice guy – when you stop playing in the whore tree."

He stood up. "I enjoy that you have so much faith in me."

I grabbed his arm and demanded to know where he was going. My tone suggested I thought he was about to abandon me. "I'm going to buy a newspaper. If I'm not back in five minutes, check the wedding chapel. That woman over there keeps staring at me."

Dropping the death grip I had on him, I peeked in the direction of his upward nod. A pretty redhead wearing a frightful apricot dress quickly looked away when I caught her eye. "Oh yeah. She wants you."

Ryan walked away without another word, returning shortly after with a newspaper in hand. "Right," he said, brandishing a pen. "How are you at crosswords?"

"Hopeless, actually."

"Don't worry about it. I'll help you." I knew his idea of helping me meant dumbing it down. "Nineteen across. Origin of the Manx people."

"You tell me," I gibed.

Ryan glanced across at me. "I don't know the answer. That's why I'm asking you."

"Do you think I know it?"

"No. Clearly I'm just humouring you."

Ordinarily his condescension would have infuriated me but this time, I had the upper hand. I knew the answer. "The Isle of Man."

I watched his eyes grow wider as he counted out the letters. "You might just be right. How could you know that?"

"The Adhene are Manx fairies." He looked totally perplexed, giving me no option but to elaborate. "In Manx folklore, fairies are thought to be fallen angels, cast from heaven but slightly too good for hell – a bit like you really."

"Speak for yourself, Charli." If he'd hoped to sound hurt, he failed.

"They're malevolent, mischievous and delight in causing misery," I added.

Ryan twisted his body to look at me, staring in a way that made me nervous. "You're such a strange girl."

We didn't get through much more of the crossword before Bente and Adam arrived. I walked as fast as I could toward Adam without running.

"We're early. I didn't think you'd be here yet," said Bente, glancing at the clock on the wall. "How long have you been here?"

I didn't have the focus to answer her. I fell into Adam's arms the second he was within reach. By that time, Ryan had joined us and answered her question. "Long enough," he muttered, trying to sound inconvenienced.

Adam looked at me for a long time, saying everything without actually speaking. For some reason, he saw things in me that Ryan and everyone else seemed to miss. His bright eyes showed no hint of nervousness or regret, and I knew what I'd known all along. He was the one for me.

When Adam finally did speak, it was to tell me how lovely I looked. I wanted to tell him the same thing but feared it might sound weird. I also wanted to grab the hem of my long dress and twirl around like a child but decided against that too.

I'd never seen Adam dressed so formally. Unlike his brother, he favoured a casual look. But he wore the dark charcoal suit and matching tie well, looking nowhere near as snobbish and untouchable as is brother.

Now that he was there, we could move forward with the formalities. License in hand, we lined up in front of the reception desk. Reaching the front of the line brought no great prize. We were assigned a number and told to wait for it to be called.

When it finally was called, it was only to sign documentation and present identification. Once again we were told to listen out for our number. It was like a long game of bridal bingo.

We headed back to the couch, acting much less antsy than the two people who were there to bear witness for us. Despite their inability to sit still, Ryan and Bente chatted easily, as they always did. It made Ivy's snide remarks about him even more intriguing. Ryan *was* a dick – just never to Bente.

"Charlotte," Adam said, from the corner of his mouth. "You don't have any flowers."

I turned my head to look at him but he didn't meet my eyes. He was focused on the latest couple to call bingo. Bride number twenty-six jumped off her couch, pulling her groom to his feet with one hand and waving her neat bouquet of red roses with the other.

How could I have overlooked flowers? Until that moment I thought I'd remembered everything. Bridal flowers symbolise emotions, values and wishes. How could I have dared to show up without any?

Finding a bouquet suddenly became more important than hearing our number being called.

"I need flowers," I announced. "We have to find some."

"Chill, Bridezilla, they sell them at the gift shop," said Bente. "I'll go and get some."

Ryan offered to go with her, leaving Adam and me alone on the couch, holding hands as we always did whenever we were within reach. We said nothing – not one word. The silence made me blissfully happy. There was only calm in my heart.

***

Bente and Ryan returned with a huge bouquet.

"It was the biggest one they had," said Bente, thrusting them at me. "Is it okay?"

I studied the mixed posy closely but Adam answered for me. "It will be in a minute."

He knew me too well. Bente gasped in horror as I began modifying my bouquet, plucking out the white carnations, pink larkspur and white sweet peas and handing them to Ryan.

"Do I even want to know what you're doing?" he asked, closing his fist around the snubbed flowers.

"They're bad luck," I explained. "Sweet peas mean departure. They're a big fat thanks for everything, I'm out of here."

"And the others?" asked Bente, curious.

"Pink larkspur." I said it acidly, as if it was a noxious weed rather than a pretty flower. "It symbolises fickleness. I don't want it in my bouquet."

Bente's sideward glance was aimed at Ryan. He dropped his head, smirking. Adam's eyes remained firmly on me, unfazed by my craziness.

"What about the other flowers?" asked Bente, pointing at the bouquet. "Do they make the grade?"

I double-checked, twisting the posy to look it over. "Yes. It's fine. Pink roses, perfect happiness; gardenias convey joy, and freesias symbolise thoughtfulness."

"Oh my God," she mumbled, shaking her head. "She's some kind of flower savant."

Ryan looked at the scrunched-up petals in his hand. "What about carnations?" he asked, frowning at me. "What's wrong with carnations?"

I shrugged. "Nothing. They're just ugly."

***

Finally our number was called. "About time," muttered Ryan under his breath. From the corner of my eye I saw Bente elbow him sharply in the ribs.

Adam took my hand and we made our way to one of the ceremony rooms. Standing in front of the celebrant was when the first hint of nervousness kicked in. Adam's palms were sweaty and my hands trembled enough to make my bouquet shake. We must have managed to look normal, though. Georgette, the celebrant, didn't seem alarmed at all.

Georgette was a pretty woman in her mid-forties, dressed in a smart but unfashionable powder blue satiny skirt suit with puffy short sleeves. The pink rose in her lapel looked jagged, and I wondered how many weddings she'd officiated wearing it.

I tried to listen to her. She was saying some of the most important words I'd ever hear in my lifetime and I just couldn't concentrate. It was as if she was speaking under water. Fearing I was missing vital information, I put my hand up.

She stopped talking. That was the moment I probably became one of the few brides in history to interrupt her own ceremony.

"Charli, what's wrong?" whispered Adam from the corner of his mouth. His eyes were still fixed firmly ahead, probably on the celebrant's half-dead boutonnière rose.

"Can we have just a minute, please?" I directed the question at Georgette, who nodded and stepped aside to give us some space. She lightly touched Adam's elbow in a sorry-you're-about-to-get-jilted gesture. Maybe she'd seen it before.

"Adam, I have to ask you something."

"Now?" He sounded absolutely terrified.

I nodded. "I have to be absolutely sure about something."

"What is it?"

"Two years, right? After law school, we move on."

It was the only part of our plan that I considered to be grey area. It was one of only two promises I needed him to make. The other was pledging to love me forever. Truthfully, I was more secure with that promise than the first. Adam had proved he could love me whether we were together or not. I just had to be sure he was prepared to do it outside of his Manhattan bubble.

He smiled. "I promise you. Give me two years here and we'll go anywhere you want to."

"Okay," I replied, a little unsteadily. "Let's get married then."

"Finally," muttered Ryan from somewhere behind us.

"Shut up," scolded Bente.

We both turned back to face the celebrant. She opened her book and continued reading as if she'd never been interrupted.

This time, I heard every word. And fifteen short minutes later we were married.

19. Fallout

I didn't keep my promise to Adam about being beside him when he woke the next morning. Sitting on the hardwood floor in the kitchen at six in the morning was where he found me.

"What are you doing out here?"

I waved my phone at him. "Working up the courage to call Alex."

Adam sat beside me, resting his back against the cupboards. "And you need to sit on the floor to do that?"

Some of the most important conversations I'd had with my father since being in New York had taken place on the kitchen floor. Sometimes I was a broken mess and sometimes I was so full of excitement I needed to sit down in order to finish my tale. I had no idea how the conversation regarding the nuptials of his teenaged only daughter would pan out. Then I looked across at the man beside me and realised it really didn't matter. Any problems Alex had were his own.

"I need to call him. I don't want him to hear it from anyone else."

"I'll call him if you want me to."

I pulled away as he made a move for the phone. "No. I've got to do this."

He kissed me lightly and walked out of the kitchen. I half wondered how I'd got so lucky and half wondered how I'd make it through the day.

It was Christmas day. Even if I lived through the conversation with Alex, I still had to endure dinner at the Décaries' that night.

I punched his name on my phone, refusing to let myself back out of calling him. He answered straight away but the line was bad. "Merry Christmas, Charli," he beamed.

"Thank you. Where are you? I can hardly hear you."

Alex was at the beach. In all the time I lived in Pipers Cove, we were *never* able to get phone reception at the beach.

Just my luck, I thought.

Alex had a different take on it – a more ethereal Blake take on it. "It must be a sign, Charli," he crowed.

Obviously the man had no idea I was about to drag him to the brink of a major meltdown. I'd done it many times before – just not quite to this extreme.

"Maybe," I agreed half-heartedly. "Dad, I have to tell you something."

"Okay." He sounded worried. My tone wouldn't have done it – the fact that I called him Dad would have been the disturbing part.

I took a deep breath and told him exactly what I'd done in four short words. I married Boy Wonder.

Alex didn't speak for a long while. At first I thought the connection had dropped out. Then I realised I could hear the ocean in the background.

"I want to know how you could possibly think that was a smart decision, Charli." His voice was monotone and flat. Clearly he was trying to keep his cool. I was grateful he was at least giving me an opportunity to explain.

"I know I'm going to want him forever."

"And a piece of paper is going to do that? Ensure that you keep him forever?"

Trying to plead my case was impossible. All I could do was beg for understanding. "Please, Alex."

"Please what, Charli? Please understand that my daughter has just monumentally screwed up her life?"

"Is that what you think?"

"You're just a kid, Charli. *My* kid." He spoke as if the whole situation was nothing less than tragic.

I decided to change tack, remove all emotion and do what I did best – rattle his cage. "Are you going to recover from this, Alex? I need to know because I'm standing by the decision I've made. I've done nothing wrong. If you'd like me to tell you some of the things I've done wrong over the years, just say the word. You'll realise then that marrying the boy I love is a drop in the ocean by comparison."

"You change your mind at the drop of a hat, Charli!" Finally, his voice was appropriately raised. "This can't be easily undone."

"I have never changed my mind about him."

"And I hate that," he groaned. "I have always hated that."

"You don't get to tell me what to do anymore, Alex. I know you hate that too."

I couldn't even be sure he'd heard my hurtful rant. The line dropped out. I tried a hundred times to call him back but couldn't get a connection. I wondered if *that* was a sign. I wished I hadn't gotten through at all.

I could tell by the look on Adam's face when I walked into the room that he'd heard everything.

I flopped down on the couch beside him, resting my head on his chest, and listening to his heart beating. I would have been content to stay there for the rest of the day – or the rest of the entire yuletide season if I'd thought that was all it would take to make the drama disappear.

"Alex will calm down," he assured me. "You weren't really expecting him to be jumping for joy, were you?"

Of course I wasn't. I was expecting the exact reaction I got. I'd even prepared for it, which made flying off the handle and saying dreadful things even more stupid. "I should have handled it better."

"Charli," he murmured, leaning across to breathe the words into my hair. "Forget about it, just for a while. Today should be about us."

I snuggled closer. "You're absolutely right," I agreed. "We should stay here all day and all night – and not go to your parents' house for dinner."

"Nice try, Coccinelle," he replied, chuckling. "You told Alex; I have to tell them."

Twisting I retrieved my phone from the pocket of my pyjama pants and handed it to him. "In my experience, these things are best handled over the phone."

Adam took the phone and dropped it on the coffee table. He pushed me back, covered my body with his, and managed to take my mind off everything other than him for the rest of the day.

With an hour to go before we were due at Adam's parents' house, I decided to try making peace with Alex one last time. I took my usual position on the kitchen floor and dialled his number.

It barely rang. Alex answered immediately.

"What do you need, Charli?" I hated his cold tone, but knew I deserved it.

"Nothing. I just wanted to apologise."

"I appreciate that, but I have to tell you, I can't deal with this right now. I need a few days to get my head around it."

I didn't know quite what to make of it. I couldn't even work out if he was blazingly angry or devastatingly hurt. Over the years I'd inflicted both emotions on him, but Alex's recovery time was usually only hours, not days.

Unable to stop myself, I burst into tears. "Please, Alex."

"Don't cry, Charli. You're supposed to be a happy bride." He sounded totally disconnected from me. For once, my crying had no effect. "I'll call you in a day or two. I love you."

Pleading with him to stay on the line would've have made no difference. He ended the call, leaving me blubbering like an idiot.

Adam appeared a few seconds later. "Please don't cry. It'll work itself out," he promised.

"It's all a big mess," I sobbed.

"No it's not. We've done nothing wrong."

"Alex hates me, and I can't wear my curly fry rings anymore." I sounded positively mental.

"Why not?" he asked, calm as always.

I shook my hand and both rings flew off my finger, tinkling as they hit the wooden floor. Adam picked them up, pieced them back together and slipped them up to the knuckle of his pinkie finger.

"I can't wear them, Adam. They're too big. I'm going to lose them."

"I don't think I can get them resized. Not without messing up the setting. I'll get you a new ring." He spoke as if it was no big deal.

Furiously, I shook my head. "No. It's bad luck. You wear the rings you were married with. That's it."

Adam slipped his own wedding ring off and rolled it between his fingers.

"What if I share my ring with you? I'll get you a ring made from the gold in this one," he suggested. "Just a simple gold band that you can wear all the time."

"You'd do that for me?"

He reached for my hand. "I can't think of anything I wouldn't do for you."

***

I wondered if the queen was dreading the idea of me being in her home for Christmas dinner as much as I was. Even Adam seemed a little keyed up. And as many times as he assured me his fidgety mood had nothing to do with his altered marital status, I couldn't quite believe him. He checked his reflection in the mirrored elevator as we rode up to their penthouse apartment a hundred times.

"Your tie is straight," I assured.

He smiled a little sheepishly.

What sort of family dinner calls for a suit and tie, for crying out loud? It was another warning bell going off in my head. Combined with the other warning bells, I had a complete orchestra ringing in my ears.

Adam reached for my hand, squeezing it reassuringly. "You look beautiful."

I looked straight ahead, studying my reflection in the mirror. My outfit came courtesy of Bente. She'd raided her wardrobe and pieced together an appropriate outfit to wear to a Décarie soiree, a long grey satin skirt and pastel pink cashmere cardigan. If I'd worn a string of pearls and horn rimmed glasses I could have passed as a librarian. If I'd perfected a scowl and skipped a few meals, I could have passed as Kinsey.

"Adam, do you really think I look beautiful?"

The mirror in front of us made it impossible for him to lie. "Always. But I think you look uncomfortable and unhappy in those clothes." I felt elated that he knew me so well. "And your hair is too neat."

"Oh, thank God," I groaned, undoing the plait and fluffing it out with my fingers. "It *was* a French braid, you know."

"I like the Tasmanian tousle better."

By the time the elevator doors opened, I'd just about made myself presentable again.

It blew my mind that he rang the doorbell.

"Your parents live here. Don't you have a key?"

"Shush," he whispered.

A lady called Mrs Brown answered the door.

I'd already conjured up a mental picture of what I expected Mrs Brown to look like. Adam talked about her all the time. She'd worked for the Décaries since he was a child, first as a nanny and then as a housekeeper when the boys were grown. Mrs Brown was the reason he hadn't learned to do laundry until the ripe age of twenty. In my mind, she was old, grey and frail. It was a terribly clichéd thought, but the only experience I'd had with nannies was with the one from *Peter Pan* - and she was a Newfoundland dog.

Mrs Brown wasn't old, grey or frail. She was a spritely woman in her mid-fifties with jet-black hair and bright pink lipstick. She hesitated briefly before greeting Adam with a warm hug. Perhaps she wasn't supposed to.

"Mrs Brown, I'd like you to meet Charli," he said, motioning toward me.

I didn't know whether to wave or shake her hand. Luckily, she made the first move, sneaking a hug from me too.

"So much better," she crooned darting her eyes between him and me.

Adam replied in French. I wanted to kick him. Mrs Brown giggled at his comment, took our coats and disappeared.

"What was that about?"

He smiled. "Nothing. She thinks you're lovely."

I didn't get a chance to demand more information. Adam slid open the huge opaque glass door in front of us and suddenly we were in Décarie land.

It was too much to take in at once. It was reminiscent of an English drawing room from a bygone era. Dark mahogany furniture dominated the room - probably all antiques worth more than some small nations. The massive glass cabinet showcasing a beautiful collection of crystal and china held my attention for a long time. I would have killed for a closer look, but was afraid to step on the spotless cream carpet.

Large floor to ceiling windows were dressed with heavy red velvet curtains and opulent swags. The four long brown leather couches positioned in the middle of the room did nothing to diminish its size. It was huge. It was also archaic, decadent and unwelcoming.

Adam must have sensed my discomfort. The vicelike grip I had on his hand probably gave it away.

"A couple of hours and we can get out of here," he mumbled, as his mother glided into the room.

"Hello darling," she said, pointing to her cheek, giving her youngest son instruction. "Merry Christmas."

Adam kissed his mother's cheek. "Merry Christmas to you, too. You remember Charlotte, don't you?"

Charlotte? I hated playing the part of Charlotte. It wasn't one I was good at. It was like trying to act a scene from Shakespeare without a script. I was never going to pull it off.

"Of course," she purred. "How are you, darling?"

"I'm fine, thank you. You have a lovely home." Somehow, I managed to choke out the rehearsed words without stammering.

"It can get a little crowded over the holidays, but we make do," she replied. I glanced around. We might as well have been standing in a museum after closing time.

"Is Ryan here yet?" asked Adam.

"Not yet. I've warned him not to bring that wretched Aubrey. We can't accommodate every drifter in town."

Adam's grip on my hand tightened, almost restricting the circulation in my fingers. It confirmed what I already knew. I was the drifter she was referencing. Fiona excused herself from the room on the pretence of checking on dinner.

Adam led me to one of the couches. It was so quiet; I could hear the ticking of a clock. I scanned the room in every direction, unable to find it.

"Is your mum really cooking dinner?" I asked, unable to imagine her slaving over a hot stove in her couture dress and six-inch heels.

"No. She has staff."

I looked across, studying his face for a long time before speaking. "Is this how you grew up, Adam?"

He broke the lock I had on his eyes and looked straight ahead. "And you thought *you* were the sheltered one. You've given me everything, Charli."

For the first time ever, I believed him. It was a surreal moment.

The queen didn't return to the room, even when Ryan arrived. I could hear him chatting to Mrs Brown in the foyer. Through the frosted glass door, I saw her silhouette lunge forward as she broke protocol and stole a hug from him, just as she had with Adam.

"About time," grumbled Adam as the door slid open. "She told us to be here at seven."

Ryan pretended to study his watch. "So? I'm fashionably late."

"At least you came without Aubrey," I jibed.

Ryan slumped on the couch opposite us as if he was already exhausted. "I came without scandal, which is more than I can say for my little brother. Have you told them the happy news yet?"

"No. Dad's not here yet," muttered Adam.

As if on cue, the door slid open again and Jean-Luc walked in. "*Ah, mes deux fils,*" he announced, clapping his hands together loudly. He beamed, genuinely happy to see his boys. "And Charli. How are you, dear?"

Dear? It was slightly better than darling but still horrid.

"Fine, thank you," I replied politely.

"Good to hear. I hope you're making yourself at home. You're welcome any time."

"Thank you," I repeated. "You have a lovely home." The insincere compliment was becoming my catchphrase.

"Do you think so?" asked Jean-Luc, glancing around the room. "I find it awfully medieval. The burden of lodging family heirlooms has limited our decorating options considerably."

Laughing probably wasn't appropriate but I did it anyway.

"We keep the suits of armour upstairs," added Adam dryly. "They creep us out."

Father and both sons laughed – disturbingly similar laughs, that dulled the instant Fiona walked into the room. She greeted Ryan with a kiss on the cheek and praise for not bringing Aubrey.

"She was busy," said Ryan. "I did invite her."

The next half hour of conversation was quiet and dull, designed purely to pass the time until the other guests arrived. Eventually Grandma Nellie arrived. Mrs Brown helped the elderly lady into the room and into the arms of her grandsons, who hugged her warmly and wished her a Merry Christmas.

Grandma Nellie was old school. In a strong English accent she demanded a glass of whiskey and ordered Fiona to turn down the heat. There was a new queen in town.

"And who might you be?" asked Nellie, staring straight at me. "One of Ryan's floosies?"

"Mother!" scolded, Fiona.

Jean-Luc and Ryan sniggered.

"No. Grandma, this is Charli," Adam said, trying to keep a straight face.

"Hello," I said politely.

Nellie squinted as she gave me the once over. "Oh yes, Adam's foreign girl."

Fiona quickly shoved a glass of whiskey into her hand. If it was a ploy to shut her up, it worked. Nellie barely said another word – except to demand another drink. As brash as she was, I liked her. There was an honesty about her that her daughter didn't possess.

As the evening wore on, Adam and I grew nervous – for different reasons. I'd caught sight of the table setting in the adjoining dining room. I'd counted four forks at each place. Alex and I would've been lucky to have four forks in our entire cutlery drawer. Dinner was going to be hardcore.

The reason for Adam's nervousness was more serious. He was preparing to tell his parents he'd married a vagrant-pauper-trollop-minx-drifter.

Our level of agitation rose just before dinner when the last of the guests arrived – dim Whit. Judging by the looks of horror on the Décarie brothers' faces, I wasn't the only one who didn't know she was coming.

There was no sneaky hug from Mrs Brown upon her arrival.

Fiona sashayed across the room to greet her as Mrs Brown showed her in. "Whitney, welcome," she crowed. "You look so lovely. I'm so thrilled you could make it."

Ryan leaned forward, grinning errantly at me. "Hold on to your hats, kids, it's going to be a bumpy ride."

"Shut up," grumbled Adam, roughly. The blank look on his face was alarming. It was as if he was completely trapped with nowhere to go.

"Come," ordered the queen, taking Whitney by the hand. "Sit with Adam."

Whitney half smiled as she sat beside him. She didn't appear shocked to see me. As far as Whitney was aware, I was someone who hung out in the whore tree with the older Décarie brother, who sat opposite me with a disgustingly smug look on his face.

Nellie leaned over and whispered to Ryan, not so discreetly, "Well, this is a fine mess."

"Indeed," he mumbled.

"I hope you don't mind me being here," said Whitney to Adam. "My parents went to St. Barts for the holidays. I'm in town alone."

"It's fine, Whit," replied Adam, insincerely.

Ordinarily it might have been fine. Adam and Whitney could've spent the evening reminiscing about old times. The only thing making it uncomfortable was the fact that his wife was in the room. I dropped my head, catching sight of the pink cardigan I was wearing, suddenly feeling the urge to tear it to shreds. I had officially become the little pink elephant Ryan had warned me about.

It was almost a relief when a Fiona finally announced that dinner was served. Adam stood first and practically ran to the table. I wasn't sure why until I saw the place cards were a little askew. Obviously he'd made some quick alterations to the seating arrangements. If his mother was annoyed that he was no longer sitting beside Whitney, she didn't let on.

Everyone took their seats and the games began.

Jean-Luc led most of the conversation. He was charismatic and interesting to listen to, which was a good thing because no one else really had much to say. Fiona played the part of hostess perfectly. It was as if she was indulging a group of strangers rather than her own children. I wondered if family get-togethers were always like that - or just when little elephants were in the room. Her reason for inviting Whitney clearly had nothing to do with her being alone for Christmas. It was a ploy to get her and Adam in the same room.

Jean-Luc asked Whitney how long her parents were expected to be away.

"About three weeks," she replied, smiling at him. "They said the weather is spectacular. I wish I'd gone with them."

She should have gone with them. I would have appreciated the rest.

"Adam, didn't you and Whitney go to the Caribbean together last summer?" asked Fiona, seizing the opportunity to mention it.

"Yes, we did," he miserably confirmed.

"We saw some of the most beautiful sunsets ever," remembered Whitney, glancing briefly at Adam.

If I'd been eating, I would have choked. The reason I wasn't eating was because I had absolutely no idea which fork to use. Ryan helped me out from across the table, picking up the fork on his far left and giving me a slight nod.

"Those are the memories worth treasuring," said Fiona, her eyes darting between Adam and Whitney.

I wondered if leaping across the table and strangling Whitney would make a memory worth treasuring. Truthfully, I couldn't be angry with her. She was just a clueless girl trying hard to win back the boy she loved - with the help and approval of his mother.

Dinner seemed to last for hours. The only person who looked more bored than me was Nellie. When she announced that she was tired and wanted to open the Christmas gifts, I was relieved.

We made our way through more sliding doors into yet another huge room. I called it the Christmas room. It even smelled like Christmas. A gigantic pine stood in the corner, decorated entirely with white glass baubles and clear twinkling lights. It was postcard-picture perfect. The mountain of gifts underneath it had such pretty wrappings it seemed a shame to undo them.

Adam led me to a tapestry-upholstered chair. His absent gesture of touching me gave Whitney the first hint that all was not as it seemed. Her face crumpled but she recovered quickly, moving to stand beside Jean-Luc. I sat on the chair and Adam stood beside me, arms folded in an unusually hostile pose.

Gift-giving in our house lasted all of ten minutes. I'd give Alex his presents and he'd give me mine. It was that simple. Gift-giving in the Décarie household was a long, drawn-out process where everyone had to observe the unwrapping of every single present. It was boring and unnecessary. The Décaries wanted for nothing.

Nellie's enthusiasm waned quickly. As soon as her glass of whiskey (the fourth for the evening) was empty, she bade everyone goodnight. Ryan volunteered to help her to her room. He was probably grateful for the escape.

As soon as they were gone, Fiona turned to Whitney. "Don't think we've forgotten about you, darling," she said, fossicking through the remaining pile of gifts. "Actually, it's a present for you *and* Adam."

Whitney looked thrilled. Boy Wonder looked appalled.

Jean-Luc walked across the room and poured himself a drink from the heaviest-looking crystal decanter I'd ever seen. Maybe it was to calm his nerves. The whole notion of a joint present seemed to suck the oxygen right out of the room.

As Whitney unwrapped the flat gift box, some papers fell to the floor. Adam scooped them up, reading them before she had a chance.

"Tickets to Europe?" he asked, outraged.

"Time away - without any distractions - will do you both the world of good," announced Fiona, looking straight at me.

Adam thrust the papers at Whitney. "Find someone to go with, Whit. I'm sure you'll have a great time."

His attitude toward her infuriated the queen. "Adam!" she hissed.

"I did warn you, Fi," said Jean-Luc. "You're meddling."

"It is not meddling," she hissed. "It's protecting my son."

"From what, Mom?" Adam barked. Fiona made the mistake of glancing in my direction, silently answering his question. "From Charli? You've got to be kidding me."

I understood none of the angry French diatribe she directed at him but I knew it wasn't kind.

"Butt out," he warned.

Fiona marched across the room, pointing at me but looking at Adam. "Who is this girl? Who is she to keep you from you family and friends?"

Oh, here we go, I thought. She'd just asked the magic question. If Adam had been waiting for the right moment to tell her his news, that was it.

He answered strongly, enunciating every word. "She is my wife."

Whitney let out a sharp gasp. Jean-Luc sculled the rest of his drink and promptly poured another one. Fiona staggered to the nearest chair as if she'd just been shot.

I sat perfectly still, unsure of what to do or where to look.

Mrs Brown, unaware of any drama, walked into the room waving my handbag.

"Your phone, Miss Charli."

My heart skipped a vital beat. It had to be Alex. He was the only person who ever called. I thanked Mrs Brown, took my bag from her and scurried out to the foyer. Alex could scream and yell at me all he wanted; it was still preferable to being in the middle of a Décarie war.

Reading the number on the screen was the only joyous moment of the whole evening. My caller was Mitchell Tate. I couldn't wait to hear his voice.

"Happy Christmas, Charli. Is it a good time to call?"

"Oh, Mitchell. You have no idea."

From where I stood, I could hear raised voices coming from the Christmas room. I did my best to ignore them. As far as Mitchell knew, nothing out of the ordinary was going on. I even managed to maintain my normal tone when Whitney rushed into the foyer in a flood of tears and grabbed her coat. "Tell me what you've been up to," I said, stepping aside as she made a bolt for the front door.

Mitchell was spending Christmas on the beach in Kaimte with the other cardboard villagers. At that point, I would have given anything to be there with him. We spoke for a few minutes about nothing important. It was a blissful escape that just didn't last long enough. Before I knew it, the call had ended and I was standing alone. I couldn't hear yelling any more, and the reason why soon became apparent.

The glass doors slid open and I was face to face with the queen.

"What do you want from my son?" she asked through gritted teeth.

I spoke slowly and truthfully. "Nothing. I love him."

"Love?" she scoffed, edging dangerously close to me, pointing her finger. "What could either of you possibly know about love? I will make sure you see not a cent of his money. Do you understand me?"

All her threat proved was how little she knew me. And that wasn't her fault.

"I don't care about the money. I just want him."

"This marriage will be annulled by the end of the week." Fiona spoke with complete certainty. "I suggest you get out of New York."

"No. That isn't going to happen."

I don't know where the sudden rush of courage came from but it certainly wasn't to my advantage. Incensed by my very existence, the queen lost all control.

In all my life, I had never been hit before. And being on the receiving end of a backhander hurt more than I imagined it could.

Immediately remorseful, Fiona reached out to me but I took a quick step back. "Oh, Charli!" She gasped. "Forgive me. I'm so sorry."

She might have meant it but I didn't trust her. She had proven herself to be an accomplished liar.

"Mother! What the hell did you do?" yelled Ryan, rushing toward me.

I didn't see from which direction he came, but could tell by the revulsion in his voice that he'd seen everything.

"I'm sorry," she repeated. "I don't know what came over me."

"Let me see," said Ryan, pulling my hand off my cheek. He took a handkerchief from his pocket and swiped it under my eye.

No wonder it hurt so much. I was bleeding. I was confused. She'd slapped me, not stabbed me. I looked at her hand and realised she'd clocked me with her massive diamond ring.

"I'm okay," I insisted.

"Unforgivable," muttered Ryan.

"I know. Oh, Charli, I'm so sorry," repeated Fiona, more desperately than before.

"Mom, get her some ice," ordered Ryan.

Fiona didn't question him. She scurried out of the room as quickly as a woman in six-inch heels could.

"Is it bad?" I asked, as soon as she was gone.

"No. You'll be fine." He pressed the cloth under my eye, making me wince enough for him to apologise. "Sorry. Listen, can I suggest something?"

"Boxing lessons?"

He grimaced. I couldn't blame him for not seeing the funny side. "Don't tell Adam about this. I know what she did was terrible, but it was a one-off. She's very upset," he told me. "Adam will never forgive her if he finds out."

I nodded and his hand moved with me. "I won't tell him."

I had a knack for bringing out the worst in people. It was practically a hobby. Realistically, I should have been thumped a million times before now.

Fiona barrelled back in to the room with a silver champagne bucket filled to the brim with ice. The absurdity nearly made me laugh out loud, but I fought against it. There was a slight chance that she meant well.

Ryan grabbed a handful of ice, wrapped it in his handkerchief and pressed it against my cheek.

"Thank you," I mumbled.

"Charli, I – " Fiona didn't get chance to apologise again. The glass doors slid open and Adam walked in.

His eyes were wide with horror. "What the hell happened?"

Fiona stared at me, probably waiting for me to rat her out.

"She's fine," assured Ryan.

Adam pushed him and the icepack out of the way, taking my face in his hands. "What happened?" he repeated, calmer this time.

I vaguely pointed to the shiny marble floor. "I slipped." It was a dangerous fib to tell. It showed Fiona that I was just as good at lying as she was. I glanced across at her. Her expression was one of total relief.

"Take Charli home, Adam," instructed Ryan, reaching for our coats.

Adam didn't argue. I got the impression he was as keen to get the hell out of there as I was.

By the time we arrived home, my whole face was throbbing and I was exhausted.

"I'm so sorry, Charli," mumbled Adam gravely – as if he'd whacked me himself. "It looks like it's going to be a nasty bruise." He stood in front of me, unbuttoning my coat. Maybe he thought I'd lost the use of my arms during my pretend slip on the floor. I shrugged out of the sleeves and he hung both our coats on the hooks by the door.

"It's not your fault. Accidents happen."

He looked at me for a long moment, searching my eyes – perhaps for the truth. Deep down, I knew he wasn't buying my story. "I should have listened when you suggested staying here," he said regretfully.

"At least they know we got married. Everything is out in the open now. Alex knows. Your parents know. It's all out there and we lived through the war."

Adam put his hand to my face, lightly skimming over the graze with his thumb. "Is this a war wound?"

If he was hinting toward a confession, it wasn't going to happen. No good could possibly come from telling him about his mother's brain snap. I stretched up to kiss him in a ploy designed to mask my insincerity. "No."

"You've never struck me as being the clumsy type."

"Adam, what exactly do you want me to tell you?"

His hand moved to my face again. "Charli, did Whitney do this?"

Poor dim Whit just couldn't catch a break.

"Why would Whitney do this? She's pissed at you, not me."

He stared at me for a few seconds before shaking free of whatever thought he was lost in. "You're absolutely right. It's absurd. I'm sorry."

I groaned. "Will you please stop apologising?"

I started to walk away but he grabbed my hand, pulling me back to his side. "I'm sorry," he said, smiling.

Linking my arms around his neck, I pressed my body against his. "Look, today needn't be a total washout. We have plenty of good things going on."

"Like?"

"Like, I'm a new bride. I have a freaking tiara to prove it. Despite everything, Adam, I am blissfully happy. We're together. That's all that matters."

"It's the *only* thing that matters," he agreed, sweeping his hand through my hair.

"I also managed to strike number eighty-one off my list of things I've never done. That's exciting. Tonight, I got my very first black eye." I said it way too proudly. "Of course, I expected it to happen during a wild pub brawl or while I was resisting arrest, so the circumstances are quite disappointing."

"Of course. How disappointing." He pulled me in impossibly close. "Just out of curiosity, what's number eighty-two on the list?"

I replied without hesitation. "Getting stung by a bee."

He pursed his lips, smiling with his eyes. "You've never been stung by a bee?"

"Nope." I tilted my head. "Not for the want of trying though."

"You're crazy, Charlotte."

"Like I've never heard that before," I replied. It was good to hear him laugh.

20. Coup de Grâce

By the next morning, I had to concede that there wasn't a whole lot of good in having a black eye.

I stood in the bathroom, staring at my reflection in the mirror. The bluish-black bruise extended from the top of my cheek to the corner of my eye. The graze made my cheek puffy and red. I looked like a ghoulish pirate.

Adam tried to play it cool when he saw it, promising me that it really didn't look too horrible. I called him out on being a terrible liar and he promptly left the bathroom without further comment.

I began to worry that it might scar. I'd never been a vain person, but permanently resembling a pirate was hardly a good look. I considered consulting a plastic surgeon. No doubt Kinsey or Seraphina could hook me up. I could sue Fiona Décarie to pay for it. Ryan could represent me. I could clean her out and steal her kingdom, just as I'd stolen her youngest prince.

The sound of Adam calling my name jolted me back to reality - and put a stop to any plans I had of ending my chaotic mental rambling with an out-loud evil laugh. The urgency of his voice suggested it wasn't the first time he'd called out to me.

"I'm here," I said, looking at him through the mirror.

He leaned against the doorframe, frowning. "I know you're here. Are you alright?"

"Yes, of course."

"Good. My mother is here." His face matched his dour tone.

"Why?"

"To make peace, I think. Please, Charli. Play nice, for me."

"I will," I promised. "Just give me a minute." I waved my compact at him through the mirror, implying that I wanted time to cover my bruises.

Truthfully, I wasn't even going to attempt it. The queen deserved to see exactly what she'd done to me in her fit of rage. As soon as Adam left, I put the compact back in the drawer, pulled my hair into a ponytail and put my game face on.

"Charlotte, darling," crooned Fiona, the second I walked into the room.

She still had her coat on. It gave me hope that she wasn't going to stay long.

"Hello, Mrs Décarie," I replied, trying to sound as if I felt as sore as I looked.

I stood beside Adam and he grabbed my hand. The reassuring squeezes he gave my fingers had almost become a secret language between us. He did it a lot when we were in hostile territory.

"Call me Fiona, please. I just wanted to stop and bring you this." She stepped forward, thrusting a poinsettia plant at me.

Adam thanked her, probably because he thought I wouldn't.

"It's lovely," I said, setting the scarlet Christmassy plant down on the edge of the kitchen bench.

It was a lie. I hate poinsettias. Besides, the idea of Fiona Décarie gifting me a flower that represented purity was more than a little odd – not that she would have had a clue about its meaning.

"Your eye looks a little better this morning."

I wondered if every word we'd ever exchange from here on in would be a whopping great lie.

Adam called her on it straight away. "No, it doesn't."

Fiona nodded. "It's true. You do look terribly wounded."

"I'll recover."

The smile she gave was tiny. "Well, as long as you're okay."

And haven't grassed on you, I added silently.

A long few seconds of silence set in. It was Adam who got a reprieve. His phone rang and he excused himself to answer it. I was jealous. I would've accepted a call from the devil himself if it had brought me an excuse to leave.

"I think we should wipe the slate clean," suggested Fiona, as soon as he was gone. "You and I should spend some time getting to know each other, Charlotte."

"Why?"

Her eyes drifted to the floor but I got the impression it was me who was supposed to be embarrassed by my question. "Because whether we like it or not, we're family now."

"Wouldn't it make more sense just to steer clear of each other?"

"This won't be an easy process if all the effort has to come from me," she snapped.

"Fine. What do you suggest?"

"I think we should meet for lunch next week - when your face is respectable again, of course."

"Of course," I said sarcastically. "You do remember why my face is bruised, don't you?"

Fiona stepped toward me to hiss her words. "I regret it terribly, Charlotte."

I felt no need to play nice anymore. If she were truly remorseful and genuine about starting over, she would handle it. "It's Charli. I'm just plain, wrong-side-of-the-tracks, Charli. Calling me Charlotte doesn't add any grandeur to who I am."

"I've noticed that my son prefers to call you Charlotte." The wretched look on her face suggested she'd just brought something awful to my attention.

"And I've noticed that you like to refer to Adam as your son. Is it a territorial thing or do you have trouble remembering his name?"

Fiona didn't appear ruffled in the slightest. "In time you'll acquire some decorum," she said calmly. "I hope you're a fast learner, for all our sakes."

"At least you realise I'm not going anywhere."

"If you're going to maintain such a nasty attitude, it's going to be impossible to move forward. You're not too ignorant to realise that."

Furiously, I shook my head.

Fiona looked past me, smiling brightly. It was a big hint that Adam was on his way back into the room.

"Darling," she crooned.

"Mom." His voice was void of any emotion.

"Charli and I are going to meet for lunch next week," Fiona said, darting her eyes between the both of us.

"Seriously?" Adam sounded as worried as I'd ever heard him.

"Of course. I need to get to know my new daughter-in-law." She didn't even choke as she said it. "Choose the time and the place, Charli. I'll be there."

If Adam was sceptical of her turnaround, he didn't let on.

It was a case of out of sight, out of mind. Once Fiona left our apartment, she wasn't mentioned again for the rest of the day.

We lazed around all afternoon. I sat on the floor, poring over the latest few hundred photos I'd taken. Adam sprawled on the couch behind me with his head buried in some textbooks, studying as always. I loved the silence. It was comfortable and calm.

What I didn't love was the fact I wasn't doing anything productive. The advice Adam received from the immigration lawyer was clear and precise. Working illegally for tips while waiting for my visa to be approved wasn't a smart idea. My new husband fired me in an instant.

It had only been a few days since my last shift at Nellie's but I was already feeling slightly without purpose. "What am I supposed to do for the next two years, Adam?" I asked, dropping a handful of pictures on to the floor in front of me.

"Love me."

"That's it?" I turned around, grabbed the book he was reading and snapped it shut, ensuring I had his full attention. "That doesn't sound too challenging."

"Possibly not," he agreed, playfully winding my ponytail around his hand.

I stared at the pile of photos in front of me. "I shall take pictures," I announced with a touch of theatre in my voice.

Adam grinned. "That's what you do."

"I'll find a gallery to display my work," I added. "I'll become a household name."

Either my ridiculous words or the dramatic spin I put on them made Adam laugh. "If anyone can do that, you can."

I got off the floor and piled on top of him, straddling his body. "World domination has always been my plan," I teased. "How about you, Boy Wonder? What's your plan?"

With both hands, he grabbed the hem of my T-shirt and lifted it up. I raised my arms as he yanked it off me. "You've always been my plan, Charlotte," he mumbled, levering himself up to kiss me.

***

After three days, I was able to convincingly cover my bruises with makeup. As soon as I was sure that I couldn't be mistaken for a pirate, I was making plans to escape the apartment.

I walked the short distance from the bathroom to the bedroom, rattling off options for a day out, but Adam didn't seem to be paying attention. He sat on the edge of the bed, tapping away at his phone.

"Are you listening to me?"

"Of course," he mumbled.

"So you would have no problem with naked skydiving today?" I asked.

He looked up, frowning. "What are you talking about, Charli?"

"It doesn't matter," I grumbled. "You're not listening to me anyway."

He reached for my hand as I passed, pulling me down on the bed.

"I am," he lied. "But I have to tell you something."

It was a cover-my-ears-and-sing moment. The first word out of his mouth was Whitney.

Dim Whit epitomised a woman scorned. Adam confessed that he'd been on the receiving end of a barrage of phone calls and text messages since Christmas night.

"After all you've done to her, she still wants you back?"

Adam shook his head, frowning like he was in pain. "No. Not exactly."

"Well, what exactly?" I practically growled the question at him. Trying to get information out of him was like pulling teeth.

"She wants to talk to me. I can't imagine what we have to talk about."

The blank expression on his face led me to believe he was telling the truth.

"And they say I'm naïve," I muttered.

"What does that mean?"

I lay back on the bed, looking up at the ceiling, unsure whether I had any business coaching him. Against my better judgement, I answered him. "Adam, don't you think you owe her an explanation? If I were her, I'd want answers."

He fell backward, laying his head beside mine, draping his arm across my chest. "I'd be happy just to know what the questions are."

I couldn't give him any more hints than I had. Adam had treated Whitney abysmally. For that reason alone, she deserved an opportunity to tear shreds off him. But besides a pound of Adam's flesh, there were other things Whitney wanted. In one particularly angry text message, she'd demanded the return of the belongings she'd left at Adam and Ryan's apartment.

To me it seemed perfectly reasonable. To Adam it was a petty grab for attention. "None of this stuff is important to her," he said waving his phone in the air. "This is purely designed to aggravate."

Doing my best to ignore his tantrum, I kept my focus on the ceiling.

"It's working, then, isn't it?"

His demeanour changed instantly. "You're right. I'm sorry. None of this is anything to do with you."

"Stop involving me then," I grumbled. "It's not hard to fix this, Adam. Go to Ryan's apartment, pack up her stuff and deliver it in person. All you have to do then is let her yell and scream for a while. Let her tell you what an insensitive jerk you are and be done with it. Just fix it, please."

Meeting with Whitney, giving her the answers she was desperately seeking and returning her possessions was the decent thing to do. The Adam I knew would have realised that from the very beginning. The Adam who'd smashed Whitney's heart to bits took a little more convincing.

Finally, I talked him round. He texted Whitney, suggesting they meet for lunch.

Her reply came quickly – yes.

***

Accompanying Adam to Ryan's apartment hardly seemed like a good day out, but I went anyway, tired of being cooped up at home. Adam disappeared as soon as we got there, moving quickly to pack the few trivial belongings Whitney demanded to have returned.

Ryan found the whole situation very amusing. "Is this your way of exorcising demons, Charli?"

The cheeky question was asked only once he was sure Adam was out of the room. He wasn't usually so cautious. I could only assume it was because he knew his brother wasn't in the mood for cheap shots.

"It's nothing to do with me." I shrugged, faking indifference. "She wants her stuff back, that's all."

"Are you sure that's all she wants back? I'm sure she couldn't care less about a few books and a hairbrush," he goaded.

"Are you going to be a pig to me all day?"

"No. I'm over it now." He pointed toward the modish lounge suite. Perhaps that was my cue to sit. I ignored him.

Adam breezed into the room a short while later, carrying a half-full overnight bag. "I should go. The sooner I get this over with, the better." He slowed his walk as he neared me, leaning over to kiss me. "I'll see you when I get home." I nodded and forced a smile. He slipped out the front door and I was left alone with the evil brother – whose mood seemed more evil than usual.

I tried to find a reason for it. "Are any crazy blonde women lurking in here, Ryan?" I quizzed, looking left to right.

"Only you," he replied, flopping onto the couch.

"I don't count."

I finally sat, sinking into the soft new couch like I needed the rest.

"You seem awfully calm considering your new husband has just left to rendezvous with his ex."

Only Ryan could make it sound so sordid. I decided to fight fire with fire. If rattling cages was the main agenda for the day, it was the perfect time to mention his tangled relationship with Bente.

"Ryan, I want to ask you something." I turned my head to look at him. Seeing him squirm didn't happen often. "What's the story with you and Bente?"

As predicted, he shifted uncomfortably in his seat. "There's no story," he insisted. "We're just friends."

"With benefits?" I hinted. "I know you… spent time with her." I couldn't think of a nicer way of describing their cloakroom romp.

Ryan shook his head, looking to the floor. "I regret getting involved with Bente," he said, choosing his words very carefully.

"Because you don't like her?"

He looked at me, frowning like I'd just sworn at him. "No, Charli. I regret it because I *do* like her."

His less than straightforward answer made complete sense to me. Bente was different from the run-of-the-mill high-maintenance girls he was used to. And Ryan, the man who insisted that love didn't even exist, could see it.

I smiled at him. "You're not so despicable after all."

"Sometimes I try not to be," he mumbled.

There were a million more questions I wanted to ask, but a knock at the door cut our conversation short. Ryan practically jumped off the couch, groaning as soon as he opened the door. I peeked over the back of the couch to see the source of his pain. Standing there, in a gorgeous full-length red coat, was Kinsey Ballantyne.

"I'm looking for Whitney. Is she here?"

"Sweetheart, so nice to see you," said Ryan. "You should have called."

"I did call," she spat. "You hung up on me."

"Oh, that's right. Perhaps that's because I detest the air you breathe."

Kinsey pushed past him, inviting herself in. I slunk down in the couch, hopelessly trying to hide. "The feeling is mutual. Look, I'm just trying to track Whit down."

"And why would you think she was here?"

Her long answer bordered on hysteria. Even without seeing her, I could tell her concern was genuine.

The last she'd heard, Whitney was planning to spend Christmas with the Décaries, still hopeful that she could work things out with Adam. Kinsey had unsuccessfully been trying to contact her ever since.

"Her parents are out of town. She's alone and I can't find her," she rambled. "Coming here was a last resort. I can't think of where else she'd be."

Better than anyone, I knew how low the pit of despair could be when you lose the one you love. Hiding away was a coping mechanism. It made me feel absolutely wretched.

"Adam doesn't even live here anymore, Kins," said Ryan, remarkably gently.

"What?" She sounded shocked. "Where is he living now?"

He had a chance to be truly nasty but mercifully, he took the high road.

"He has a new apartment. Actually, Adam pretty much has a new life."

Predictably, Kinsey demanded an explanation. I couldn't leave it up to Ryan to explain. He would either lie or tell the truth. Neither scenario was pretty. Abandoning my cowardly hiding spot, I stood up, catching Kinsey so unaware that she jumped.

"Ugh! Do you make a habit of listening in on private conversations?" She didn't wait for an answer. She turned her attention to Ryan. "You should keep a tighter leash on your dogs."

"You're in my house," reminded Ryan menacingly. "Behave."

"Look, do you know where Whitney is or not?"

Ryan glanced at me. "Do you know what a coup de grâce is, Charli?"

"You know I don't," I mumbled.

His ensuing smile was positively evil. "It's a stroke of mercy, a deathblow used when putting someone out of their misery. Please put an end to this stupid charade."

There was no reason not to. Whitney already knew the truth. The only objective I had behind keeping my relationship with Adam secret was to preserve her feelings. I failed. Her feelings were obliterated anyway.

"Are you high?" barked Kinsey. "What the hell are you talking about?"

Ryan took a very measured step toward her, leaning forward as if he was about to whisper something. "If I tell you, you have to listen. I'm only going to tell you once. Traditionally, a coup de grâce is one shot."

Kinsey folded her arms and tapped her foot on the floor impatiently. "Get on with it then."

He motioned toward me with his arm. "Meet Charlotte Décarie." For a split second, I considered flipping the couch and using it as a barricade. I was probably about to need it.

Kinsey stared at me, clearly confused. "A cousin or something?"

Ryan spoke very slowly. "No. Adam's wife."

The coup de grâce was successful. She walked out the front door without another word.

***

That afternoon I spent a lot of time compiling a mental list of questions I *wouldn't* ask Adam when he arrived home, fearful of what I might learn. I was sitting on the couch, pretending to read a magazine, when he walked in the door. I held my tongue, saying nothing until he did.

"I'm glad you're here." He leaned down and kissed me before flopping beside me.

"I'm legally obligated to be here," I replied, trying to mimic his usual formal diction.

The lock he had on my eyes lasted much longer than usual. I used the time to assess his mood. Adam looked tired but otherwise unscathed.

"You're so beautiful," he said, tucking my hair behind my ear.

It was my turn for a silent stare, which didn't faze him in the least. "How was lunch?"

"It was fine. We ate sandwiches." His smart aleck answer had left me with nowhere to go but to call him out on his stinginess.

"Classy."

Adam grinned. "You didn't let me finish. We ate sandwiches at the airport while we waited for her flight to be called. Whitney decided to get away for a while. She's meeting her parents in St Barts."

I was relieved. I couldn't pretend otherwise. "Time away will be good for her."

"She doesn't want to be in town when word gets out that...."

I dipped my head as his voice trailed off. "Just say it, Adam."

"Her words, not mine, okay?" I nodded, giving him a green light to insult me. "She doesn't want to be around when word gets out that I married the whore I dumped her for."

I actually winced as he said it. Adam rubbed his hand up and down my arm in a feeble attempt to comfort me.

"Is that what she thinks happened?"

Adam shook his head. "Nothing I said would've helped, Charli. Whitney needs a villain."

"I'm tired of being the bad guy, Adam," I muttered.

He pushed me backward into the cushion. "It'll pass, I promise. At least we're not trying to protect anyone's feelings anymore. The whole world can know –"

I covered his mouth with my hand, cutting his sentence short. "The whole world already knows. Kinsey found out."

Adam groaned, burying his head in my shoulder. "Excellent."

21. Finding Balance

Days had passed since I'd seen Bente. Keen to catch up, we made plans to get together at Nellie's before opening.

The weather was horrific, but Adam's best efforts at dissuading me from going fell on deaf, frozen ears. Because of the recent heavy snowfall, the walk took double the time. It wasn't even pretty snow. It was dirty, sludgy and wet. The overcast sky stole the daylight, making the early afternoon seem like night. I arrived at the closed restaurant looking like something a cat had dragged in.

Bente was alone inside, setting tables for the evening service. I pounded on the door and she rushed to open it.

"Welcome, stranger," she greeted, throwing a handful of cloth napkins at me. "Don't drip on my floor. That would be a lawsuit waiting to happen."

I followed her across the room, trying to pat myself dry. "Anyone prepared to go up against the Décaries deserves a multi-million dollar payout."

"Ooh, Charlotte," she drawled, cupping her hand to her ear. "Is that the sound of someone changing their tune?"

I grinned. "Not at all."

Bente heaved a sigh. "That's a shame. I was hoping for some juicy gossip. This place has been dead since Christmas."

"I didn't say I didn't have juicy gossip."

That vague hint was all it took for Bente to abandon the table settings and run to the kitchen. I wasn't surprised; I'd seen that manoeuvre before. I pulled out a chair at the table nearest the kitchen door, waiting for her to return.

"Chocolate cake," she announced, crashing through the swinging door to the kitchen. "It's no pecan pie, but it will have to do."

"How do you know I even have gossip worthy of chocolate cake?"

"Well, for starters, you have an impressive-looking shiner." She pointed at my eye. "That's got to be a great story right there."

The hour I'd spent covering it up with makeup had been pointless. The snow had washed it all off.

"It's not what you think."

Bente took a huge bite of cake and closed her eyes in ecstasy. "You don't know what I think; but I must say, a newlywed bride with a black eye is never a good look. People could easily get the wrong impression of your frog."

"I know." I'd spent many days cooped up at home for that very reason. "But Adam would never –"

"Relax, Kemosabe. He's a frog, not a thug. I want the real story."

The real story was worthy of far more than chocolate cake. I filled Bente in on the whole sorry saga, starting with the slap from the queen and ending with Whitney skipping town. "So all in all, it's been a rough week."

"You're telling me!" shrieked Bente gleefully, taking far too much delight in my misery. "Do you think Fiona got it all out of her system? Is it happy families from here on in?"

"I doubt it." I poked my piece of cake. "I think she was more concerned that I'd tell Adam, rather than the damage she'd done to me."

"She really didn't take the news well, did she?" Bente's tone was uncharacteristically sympathetic.

I continued my tale of woe, explaining how no one had taken the news well. My father was so furious that he was unwilling to deal with me. Alex's promise of calling me after a few days was the first he'd ever broken. I hadn't spoken to him in nearly a week. Whitney was convinced I'd found a way of breaking up her perfectly happy relationship with Adam. To her, I was nothing more than a home-wrecking whore. "How can someone be so blissfully happy and yet so miserable at the same time?" I smiled to dull the gravity of my question.

A slight frown crept across Bente's face. "Can I give you a little advice?"

"Please, do."

"Trying to convince people that you've done nothing wrong would be a whole lot easier if you both stopped sneaking around as if you have."

"I don't fit in with these people, Bente. His family and friends are never going to accept me." I pushed my plate of uneaten cake to the centre of the table. "All I want is Adam. I'd be content to hide forever if it meant having him all to myself."

I knew how selfish and unrealistic it sounded. I wasn't expecting Bente to tell me anything otherwise. "So his friends are douche bags." She shrugged her shoulders. "There's no way around that, but for some weird reason, Adam likes them. You're going to have to make more of an effort to fit in."

"I can't see it happening."

Bente picked up a saltshaker and poured a stream of salt on to her empty plate, followed by two packets of sugar. "Imagine that this salt is the purple circle," she said, stirring the grainy pile with her finger. "And the sugar is his family."

"Because they're so sweet?" I asked.

Bente walked to the information station and returned with a tall wooden pepper mill. "You can be the pepper – hot and spicy."

I rolled my eyes. "What is this visual display in aid of?"

She twisted the mill, covering the plate with flakes of pepper. "Bear with me." Again, she stirred the pile with her finger. "Adam's whole world is on this plate – his friends, his family and you."

"Okay," I dragged out the word, still unsure of the point she was trying to make.

Bente pushed the plate toward me and ordered me to separate the grains.

I looked down at the concoction, shaking my head. "You know I can't."

"Of course you can't, Charli. And neither can he. Adam is constantly trying to pick pepper out of salt. No one can keep that up for long. You're going to have to change your ways."

22. Legends

Our New Year's Eve was meant to be a quiet affair. My eye hadn't quite healed and Adam was suffering a mild case of the flu.

Eating dinner by candlelight was my idea. We sat side by side on the floor, using the coffee table as a dining table. The mushroom risotto I'd attempted hadn't gone exactly to plan. I was hoping that the dull light might make the gluggy mess seem less horrid. Adam never mentioned it. I wondered if he thought it was beyond even false compliments.

"If you don't eat it all, you can't have dessert," I teased, bumping his arm.

He set his fork down on his plate. "I have something for you."

"A fillet steak?" I asked, only half-jokingly.

"No, not quite." He reached into his jeans for a small black box. He set it on the table and we stared at it as if it was about to explode.

"What is it?" For some reason, I whispered the question.

"It's your new ring."

"Well, can I see it?"

His pained frown confused me. Unless he'd managed to have the ugliest gold ring in the history of rings made, I saw no reason for his hesitation. I didn't bother waiting for an answer. I picked up the box and flipped open the lid. There were two plain gold rings inside. The gold from Adam's wedding ring had been used to make a simple thin band for me; his altered ring was about half the original width.

"What do you think?" he asked, picking up his fork and stabbing at the mush on his plate.

I took my ring out of the box, slipped it on my finger and flapped my hand. "It fits like a glove," I replied. "I'll never take it off."

"I'm glad."

His dull tone annoyed me. Perhaps his stuffy head was to blame. Or maybe the horrid risotto was sucking the life right out of him. "You don't sound glad, Adam."

Still looking slightly tortured, he shrugged. "I like the other ones better, that's all."

I sidled closer to him, snuggling in, linking my arm through his.

"I love my curly fry rings. You know I do. I just can't wear them. This ring is perfect for me."

I held my hand out, wiggling my fingers. He slowly shook his head. "Nothing about a plain gold band is special."

I was furious. It was one of the few joyous moments I'd had that week, and he was ruining it with the superficial opinion that it wasn't grand enough. I released my hold on him and straightened. "To me, it's special. I don't want a big flashy ring." I slipped the ring off my finger, put it down on the table and stood up, towering over him for once. "And if you want the truth, I'm not so keen on the big flashy life that comes with the big flashy ring either."

He lifted his head to look at me, looking positively wounded. "What does that mean?"

I wanted to tell him exactly what it meant. I was having major issues when it came to adjusting to life in his world, most of which he was oblivious to. But I didn't. I walked away.

I learned something that night.

Adam wasn't a chaser. My father was a chaser. Every spat I'd ever had with Alex ended with me storming out of the room. Minutes later he'd follow me, attempting to either calm me down or continue the argument.

Adam didn't follow. He left the apartment, which was nothing less than I deserved.

He left because he couldn't deal with me. The list of people who were prepared to deal with me was becoming shorter by the day. It seemed like a good idea to try bumping numbers.

I called Alex.

"Hi Charli," he greeted, answering on the second ring.

"Hello Father." I was thrilled that he sounded pleased to hear from me. "I miss you."

"You can come home any time you like."

As tempting as his offer was at that moment, I had no intention of jumping ship.

"What are you doing for New Year?" I asked, changing the subject.

Alex explained that he and Gabrielle were spending a few days in Hobart. "We're going to watch the fireworks on the waterfront."

My heart ached for home – just a little. As a child, Alex took me to Hobart every New Year's Eve to watch the fireworks. I was glad he'd kept up the tradition.

"I guess you and Adam are heading to Times Square?"

"I'm not sure what our plans are yet," I lied.

I knew exactly what my plans were. I just didn't think Alex needed to hear how I was going to see the New Year in alone because my bad behaviour had driven Adam out of the apartment.

"Are you happy, Charli?" Alex asked, perhaps sensing something was amiss.

"I'd be much happier if I heard from you once in a while."

"I haven't had much to say to you lately."

"Are you still mad?"

"I'm still disappointed," he replied after a long pause. "I'm still trying to get my head around why you think getting married was a good idea."

We were about to repeat mistakes of old. Ending the conversation before one of us said something regretful seemed sensible – mainly because the regretful comments usually came from me.

"Alex, I have to go. It's getting close to midnight."

He wished me a Happy New Year and promised to call me in a few days. It was a promise I wasn't sure he'd keep. The distance between us lately wasn't just geographical.

I really didn't want to be alone at midnight, but as the minutes ticked by it seemed likely. I grabbed a blanket off the bed and rugged myself up on the couch. It was a position I held for only a moment. I couldn't stand the sight of the two plates of ghastly risotto still sitting on the coffee table. I carried them to the kitchen, scraped them into the bin and set about making a pot of tea. That's where I was when Adam walked in the door, a few minutes before midnight.

He made no effort to come any closer than the edge of the kitchen – probably worried about the reception he'd receive. I wanted to speak but couldn't summon words. I hoped he was silent for the same reason. The mutual stare down lasted an uncomfortably long time before he finally made a move that was well worth the wait.

He walked over to me and lifted me onto the kitchen counter. Wedging himself between my legs, he took my face in his hands.

His long lingering kiss was the sweetest sign of forgiveness. The way I kissed him back was my silent apology.

Not one single word was spoken until morning.

***

Adam presented me with my new gold ring for a second time over breakfast – just as casually as he had the night before.

"I'm still not happy with it, but something is better than nothing."

I slipped it back on my finger, ignoring his misgivings. "I love it. Even if you don't."

Nursing a mug of hot coffee with both hands, he looked down, shaking his head. "I love you. The ring is unimportant."

"No good comes of being weighted down with jewels anyway. It's a tragedy waiting to happen."

Piquing Adam's curiosity with just a few words was ridiculously easy. It always had been. And I loved that about him. "Charlotte, what on earth are you talking about?"

"Greek Cypriot fairies." I held two fingers in the air. "Two sisters, Dorcia and Effie."

Adam took a sip of his coffee, set it on the counter and glanced at his watch. "I want to hear this tale but I really have to go."

The work at the new restaurant was completed, and the grand opening was just two weeks away. Adam wasn't anywhere near as amped up about it as his brother, but he needed to be there that morning to sign off on the project. That was the reason behind the stuffy suit and tie he was wearing. I had nowhere to be that morning. That's why I was still wearing my pink monkey print pyjamas.

I shrugged. "I'll tell you about it another time."

I began walking away but he caught my hand as I passed, pulling me to a stop. "Not so fast, Charli. If you don't tell me now, I'm going to be wondering about it all day."

"Curious little thing, aren't you?" I teased, leaning in to straighten his tie.

Adam raked both hands through my bedroom hair and rested them on my shoulders.

"Enchanted is what I am," he whispered, leaning in dangerously close. "Tell me."

I sighed as if explaining it was a chore. "The sisters were nothing alike. Dorcia was materialistic and vain. Her sister, Effie, was the complete opposite. When it came to choosing husbands, Effie married for love. Her husband, Abraxas, was a lowly carpenter, but she loved him with her whole heart."

"How do you remember all of these stories, Charli?"

"Shush. Do you want to hear it or not?"

He moved his hand, checking the time on his watch again.

"I am so late," he muttered, smiling. "Keep going."

"Dorcia married Xenon. She didn't love him at all, but he was filthy rich. Impossibly rich. *Décarie rich,*" I teased. "Effie's wedding ring was a simple gold band like this one."

I wiggled my fingers at him and he rolled his eyes. "Poor girl."

"Dorcia wore a huge solitaire diamond that sparkled brilliantly," I continued. "Xenon showered her with other diamonds too - earrings, necklaces, bracelets -"

"Where's the tragedy, Charli?" asked Adam, trying to hurry the story along.

"I'm getting to it. One day, the sisters decided to visit their family on a neighbouring island. The only way they could get there was by boat, but during the trip something terrible happened."

"Oh, no," he crooned in mock horror.

I changed my tone to match the theatre in his. "The boat sank and the girls were forced to swim for their lives."

"Did they make it to shore?"

I smiled purely because he'd asked the question. "Effie did. But Dorcia's vanity got the better of her. She refused to abandon her jewels. When she hit the sea, all her diamonds soaked up the water, making them even heavier. She sank like a stone and drowned."

His frown grew more concentrated as he thought it through.

"Are you doubting the legend, Adam? Every time someone claims not to believe, a fairy falls down dead. You don't want that on your conscience, do you?"

He shook his head, his hand on his heart. "Never."

"There's proof that it's true, you know. Dorcia's jewels can still be found - only they're not diamonds anymore. They're aquamarines - jewels tinged the same colour blue as the oceans of Cyprus."

Adam's arms slipped around my waist. "I am so in love with your mind."

It wasn't a question. I didn't have to speak. Instead, I pressed my lips against his, secretly willing him to stay home with me.

It didn't work. Adam met Ryan at the new restaurant as planned - albeit half an hour late thanks to Dorcia and Effie.

23. Gold Digger

Life moved quickly in New York. Sometimes I had trouble keeping up.

The holiday season was over and Adam's classes resumed just a few days into the New Year. That meant we were back to stealing time together whenever his hectic schedule allowed.

My eye had completely healed. As happy as I was not to resemble a pirate any more, there was a downside. I no longer had an excuse to put off my lunch date with the queen. Adam had sworn that she'd turned over a new leaf, promising that she'd been nothing but kind about me in the few times he'd spoken to her since Christmas.

To say I had doubts was a massive understatement. I chose to meet her at Nellie's. It was hardly neutral territory, but it was a place I felt comfortable. Obviously, Fiona didn't feel as secure. She brought backup.

I didn't know the woman. They were sipping champagne and giggling like schoolgirls, at my favourite table near the window. Spotting me immediately, Fiona waved me over.

I walked slowly, giving her friend ample opportunity to look me up and down.

"Charli, darling," Fiona sang, standing when I reached the table. "How are you?" She lunged forward, kissing my cheeks.

"Fine, thank you."

"Wonderful. I'd like you to meet someone." Fiona grabbed my elbow and angled me toward the woman, positioning me as if I was on display. "This is Mrs Pennington, a dear friend of mine."

I spent a few seconds sizing her up, just as she'd done to me. There was something extraordinarily odd about her face. It dawned on me that it was her mouth. Mrs Pennington's lips were so pumped up they were disproportionate to the rest of her face.

Politely, I shook her hand. "Nice to meet you. Are you joining us for lunch?"

"No, I won't impose. I'm meeting another friend here shortly."

I nodded, unsure whether I was relieved or not.

Fiona hooked her arm through mine, pulling me closer to her side. "Isn't she beautiful?"

"Stunning," agreed Mrs Pennington, smiling as best she could with her fat lips. "Adam has wonderful taste."

It was an uncomfortable exchange that thankfully didn't last long. Mrs Pennington's friend arrived, and she excused herself. Fiona smiled at me, pointing at the newly vacant chair. "Please, sit down. Champagne?"

I sat, resting both hands in my lap, trying to remember my manners. "What are we celebrating?"

"Darling," she cooed, "we don't need a reason to drink champagne."

I held off on the alcohol, preferring to keep a clear head. Fiona's expression soured when I called Taylor over and ordered a pot of tea. Perhaps that was bad manners.

Conversation eventually began to flow. The queen was fairly curious about me, which was good. As far as I was concerned, I was quite interesting. "I can understand how Adam is charmed by you. I just don't understand why he felt the need to marry you."

At least her blunt statement was honest. It was easier than having her pretend to like me.

"He loves me."

"I was extremely hurt to find out that my son got married in secret."

I knew how crushed Alex was. Her pain was genuine. "Weddings are supposed to be joyous occasions that are shared with family and friends."

"We didn't want a fuss and we didn't want to wait."

She avoided my eyes as she asked the next question. "Do you have immigration issues, Charli? Is that the reason for the rush?"

I shook my head and told half a lie. "No. As far as I know, there are no issues."

Her expression barely wavered and I suddenly felt wide open.

I had no idea what my immigration status was. Adam told me he was going to seek advice from his father – and hadn't mentioned it since.

"May I see your ring?" she asked, catching sight of my finger.

I couldn't have said no if I'd wanted to. She reached across the table for my hand, tightening her grip as she studied the simple ring.

Explaining that the plain gold band was a substitute for the hellishly expensive diamond rings that I struggled to wear might have appeased her, but I couldn't be bothered. I owed her no explanation.

I reclaimed my hand and began twisting the ring on my finger. "It's pretty, isn't it?" She nodded and gave a forced half-smile. The weak gesture infuriated me and I knew I was dangerously close to saying something regretful. I had to get out of there. "Will you excuse me for a moment?"

"Of course."

I escaped to the bathroom to pull myself together. I pushed the stall door closed, sat down on the toilet and pulled in a few deep breaths, trying to calm myself down. I couldn't seem to shake the feeling that being so frank with Fiona was a mistake.

My fears were confirmed a moment later when Mrs Pennington and her lunch date walked in. They couldn't even stop talking long enough to take a bathroom break. I wasn't overly surprised that they were talking about us.

Not content with eavesdropping, I peeked through the tiny slit at the edge of the stall door. The women stood at the mirror, touching up their makeup.

"You know what Fi is like," said Mrs Pennington. "She'd protect her boys to the ends of the earth. She's determined to put an end to this."

"I imagine she would be," commented her nosy friend.

"She looked into the girl's background. Needless to say, it's quite colourful. Are you ready for it?" Mrs Pennington teased, cackling like a witch.

"Of course!"

Even I wanted to hear the answer. With a build up like that, it was bound to be good.

"She's the bastard child of a small town shopkeeper. She never even graduated high school."

Her cruel and ignorant words burned through me but I had no choice but to stay put and ride out the character assassination.

"And she landed a Décarie boy?" asked her friend, incredulous. "Good God! The girl must be rubbing her hands in glee."

"It's not hard to see why he's so smitten with her. She's quite pretty - but awfully strange."

"Oh, do tell!"

Yes, trouty old witch, do tell, I agreed mutely.

"Well, Fiona said she's penned all sorts of strange ramblings on the walls of their apartment. The poor woman is beside herself with worry. And to top it all off, there's no pre-nup." Mrs Pennington leaned closer to the mirror, pursing her inflated lips and reapplying her lipstick before continuing. "She has no legal avenue to take. Jean-Luc has been no help. He told her to stay out of it and wait for Adam to come to his senses."

"I sincerely hope she doesn't clean him out before then. I've seen it so many times. I've done it twice myself."

Both women burst into giggles.

"I would say that over the coming months, Fiona's going to find out exactly what the new Décarie wife is made of. She'll make sure of it. If it's money the girl is after, she's going to have to work for it."

I felt sick.

The queen needed to learn to keep her mouth shut. I imagine she'd put a lot of thought into tearing me down in the last few weeks. I wondered how she'd feel knowing that her family drama was bathroom fodder for her so-called friends. Part of me wanted to go back to the table and tell her all about it. A bigger part of me was just thankful for the heads-up.

As soon as the ghastly women left the bathroom, I headed back to the table.

"I was beginning to think you'd slipped out the back door," said Fiona, only half jokingly.

I hoped my forced smile looked normal. There was no need to call her on her wickedness just yet. I would bide my time and pretend to be as blind to the truth as she expected me to be. I endured only another few minutes with her before complaining of a headache and making an excuse to leave.

"I think I just need to lie down for a while," I told her, reaching for my bag.

"Of course, darling," she purred, faking concern. "You should go."

I decided to walk. The icy winter chill was warmer than spending time with the queen. Besides, I was in no hurry to get home.

Adam was hinging a lot on my lunch date being successful. It was as if he thought all fences could be mended in a few hours – providing we both played nice. From what I'd just learned, mending anything would be impossible. We were on the brink of war.

One block from our building was a row of very exclusive boutiques, none of which I'd ever paid any more attention than a quick glance on my way past. Today wouldn't have been any different – until Kinsey nearly bowled me over as she stepped out of a doorway. Seeing her wasn't exactly shocking. The Manhattan bubble could be just as small as the seaside town I hailed from at times.

"Watch it!" Kinsey scolded.

"Excuse me," I muttered, leaning down to pick up the shopping bag she'd dropped.

"Oh, Charli," she said, abandoning the choler. "I didn't realise it was you."

I handed her her bag. "What difference would it have made? Once a rude bitch, always a rude bitch."

Kinsey actually seemed offended by the venom I was directing her way. For some irksome reason, I apologised.

"It's fine. I'm glad I ran in to you, actually." Her chirpy tone grated on me. "I had coffee with Adam this morning."

"See? I do let him out to play occasionally."

Kinsey pursed her glossy lips to form a tight, false smile. "We miss him, you know."

"I don't stop Adam from doing anything. If you haven't seen him enough of him lately, talk to him about it."

Already tired of the conversation, I began walking away. Unfortunately, she walked with me. "We're having a get-together tonight. You should both come."

"I'd rather eat broken glass," I told her.

Kinsey grabbed my arm, pulling me to a stop. I shrugged free, frowning to let her know she'd overstepped the mark.

"Look, don't you see what you're doing? You're forcing Adam to choose. He's obviously happy with you, he married you." She pulled a face, suggesting it was the most ludicrous move he'd ever made. "But he has friends who miss having him around. I know you think we don't like you –"

"You *don't* like me."

Kinsey sighed, buying herself more time to string the appropriate words together in her head. "Please come tonight," she urged. "Adam will appreciate the effort we're all making."

"I'll mention it to him." It was the most I could promise. Bente had already pointed out my selfish behaviour, but changing my ways was harder than anticipated.

"Great," said Kinsey. "It's nothing fancy. Just a few drinks and pizza."

"I'll mention it to Adam," I repeated, refusing to commit to more than that. I started walking again. Although she didn't follow, Kinsey called out, forcing me to turn around.

"If you don't show up, I'll assume you didn't tell him. That will mean only some of us are making an effort to call a truce, Charli. That might not look good for you."

I should have known her moment of civility would be fleeting.

"I'll keep that in mind," I told her, walking away for the last time.

***

As expected, Adam wasted no time in quizzing me about my day. I'd barely made my way in the door and was kicking my shoes off when the questions began.

"Are you alright?"

"Of course. Why?"

"Mom said you left Nellie's with a headache."

It wasn't surprising that she'd spoken to him already. I just had to figure out *what* she'd told him.

"I'm okay now."

"Well, you look okay. How did lunch go?"

What was I supposed to tell him? Would it have been fair to tell him that his mother was a horrid, two-faced schemer who was doing her level best to oust me from his life? No, probably not. Would he appreciate knowing that she'd gone to the extent of doing a background check on me, or that we were now juicy bathroom conversation because of it? Absolutely not. Telling him anything at all would have been just plain cruel.

"It was fine."

"I'm happy you sorted it out," he murmured, sweeping the back of his hand down my cheek.

"Me too," I lied.

Adam followed me as I walked through to the kitchen. He picked up the stack of mail off the counter, thumbing through it until he found the envelope he was looking for. "I have something for you," he said, waving the envelope at me.

I snatched it from him. "Sounds ominous."

"It's nothing bad, I promise."

I tore it open without reading it. Inside was a black credit card in the name of Charlotte Décarie.

"Thank you," I said sarcastically. "It's just what I've always wanted."

He'd inadvertently just made trying to convince his mother that I wasn't a gold digger impossible. Why would she ever believe it? I had shiny, probably limitless credit card with my name on it – well, Charlotte Décarie's name on it.

I wasn't even sure who Charlotte Décarie was. All I knew was that she'd almost done away with Charli Blake.

My scorn should have been obvious but he stepped toward me, snaking his arms around my waist. "You're so pretty when you're being disgusted by Décarie money," he teased.

If I were brutally honest, I'd have to admit to being disgusted by much more than the Décarie money. As far as I was concerned, the only good thing to come out of that family was him - and possibly Ryan, on a good day.

I pulled open a drawer and dropped the card inside, bumping it closed with my hip.

Adam looked surprised. "You'll need it, Charli."

"I know where it is, if I do. Can we change the subject, please?"

Adam didn't skip a beat, shifting the conversation to our plans for the evening.

"I'll cook you dinner and we'll have a quiet night in." His cheeky expression implied a different agenda.

"How about we go out?" I suggested.

His perfect grin was wide and bright. I might as well have been offering him a trip to the moon - or parole. That realisation made me cringe a little.

"Where would you like to go, Mademoiselle?"

"Well, I ran in to Kinsey today," I mentioned, speaking as if I'd only just remembered it.

He frowned. "So did I. I ended up having coffee with her and Parker between classes."

"I know. They're having a get-together tonight and asked if we'd like to go. Nothing fancy, just drinks and pizza."

"They never mentioned it to me."

"Maybe it was a last-minute thing."

"Maybe." He didn't sound convinced. "Do you want to go?"

As hard as I tried, I couldn't think of a reason not to. I'd been keeping him to myself for far too long.

24. Losing Numbers

One of the things I loved most about living in New York was that we walked just about everywhere. We bundled up in our thickest coats and ventured into the cold night.

We'd walked quite a distance before Adam asked me where we were going.

"Did Kinsey say they were going to be at her apartment or Parker's?" he asked, blowing a warm breath into his clenched fist.

"She didn't say." I'd wrongly assumed they lived together.

He took his phone out. "We should probably find out where we're going. I'll ask Parker."

I bounced around on the spot, trying to keep warm. "Walk and text, Adam. It's freezing."

We continued walking again until his phone beeped with a reply.

"Oh, Charlotte," said Adam gravely, slowing his walk as he read the message.

"What's wrong?" I grabbed his arm, forcing him to a stop.

He reached for my hand, probably to stop me bouncing around. "What did Kinsey say their plans were?"

"Drinks and pizza."

Bafflingly, his wry grin broadened. "They're having *drinks at Pieza,*" he corrected. "It's a club not far from here."

Emphatically, I shook my head. "No. That's not what she said."

"Shall we just go home?"

"Can't we just go to Pieza?"

"We're a little too casual," he explained, looking down at his faded jeans and well-worn coat. "It's a pretty upmarket club."

I shrugged. "I don't care. We should go. Will we get in dressed like this?"

He shook his head but the smiled remained. "I think I can get us in. You realise we're way underdressed though, right?"

I really didn't care. I hadn't misheard Kinsey. She'd made a point of telling me it was nothing fancy. If she was playing games in hope of embarrassing me, it wasn't going to work. I would have felt more out of place in a dress and heels than jeans and boots, regardless of how everyone else was dressed.

True to his word, Adam got us in. All he had to do was sweet-talk the woman bouncer at the door. She unhooked the velvet rope and ushered us in, shamelessly winking at Adam as he passed.

I hated the whole atmosphere of Club Pieza.

The loud music pulsed through me. Overhead strobe lights worked the crowd. The tight grip Adam had on my hand did little to save me. Bodies thumped and jerked into both of us as we manoeuvred our way through the club in search of his purple circle teammates.

Finding them took no time at all. They were upstairs in the VIP section, hidden away at a private table.

"Hey!" greeted Parker as soon as he saw us. Adam dropped my hand to receive the back thumping hug that guys are so fond of. Parker toned it down for me, kissing my cheek as if he knew me. "I'm glad you could make it."

"Didn't you think we would?" asked Adam, glancing at Kinsey.

"We weren't sure," she said. "Charli was a little non-committal. Still, it's nice to see you dressed up for us." She looked me up and down.

"Drinks and pizza, Kins?" asked Adam.

Her expression was the guiltiest I'd ever seen, confirming what I knew. Kinsey had tried setting me up. At least Adam knew it too.

I decided very early in the evening that if I couldn't beat them, the only option I had was to join them. Kinsey, Sera and Jeremy shuffled along the narrow booth seat making way for me to sit down. Adam remained standing, talking to Parker.

The loud music made it hard to hear each other speak. Snide whispers were impossible to catch, which was probably a godsend. I got the impression there was a lot of it going on.

"Charli, would you like something to drink?" asked Jeremy, pointing to the copious bottles of wine on the table. "Champagne maybe?"

What was it with these people and champagne? Where I came from, champagne was for special occasions. Then again, so was wearing mascara, but I'd found myself doing that a lot lately. Maybe I was turning into one of them. I shuddered at the thought and quickly declined his offer, settling for a beer instead, to Kinsey's disgust.

Small talk was exactly that - only smaller. Jeremy tried hard, asking me every polite question he could think of. Unfortunately, my answers were as short as his questions, so conversation soon dried up. The lull didn't last long. Kinsey jumped right in, asking me all sorts of things that I would never have considered answering if not for the two beers I'd consumed.

"Is that everything?" I asked wearily. "Is there anything else you'd like to know?"

"Just one more thing," said Kinsey, leaning in close. "Adam belongs to one of the wealthiest families in Manhattan. Why are you wearing an eighty dollar wedding ring?"

I glanced down at my hand, wiggling my fingers. "Is that all it's worth? He told me he paid a hundred for it."

Kinsey burst into a fit of patronising giggles. Jeremy tried shushing her to no avail.

Perhaps sensing a drop in the level of good manners, Adam reached for my hand, pulling me to my feet. "Are you done playing?" he asked, leaning down so I'd hear him. "We can go if you want to."

I felt utter relief. Parker walked over, interrupting by handing us both another drink. "I've got to tell you," he began, "I'm still trying to come to terms with the news that you sneaked off and got married."

"Don't take it personally." Adam grinned at me. "We had to do it quickly, before Charli changed her mind."

Parker stared at me strangely – like he was trying to see further than my eyes. "Adam, how can you be so sure she's the one?"

"Look at her. How could she not be the one?"

Parker smiled. "I'm happy for you, man." He patted Adam on the back.

At that point I wasn't sure how I felt about Parker. He was charming in his way, but something about him made me distrust him. He pulled me aside a short while later and I used it as an opportunity to figure him out a little more. We stood side by side, leaning against the railing, looking at the crowded dance floor below.

"Do you dance, Charlotte?" Parker asked, leaning in much too close.

"It's Charli, and no. I definitely don't dance."

"Me neither. But I thought it would be polite to ask."

"Well, you're nothing if not polite."

He twisted his body to look at me. I kept my eyes on the floor below, focusing on an extremely drunk girl jiggling around in a tight sequined dress. I couldn't help smiling. Her butt looked like two pigs fighting in a sparkly sack.

"Do you see this whole marriage thing as a long-term deal, Charli?" he asked.

"Why not?" I asked, faking apathy. "Adam's a great choice for a first husband."

He smirked. "Adam and Whitney were together for a long time. It was amazing how quickly he dropped her in favour of you. He never used to be fickle."

"To be honest, Parker, I could care less about Whitney – or the rest of his friends for that matter."

"Ouch," he muttered. "We're just trying to be friendly."

"No, you're not. You've been testing me since I got here. Your girlfriend expected me to be embarrassed by the so-called mix up in the venue tonight. But I'm guessing you know that already,"

"Maybe I did." The dark edge to his voice unnerved me. "Adam is our friend. We like having him around. Luckily, we're patient."

"What's that supposed to mean?"

"It means we're happy to bide our time. I think he'll tire of you."

"Time will tell, I guess," I replied, fighting to keep my tone strong.

"Adam told me all about your two-year plan. It's fascinating."

"Is that so?"

"Absolutely." He leaned so close, I could feel his breath on my neck. "But you should know something. Adam is New York through and through. If you knew anything about him, you'd know he's never going to leave here. And if you can't adjust to that, you'll be sent packing with a one-way ticket back to the gutter he found you in."

I turned around, searching for Adam. He sat in the booth, wedged between Seraphina and Kinsey.

Noticing me, he winked. I forced a smile that must have looked odd. He nodded, excused himself and walked over. "Everything okay?" he asked, draping his arm around my shoulder.

"I'm just tired."

"Yes. You should take your bride home, Adam. She looks a little weary." Parker's fake concern made me want to retch.

I pulled Adam by the hand to get him moving. Getting out of there took another ten minutes. By the time we'd said goodnight to everyone and manoeuvred our way through the crowd, I'd well and truly reached my New York limit for the day.

***

Just before six the next morning, the sound of Adam's blaring alarm filled the bedroom. I'd been awake for a while so the annoyance was all his. He groaned, reached across and thumped his hand on the alarm to stop it beeping. I rolled to the side, resting my head on his warm chest, hoping to keep him in the cosy bed for a while longer.

"Stay with me today?"

Adam tangled his hand through my hair. "I can't, Charlotte," he murmured. "I wish I could."

"What if I told you I needed you to?"

"Then I would stay." His free hand moved to my forehead. "Are you sick?"

Sick and tired is what I was. Having to justify my New York existence at every turn was draining me. But it wasn't a good enough reason to keep him from attending class.

"No," I said flatly. "I'm not sick."

The old adage that a problem shared is a problem halved didn't seem applicable. I wanted to tell him the reason for my dark mood, but coming clean and admitting that I was on his mother's hit list wasn't an option. Even Ryan had asked me not to tell Adam. Obviously he knew that ugly can of worms was pressurised.

Trying to fit in with his friends wasn't working out so well either. It was not a plan I'd put my heart and soul into. Cheap shots and bitchy comments on my part had shut down any chance of being accepted from the very beginning. Not that being denied membership to the purple circle bothered me, but keeping up the façade that all was well was going to become tiresome.

"I'll try and get home early. We'll do something special, just the two of us," he suggested.

Every second we spent alone together was special. It was the time I spent with other people that was slowing destroying me, from the inside out.

"I don't need special. I just need you." Hopefully, he'd realise it was the same thing.

Adam shifted, pressing my body into the mattress as he rolled on top of me. "Okay, we'll do something un-special," he teased. "Something ordinary."

I allowed a slow smile to creep across my face. "Something un-flashy and un-Décarie."

He dropped his head. "Are you craving the mundane, Charlotte?" He murmured the question against my bare skin, making me shudder.

I fisted my hands through his hair, drawing his face back to mine. "I'm craving low-key and normal."

"I'll see what I can do," he replied, before kissing me in a way that reminded me why everything I endured was not without reason.

"I'm going to write it on the wall, Adam," I warned, breaking free of his lips. "If it's on the wall, it becomes a promise."

"Fine by me," he murmured.

***

In my estimation, getting home at five o'clock is not early. Too happy to have him home, I didn't argue the point.

"Are you ready to go?" he asked, the second he was in the door.

"Go where?"

"To find normal."

"Do you even do normal, Adam?"

He grabbed my coat off the hook and held it out to me, smiling brightly. "I guess you'll have to wait and see."

The weather was the only part of the afternoon that was bleak. We ended up at the rink at the Rockefeller Centre. I'd been there a few times before - as a camera-wielding tourist. The Prometheus statue had disappointed me each time. Statues aren't great subjects for photographers who liked to capture moments in time. The united nation flags circling the rink were a much better muse, especially on windy days.

But there would be no photography today. We were there to ice skate - something that should have rated highly on my never-done list.

As expected, Boy Wonder was much steadier on his feet than I was. He slowly skated backwards, pulling me along.

"You've done this before, Adam," I accused, stating the obvious. His grip on my hands was the only thing stopping me from crashing to the ice in a heap.

"Once or twice. Never with anyone as pretty as you though - or as uncoordinated. For a girl who balances on a plank in the ocean with ease, you're remarkably clumsy on ice," he teased.

"Just so you know, when I fall I'm taking you with me." I wobbled a bit, and he moved quickly to steady me.

"Bend you knees and lean forward, not back," he instructed, daring to laugh at my near-slip. "I won't let you fall."

Ice skating, much like my New York life, was all about finding balance. And I found that both were easier if I focused only on Adam.

If he found it odd that I was staring at him, he didn't let on.

I was about to claim to be getting the hang of it when an obnoxious boy whizzed past us, far too close to be doing anything other than being a brat.

"Hey!" yelled Adam, grabbing a fistful of my coat to save me from falling. "Slow down, jerk!" The boy turned back, smirking wryly at the reprimand. We got the last laugh when an employee collared him as he went round and ordered him off the ice. Adam turned his attention back to me. "You okay?"

I smiled, but he didn't loosen his grip. "Almost came a cropper."

"Came a cropper," he repeated, badly imitating my accent. "Is that even English, Charlotte?"

Laughing was a mistake. It signalled the end of my skating streak. Not even Adam could save me as my butt thudded down hard on the cold ice.

"Okay," I whimpered. "Enough now."

From behind, he hooked his arms under mine, levering me to my feet. He turned me around to face him. "I'll take you home," he said regretfully. "Seeing you get your ass kicked wasn't part of my master plan this morning."

My arse had been kicked much harder than that lately, and it wasn't anywhere near as enjoyable as having it happen while ice skating with the boy I loved.

I linked my arms around his neck, mainly for support.

"So what's your master plan for the rest of the evening?" I asked suggestively.

"I'll take you out for dinner. Somewhere special."

"Normal is the theme of the day, remember?"

"Okay, I forgot," he replied. "A long walk and soup from a plastic cup?"

I shook my head and tightened my grip on his neck. "No, not soup. I want one of those quesa-thingies."

"Quesadillas?" he guessed.

"Yes. Is that even English, Adam?"

He laughed. “No, Charli. I’m fairly sure that’s Spanish.”

25. Tomorrow, The Louvre

I wasn't really sure how I'd got roped in to babysitting Fabergé for the day.

It started with a frantic phone call from Ivy. I stood in the kitchen, absently stirring my mug of tea while I listened to her drama-filled explanation of why she urgently needed a sitter. She was due to attend a pageant seminar downtown that morning, but her regular sitter had fallen ill.

"Can you please watch her?"

"Ivy, what's a pageant seminar?"

"I have no time to explain," she huffed in her usual curt manner. "Will you take care of Fabergé or not?"

It was impossible to say no. Ivy had made me the most beautiful wedding dress in the history of all brides – for free. I probably owed her a few months of babysitting. "Can you drop her off?"

"Yes, I can."

I was about to give her our address when there was a loud knock at the door. Cradling the phone between shoulder and ear, I held my mug of tea with one hand and opened the door with the other. I was stunned to see Ivy and Fabergé. "Wow. You're here now."

"Of course we're here now," said Ivy, bustling past me, Fabergé in tow. She dumped Fabergé's bag down on the couch and rattled off a list of rules as she made her way back to the door. "No junk food, no TV and don't let her squeal."

"Why would she do that?" I asked, a little afraid.

"She likes to squeal." Ivy slung her handbag over her shoulder and shrugged. "But it ruins her singing voice and we're hoping to clean up in the talent section of the Pickle Leaf Pageant next week."

I nodded, utterly terrified. Small children were a mystery to me.

She hugged little Fabergé tightly, telling her she'd return soon. I prayed she was telling the truth. Ivy disappeared out the front door as quickly as she'd breezed in, making the number of minutes she'd spent in the apartment less than three.

I looked down at my little charge, wondering how on earth I was going to keep her entertained all day, when without warning she opened her mouth and squealed – a horrible, high-pitched scream that made me spill my tea down the front of my shirt. By mid-morning I was exhausted and Fabergé's singing voice was probably cactus.

"Fabergé, what do you like to do?" I asked, at my wit's end.

Her mop of brown curls bounced wildly as she jumped around on the couch. "Cartoons."

I would've broken Ivy's no television rule in a flash – if only we'd had one. A knock at the door a few minutes later made *me* want to squeal with joy. Convinced it was Ivy, I jumped off the couch and bolted to open it.

"Oh, it's only you," I said disappointedly.

"Oh, my feelings are hurt," mocked Ryan, holding his hand to his heart.

Slamming the door was tempting but I couldn't bring myself to do it. "What do you want?"

"I need a favour."

I wasn't sure I could handle doing any more favours that day. I'd reached my charitable limit. On the plus side, the favour he needed might involve leaving the apartment.

"What do you need?"

"I'm having some artwork delivered to the new restaurant today," he explained. "I need to choose some prints for the walls. I was hoping to get your opinion."

My eyes narrowed with suspicion. "Why?"

Ryan sighed heavily, probably regretting ever knocking on the door. "Because you're arty and fluffy and good at that kind of junk."

I hissed through my teeth, "You think I'm fluffy?"

"No, of course I don't think you're fluffy. I think you're... whimsical," he amended, turning on the Décarie charm. "Please, Charli. Just help me out."

"It's going to cost you, Ryan."

He grinned errantly and I couldn't help smiling back. "Name your price."

"A TV. No, a huge TV," I revised, waving my hands around for effect. "And it has to be delivered today."

The confused frown that swept his face lasted only seconds. "Has the novelty of marriage worn off already?" he asked, barely composing himself.

"Fine," I grumbled. "Pick your own artwork."

I pushed on the door, attempting to close it in his face, but he stepped forward, wedging his foot in the way.

"Okay, okay. I'll buy you a TV." I glared at him, prompting him to clarify his offer. "A huge television that will be delivered today – at any cost."

"Love your work, Ryan." I quipped, spinning around to face the little girl who was sitting on the couch, munching her way through a bag of contraband chips. "Grab your coat Fabergé, we're getting out of here."

Ryan pushed the door wide open and stared at the tubby little girl rushing toward me, dragging her coat behind her. "What on earth is that?" he asked, pointing at the toddler behind me.

"*That* is a Fabergé." I scooped her into my arms. "And she'll be accompanying us."

He shook his head, frowning. "No."

"Take it or leave it." Standing my ground was remarkably easy. I'd been run ragged by a three year-old all morning and yet I somehow still had the upper hand.

"Fine, pack up your munchkin and let's go. I have a driver waiting."

It didn't take long for me to realise that Ryan had a fear of small children. Fabergé was his Kryptonite. He spent the short drive to the new restaurant trying to restrain her as she bounced around the back seat of the car - without actually touching her.

"Can't Bente watch her?" he asked, dangling his bunch of keys in front of Fabergé as if that would calm her down. "She *is* her aunt."

"Obviously not. That's why her mother called me."

"Phone?" Fabergé asked Ryan.

"Kid, I am not giving you my phone."

Fabergé responded with an ear-splitting squeal. Giving in instantly, he reached for his phone and handed it to her.

"Girls always get the better of you," I muttered, looking out the window to hide my smile.

A lot had changed at the restaurant in the few weeks since I'd last been there. The blue construction door and scaffolding were gone, and the inside had been transformed in to a bright, albeit empty, space.

We had the run of the place, and Fabergé made the most of it. Her squeal echoed around the empty space; she obviously liked the sound of it.

"Please, shut her up," begged Ryan.

"How?" I hissed, as annoyed as him.

He called her over and held out his phone, pulling it back as she made a grab for it. "If I give you this, you have to be quiet, okay?"

Fabergé nodded and the deal was complete. She sat on the travertine floor, randomly pressing buttons.

"Well done, Ryan," I praised, genuinely impressed. "So where is this artwork you want me to see?"

He pointed to the far side of the room and I wondered how I'd missed it. Six large canvases wrapped in brown paper leaned against the wall. "I only want three," he said, walking toward them. "Choose the best ones and I'll send the rest back to Adam."

"What does Adam have to do with this?"

"He knows the artist." He smirked as he spoke. "He promised he'd get us a good deal."

Ryan tore the paper off the first picture. I recognised it immediately. The large black and white cityscape photo was one I had taken during my first few weeks in New York. Pride overtook me and I could feel myself beaming like an idiot. "That looks incredible!"

Ryan folded his arms and took a step back, studying it for a moment before turning his attention back to me. "I love your humility."

"You really want to display these here?"

He nonchalantly shrugged. "It was Adam's idea but they're actually not too bad."

The mere fact that they were in the restaurant was a huge compliment. If he didn't like them, he'd say so. Ryan wasn't renowned for protecting people's feelings.

"I had no idea he planned this."

"I know. I think he had grandiose ideas for the big reveal. It probably involved mood lighting and roses, but I don't think he really needs the brownie points, Charlotte. Do you?"

"No. He's amazing."

"Oh, please! Amazing and preoccupied. He should have moved faster. I need this done now, which is why we're here. The furniture arrives tomorrow."

Ryan moved quickly, tearing the paper off the remaining pictures. He walked over to me, folded his arms and instructed me to pick the best three.

"I love them all."

"You can't have them all. Pick three."

"No. I love them all."

Ryan pinched the bridge of his nose with his thumb and forefinger. I wondered if I was causing him pain. "Fabergé is more reasonable than you."

The mention of her name reminded me that she was there. I spun around to check on the little girl, relieved to see her still sitting on the floor, happily playing with the phone.

"Ryan, it's a big place. There are four walls," I waved my arms around the vast empty space. "Hang them all." I pouted a little but I'm sure it did nothing to help my cause.

"If I agree to that, this whole afternoon is a waste of time. I didn't need to bring you and the munchkin down here at all."

"An expensive waste of time," I taunted.

"Why?"

"You owe me a TV."

***

The afternoon was much better than the morning. Ivy was getting out of a cab just as we pulled up to my building, so I didn't even need to take Fabergé back to the apartment.

"Has she been good?" asked Ivy, pulling her out of my arms and into hers, protectively cradling her as she glared at Ryan.

I'd forgotten how much she disliked Bente's cloakroom buddy. I stood a little closer to him, hoping that if she tried smacking him, I'd at least made the access more difficult.

"Fabergé was perfect," I replied, embellishing her behaviour report.

"No squealing?"

"None."

I doubt she believed me but she didn't press the issue. Ivy had something else on her mind. "I need your help with something else," she told me. "And there's no point saying no because I've already volunteered you for the job."

I actually liked Ivy's harshness. It left absolutely no room for misinterpretation.

"What job?"

"I'm hosting a pageant seminar of my own next week. We need a photographer so the girls can build their portfolios. You'd be perfect."

Taking pictures of hyped-up toddlers in jewel-encrusted dresses was madness. I accepted the challenge immediately.

Clearly in a hurry, she thanked me, gave Ryan another blistering glare and got back into the cab. I waved to Fabergé as they drove away. Fabergé waved back with one hand – and tapped Ryan's phone on the car window with the other. Mercifully, he didn't see it. He was too busy making his way back to his waiting car, in just as much of a rush to escape as Ivy.

"So rude," I muttered, pretending to be annoyed that he was doing a runner.

"What?" he asked, turning to face me but not slowing his walk. "Do you want me to walk you to your door?"

I grinned at him and he smiled back at me. "Bye, Ryan."

"Au revoir, Tinker Bell."

My usual chat with Marvin before heading inside was purposely short. As soon as he mentioned that Adam had arrived home, I was edging toward the door.

As soon as I opened the apartment door, I barrelled toward him, practically leaping into his arms. Adam moaned, staggering back like I'd knocked the wind out of him. We both fell in a heap on the couch, landing in a position I couldn't have planned better if I'd tried.

"I love you so much," I declared fervently. His body shook beneath me as he chuckled. "Adam, you're not supposed to laugh."

"You said it as if you've only just realised it," he said, expertly unbuttoning my coat with one hand.

"No. I've known it all along." I shrugged free of my coat and threw it on the floor. "I went to the new restaurant today, with Ryan."

"He showed you the prints, didn't he?" he asked, leaning in close to me. "I wanted it to be a surprise."

"I was surprised. They looked beautiful."

His lips found mine, a deep sweet kiss that put the conversation on hold for a moment. "They're beautiful pictures, Charlotte," he murmured. "The whole world should see them."

Having them hanging on the walls of a trendy Manhattan restaurant was as good as any gallery showing. "Today, downtown Manhattan. Tomorrow, The Louvre," I breathed.

"I don't doubt it for a second." He moved to kiss me again. "Sooner or later you'll conquer the world."

"I'm going to start by conquering the pageant world," I said theatrically.

He moved his head back, buying enough space to look at me. "You're going to enter a pageant?" He sounded worried. His frown disappeared as I explained Ivy's offer.

"I think it might be fun. At least I'll be busy."

"I think it's a great idea."

I craned my neck and tangled my fingers through his hair as he kissed me, getting caught up in a moment I hoped would last the rest of the afternoon, but unfortunately it was short-lived. The interruption came via an unexpected visit from Colin, our long-suffering courier. "I have a delivery for Mrs Décarie," he said cheerily.

Overlooking the fact he'd called me by my witchy mother-in-law's name, I signed for it, no questions asked. I wasn't the least bit curious about the big box that sat blocking the doorway. I knew exactly what it was. Adam, however, had no clue.

"What is it?" he asked, dragging the box inside so we could shut the door.

"It's a TV."

He looked at me, cocking one eyebrow. "Am I boring you, Charlotte?"

I leaned forward, grabbing a fistful of his shirt, pulling him against me.

"Not even close."

26. Glass Houses

Adam was about to leave the next morning when Ryan turned up, beating on the door like he was trying to bash it down. I knew it was Ryan because he'd called ahead, warning Adam to stay put until he got there.

"Dick," muttered Adam, heading toward the door to let him in.

As soon as the door opened, he stormed in, waving a stack of papers at his younger brother. "Do you have any idea how much money you've just cost us?"

Adam didn't seem at all bothered. He closed the door, strolled past Ryan and headed to the kitchen. I remained on the couch, trying to figure out what was going on. Maybe Adam had looted his apartment again and forgotten to tell me. "*I* didn't cost us anything."

His lax tone infuriated Ryan, which wasn't necessarily a bad thing. His ensuing tirade gave me a chance to work out the source of his rage.

The liquor license for the new restaurant hadn't come through. Adam was supposed to organise it. Ryan contacted the liquor authority to chase it up – only to find out there was no record of an application ever being lodged.

"You put the opening back another two weeks, Adam. All because you never got the paperwork in!"

"Ryan, I posted it days ago."

The growing pit in my stomach was torturing me. Adam wasn't lying. As far as he knew, it had been sent. He'd given me an envelope to post a few mornings earlier when I was on my way out the door. Once I'd slipped it into my coat pocket, I hadn't given it another thought.

I was forgetful, but not a coward. I walked to my coat and reached into the pocket, retrieving the envelope. "I'm so sorry. I forgot all about it."

Ryan snatched it out of my hand and began waving it at me. "Way to go, Tinker Bell. You've just cost us thousands in lost revenue."

Adam snatched the envelope from Ryan and thumped it against his chest. "Leave her alone," he warned. "It's not her fault."

"It's absolutely her fault," Ryan insisted, following up with an angry French diatribe.

"English!" My demand fell on deaf ears. Adam joined the French squabble, raising his voice to match his brother's.

I couldn't stand it. Knowing Adam was bordering being late for his first class of the day, I grabbed his coat and thrust it at him. "Go!"

"No. He can go," he replied, gesturing to his brother with an upward nod.

I turned my attention to Ryan. "Get out."

"No," he snapped.

"What do you want from me, Ryan? Blood?" I yelled, exasperated. "I said I was sorry."

"You are a square peg, Charlotte," said Ryan. "Sooner or later, you're going to realise that New York - and everything in it - is a round hole."

"Enough," chided Adam.

"No, it's fine." I kept my eyes firmly on Ryan. "Let him get it off his chest."

"I know that none of this is important to you," growled Ryan. He waved his arms at the room, but was clearly referencing a much bigger picture. "But we can't all live our lives being guided by astrological charts and fairy stories. Some of us have direction. Some of us grow up. You can be as scattered and ethereal as you want to be, but don't ever let it impact on me. Got it?"

"Oh my God," muttered Adam, appalled. "Ryan, get out."

"She's detrimental to your brain function, Adam!" Ryan tapped the side of his head. "Collecting seashells on a beach is where you're going to end up. That's all she aspires to, and you're so besotted you'll be right beside her, holding the bucket."

Adam opened the door, and pointed to the foyer. Thankfully, the angry evil brother stamped out without another word. Adam slammed it behind him. He pulled me into his arms, resting his chin on the top of my head. I could hear his heart beating - much faster than normal. It betrayed his unruffled demeanour.

I selfishly wondered if a run-in with Ryan was traumatising enough to make him stay home for the day - something I tried every morning. Trying my luck, I asked him to skive class and hang out with me.

"I can't. You know I can't," he whispered.

I leaned back, untangling myself from his arms. "You should go, then. You're going to be late."

I didn't crumple until Adam was gone. I took a long shower, letting the hot water stream over me until the skin on my fingers shrivelled. I used the time to work out my next move.

Until now, Ryan Décarie had always been on my side - even when I was wrong. It was beginning to seem like my life was a game that I was never going to win. The rules kept changing.

Living in New York was like owning a fabulous pair of sparkly shoes that were two sizes too big. Obviously, I was never going to grow into them. But I loved the damned shoes. I just needed to figure out how to walk in them.

***

Time alone wasn't always good for me, but I used that day well, painting our graffitied wall back to white. The look on Adam's face when he saw it that night wasn't one of approval. He seemed to take it personally, as if erasing the writing meant the dreams were gone too.

"Why, Charli?" he asked, slumping on the couch. "If this is because of something Ryan said –"

"I wouldn't give him the satisfaction."

"Then why?"

I wriggled into his arms and rested my head on his chest, staring at the stark white wall before answering. "Too many people have seen it. Your mother has seen it. She thinks I'm disturbed. Those words were meant only for us."

"She does *not* think you're disturbed."

If only you knew, I thought, unwilling to venture further into a conversation about the queen.

"Ryan saw it too. That's why he called me Tinker Bell."

Adam absently wound a lock of my hair around his fingers while he mused. It was his version of the airhead twirl. "Considering how angry he was, he could have called you much worse. You got off lightly."

"I'm glad you found it amusing," I replied.

"I found it intolerable, Charlotte," he said, grimacing. "And I can guarantee it won't ever happen again."

"So can I. I don't need you to fight my battles."

Adam pulled me in close again. "Why does everything have to be a battle?"

If only he knew.

***

Avoiding Ryan might have been easier if I'd stayed away from Nellie's, but hanging out with Bente occasionally, setting tables before dinner service, helped preserved my sanity. She was the only person privy to every little thing that went on with my life. Sadly, Bente knew more than Adam.

"I told you he's a jerk. Don't take it so personally" said Bente on hearing the details of Ryan's rant. "He didn't have to be mean. He just *likes* to be mean."

I had no option but to agree with her, but felt incredibly sad about it. Team Charli could hardly afford to be losing members.

"Yeah, well, I won't put up with it."

"Are you planning to talk to him about it?"

Abandoning the place settings, I stared across the table at her, shocked that she'd even asked the question. "I wouldn't waste my breath on Ryan Décarie."

"You might want to leave now, then," she suggested, pointing behind me with the forks in her hand.

I turned to see Ryan on his way through the front door.

"What's he doing here?" I sounded more panicked than irate.

"He owns the place," Bente pointed out. "He comes here almost as often as you do."

I wanted to bolt, but refused to give him the pleasure. Instead I continued setting the table. Following my lead, Bente offloaded the stack of forks she was holding and began fussing with the already perfectly placed white napkins.

Ryan appeared by my side a second later, greeting us both cheerily – like the argument we'd had a few days earlier had never happened. "Good afternoon, ladies."

Knowing I had nothing pleasant to say, I ignored him. Bente was more forgiving. "How are you, Ryan?"

He frowned across the table at her, probably trying to figure out the reason for her smile. "Great. Why?"

Dishing out the silent treatment was impossible for me. I dropped my stack of cutlery, making the entire four-place setting rattle. "There is something seriously wrong with you," I growled.

"What am I missing here?" he asked, eyes darting between Bente and me.

"A sense of decency, a conscience – shall I continue?"

"Okay, I'm out of here," announced Bente, throwing both hands in the air and backing away. She slipped through the kitchen doors, leaving me alone with the object of my wrath.

"Is this about the other day?" he asked, infuriating me even more. "I was angry, Charli."

"And that makes it alright? You said some terrible things to me."

"I was angry." He said it slowly, as if I'd misunderstood him the first time.

I looked straight at him, speaking as slowly as he had. "There is just no good in you."

"Look, if I'm the reason for your black little mood – "

I'd heard enough. I cut his condescending sentence short by pushing past him and making a dash for the front door.

"Stop, Charlotte," he ordered as I made a grab for the door handle. Heeding his obnoxious demand was weak but I did it anyway, turning to face him. "Your feelings are hurt."

"You think?"

"I'm sorry." His words sounded strange. I imagine it was because he'd never said them out loud before. "Charli, I was upset with you. It doesn't mean anything."

I begged to differ. "You meant everything you said."

"I didn't mean any of it."

I had to accept that Ryan truly didn't think he'd done anything wrong. I didn't really believe there was no good in him. Some days it just seemed that way.

"Bente was right," I said, making another grab for the door handle. "You're a dick."

"Wait – Bente thinks I'm a dick?"

I turned back to face him, smiling because I couldn't help myself. "She absolutely does, Ryan."

His handsome face looked so crestfallen that I almost felt sorry for him. "That's terrible news. How do I fix that?"

"Hello," I cooed, clicking my fingers at him. "One drama at a time, please."

He ignored me, still stuck on his train of thought. "I like Bente."

It was laughable. The man with the biggest vocabulary in history had been reduced to three word sentences. "Whatever shall you do?"

My jibe was wasted on him. He was barely listening. After a few seconds, he walked toward the kitchen, whacking the doors with both hands as he pushed them open.

I was too curious to leave – even at the risk of appearing pathetic for staying put. He crashed back through the swinging doors just a minute later, looking as smug as I'd ever seen him. "Your fairy powers of perception are wrong, Tinker Bell." I scowled at the nickname. "Bente just agreed to go out to dinner with me."

I bit down on my lip, determined to hide the fact that I was secretly pleased. "Where are you planning to take her?"

"That's for me to know and you to find out when she calls and tells you all about it."

"Better make it good then," I told him, pulling the front door open.

"Charli," he called. I turned around. "For what it's worth, I am sorry I hurt your feelings."

I believed him, but he had a long way to go before I'd let him think he was forgiven. "It changes nothing, Ryan. You're still a dick."

I walked out of Nellie's feeling slightly vindicated. Ryan Décarie would probably never change his ways. But girls who live in glass houses probably shouldn't throw stones.

27. Showpiece

With only a few days before the restaurant's grand opening, Ryan's diva-like demands on Adam's time ramped up to stellar levels. The meetings, paperwork and phone calls were incessant. It felt like I'd hardly seen him in days, and my irritation was obviously beginning to show.

"Keep tomorrow free," said Adam, chastely kissing my forehead as he made his usual morning bolt for the door. "We'll spend the whole day together."

"I'll cancel my other engagements."

I couldn't even be sure he'd heard my sarcastic comment. The front door closed and he was gone.

Unlike Adam, I was time rich, but for once I had plans too. It was the day of Ivy's pageant seminar. Having no idea what to expect, I convinced Bente to accompany me as moral support.

I needn't have worried. It was hardly a big-ticket event. Ivy's little home was more cluttered than usual. Little girls ran amok through every room, squealing just as painfully as Fabergé.

"How long do you expect this to take?" Bente whispered as we walked down the hall in search of Ivy.

"I have no idea," I replied, nudging a little girl in a princess dress out of the way.

Ivy appeared out of nowhere. "Charli, it's about time. I've set up for you in the sewing room," she babbled. "What do you need?"

"A stiff drink," muttered Bente invoking a searing glare from her sister.

"Nothing. Just room to work," I told her, smiling.

I'd always been a little afraid of Ivy – which probably explained why I made Bente walk ahead of me as we followed her down the hall to the sewing room.

Setting up my equipment had the same effect as the Pied Piper playing his flute. Little girls and over-enthusiastic women started lining up at the door.

"How much is this session?" asked the woman first in line.

"Err, nothing. I'm doing it as a favour to Ivy."

"I hope you take a decent picture," she said sceptically, stroking her hand through her little girl's auburn mane as if she were a pony. "We were offered complimentary hair and makeup at a seminar in Boston. It took weeks of conditioning treatments to right *that* little problem."

A few mothers further down the line murmured in agreement, and I wondered exactly what *that* little problem had been.

"The whole photo shoot is free," growled Bente. "What more could you want?"

Ivy pushed past the growing queue and stood between Bente and the woman. "They'll be amazing, Pia," she crowed, in the friendliest tone I'd ever heard her use. "Charli has taken photos all over the world."

Yeah, of rolling waves and beaches, I thought. Snapshots of spoiled pageant princesses were a first. It didn't seem like a good idea to mention that, though.

"Then we'll expect good pictures," said pushy Pia, staring at me.

The pageant mothers were a tougher crowed than Kinsey, Parker and Whitney all smooshed together. Pia could have come close to giving Fiona Décarie a run for her money. After three long hours I'd photographed all but one little girl. I'd dealt with tantrums, diva behaviour and tears - mostly from the mothers. Bente was barely holding it together. Her biggest task had been taping the black velvet backdrop to the wall every time it fell down, which was often. She'd resorted to swearing at it every time it happened. It was hardly a professional setup, but I had to admit it was the most fun I'd had for weeks.

The last muse and her mother stepped into our makeshift studio.

"This is Amber," announced the woman proudly.

"Hi, Amber, you're looking pretty today," I told her.

"I know," said the girl, displaying conceit far beyond her three or four years.

I spun to face Bente so Amber's mother wouldn't catch me smiling. Bente wasn't so polite. She laughed out loud, appalled. I turned my attention back to the little girl on the stool in front of me. "Are you ready?"

She nodded.

Her mother took an industrial sized can of hairspray out of her handbag and practically fumigated the room with a ten second burst of spray aimed at her daughter's head. Bente coughed. I stuffed my camera up my shirt, trying to protect the lens. "We're aiming for a natural look," said the woman. "Can you do that?"

I stared blankly at Amber. There was absolutely nothing natural about the child. Her skin was so bronzed it was practically metallic. I suspected her white-blonde hair had come out of a bottle too.

"She's not a miracle worker," snarled Bente.

I watched the woman's expression crumple. "No problem at all," I assured her hastily. "Natural it is."

It was a bold promise that ordinarily I wouldn't have felt comfortable making. Bente waited until we were alone before calling me on it. "How much editing are you going to have to do to make that kid look natural?"

"She had absolutely no makeup on. That *was* her mother's idea of natural. I'll make her look a little less shiny than the tinfoil complexion she has now, and her mum will be rapt."

Bente tore down the sheet of black velvet and folded it up. I continued packing up my camera and laptop.

"You seem happy today."

"I am happy. Today was great fun. I might do it again."

"Any time you want, Charli," announced Ivy, walking in. "You were a big hit."

"They haven't even seen the pictures yet."

"It makes no difference. They liked you." She pointed at her sister. "You, not so much."

"Like I care."

I knew Bente's day had been rough. I finished packing up and got her out of there as quickly as I could. Most of the journey back to Manhattan was spent chatting. It was the first chance we'd had all day to really catch up. High on the agenda was her date with my evil brother-in-law. "You've told me nothing," I chided, nudging her.

"It went well."

"That's it?" I asked. "That's all you're going to give me?"

"What do you want to know?"

"Er… everything."

Her story was fairly short. Ryan had taken to her to a flash restaurant somewhere downtown. He looked good, he smelled incredibly good and he behaved like a gentleman. "It was nice," she told me.

"Did you spend the night with him?"

My boldness didn't shock her. "No. Like I said, he was the perfect gentleman."

"Did you *want* to spend the night with him?"

"Charli!" Her attempt at rebuking me was mediocre at best – especially considering she went on to answer my question anyway. "I would have, if he'd asked."

There was a reason he didn't. Ryan actually liked Bente. I hoped she'd connect the dots and realise that. It wasn't my place to tell her.

"Are you going to go out with him again?"

"If he asks me, I will."

As brash and brave as Bente was, I knew she'd never make the first move. It was all up to Ryan.

"I hope it works out, Bente," I whispered.

"Hope's got nothing to do with it," she replied, grinning like she'd already won the prize.

Bente was half an hour late for her shift at Nellie's by the time we got there. Someone else had set the tables, and the restaurant was minutes away from opening. Paolo flew out the door the minute Bente arrived, and she set about doing whatever it was she did when she actually worked.

Adam and I had made plans to meet there for dinner. He arrived soon after we did, greeting me with a long, desperate kiss that implied we'd been apart for too long. He led me to the table furthest from the front door.

"Are you on the run?"

Adam pulled out my chair. "No, I just want you all to myself," he replied, sitting opposite me. "Tell me how your day went."

For once, I was excited to tell him about my day – so excited that I managed to do it in one ridiculously long rant. "It was great! The kids were cute – all painted up but still cute. The mothers were drama queens, but I handled them. And through all the craziness, I still managed to take some decent pictures. Even Ivy was happy, and Ivy is *never* happy."

"Take a breath, my little rebel without a pause," he ribbed.

"It was such a good day, Adam," I said, calming my tone.

He smiled. "I like seeing you like this."

"I imagine you probably enjoy seeing her naked too but there are some things I just don't need to know," interrupted Bente, pen in hand, ready to take our order.

"Can we have a few more minutes, please?" asked Adam.

"I think that can be arranged," she replied, disappearing as quickly as she'd arrived.

"Wow. She's in a pleasant mood."

"Bente didn't enjoy her pageant seminar experience as much as I did," I explained.

We were halfway through our meal when I caught something from the corner of my eye that might have added to Bente's prickly mood. Ryan - who hadn't said a word to us all night - was standing by the podium talking to a blonde woman pretty enough to be in his posse.

Adam noticed my preoccupation immediately. "What's going on?" he asked, turning to see for himself.

"Who's that girl with Ryan?"

"That's Yolanda."

"The interior decorator? What's she doing here?"

"I have no idea, Charlotte," he said, grinning. "Why don't you go and ask her?"

I rolled my eyes at his ridiculous suggestion. "Not a chance."

"We hired Yolanda to do the interior fit-out for the restaurant," he explained, putting me out of my misery. "They're probably talking business."

I wasn't convinced, but left quizzing Ryan about it until we were on the way out. "Ryan, are you going to see Bente again?" I turned around and slipped my arms through the sleeves of my coat as he held it out for me.

"I saw her five minutes ago." Even without seeing him I could tell he was smiling.

"Wise guy," I muttered.

"I have something for you," he announced, reaching into his breast pocket. Like the juvenile he was, he waved the envelope in front of my face until I snatched it from him. It was full of money. I was perplexed, having no idea what it was for.

"Have you sold your soul, Ryan?" I asked in my best witchy voice.

He grinned. "If I had, it would've been for more than the eight hundred bucks in that envelope."

"So what's it for then?"

"I sold two of your pictures that we hung in the restaurant. You're going to have to send some more over."

"Who bought them? More to the point, *why*?"

"Yolanda bought them. She saw them at the restaurant and thought they'd be perfect for an apartment she's decorating."

"So you sold them? Just like that?"

Ryan frowned. "Everything has a price, Charli. I thought you'd be pleased."

"I am. I'm thrilled."

"Thrilled about what?" asked Adam, catching the tail end of the conversation.

Ryan told him. "She really wanted them. I should have charged her double."

"I'm not sure they were even for sale," said Adam smiling uneasily.

"Sure they were," I replied. "I just didn't realise it."

***

It had been a fabulous day that I had no plans of ending once we'd left Nellie's. I instigated the amorous behaviour in the elevator on the way up to our apartment. The object of my affection – although blindsided – didn't try dissuading me. We practically fell through the apartment door, lips locked and dangerously close to being indecent, and bumped into a large piece of furniture that hadn't been there when we'd left that morning. Colin the delivery guy had struck again.

"Do you know anything about this?" asked Adam, still breathless.

I looked at the glass-topped dining table and four black leather chairs blocking our path.

"Not a thing," I replied, bewildered.

Adam noticed a card on the table and picked it up, groaning as he read it. As soon as I saw the flowery picture on the front of the card, I knew it was from the queen. His sour expression confirmed it.

"It's from my mother."

"I know. Why?"

He folded the card in half and slipped it in to his pocket. "No real reason. She noticed we didn't have one."

I couldn't quite believe him. His lame explanation made no sense.

On the guise of picking up where we'd left off, I pressed my body hard up against his, kissing him intently enough to slip my hand into his pocket and retrieve the card without him noticing.

As soon as it was in my grasp, I broke our embrace.

"Don't read it, Charlotte," he warned gravely.

I couldn't help myself. "Darling," I began, in my best English accent, "perhaps you might encourage Charli to use this suite well. Good etiquette is an important part of life."

"I warned you not to read it," he said weakly.

"She wanted me to read it," I replied, dropping the card on the table. "I knew I shouldn't have combed my hair with my fork at lunch the other day."

Adam stuffed his hands in his pockets. "Would you believe me if I told you she meant no harm?"

"Like a poisonous snake that didn't mean to strike?"

Adam lurched forward, pulling me into his arms. "Forget about my mother," he urged, breathing the words into my hair.

"Will you send it back?"

"Charlotte, I'll send it to the moon if it makes you happy."

***

If Adam had sealed his promise of spending the next day alone together by crossing his heart and hoping to die, he would've been a dead man by breakfast. Ryan called early, demanding a meeting to sign yet more paperwork. With a tight hold on my hand, Adam practically pulled me through the front door of the empty restaurant.

Dragging my feet gave me a chance to have a look around. Yolanda had come through for them in a big way. The attention to detail was superb. I loved everything about it, from the lavish floral arrangements to the big pillar candles. The square tables and high-backed chairs were complemented perfectly by pristine linens and white tableware. It represented the Décarie brand perfectly. Much to my amusement, it also made Nellie's look like a low-rent diner.

"Ten minutes and we'll be out of here," promised Adam.

The thought of Ryan interrupting my day for even a minute was annoying. "He's not even here yet," I grumbled. I sat at the centre table, looking up at the mammoth chandelier above me. "Can we turn the light on?"

Adam crossed the room and a flicked the switch on the wall, sending warm light flickering around the room. "Not bad, huh?"

I played down its beauty with my stiff reply. "It's okay."

"Just okay? It played a big part in naming this place. It had better be impressive."

"What *did* you call this place?"

Adam grimaced. "I didn't call it anything. Ryan named it." His expression was positively sour, piquing my interest.

"Tell me."

Adam pulled out the chair closest to me and sat down. He looked up at the chandelier, scowling again. "The sign goes up tomorrow. Wait until then."

"No. I need to know now. It can't be that bad."

He gave in instantly. "He called it Crystals."

I cracked, covering my mouth with my hand in a silly attempt at hiding my smile. "It sounds like a strip club or a new age healing clinic."

"Don't tell Ryan that. He put a lot of thought into it. We spent thousands of dollars on that light fitting. I think he wants it to be the showpiece."

The chandelier *was* the showpiece. It was grand and beautiful. No one needed a sign on the building to realise it.

"There are so many legends he could have drawn inspiration from. The best name he could come up with was *Crystals*?"

"I don't think he knows any inspiring tales about crystals," said Adam, grinning across at me.

I shook my head. "I wouldn't expect him to. I'll bet he knows a few inspirational girls called Crystal though."

Adam laughed darkly. "Probably."

"Chandeliers are the ultimate billet-doux," I announced whimsically. "Love letters."

He managed to smile and frown at the same time. "I know the translation, Charlotte."

"I thought you might."

"But I don't get the connection between a chandelier and a billet-doux."

I quickly glanced around the room, making sure Ryan was nowhere in sight. The last thing I wanted was to be caught out recounting one of the many stories in my repertoire that he found so strange.

The coast was clear.

Adam sat quiet and interested, listening to the tragic story of Mathilde and Eric.

"They had four little children and no money, so Eric worked very hard as a fisherman, sometimes for weeks on end. The family lived in dilapidated shack at the top of a cliff overlooking the bay. It was freezing in winter and unbearably hot in summer, but Mathilde refused to move to another house on lower ground."

"Four kids, no money, ramshackle house. The woman must have been a glutton for punishment," teased Adam, ticking off her troubles on his fingers.

"She loved that house because she could see Eric's boat in the bay while he was out fishing. And because she was clever, he could see her too.

It started with a lantern that she hung from the porch. It was a little flicker of light that he could see all night long from his boat. Mathilde told him that every time she thought of him while he was at sea, she'd attach a crystal bead to the lantern, making the light flicker just a little bit brighter. It was her way of sending him love. It was a long distance billet-doux."

"I like that story," Adam murmured.

"That's not the end," I said, shaking my head. "After a long fishing trip one winter, Eric never made it home."

"Let me guess," said a sarcastic voice from somewhere behind me. "The boat sank in rough seas and she never saw him again."

I didn't need to turn around to know it was Ryan. I straightened. Ryan dropped a stack of papers and joined us.

"I guess you'll never know," I told him.

"Pay no attention to him, Charli," urged Adam. "Finish your tale."

"There's no need to finish it on my account," said Ryan, checking the time on his watch.

"Trust me. You're going to want to hear the end of the story," insisted Adam. "If you don't, it's going to torture you for the rest of the day."

Ryan squinted at me. "That probably *would* be one of your magical powers - stealing lucid thoughts."

"Amongst others," I said, pulling a face at him.

"Continue," Ryan demanded.

I looked at Adam as I spoke, ignoring the evil brother as best I could. "Poor Mathilde was heartbroken."

"Maybe he just wasn't that into her and he took off with a mermaid or something," suggested Ryan.

"Shut up," scolded Adam.

I could feel my temper giving way but I continued. "Convinced he was still seeing the light from far out at sea, Mathilde continued attaching crystals every night. Eventually her children all grew up and left home, leaving Mathilde alone with her grief."

"Did they ever go back and visit?" Ryan's curious question floored me. I looked across at him, grinning as if I'd just accomplished something huge. His sheepish expression led me to think maybe I had.

"Not for years and years – long after Mathilde had died. The old shack was worse than ever, barely standing. But still hanging from the porch was the lantern with thousands of crystal beads hanging from it – every one of them representing a moment when she'd professed her love for Eric. It was a crystal billet-doux."

I was used to the faraway look Adam gave me after hearing my stories, but the stare from Ryan was plain unsettling. After a long while he snapped out of whatever thought he was lost in, pushed the stack of papers and a pen across to Adam and asked him to sign.

Adam flicked through pages, scrawling his name but reading nothing. "That's it?" he asked, handing the pen back to Ryan.

"Yeah, that's it."

"Great." Adam stood up and pulled me to my feet. "We're out of here."

We were almost to the door before I turned back to Ryan. He was still sitting at the table, absently clicking the lid of the pen in his hand.

"Bye, Ryan," I called.

He didn't look at me. "Au revoir, Tinker Bell," he mumbled.

28. English Rose

I wasn't sure how I felt about attending the grand opening of Crystal's restaurant. The crappy choice of name was sure to be a bad omen. Maybe that's why a kaleidoscope of butterflies had set up home in my stomach.

"Adam, what if no one shows up tonight?" I asked, looking at him through the bathroom mirror.

He continued fussing with his tie. "Ryan will cry."

"Are your parents going to be there?"

"Yes. I think it's safe to say they will definitely show."

The raging butterflies suddenly multiplied. Just the thought of seeing Fiona Décarie was pressure in my day. I hadn't seen Jean-Luc since Christmas, and that suited me just fine. For all I knew, he loathed me just as much as the queen did.

Not only was I going to have to deal with the king and queen, Parker and his minions also made the guest list. I couldn't even whine about it. They were Adam's friends – the very same friends who couldn't stand the sight of me. The feeling was mutual, but as far as Adam knew we were all getting along just fine. The tangled web I'd woven was beginning to strangle me.

Getting out of the confined space of the bathroom, I headed back to the bedroom and sat on the edge of the bed. Adam followed, crouching in front of me. "Is something bothering you, Charli?"

I hate your fake friends! I despise your scheming mother! And I'm tired of pretending otherwise. Those were the words I wanted to scream, but my actual reply was more polite. "Other than the name of the restaurant, no."

He reached over to his dinner jacket that was laid out on the bed, and retrieved his phone from the pocket.

"I was going to leave it as a surprise, but I'll show you now." He tapped the screen a few times and handed it to me. "I got this message from Ryan this afternoon."

It was a picture of the outside of the new restaurant. In big brass letters was the name.

"Billet-doux," I marvelled.

Adam smiled brightly at me. "Ryan's idea. You managed to inspire the uninspirable."

"Maybe there's hope for him yet."

***

The gala opening of Billet-doux the grandest event I'd ever attended. It was also the first time I'd seen the chandelier lit up at night. It filled the entire restaurant with a warm glow that bounced off every surface. Soft classical music filtered through the room, and extraordinarily well-dressed people milled around, chatting, laughing and eating little canapés that looked too perfect to be real.

Ryan's proud glow was almost as bright as the chandelier. I spotted him the instant we walked in, but that was as close as I got to him.

A middle-aged woman wearing a red velvet dress and the biggest ruby necklace I had ever seen collared Adam at the door. "Your mother is positively beaming with pride tonight, young man. You've done her extremely proud."

I quickly scanned the room, but couldn't see her anywhere. It was annoying that she'd rated a mention. Fiona had had nothing to do with Billet-doux.

"Thank you," replied Adam politely. "Ryan did most of the work. Mrs Scholl, have you met my wife, Charlotte?"

She extended her hand. "What an absolute pleasure," she said, dragging out the words.

Adam excused us both and we edged into the restaurant. We had the same false conversation a hundred times. Curiously, everyone seemed to know about me. I knew no one – until we stumbled upon the poison ivy league sitting at a table in the far corner.

Until Bente arrived, hanging out with them would have to do. Kinsey was thrilled to see Adam. Presumably, having one of the guests of honour at her table would elevate her status colossally. "Come, sit," she ordered, kissing his cheek without actually making contact. Although uninvited, I sat too.

"You look gorgeous, Charli," complimented Sera, leaning across to whisper the words. "I love your dress."

I loved my dress too. Ivy had worked her magic again, knocking out a pretty A-line black satin dress in just an hour and a half. Having my own dressmaker at the ready had its advantages. It also meant that my shiny black credit card still had a home in the kitchen drawer. Proudly, I'd never once had to use it.

"Thank you; your dress is nice too." One thing those girls never lacked was style. It was only charm and good manners that seemed to escape them.

Adam appeared to have found his place for the evening. He did his absolute best to include me in the conversation but I wasn't clued up on a lot of the subject matter. Not only were the purple circle mean and self-absorbed, they were an incredibly boring bunch of people. I had no clue what Adam saw in any of them. From my seat in the corner, I kept an eye on the door, silently cursing Bente for being late. Finally she arrived, wearing a pretty Ivy creation in blue organza. I excused myself and rushed to meet her, practically dragging her to the first empty table I found. "I was beginning to think you weren't coming," I said, forgiving her tardiness instantly.

"Fear not, Kemosabe. I'm here now. Where's your frog?" I motioned toward Adam with an upward nod. "Oh, he's with his little friends."

"Can we be nice, please? You'll undo all my good work."

"Don't tell me you've been making an effort."

"When in Rome, do as the Romans do, right?"

"You're such a good wife, Charlotte."

"Will you come over there with me?"

Bente giggled. "You've got to be kidding. Not a chance."

I looked back at the purple circle, catching Adam's eye immediately. He smiled suggestively at me and I responded with a let's-get-out-here smile of my own. Both of us knew it wasn't going to happen. We were stuck there for the night.

I turned my attention back to Bente. "Well, do you know anyone else here?" I asked, grasping for an alternative.

"Where's Ryan?"

I looked around. "No idea. He was here a second ago."

"Well, if we can't torment the host, we'll drink his wine and stuff our handbags with as many hors d'oeuvres as we can carry. Let's go to the bar."

I giggled at her absurd plan. "I'm pretty sure it's all free tonight, Bente."

From the bar we had a perfect view of the mezzanine area that Ryan had elected to keep closed for the evening. Tragically, we also had a perfect view of the mystery blonde woman he was up there fooling around with.

I didn't think Bente had seen, until she let out a disgusted grunt, put her glass of wine on the bar and stormed off. Following her seemed like the right thing to do.

"Bente, wait," I called, grabbing her arm to slow her walk.

"Charli, it's fine," she insisted, shrugging free of my grip. "I just need a minute."

We ended up in the bathroom.

"I'm sorry." I had no idea what else to say.

"Don't be. I'm not."

I didn't believe her for a second. Bente was crazy about Ryan. I was certain the feeling was mutual, but for some stupid reason Ryan just couldn't follow through.

"I know how he feels about you. He's just afraid."

"He's just a douche bag," she replied, beginning to cry. "He always has been."

I searched my tiny clutch bag for tissues, then remembered we were in a bathroom. I swiped the entire box of tissues off the vanity and handed them to her.

"I'll talk to him."

"And tell him what?" she sniffled. "This isn't high school, Charli. He's not going to change, and it's about time I stop expecting him to."

I nodded. "Well, let's just go back out there and pretend we didn't see anything."

Bente honked into a handful of tissues. "No. I'm going home. I'm not going to pretend anything, Charli. That's your forte, not mine."

Her comment stung more than I let on. Pretending everything was fine *was* my specialty of late. And I was close to living a complete lie because of it.

"Okay," I offered, "I'll sneak a bottle of wine from the bar and we'll stay in here all night."

"Deal," she replied, laughing through her tears.

I ordered her to stay put and headed back to the party, making it as far as the bar.

"Can I help you with something, Mrs Décarie?"

I spun around, expecting to see the queen standing behind me before realising the barman was talking to me. "Oh, um, yes. A bottle of merlot, please."

"A whole bottle?"

Foolishly, I amended my order. "Two, actually."

Wisely deciding against questioning me any further, he placed two bottles of wine on the bar. I snatched them, thanked him and bolted back to the bathroom.

Bente had given into the misery by then. She was sitting on the floor with her back against the wall, smoking a cigarette. I set the wine down beside her and started waving my arms around, trying to clear the smoke. "You can't smoke in here," I chided.

"I'm pretty sure I can do anything I want to."

Setting off the smoke alarms and clearing the building probably *would* have brought her a little joy at that point. I was usually the first one to err on the side of wickedness, but for once I hesitated. Ryan was an ass, but he didn't deserve to have his party shut down.

I sat beside her, took the cigarette out of her hand and handed her a bottle of wine. She couldn't burn the place down with merlot.

My track record for being a good friend wasn't exactly stellar. I was happy to be there in Bente's hour of need - right up until the bathroom door opened and I was caught red-handed by the queen.

Considering the height of our heels and the short length of our dresses, Bente and I scrambled to our feet remarkably quickly. I ran to the sink and extinguished the cigarette under the running water.

Fiona looked aghast. "You trashy little minx!"

"It's not what you think, Mrs Décarie," Bente exclaimed. "Charli has done nothing wrong."

Fiona stepped into the room, furiously wagging her finger. There was a fair chance I wasn't going to get out alive.

"Everything this girl does is wrong," she growled. "Just who do you think you are? You're married to *my* son. Do you understand what that means?"

"I'm beginning to," I muttered.

"You're a disgrace, Charlotte," barked Fiona. "If you think for one second I'm going to sit back and accept this vile situation, you're sadly mistaken."

"Mrs Décarie, please," said Bente. "Just stop."

The brunt of her anger was reserved entirely for me. The queen didn't pay Bente an ounce of attention, which was unfortunate. If she had, she might have realised that Bente's pleading had something to do with the fact that two women now stood in the doorway behind her, hanging on every word.

"I rue the day Adam met you," she declared, doing her very best to menace me. "You're nothing more than an unrefined little bitch."

A collective gasp from her audience of two alerted her that they were there. She glanced at them before spinning back to face me, looking one part mortified, one part trapped rat.

"Pull yourself together and find Adam. Do not leave his side for the rest of the evening," she ordered, leaning forward to whisper her command.

"Let's go, Charli," mumbled Bente, nudging me toward the door.

My grip on Bente's arm as we wove toward Adam was vice-like. "Say nothing to Adam about this," I warned.

"Would you rather he heard about it from his mother?" she hissed.

"She won't breathe a word." I was almost certain of it. Past history told me Fiona wasn't likely to squeal.

"Why do you let her treat you like that, Charli?" I had no answer. My reasons for keeping quiet were becoming hazier by the day. "Adam needs to know his mother's a bitch."

"Not tonight," I replied, demanding she keep quiet.

Adam was pleased to see me, blissfully unaware of anything that had just happened.

"Sorry," apologised Bente, thrusting me toward him. "I stole her away."

"Understandable," said Adam, reaching for my hand. "She is gorgeous."

From then on, minutes ticked by like hours. The only person having a worse evening than me was Bente. I wasn't surprised when she left early. If I thought I could have, I would've escaped with her. Things went from bad to worse when Adam suggested we go and chat with his parents. I agreed, unable to come up with a plausible reason not to. I looked across at the Décaries. Fiona was doing all the talking. Jean-Luc nodded occasionally. I knew exactly what she was telling him.

My eyes were firmly on the queen as we approached. Her lips moved a mile a minute as she whispered to her husband, probably trying desperately to get the whole story out before we got there.

"Darling," she crooned, pulling herself together the instant Adam was near.

He leaned down and kissed her cheek. "How are you, Mom?"

The witch answered him in French. The frown Adam flashed me proved she'd said nothing good.

It was Jean-Luc who moved quickly to smooth things over. "Your pictures are fascinating, Charli," he said, gazing at my prints on the wall behind me.

"Thank you."

"You have an outstanding eye for detail."

"Thank you."

"They complement the décor beautifully."

"Thank you."

Understandably, Jean-Luc gave up making small talk. I was barely concentrating. All my focus was on Fiona and the unusually cross look on her youngest son's face. I could only imagine what she'd told him. The bigger worry was why she'd opted to tell him anything. Her usual modus operandi was to say nothing at all and torment me later.

"Charli and I are going home," Adam announced bleakly, after a minute.

His mother lurched forward, kissing both of his cheeks. Jean-Luc did the same to me, probably so she wouldn't have to. For the first time ever, Adam didn't reach for my hand. I was glad. If he had, I would've resembled a child being led out of the room in disgrace.

It didn't take a genius to work out that he was unhappy with me. I waited until we were home before questioning him about his conversation with his mother. Amazingly, Fiona had stuck reasonably close to the facts – leaving out only the horrid name-calling and threats made on her part.

"What were you thinking?" he asked, loosening his tie and dragging it off his neck.

I kicked off my heels and followed him down to the bedroom, explaining how Ryan's bad behaviour had sent Bente to the brink. "She was really upset about it."

"So you thought smoking cigarettes and downing wine straight from the bottle in the bathroom would cheer her up?"

"No, of course not." I continued struggling to reach the zip on the back of my dress. Adam shrugged off his jacket and dropped it on the bed. "I was just trying to be a good friend."

He threw his arms up in exasperation. "What a grand situation for my wife to be in," he announced scathingly. "It's no wonder people get the wrong impression of you."

"Let me tell you something, Adam," I said, pointing at him. "I don't care what people think of me."

He sat down on the edge of the bed, rested his elbows on his knees and ran his hands through his hair. "You should care."

"Well, I don't," I insisted, making one final grab for the zip on my dress. He finally stood up, spun me around by the shoulders and unzipped it.

"Did you happen to notice who my mother was with when she sprung you?"

I shrugged, let my dress drop to the floor and stepped out of it. "There were two women I didn't know either of them."

Adam turned me around to face him. "One of them was Antonia Roberge. Her daughter Tilly was at the party too."

I had no idea why he was telling me the ins and outs of the guest list. "So?"

"So, Tilly writes a tasteless little online blog. It has a ridiculously large following considering it's nothing but tabloid garbage." I stared blankly at him, still clueless. "You don't get it, do you? Antonia would've been champing at the bit to tell Tilly all about the wayward new Décarie wife."

For a man who claimed not to care about what others thought of his decisions of late, he was taking things awfully seriously. What was the worst that could happen? Tilly Roberge could pound me in her blog by telling the whole world what an unsavoury redneck I was. Fiona would be vindicated and I'd still be in the land of not-giving-a-damn.

"Adam, why did Fiona tell you about it? I mean, you would've found out soon enough anyway. As soon as that girl updates her blog, my name is mud."

"She wants me to try and stop that from happening," he explained wanly. "She doesn't want you to be embarrassed."

His answer made absolutely no sense. Fiona would jump at the chance to see me publically humiliated. I drew in a long breath, trying to figure it out.

The real reason for her concern finally hit me. Tilly's mother hadn't seen the merlot and cigarette debacle. All she'd seen was the queen bombarding me with insults. Her inability to control herself when it came to chewing me out had backfired. She'd made the mistake of doing it in front of an audience.

If Tilly Roberge's blog ever saw the light of day, Queen Fiona might not come out smelling much like an English rose.

29. Second hearts

We ended up at a small café in Greenwich Village for breakfast the next morning. It was an eclectic little place, nestled between a bookshop and travel agent. If I'd thought for a second we were there by chance, I would have praised Adam on his choice of venue, but judging by the incessant text messaging he'd been engaged in all morning, breakfast in the village was part of a plan I wasn't privy to.

"Why are we here, Adam?" I asked, bleakly.

He shrugged. "I thought we'd try somewhere new."

I wasn't buying it. He usually favoured quiet tables in the corner. Opting for a table at the window closest to the door was a huge clue that something was amiss. Darting his eyes toward the door every time someone walked in also blew his charade to pieces.

"Tell me the truth," I pressed. "Who are you waiting for?"

Adam confessed instantly. "Sera. She's sort of friends with Tilly."

"Tilly? The mean blog girl?"

He nodded. "I'm hoping we can have a quiet word and convince her not to tell any tales about last night."

I was furious. Nothing had been mentioned about the bathroom drama at Billet-doux since the night before. Frankly, I assumed the cold light of day had put everything in perspective.

"This is so stupid," I muttered. "I can't believe you dragged me all the way down here for this."

"Trust me, Charlotte. You do *not* want your name in that blog."

Little did he know he wasn't there to protect my honour. The only one likely to be damaged by the bad press was his mother.

Eventually Seraphina breezed through the door, making a beeline straight for our table. Mean blog girl sashayed in right behind her, flicking her long blonde hair off her shoulders and glancing around the café – probably wondering why no one was bowing down and kissing her feet. The whole entrance was reminiscent of a cheesy shampoo commercial.

Both girls smiled brightly as they approached. Adam stood, did the dumb double kiss thing and invited them to sit down. I remained seated, too furious to even pretend to be polite. The whole situation was contrived and absurd.

"Charli, this is Tilly Roberge," Adam announced.

Tilly extended her hand across the table, which I met with a firm, unladylike shake. "Nice to meet you," she crooned in a sickly sweet tone. "I've heard so much about you."

Adam flashed a panicked glance at Sera who seemed to be trying to reassure him with a faint smile.

I stared at Tilly for an abnormally long time – which didn't faze her in the least. She probably thought I was in awe of her. "Have you now?"

Adam didn't appreciate my loaded question. He frowned at me. I stood my ground by frowning straight back. My intentions just weren't honourable. I wasn't about to shower the cocky girl with false compliments and polite conversation in the hopes that she'd change her mind about hammering me on her website.

"Tilly was at the opening of Billet-doux last night," said Sera, stating the obvious.

"I know."

Like Adam, Sera tried pulling me into line with a prickly glare.

"You must be so pleased that Adam's ventures are so successful, Charli. First Nellie's and now Billet-doux," exclaimed Tilly.

I ignored her, but continued staring at her as if I was somehow disturbed. Sera jumped in again. "Charli had a lot of input with Billet-doux. She came up with the name, and all the pictures on the walls are hers."

"Tell me, Adam," purred Tilly, alternating her pointed finger between the two of us. "How did you meet? I mean, you're such an unlikely couple."

I'd reached my limit. Who the hell did this girl think she was? Until the night before, I'd never even heard of Tilly Roberge, and yet Adam squirmed as if he had no choice but to answer her question. I had the sudden urge to thump him.

I looked straight at him. "Adam, don't you dare answer her."

Tilly laughed. It was an irritating, condescending cackle. "Wow. That's cute. You're touchy, aren't you?"

"Look, Tilly, I know exactly what you're all about," I muttered.

"Do you?" she asked pompously.

"Adam and Sera seem to think it's important to try and stay in your good graces – as if that's some kind of guarantee that you won't trash us in your blog. After all, image is everything, right?"

Tilly smirked at me, changing my mind about who I wanted to thump. She now topped my list.

"Charli," mumbled Adam, displeased.

"No, no, it's fine," soothed Tilly. "Let her speak."

"I don't need his permission to speak."

"And I don't need anyone's permission to write," she replied. "Everything in my blog is the truth. It's freedom of speech. If your family's image is somehow tainted by that, then you should all consider behaving more appropriately."

She dropped her eyes to the table and smiled, riling me even more.

I let out a long sigh, unhappy with the realisation that annihilating her also meant protecting the evil queen. I forged ahead anyway. "For some reason, people get the wrong impression of me," I complained. "They assume that I'm stupid." I tilted my head to the side and blinked spastically, adding validity to their claim. "Perhaps it's my accent."

Knowing I was up to no good, Adam slowly shook his head at me. I ignored the silent reprimand and focused only on Tilly. She leaned back in her chair and folded her arms. "Well, you have a chance to set the record straight right now. The floor is yours."

Tilly Roberge represented every bitchy girl I'd met since being in New York. The decision to wipe the floor with her came easily. "Why should I set anything straight, especially to you? You're nothing to me."

"Charli, please," Sera mumbled, mortified.

"I'm just putting it all out there. Crucifying others with her words gives her power. Belittling others makes her feel better about herself. It's how she deals with her own insecurities."

Tilly's expression flashed the first hint of anger. "You should tread carefully, Charli," she warned.

"You're extremely insecure, Tilly." I spoke gently, as if breaking the news to her. "And it makes you do silly things."

"What are you talking about?" she sneered, folding her arms defensively.

I stood up, preparing to leave. Adam and Sera stayed put, content to go down with the ship they assumed was sinking.

Resting one hand on the table, I leaned closer to Tilly. "I saw you up on the mezzanine with my slutty brother-in-law last night," I revealed, lowering my tone. "Who knew you were such an exhibitionist? Imagine how damaged *your* image would be if *that* became public."

Her cheeks blushed crimson, instantly realising I had serious dirt on her.

I'd recognised Tilly as being Ryan's make-out buddy the second she walked into the café, but it wouldn't have even rated a mention if she weren't so hell-bent on being a bitch.

"Are you threatening me?" she asked, angrily.

"Absolutely not," I replied, shaking my head. "I'm merely setting the record straight, just as you invited me to do."

"Is that so?" Her bravado was false. Her voice shook as she spoke.

I took it up a notch, practically growling at her. "Don't underestimate me, Tilly."

I straightened my pose and took half a step back, surveying the damage. Sera and Adam sat wide-eyed and silent. Tilly remained stoic, but at least her horrid smirk had disappeared. Grabbing my coat and storming out while they were still silent was a great move. It allowed for the cleanest getaway in history.

I clambered into the back seat of our waiting car, giving the unsuspecting driver such a fright that the newspaper he was reading flew in three different directions.

"Drive, please," I ordered.

"Shouldn't we wait for Adam, Miss Charli?"

"Look… Randy," I said, squinting to read his name badge, "I've had a really rough morning and I'm sure you're sick of sitting here waiting for us to finish breakfast. Am I right?"

Poor Randy didn't know whether to answer me or not. "Where would you like to go?"

"Home, please."

"As you wish."

As I wish, I repeated in my head. If things had panned out as I'd hoped when I cashed in wishes for a life in New York with Adam, things would've been much simpler.

***

I expected Adam to be brutally furious with me when he arrived home. I'd never actually seen him brutally furious, but ditching him at the café *was* pretty poor form. He walked in the door and hung his coat. I stood in the kitchen, trying to gauge his mood as he walked over to me.

"You left before your tea arrived," he said, handing me a takeaway cup that was amazingly still warm.

"Thank you."

"I figure it was the least I could do. Annihilating the prima donnas of Manhattan is probably thirsty work." Adam leaned his back against the kitchen counter and folded his arms. "I wasn't expecting you to make such light work of her, Charlotte."

"What were you expecting me to do, exactly? Beg for mercy? Cry a little?"

He knew better than that, which is exactly why he hadn't told me the real reason for our excursion until we got there.

"I didn't expect to get caught up in one of your games," he chided. I took the lid off my tea and poured it down the sink. It was all I could do to stop myself throwing it at him. "Why didn't you tell me you had that kind of leverage over Tilly?"

"I didn't even know who she was until she arrived. I wouldn't have even mentioned seeing her with Ryan but – "

"But what?"

Cutting me off was unnecessary. It was an annoying ploy designed to make me feel childish.

I took a step toward him but Adam's pose didn't waver. He remained leaning against the counter with his arms tightly folded.

"Bitchiness begets bitchiness," I said spitefully. "It's an art I've had to master to survive here."

He shook his head, riled by me. It was the first time I'd ever seen such an angry expression on his perfect face. "No one twisted your arm and forced you into the bathroom with a bottle of wine, Charli. You wouldn't have to be on the defence all the time if you'd just…."

I took it upon myself to finish his sentence. "Conform? Behave myself?"

"Something like that." His answer was barely more than a mumble.

Something inside me gave way. I couldn't stave off the hurt and frustration any longer. I picked up the wet dishcloth off the sink and socked it at him. It splattered against his shirt, leaving a big wet patch before falling to the floor.

"You have no idea what I've been through in the last few months!" The words raged out of me. I flung open the cupboard closest to me, grabbed a roll of paper towel and threw that at him too. "Toeing the line was never an option, Adam. I've never been given the chance."

If I'd been Whitney Vaughn's doppelganger, I still wouldn't have been accepted by his spiteful mother and awful friends. They all loathed me. I stared at him for a long time, trying to figure out what would change between us when he found that out.

"I know this hasn't been an easy transition for you, Charli," he said, dabbing the front of his shirt with the paper towel. "I see that."

"Do you see your so-called friends tearing me down at every opportunity?" I asked dully.

"They've tried hard to include you."

His obliviousness made me want to throw up. "Keep telling yourself that, Adam."

"Is there more to it?"

I didn't hesitate; blurting out every misdeed his friends had subjected me to. By the time I was done, Adam knew exactly how the purple circle really felt about me.

He frowned. "Why haven't you told me any of this before now?"

Frustrated tears welled in my eyes and I looked to the ceiling, trying desperately hard to stop them brimming over. "Because I love you."

"So you lied to me?"

"You don't know the half of it," I sniffed.

"Tell me *all* of it."

I quickly realised I couldn't do it. Finding out how awful his mother was would solve nothing. I compromised with myself, deciding to give him only snippets of the bigger picture. He didn't need to know how malicious and cruel she was. He only needed to know that she wanted me gone. "You mother hates me."

Adam groaned, locking his hands behind his head as if his brain ached. "Don't you think you're blowing things a little out of proportion?"

In the steadiest voice I could muster, I told him about the conversation I'd overheard in the bathroom at Nellie's on the day I went to lunch with the queen.

"You're spending a lot of time in bathrooms lately," he noted humourlessly.

"Nothing Tilly Roberge planned to write about me would have been new, Adam. Fiona's been spreading the word for weeks."

He frowned. "She was very concerned for you when she thought you were going to end up in that blog."

I shook my head sadly. "You're an idiot. An absolute, dead-set idiot."

Adam seized my face in his hands and tilted my head, forcing me to look at him. "Stop crying and calm down."

It was a stupid thing to say. I wasn't capable of calming down. I dug the heels of my palms into his chest, pushed him away and let loose. "Don't you see? Fiona was trying to save her own skin! Tilly's mother didn't see me doing anything wrong. She walked in on your mother screaming at me, roaring about how much she despises me. That's what was going to end up in the stupid blog."

Adam stared at me for a long moment, processing my words. "Why protect her then?" he asked, still perfectly calmly. "Why bother silencing Tilly?"

I huffed out a sharp breath. "I guess I just couldn't pass up an opportunity to destroy her. She deserved to be shut down."

He shook his head. "I don't know what you want me to do about this."

"All you have to do is tell me that you believe me."

Adam took a few steps forward and kissed my forehead. But he said nothing. And it crushed me.

I had to get out of the apartment. I wanted to be where there was no noise, no trouble and no Adam.

Inexplicably, the laundrette was where I ended up – with Adam in tow, because lugging a bag of laundry three blocks was beyond me.

We sat side by side on the row of plastic chairs, mindlessly watching our clothes slosh around in the machine while we waited.

"I want you to know that I didn't mean what I said," Adam murmured, entranced by the spinning clothes in front of us. "I would never want you to conform. It would be like ripping the wings off a butterfly."

It was a sweet thing to say, but still implied I'd done something wrong.

"It's unfair that I love you the way I do," I said bleakly. "My second heart will be black by the time I'm through with it."

Adam turned to look at me, silently quizzing me with his eyes.

I sighed, unwilling to explain. "Never mind." The machine stopped spinning. I grabbed a trolley and began pulling the clothes out.

"Please tell me," he urged.

I stuffed the wet clothes into the dryer and slammed the door. "No. You'll have to figure it out."

He pulled out a handful of coins and pumped them into the machine. "And if I can't?"

I shrugged, highlighting my indifference. "Then I guess you'll never know."

He turned to me, drawing me in close. "I love you, Charli," he said, leaning his forehead against mine. "And if I've let you forget that today, I will tell you a hundred times more."

30. Effort

The rest of the weekend passed without incident, and Monday morning rolled around quickly. Nothing had been resolved, but it was easier to make believe everything was fine when it was just the two of us.

"Charli, what do you have planned today?" asked Adam, rushing around the bedroom searching for something to wear.

I stayed in bed. I had nowhere to rush to. "Promise not to judge me?"

He stopped searching and turned to face me. "Of course. What do you have planned?"

"I'm going to have my nails done with Seraphina," I replied in a tiny voice.

"You're kidding me. How did that come about?"

I wasn't entirely sure. She'd completely blindsided me with a phone call the day before, suggesting that we get to know each other better. "Before I knew what was happening, I was agreeing to a play date."

"Sera's a sweet girl, Charli. You'll be fine."

I had to concede that Seraphina had never been particularly hostile toward me. "Time will tell, I guess," I replied. "What do you have planned?"

"Well, for starters, I need to find a shirt."

I pointed to the laundry basket. "Then what?"

"Research and study," he replied, dragging a T-shirt over his head.

"You're such a boring man," I teased, dragging out the words. Without warning, Adam pulled the warm covers off me, grabbed my ankles and dragged me down the bed. "I'm sorry." He murmured the words against my bare stomach, sending a hot rush right through me. "I'll try harder not to be, starting now."

***

I wasn't exactly a nail salon virgin, but I'd never had my nails done in a salon that served complimentary champagne at the door. Sera arrived late, leaving me to fend off the overzealous technician by myself. His name was Zahn, and he scared the living daylights out of me. The tight-fitting black turtleneck, black skinny jeans and diamante studded belt was a very brave look, considering he was about fifty pounds overweight.

"Come! Sit! Sit, darling!" he commanded, jiggling toward me as I walked in. I didn't have a chance to protest. He grabbed my hand and led me to the nearest chair. "What is it you want from Zahn?" he purred, examining my hands under the bright desk lamp.

"A manicure?" I actually sounded unsure.

"What do you do with these hands, darling?" he asked, stroking my palms like he was petting a cat. "Cart bricks?"

As luck would have it, that was the moment Seraphina showed up. Zahn momentarily forgot about me, dropping my hands and running to take Sera's coat. "Hello Zahn," she greeted, air kissing both of his cheeks.

"Seraphina, ballerina," he cooed, giggling like a little girl.

Sera wriggled free of him, made her way down to me and sat down on the chair beside me. "Hi Charli. How are you?"

"A little frightened," I whispered, making her chuckle.

There was no escaping Zahn. Considering the over-the-top greeting Sera received, I thought he'd ditch me in favour of her. But he didn't. A girl called Jojo with spiky pink hair, two studs in her eyebrow and pink Beats headphones covering her ears sat down and went to work on her.

"I'm really glad you decided to come," said Sera. "I wanted to be sure you were okay after that horrible episode with Tilly. She does a lot of damage."

I didn't look at her as she spoke. "Thanks, but I wouldn't say she's the worst I've had to deal with since I've been here."

"Fitting in hasn't been easy for you," she agreed.

"Nope. You're a tough crowd."

Zahn giggled, a girly shrill that reminded me of Fabergé. I realised I probably shouldn't have been talking so freely in front of him.

Jojo couldn't have heard a word. We could hear the loud music thumping through the big headphones she was wearing.

"I know it's no excuse but, well, you took us by surprise. One minute Adam was with Whitney and the next he was married to you."

"Scan-da-lous," interjected Zahn. I wiggled my fingers to get his mind back on task.

"It seemed so out of character for Adam, which can only mean one thing," she mused.

"What, darling? What does it mean?" Zahn asked the question as if hearing the answer meant the difference between life and death.

"He loves her, Zahn."

"The feeling is mutual," I said, ignoring Zahn's coo of approval. "I love him."

We were quiet for a while, but the silence wasn't awkward. I felt no need to impress Sera. I'd already made the decision that she'd have to take me at face value. It was a stance I probably should've adopted the second I arrived in New York.

"Why did you get married? How can you be sure he's the one?" Sera didn't sound cynical, just curious. "What if you break up?"

I shrugged. "It won't matter. He'll still be the one."

My words stunned her into silence. Even Zahn was quiet.

I drew in a long breath, debating whether or not I should elaborate. I decided to throw it all out there and let her decide if I was crazy or not. "I'll tell you the whole story if you want to hear it."

Seraphina nodded, smiling eagerly.

Zahn squeezed my fingers so tightly I thought he was going to break them. "We want to hear ev-ery-thing, darling," he enthused.

It wasn't a tough story to tell. I liked the story of Adam and Charli. Apparently Zahn did too. He burst into tears halfway through the tale, blubbing so uncontrollably that I had to wait for him to pull himself together before continuing.

"So you searched Africa, looking for him," he breathed. His exotic accent seemed to slip along with his concentration. I suspected that Zahn from Europe was actually Gary from Brooklyn, but held off on calling him on it.

"Ah, no," I corrected. "I was on a surfing trip in Africa. Adam has always been in New York."

"Yes," said Sera giggling. "Searching Africa would've been pointless. I can't imagine Adam hanging out somewhere like that."

Nor could I, and that realisation was a dull but constant hum in my head.

"I'm hoping to change his mind."

Seraphina glanced at me and smiled, albeit uneasily.

My story wasn't the only one told that day. I learned that Sera wasn't particularly fond of her circle of friends.

"I love Jeremy, of course. Whitney and Adam have always been sweet to me, but I wouldn't trust the others as far as I could throw them." She shuddered and I was suddenly keen to know more. Zahn was too, saving me from appearing nosy by demanding that she elaborate. "Tell us ev-ery-thing, darling."

Apparently Kinsey's career in bitchiness was long. She'd done everything from passing off Sera's college assignments as her own to hitting on her boyfriend. Sera's revulsion for Parker stemmed from the hundreds of times he'd made a move on her.

"He's a smarmy low-life," she growled. "But I figure Kinsey deserves him." Zahn threw his greasy blonde head back and cackled. Sera and I laughed too, mainly at Zahn. There was nothing funny about her story. At times she'd been just as tormented by them as I was.

I left the salon with new nails and a new opinion of Seraphina Sawyer. I understood her a little better. Hopefully, she felt the same. If not, I'd just given her a whole lot of ammunition to use against me.

***

I didn't go straight home. I'd received a curious phone call from Adam asking that I meet him outside a café all the way down near Battery Park.

"Take a cab and make sure you wear something warm," he instructed. "Oh, and Charli?"

"What?"

"I love you."

I would've returned the sentiment, but in true New York style, he'd already ended the call.

Peak hour traffic in Manhattan is abominable. The long cab ride seemed to take forever so I cut the journey short and walked the last few blocks. Needless to say, I was late.

"Where have you been?" asked Adam urgently, striding toward me. "I thought you weren't coming."

"Of course I was coming. It just took a while." He wrapped both arms tightly around me. "What are we doing here?" The financial district wasn't usually one of our haunts. I leaned back, needing to see his eyes.

He squinted mischievously, making the manoeuvre totally worthwhile. "I have a surprise for you."

I didn't ask what. It was never going to be a bad surprise. I just held his hand and tried to keep up as he marched along the footpath. We ended up in front of an office building with front doors so tall a car could've driven through the with ease. Adam led me across the marble foyer to a reception desk that looked lost in the wide open space.

Curiously, the woman at desk knew him and greeted him by name. "I'll call ahead and make sure your father is in," she offered, reaching for the phone.

Adam smoothly protested. "No, no. It's fine. I was hoping to surprise him."

We were in the building that housed Jean-Luc Décarie's law offices. It was a crappy surprise, after all. I'd enjoyed the few days reprieve we'd had from his family.

The receptionist smiled. "Go on up then," she permitted, pointing toward the row of elevators.

I said nothing. I trailed behind as he led us into the elevator. The doors closed and I stood studying the brass plate on the elevator wall. "Décarie, Fontaine and Associates. Level forty-three," I read.

Adam hit the button for the roof level. "We're not here to see my dad."

"What *are* we here to see?" I asked, feeling curious and relieved at the same time.

He glanced across at me, wiggling his eyebrows. "We're here to see magic on the roof, Charlotte."

The rooftop was a restricted area. The elevator stopped a floor below and an audible recording told us it was the end of the line. Adam reached into the pocket of his coat, pulled out something that looked like a hotel room card and swiped it along the keypad. The elevator hummed and we continued the short journey upwards.

"Did you steal that card?" I asked, thrilled by the prospect.

"The harder the access, the sweeter the find, Charlotte." It was the same statement I'd made to him a million years ago when we were scaling a fence to get to a private stretch of beach in Pipers Cove. It reminded me of how much he loved small details.

The freezing cold air hit me the second we were outside, and I lingered by the door. "Come and see," Adam urged, waving me over as he walked to the fenced off edge. "It's incredible."

"I can see it from here," I lied.

He abruptly forgot the view and turned to face me. "Are you frightened?"

Until then, I didn't think I had a problem with heights. I'd changed my mind somewhere between the sixtieth and seventieth floor. "A little bit," I conceded. "We're a long way up."

Adam ambled back to me as if he was using the time to plot his next move. He reached for my hand and led me to what looked like a big metal air-conditioning box in the centre of the roof. We sat down and I snuggled into him. The humming box was warm, working hard to heat the offices below.

"Better?"

I nodded. My legs had stopped shaking, probably at the realisation that we could no longer accidentally tumble off the edge. I couldn't even see the edge any more.

"It's a pretty view," I told him, looking at the skyline ahead.

"We're not here for that view," he said enigmatically. "We're here for *that* view." He pointed upward and I looked to the hazy sky.

"The clouds?"

"No, the stars. We're a bit early, I guess."

I cast my mind back to the conversation we'd had that morning. It occurred to me that his day of research and studying had nothing to do with his class work. I turned my head, smiling at him. "You researched second hearts, didn't you?"

"You knew I would." He grinned. "You want to hear what I learned?"

Enjoying the warmth, I lay back on the metal box and looked to the sky. "Of course I do."

Adam had found out something I'd known to be true for a long time. Fairies gift new babies a second heart when they're born.

"They're shiny and silver and stay with us until we die," he recited, lying down beside me. His head was turned toward me, but I kept my focus on the overcast sky above.

"I'm very impressed."

"The fairies reclaim them once we die," he added.

"Then what?"

His hand reached across my body, slipping inside my coat and coming to rest on my heart. His cold skin sent a shudder through me, but I made no attempt to move out of reach.

"They hang them in the sky. They become stars," he whispered. "They're picky though, the fairies."

"Really?"

"Yeah. They only take the brightest hearts. If they haven't been treasured and looked after, the hearts become blackened and tarnished."

I let out a long breath that came out in an unsteady shiver. "That's the tragedy."

"Yeah. No one wants their second heart to become the rattling ball in a can of spray paint."

I frowned at him. "Is that what happens to them?"

Adam laughed, hard enough that his hand trembled on my chest. "No. I'm lying about that part. I couldn't find what happens to the reject second hearts."

I turned on my side, cuddling into him as if we were in bed rather than lying on an air conditioner box seventy stories above the street. "Well, it's my understanding that they polish them up and reuse them. Fairies are big on recycling."

He reached forward, stroking my cheek with the back of his free hand.

"These stories sometimes confuse me."

"Why?"

"Well, how do you know which is the truth? Are stars stuck in the sky serving a punishment, big rocks that splinter into diamonds or second hearts?"

"They're whatever you believe they are," I replied. "That's the beauty of magic. There are no rules."

He leaned in, pressing his cold lips against mine. "You have no idea how lovely you are, Charlotte."

Hanging out on the top of the office building was the best few hours we'd spent together in a long time. It was a true escape from the busy city.

We didn't stay to see the stars. Getting locked up there after business hours was a bigger risk than either of us was prepared to take. But skipping out early dulled none of the magic. Both of my hearts were positively gleaming.

***

It had been a good week. Drama had been at a minimum and attention from the cute French American boy had been at a premium. That was why I was caught off guard by the huge bouquet of flowers on the dining room table that morning. I knew they weren't from Adam. Gifting me ostentatious floral arrangements wasn't his style.

"They arrived a few minutes ago," he said, sidling up behind me. "Mom sent them."

The way he kissed the back of my neck usually set me on fire, but his touch was powerless. I was too focused on the stupid flowers. "Why would she do that?"

"It's her way of apologising. She also wants to take you to lunch." I backed away, fighting the sudden urge to set fire to the flowers, and uselessly tried to wrestle free of his grip. "Why, Adam? It's just asking for trouble."

He didn't seem to pick up on the terror in my voice. I was beginning to suspect Adam saw only what he wanted to.

"At least she's making the effort."

"Don't you wonder why she's making the effort?"

"Please, Coccinelle." His technique of breathing the words into my neck was nothing more than trickery. It made protesting impossible. "Just meet with her and sort it out. For me."

It would only be for him. It was only ever for him. If it were up to me, Fiona and I would never cross paths again.

31. Snookered

The queen decided we would meet at a fancy restaurant called Palmeraie. I'd never even heard of the place. Studying the map Marvin had drawn me, I realised it was going to be a long walk.

More than happy to be late, I meandered ridiculously slowly, as if headed to my own execution. I had no idea how I was going to handle her. All I knew was that this would be my very last attempt at calling a truce.

The only advice Adam had given me was wardrobe-related. "Palmeraie is very up-market. You should wear a dress."

As unhelpful as his advice was, I arrived at the restaurant wearing one of the only three dresses I possessed.

Choosing between outfits wasn't difficult. I doubt my new mother-in-law would have appreciated seeing my gorgeous wedding dress that late in the game. My black cocktail dress was probably a bit over-the-top too. My other dress wasn't anywhere near as special, but far more appropriate. The cowl neck wool dress was itchy beyond belief, but I tried hard to hold myself together. Fiona had already formed the opinion that I was a vagrant pauper. I didn't want to give the impression that I had fleas too.

I saw her as soon as I walked in, sitting at a table near the window, decorously sipping a glass of wine while she waited.

Escorted by the maître d', I approached. Fiona stood up, greeting me with the fake little double-kiss that the Décaries are so fond of. "Hello, darling," she greeted. "Sit down, please."

Said the spider to the fly.

The maître d' pulled out my chair and I sat down, trying to appear more settled than I felt. "I'm sorry I'm so late."

"I am just pleased you agreed to come."

"Did you think I wouldn't?"

Her eyes dropped to the table as she absently rolled the stem of the wineglass with her fingers. "You bring out the worst in me, Charli. The frustration caused by the choices my son has made is insufferable."

"You need to find a way around it, Fiona," I suggested. "I'm not going anywhere."

"You really do love him, don't you?"

"With all that I have."

"But you have nothing, Charli," she said bleakly, cutting me down. "That is what concerns me."

An unbearable silence set in. Fiona's eyes kept glancing at the door like she was hoping someone would show up and rescue her.

"Am I keeping you from something?"

Perhaps embarrassed by being caught out, her eyes drifted back to mine and I had her undivided attention – for about three seconds until the person she'd been waiting for walked through the door.

"Oh, look who's here." Her acting was as bad as I'd ever seen.

I looked, to see Whitney flounce in. It felt like days since I'd last seen her, running out of the Décarie house in a flood of tears, but in truth she'd been gone for over a month.

I used the time it took Whitney to make her way to our table to stare down my mother-in-law. Anyone who didn't know Fiona Décarie would think she was stunning. Her long dark hair, unusual cobalt eyes and flawless skin personified beauty. On the outside, she was gorgeous. On the inside, she was rotten to the core. I might as well have been sitting opposite Cruella de Vil.

"Fi, how are you?" crooned dim Whit in a syrupy tone.

Fiona stood up, did her double-kiss routine and hugged her as falsely as she kissed her. "I'm wonderful, Whit, just wonderful." She vaguely waved her hand in my direction. "You remember Charli."

I wondered if giving them a round of applause would alert them to the fact that I knew they were both acting. Instead, I went along with their game. "Hello, Whitney."

"Please, join us for lunch," suggested the queen. "You don't mind, do you, Charli?"

I shook my head, giving Whitney all the encouragement she needed to pull out a seat. "I can't believe we ran into each other like this," marvelled Whitney, patting Fiona's arm.

"Neither can I," I said tartly.

"Show Whitney your lovely wedding ring, Charli. She'd love to see it." I volunteered my hand across the table – not because Fiona demanded I do so but because I knew she didn't think I would.

Whitney frowned as she studied it. I didn't care one bit. To me, my simple gold band was much more than lovely. It symbolised the very best thing in my life.

"Adam gave me this bracelet for my birthday last year." Whitney thrust her hand across the table, waving it so close to my face that I had to lean back to see the garish bracelet she was flashing at me. "Four carats, total."

"You win then, I guess," I replied.

The conversation was ridiculous. Apparently the queen agreed, moving to change the subject. "Let's order. I'm famished," she announced.

I knew lunch would be an ordeal, purely because of the company I was with. What I didn't know was that the agony would be drawn out over four courses of food and two bottles of champagne. It was asinine. The waiters ended up clearing the table of enough food to feed a small army. Much to my relief, most of the champagne got left too. It was hard enough dealing with them sober, let alone tanked on hundred-dollar bubbly.

I was merely an observer. I contributed nothing to the conversation. I didn't know any of the people they gossiped about. I had none of the to-die-for handbags Fiona had picked up in Soho. And I had never set foot in the five star resorts Whitney recommended to Fiona for her next vacation to St Barts. I did, however, know of a great half-star backpackers hostel in Madagascar that had Internet access on Tuesdays.

Fiona stood up and made polite - but obviously fake - excuses to leave when lunch was over. Whitney stood too. I stayed put.

"Call me and we'll do lunch next week," she instructed, kissing both of Whitney's cheeks.

"Absolutely," she beamed. "We'll catch up on all the scandal."

Considering they'd just spent the last two hours gossiping, it was easy to read between the lines. I was the scandal.

Fiona turned her attention to me. "Charli, please give my love to Adam."

"I will. Thanks for lunch."

"No, thank *you*. It means the world to me that you came." She almost sounded genuine, but killed it by leaning down and kissing my cheek.

Being left alone with Whitney was a fate worse than death, possibly because I was forced to admit to some truths. I had no idea how it was going to pan out, but one thing was certain: there were a few things dim Whit wanted to get off her Escada-clad chest.

"You must feel very uncomfortable," she said flatly.

I was wearing a wool dress. I was very uncomfortable, but I knew that wasn't what she was referring to. "We all have a cross to bear, Whitney."

"Do you think he's worth this?" she spat. "It's always going to be uncomfortable for you. It's never going to be over."

Whitney's attempts at menacing me were subpar at best.

"It is over," I insisted. "You need to preserve what little sanity you have left and move on."

If I'd thought I could handle it with a little more tenderness, I would have given it my best shot. I was beginning to think Adam was so cold toward her because he needed to be. She just didn't get it.

"You're a temporary glitch, Charli. He's invested nothing in you. Not even a decent ring." She leaned down to hiss the words across the table.

Replying calmly and quietly was my best defence. "Whitney, it's over."

She said nothing for a long time but her hard demeanour was beginning to crack. Angry, frustrated tears welled in her brown eyes. I didn't take any delight in seeing her cry - but at least it proved she was human.

"You're temporary," she repeated, sounding more like she was trying to convince herself than me. She drew in a sharp breath, composing herself. "He'll never leave here, Charli. You won't convince him to throw his life away for you."

"It's really none of your business."

The smirk that crossed her face was positively wretched. "I don't know what you two actually talk about, other than rainbows and puppies." She punched out one hard laugh which was one more than her ignorant comment warranted. "Adam has much bigger plans than you."

"Really?" I drawled.

Whitney slid her chair back and stood up, leaning down to bully me with her quiet words. "You're trash, Charli. And eventually, trash gets put out."

I let her have the last word. She picked up her to-die-for handbag and walked out the door.

Mentally, I was exhausted. I sat for a minute trying to figure out whether I wanted to laugh or cry at the absurdity of my day thus far.

I didn't notice the waiter approach the table. "Will there be anything else today, Miss?"

"No, thank you."

He smiled, nodded his head, placed a small black folder down on the table and walked away. A wave of pure dread washed over me. I lifted the cover of the folder just enough to see the amount of the bill inside. It was just shy of four hundred dollars. There was no way I could even come close to covering it. I couldn't even cover the tip.

I suddenly recalled Fiona's parting comment to me when I thanked her for lunch. "No, thank *you*."

I'd been set up. Cruella de Vil and her trusty sidekick had completely snookered me.

Discreetly glancing around the restaurant, I considered my options. Approaching the maître d', explaining the situation and offering to do the dishes until the tab was settled wasn't an option. Firstly, it would take a million years to work it off and secondly, I was in the wrong part of town to expect such a deal could ever be negotiated.

Calling Adam was my best bet, even if it meant enduring a lecture about not carrying my credit card for emergencies like this. He answered straight away. "Charli, I'm in the middle of class," he whispered, unimpressed by the interruption.

"I know. I'm sorry. I really need you to come down here and get me."

"What are you talking about? Why?"

"Please, it's important."

He groaned. "Look, I take it things aren't going well. You're just going to have to deal with it. I'll see you at home later."

I doubted I'd be home any time soon. Rikers Island Jail had a bed with my name on it. I was just about to explain why I needed him there so desperately when a waiter appeared beside me and picked up the black folder. Realising it was empty, he quickly placed it back on the table.

"On second thoughts, can I order a pot of tea, please?" I asked him, desperately stalling for time.

"Of course, Miss," he replied, walking away.

To my detriment, Adam heard my request. "Charlotte, drink your tea," he said sarcastically. "I love you. I have to go."

He hung up on me. And when I tried calling him back, it went straight to voicemail. I considered calling Bente, but wasn't sure she'd be able to scrape together that much cash in a hurry. Ryan was my last hope.

"I have a meeting in a few minutes, Charli. It's not really a good time."

"Ryan, please. I need you to come down to Palmeraie." I was practically begging.

Unlike his brother, he didn't ask why, which was a good thing because the waiter reappeared at the table to serve my pot of tea and amend my bill. Ryan told me to stay put – as if I had a choice – and promised to be there within the hour.

I dragged my tea drinking out a ridiculously long time. It was stone cold by the time I'd finished, and panic was beginning to set in. From the corner of my eye I noticed the maître d' standing at the podium, having a sly conversation with the waiter who'd served me. I was in a whole world of trouble.

Over an hour had passed since I'd spoken to Ryan. I had been at Palmeraie for nearly four hours. The unwavering stare-down by the maître d' catapulted me to the point of hysteria. Breathing suddenly became a task I had to concentrate on, which meant I noticed nothing going on around me, including Ryan finally walking through the door. I jumped as he said my name, leaping out of my seat and throwing my arms around his neck.

"Ow, Charli, I need to breathe," he said, loosening my grip with both hands.

"Oh, I'm sorry. I'm just so glad to see you."

Ryan sat down, reached for my hand and pulled me down onto the chair beside him. "Why? What's the problem?"

I did my best to explain everything to him, ending with the obvious. "I can't pay the bill."

"You do realise your husband is loaded, right? Lunches at Palmeraie are supposed to be chump change."

Again, the waiter approached our table. I didn't feel anywhere near as nervous as I had the last time he appeared beside me. "Miss, management have requested that you settle the bill now."

"Oh, that's too bad," cooed Ryan. "We were just about to order cocktails."

"Sir, the young lady has been here for over four hours."

Ryan looked across at me, grinning wickedly. "Lush."

"There was some concern as to whether she could cover the tab," said the waiter.

Ryan reached into his breast pocket and pulled out his wallet. He placed his credit card in the black folder, snapped it shut and handed it to him. "I think it's obvious that she can, don't you?"

The waiter dipped his head and backed away, scurrying back to the podium to process the payment.

"Thank you," I breathed.

"My pleasure," he replied. "So how did you work your way in to this fine mess?"

I paused for a second so my words would be true. "Your mother and her little underling set me up."

"You're going to have to elaborate, Charli."

I drew in a deep breath before launching in to my explanation. Ryan sat motionless and stone-faced, allowing me to finish the tale unchallenged.

"The irony is, they didn't have to put so much effort in to humiliating me. I wouldn't have been able to cover the first bottle of champagne."

Ryan frowned, dropping his line of sight to the table. Dipping my head, I chased his eyes.

"It wasn't about humiliating you, Charli," he said quietly. "They were trying to raise the charge from petty theft to grand larceny. That's a felony."

Nothing he said made any sense to me and I had no choice but to admit it – even at the risk of him having to dumb it down for me. "I don't understand."

"I had a casual conversation with my mother a few days ago. She asked me about the likelihood of you having your visa approved," he explained. "I told her it seemed pretty cut-and-dried. You obviously love each other, have plenty of money and no criminal convictions."

His words were like a spear through my heart. "She wants me gone so badly that she'd set me up?" I asked, beginning to cry.

Seeing I was on the brink of a meltdown, Ryan reached across the table, covering my hand with his. "Please don't cry. I hate it when girls cry. It reminds me of what a jerk I am."

" At least you're here. Adam wouldn't come."

"You mean I wasn't your first choice?" His sad tone was completely false, and his over-the -top gesture of hand to heart made me laugh through my tears. "I'm crushed."

"Don't be. You would've been my phone-a-friend from jail if they'd arrested me."

"Well, crisis averted. No one's getting arrested today."

"Can we get out of here please?" I asked, exhausted.

"Absolutely."

***

I wasn't up to the long walk home. I was utterly battle weary, and the dark, icy afternoon matched my bleak mood. I was relieved when Ryan insisted I take his driver.

I stripped off the second I was in the door. My itchy, uncomfortable dress hit the floor before I made it to the end of the hallway.

"Charli?" Adam called, probably following the trail of discarded clothing down to the bathroom. I hadn't even realised he was home. I almost wished he wasn't. I had nothing nice to say to him. I turned on the shower and stepped inside.

It took Adam all of two seconds to realise I was ignoring him. "You're upset with me."

"Genius," I muttered.

"Look, I couldn't just drop everything and come running because your lunch date with my mother wasn't going well."

His superior tone was the first mistake he made. Mentioning his mother was the second. I cleared the foggy shower screen to see him.

"I needed you there."

"Always drama." He rolled his eyes, making his third mistake.

Adam's arms were outstretched, holding a towel for me before I even finished turning the water off. I snatched it from him, wrapping it tightly around my body. His decision to follow me down to the bedroom made silent brooding impossible. "Go away."

"I'm not going anywhere. Tell me why you're so upset."

Throwing open the closet doors, I searched for something to wear. I didn't care what it was – providing it wasn't wool. I settled on jeans and a T-shirt. I made him wait until I was fully dressed, which he did patiently, bugging me even more.

"Your mother is an evil, nasty woman." I said it hatefully, meaning every word.

Adam sat down on the edge of the bed and groaned out a long breath. "What has she done now?"

It took me a long time to explain it to him. I embellished nothing. The story was so ludicrous that I didn't need to. Like Ryan, Adam sat silently throughout my rant. "She's so desperate to get me out of your life that she tried to have me deported."

"You're mistaken, Charlotte," he said dully.

"No, Adam. Whitney wasn't there by coincidence. They didn't order hundreds of dollars worth of food for no reason. They set me up. Fiona knows I don't use that stupid card you gave me. I made it easy for her."

"No."

We'd somehow stepped in to very dangerous territory. He didn't believe me. "How else would you explain it?"

Adam stood up, taking an angry step toward me. "I can't explain it. You're mistaken."

I threw my arms up in frustration, slapping them down loudly on my sides. "Then you've just killed us. If you don't believe me, we have nothing! I'll take whatever is dished out to me providing you're on my side. I won't do it by myself. I have no reason to."

"You're talking about my mother!" he yelled, walking out of the room.

I couldn't help following him down to the kitchen. I was nowhere near done with him. "I *am* talking about your mother," I spat, rounding the doorway. "I'm *finally* talking about your mother."

Adam threw open a kitchen drawer, took out the unused credit card and marched over to me, tucking it into my back pocket.

"There was no need for this drama. In future, carry the damned card with you."

The noise that escaped me was nothing short of a guttural growl. "How can you be so oblivious? You see only what you want to."

"Stop this," he begged.

Something clicked in my head. I was done protecting the evil queen. I'd always glossed over the extent of her malice toward me but couldn't see any point in maintaining the charade anymore. She was killing us.

"It was your mother who gave me the black eye on Christmas day," I confessed bleakly. "Something about me infuriates her so much that she thumped me."

Adam staggered back a step, staring at me in wide-eyed horror. "Why haven't you told me this before?"

"Because she's your mother," I muttered sourly. "And because Ryan asked me not to tell you."

Adam recovered quickly. "Get your coat, Charlotte," he ordered.

"Where are we going?"

I wasn't entirely sure I wanted to hear the answer.

"We're going to put an end to this, right now."

32. Pound Puppy

Adam Décarie was the gentlest person I knew, but there was no mistaking his rage as we rode the elevator up to his parents' penthouse. I stared at him through the mirrored wall, trying to figure out what was going to happen when we got there.

"Adam, don't do anything you'll regret later," I urged, trying to keep my voice steady.

"I thought you'd be happy with this outcome," he muttered, staring blankly at me through the mirror.

What outcome? I wasn't even sure what was happening. I was, however, wishing I'd kept my big mouth shut.

Adam didn't knock to announce his arrival as he'd done the last time we were there. He barrelled through the unlocked front door as if he was the king rather than one of the princes. I had to run to keep up.

Mrs Brown missed Adam's entrance but walked into the foyer in time for mine. "Miss Charli," she said, wide-eyed and worried. "What is the matter?"

I didn't quite know how to answer her, but gave it my best shot. "Adam is here to see his mother. Is she here?"

My question was redundant. I could already hear raised voices from the lounge room. Mrs Brown abandoned me in an instant, running into the room to find the source of the commotion.

The second I passed through the opaque glass doors, I knew there would be no going back. My eyes scanned the room, searching for Adam. He was standing near the windows with his back to his mother. Perhaps he couldn't bear to see her so distraught. Even I was having trouble with it. Fiona sat on the edge of the couch, weeping into her hands. Mrs Brown rushed to her side, doing her best to comfort her by patting her knee.

"I will never forgive you for this, Mom," admonished Adam.

"You're making such a dreadful mistake," she wailed. "This girl will never be to our standard." She pointed across the room to me, reminding me that I was the enemy.

Adam shot her a look of sheer poison. "I don't like our standards."

Fiona let out a weird raspy sob. Mrs Brown put her arm around her, glared at Adam and spouted a few sentences in French. Adam replied in the same rough tone, using the same secret language. The whole situation was absurd, especially now that I'd lost track of the conversation. I just wanted the end to come quickly.

Fiona composed herself by taking in a deep breath, shrugged free of Mrs Brown and stood to face up to her son. I was almost grateful for the change in her demeanour. She was actually easier to handle when she was furious.

"If you choose to throw your entire life away on this girl, be my guest."

"What is it about her that you despise so much?" asked Adam. "It can't honestly be Charli's background. You've obviously forgotten that you started out as the product of a single mother, living in a council flat." He mimicked her English accent perfectly.

I heard a sharp gasp - then realised it had come from me. I had no idea that her class one pedigree had come via Jean-Luc. She'd been behaving like a lowly pound puppy because deep down, she *was* one - just like me.

"Look at what you've done," she yelled at me.

I frowned, unsure of what she was accusing me of.

"Don't even talk to her," warned Adam roughly.

"She will never fit in here," Fiona scoffed, stepping even closer to him. "The girl doesn't belong here."

I totally agreed with her - but it didn't seem like the right time to mention it. If someone had burst into the room at that very moment and offered me a ride to the airport, I would've jumped at the chance.

"If you knew anything, you'd realise how lucky you are to even know her," Adam ranted. "How sad it is that you've never given yourself that chance."

The queen looked far from regretful. She looked as if she was close to lynching the both of us. "*Jamais*," she hissed, unrepentant.

"Then you lose me too," he said sadly, already walking away from her. He reached for my hand as he passed and began leading me toward the door.

"If you walk out of this house, you will never be welcome here again, Adam!"

"I wasn't planning on coming back." He didn't even slow down.

As good as it felt to be on the winning side for once, I knew Adam was on the verge of permanently damaging something very important. I couldn't let him do it.

"Wait," I muttered, pulling my hand free of his as we got to the door. I turned back to face Fiona. "You're going about this all wrong," I told her. "It's like you're trying to do away with me by drinking the poison yourself. You're the only one who's getting hurt."

"Is that what you think?" she asked, circling the couch like a prowling lioness. "Stupid, obnoxious girl."

She sat back down and I felt safe enough to take a few steps back into the room. Adam stayed put near the doorway. "I think you know you're about to lose your son. And you love him as much as I do. And you loved him first. You shouldn't let him walk away."

Fiona looked away ostentatiously, saying nothing, incensing Adam all over again. "We're out of here, Charli," he said already halfway out of the room. "She's not listening."

"Please don't let him do this," I begged.

She glared at me as if I'd already stolen him away. "Go," she snarled.

She left me with no choice. I turned and walked away, feeling much less victorious than I thought I would.

***

Stepping out on the street felt like surfacing after a long stint under water. Breathing became a whole lot easier, but the exhaustion that comes after nearly drowning remained. Adam didn't seem to be faring much better.

"Are you okay?" I asked.

His grip on my hand tightened and he quickened his pace, forcing me to skip forward to keep up. "No. I'm not okay," he said roughly.

I yanked on his hand, pulling him to a stop. "Your mum will calm down, Adam." It was a stupid, unqualified statement to make. I had no idea how long the woman could hold a grudge.

"I couldn't care less, and nor should you." I was confused by his anger. "You should be thrilled things ended the way they did. Now you'll never have to deal with her again."

"You'll regret cutting her off. The way you're acting proves that you already do."

He shook his head, glaring at me. "I don't understand you at times. She behaved terribly and you just put up with it."

"I tried to tell you. You told me I was overreacting."

"Were you planning to just endure her wrath indefinitely, Charli?"

"No, Adam" I spat. "I was prepared to keep it up for two years."

He locked his eyes to mine, deliberating. "I really don't deserve you."

"I love you, you idiot! Whether you deserve me or not!"

He looked absolutely stunned. "You were right," he said finally. "The way you love me *is* unfair."

He walked away then, never once turning back to see if I was following. Boy Wonder left me standing alone on Fifth Avenue, feeling as though the whole sorry saga was somehow my fault.

My next move bordered on lunacy. I tried my hand at retail therapy. I slipped into the first boutique I came across, whipped out the evil black credit card and used it to buy a ridiculously expensive dress that I didn't even like.

It wasn't therapeutic at all. It wasn't better than sex and it wasn't better than chocolate. I found it to be self indulgent and boring, which brought me great hope. In my mind, it meant that Charli Blake hadn't been completely consumed by Charlotte Décarie and the stupid world she lived in.

***

Days passed without any mention of the queen. Adam went about life as if nothing out of the ordinary had happened. He studied as hard as he always did and loved me as much as he always had.

I didn't mention that I'd received a phone call from Jean-Luc's office demanding a meeting with me that morning. All things Décarie were seemingly taboo lately.

I was officially a fool. I sat in the reception area on level forty-three of the massive office building, shaking like a leaf. I was terrorising myself. No one forced me to jump every time the Décaries beckoned. For some reason I just did it.

Coming to my senses, I picked up my bag and made a quick dash toward the elevator, only to have the receptionist call out to me as I passed her desk.

"I can't wait any longer," I told her, unapologetically. I thumped the button on the elevator over and over as if that would somehow hurry it up. But it was futile. The doors opened and I stood face to face with the king.

I often wondered if Adam and Ryan saw their future when they looked at their dad. He was a strong mix of both of them, and just as handsome – probably even more so, if I was being honest. His hair was a little darker than Adam's, lightly flecked with grey at the temples. He shared Ryan's warm brown eyes and penchant for expensive suits. I didn't know him well enough to decide whether he was arrogant like Ryan or low-key like Adam.

"Dear Charli. How are you?" he asked, alternating glances between the compendium of papers in his hand and me.

I was about to reply but he walked straight past me, heading toward his office. Evidently, he was self-important like Ryan. "You're not going to stop walking long enough to hear my answer?" The brash question tumbled out of my mouth. I was too miffed to even bother trying to censor it.

Jean-Luc stopped dead in his tracks and turned to face me. "Of course. Forgive me," he said quietly. "Charli, how are you?"

"I'm a little upset actually," I said, continuing with my brutal run of honesty. "You asked me to meet you here at nine. It's almost half-past."

The receptionist must have thought this was compelling viewing because the incessant tapping of her long nails on her keyboard halted immediately. Jean-Luc smiled at me but I held my ground. I'd come too far to back down and apologise for my Décarie-strength arrogance. "I apologise for my tardiness." He spoke slowly, choosing his words very carefully. "If you don't have time to meet with me now, perhaps we could reschedule for another day."

"No. I'd like to get this over with now."

I didn't even know what *this* was but I knew it wouldn't be good. Fiona's recollection of the vicious run-in with her son would have been an Oscar-worthy performance. And all blame would have been lumped squarely on me.

A frown flashed across Jean-Luc's face but he recovered quickly, opening the door of his office and ushering me in ahead of him.

It was impossible not to be impressed. The large room was as big as our whole apartment. The floor to ceiling windows boasted a view almost as good as the one from the roof.

"Take a seat, please," he said motioning toward a big leather chair opposite his desk. "If you can draw yourself away from the view." He sat in his chair and pulled it closer to his desk. He picked up a pen and began writing something on the stack of papers he'd brought in with him. "I am constantly distracted by the window," he complained jokingly. "It's hard to get any work done in here."

I found it hard to believe anything distracted him. Even as we spoke, he was preoccupied with the work on his desk.

Ditching the scenery, I crossed the room and sat opposite him, immediately noticing an envelope on his desk that *almost* had my name on it.

Charlotte Blake-Décarie.

I wondered who'd decided to hyphenate my surname. I hadn't even made that call yet. "Is that for me?" I asked, pointing to it. "Is that what you summoned me here for?"

"Yes, it is," he confirmed, smiling the killer Décarie grin. My mind went in to overdrive, imagining what was in the envelope. Divorce papers, perhaps? Maybe he planned to dangle me by my ankles from his office window until I agreed to sign them. Or money. That seemed more like the Décarie style. He was about to try paying me off. I wondered how much he thought it would take to get me out of his son's life.

Being constantly on my guard was beginning to take its toll. I sank back in my chair and stared at the patriarch of the most evil family on earth. "I don't want it. I'm not taking it."

"Charli, I –"

"Please, please just stop this," I begged. "I love Adam. I came from the other side of the world to be with him. Surely that proves that my intentions are good."

Jean-Luc pushed his chair back slightly, putting more space between us. He didn't seem angered or offended by my outburst, just confused. "Who doubts your intentions?"

I groaned at his stupid play at obliviousness. "I'm so much smarter than you all give me credit for but I don't want to fight with you people anymore." The words hitched in my throat and I fought against crying. Even I was worried that I was having some kind of breakdown. I buried my face in my hands, wishing I'd stayed in bed that morning.

"Charlotte, what is wearing you down?" he asked gently.

Jean-Luc Décarie was a lawyer at the very top of his game. I was probably the easiest hostile witness he'd ever cross-examined. I was so beaten down, I would have told him anything he wanted to know.

I forced myself to lift my head and look at him. "I just want to love your son. I shouldn't have to fight his family for the right to do that."

"No, you shouldn't," he agreed. "My wife took it upon herself to draw some very unreasonable lines in the sand."

"Look, I realise I'm seriously flawed. I don't have the education or the upbringing you wanted Adam's wife to have. And I'm certain you didn't even want him to have a wife at twenty-two, but I love him. I can't even begin to tell you how much – "

"I understand that, Charlotte – "

"No, you don't." I shook my head, drumming my finger on his desk. "I've given up everything to be with him. I haven't seen the ocean in months… and I miss the ocean. I miss my father dreadfully. For the time being, I've given him up too. And yet as long as I have Adam, I'm still ahead."

Jean-Luc leaned back in his chair, resting his hands behind his head while he mulled over my rant. I didn't care whether I'd managed to change his opinion of me or not. At least I was putting up a good fight. "Would you like to know what's in the envelope?"

"You mean, would I like to know *how much* is in the envelope?"

He laughed loudly, in a way that reminded me of Adam. "Do you think I'm about to try paying you off? Oh, dear girl, your opinion of me is incredibly low."

"You haven't given me much to work with."

He smiled slowly. "I see what my sons see in you."

It bothered me that he referenced both sons, but I let it slide. "Please, just tell me what's in the envelope."

He picked it up and dropped it in front of me. I wasted no time, roughly tearing it open to access the letter inside. Jean-Luc explained it before I'd even got through reading it. "Your visa has been approved," he announced. "I pulled a few strings." Bizarrely, I began to sob as if I'd just found out I was being deported. "My son's happiness is paramount to me, Charli," he said, pulling a black silk handkerchief from his pocket and thrusting it at me. "My wife didn't handle the situation well, but her priorities are the same as mine." I nodded but said nothing, prompting him to continue. "I implore you to work this out."

"I'll try," I promised, eliciting another brilliant smile from him.

"Outstanding."

***

I'd been home for over an hour before Adam arrived. Too antsy to show any form of restraint, I hurled myself at him the second the door opened, flinging my arms around his neck and hitching my legs around his waist. He groaned, but the protest was weak. He responded to the ambush by kissing me, just as urgently as I'd thrown myself at him. By the time he'd walked us down to the end of the short hallway, we were in danger of never speaking again.

"Stop for a second," I breathed, giving no indication that that was what I really wanted him to do.

"Stop what?" he murmured, kicking the bedroom door open with his foot.

"Adam, please. It's important."

He surrendered by dropping me on the bed in a messy heap. I took a few seconds to try and steady my breathing. His tactics were a little different. He paced around the bedroom, ruffling his hands through his dark hair, trying to pull himself together. "What could be more important that this?"

I doubted I was in any fit state to answer him. I held the letter out to him.

Adam grabbed it and quickly read through before tossing it aside and lunging forward. I couldn't have escaped if I'd wanted to. And I definitely didn't want to.

"So, you're stuck with me," I told him, murmuring the words into his ear.

"It's a mutual predicament, Charlotte," he breathed.

33. Billet-doux

Adam wasn't exactly renowned for off-the-wall ideas. In fact, I imagine the one he came up with over breakfast the next morning was his very first. It involved a trip to the offices of Décarie, Fontaine and Associates, and a meeting with Ryan at Billet-doux.

We arrived at the restaurant just after three – ten minutes late, just to be annoying. Adam pounded on the door and Ryan eventually appeared to unlock it. "Nice of you to make it," he chided, stepping aside.

"Nice of you to fit us in," replied Adam, still sore that he'd made us book an appointment to see him.

I loved being at Billet-doux when it was empty. It was pretty and grand and always smelled like fresh flowers. Maybe that's why Ryan belonged there. He was pretty and grand too.

"What's this all about?" Ryan asked, pulling out a chair at the nearest table. "I get the feeling that it's going to be as ridiculous as always."

We followed his lead and sat. Adam's poker face was impressive, but something about my expression made Ryan nervous. "What did you do this time?" he asked, squinting at me with suspicion.

Adam answered for me. "She hasn't done anything. Her visa has been approved."

Ryan's expression relaxed a little, and he smiled. "I heard. Congratulations, Charlotte. I guess that'll make mother's attempts at getting you thrown out of the country a little trickier." Adam's glare had no effect. "Sorry, fairy pants," he said insincerely. "Too soon?"

Ignoring his comment, Adam forged ahead. "We've decided to make a few changes. I've got next to no time on my hands and Charli has plenty."

Pre-empting his next sentence, Ryan looked at me and groaned. "You want your job back."

Even from the corner of my eye, Adam's grin was blinding. "She doesn't need her job back. She now owns my half of Billet-doux."

Ryan nearly choked. I'd never seen him stunned into silence before, and I knew just how much fun rattling his cage could be.

Adam pushed a stack of paperwork across the table toward him. Ryan thumbed through them too quickly to have read any of them. "No, no, no," he protested. "I *like* working with you, Adam. You never come here. You don't argue. You're a *silent* partner. I *like* silence. Charli doesn't do silence." He pushed the papers back to Adam as if that was all it would take to make them go away.

Adam slid them straight back. "Charli will be good for this place. She has some great ideas."

He was lying. All I had was a couple of half-baked ideas and an urge to do something productive.

Obviously realising he wasn't making any headway with Adam, he turned his attention to me. "Look, Charli, sweetheart," he began, in his usual superior tone. "You're very pretty."

"What's that got to do with anything?" asked Adam gruffly.

"Let me finish." Ryan's eyes never left mine. "You're very pretty and you're very arty. But those attributes aren't applicable to the running of a successful restaurant. You need to broaden your horizons." For some strange reason, he started flapping his arms like he was trying to fly. "Find a glitter shop somewhere and make Adam buy it for you. Please, just tear up the papers and hand ownership back to your husband."

"No," I said simply.

Ryan dropped the calm demeanour instantly. "You and I are never going to work." The words raged out of him.

"Why not?" asked Adam, grinning like an idiot.

"Because I am not enamoured by her like you are. She's going to show up here and torment me on a daily basis."

"I'll make a deal with you, Ryan," I suggested.

He gestured wildly at the stack of papers. "You've made enough deals for one day, wouldn't you say?"

"Just hear her out," urged Adam. "Let's face it, you really don't have much choice."

Ryan slumped back, looking close to beaten. I seemed to have that effect on a lot of people lately.

"Billet-doux closes at two and opens again for dinner at six," I said, in my best businesslike voice.

"It does," he agreed wearily.

"Let me run service for those few hours, just for one day."

"And serve what? Fairy food?" He thought he was being witty but he was closer to the mark than he could ever have anticipated.

"Yes," I agreed, deadpan. "Fairy food."

"Oh my God." Ryan slapped his palm on his forehead. "You'll bury us in a week."

"Just give me a chance, Ryan. It's only four hours."

"I'm going to get this contract checked out," he said waving the papers at both of us.

"It's perfectly legal," explained Adam, shrugging his shoulders and grinning like a complete villain. "Dad drew up the paperwork. Face it brother, you have no choice but to let her in."

Ryan folded his arms across his chest, staring at me like I was his worst foe. "When do you plan to put this ridiculous plan into action?"

"Give me a week. All you have to do is show up here one week from today at two o'clock."

"I don't have a choice, do I?"

"None whatsoever," replied Adam, smugly.

***

It only took a day for me to come to the realisation that I might have bitten off more than I could chew. Ryan had demanded a silent partnership. I learned pretty quickly that it was a one-sided arrangement. He'd called me at least five times, wanting to know my plans for Billet-doux. I assured him that everything was under control and then hung up on him, like a true New Yorker. My bravado was a complete act. I had a potentially awesome plan but seemed to flounder when it came to putting it into action.

Desperation makes you do strange things, which is the only explanation I could come up with for ending up at the queen's door.

Mrs Brown looked positively alarmed when she saw me – so unnerved that I found myself promising that I wasn't up to mischief. "I just need to see Fiona for a minute."

"I would never turn you away, Charli," she told me, ushering me into the foyer and taking my coat. "But please…"

I finished her sentence as her voice trailed off. "Don't make eye contact and speak only in hushed tones?"

Mrs Brown brought her hand to her mouth to smother her giggle and showed me through to the lounge.

The queen kept me waiting an outlandishly long time. Finally she breezed in and pretended to be surprised to see me. "Charli. What are you doing here?"

"I need to ask a favour," I said, wincing like a coward.

Fiona sat down on the couch opposite me, looking calm enough for me to think I wasn't entirely wasting my time.

In a long monologue, I explained that I was planning a fairy themed high tea at Billet-doux. "My friend Ivy has been spreading the word. It's completely booked out. Thirty little amped-up fairies are going to show up at Billet-doux expecting cakes, finger sandwiches and tea."

"So what do you need from me?"

"Some help. I have to organise a menu and table decorations. Ryan will string me up by my feet if I can't pull it off," I said, sounding aptly terrified. "Fairy parties are generally classy and elegant affairs. I can't think of anyone better than you to help me with it."

"But why?"

I slapped both hands down on my knees, preparing to kill or be killed.

"Look, I know I'm not your favourite person but I have no hidden agenda. I just need the input of someone who actually knows what they're doing. That would be you."

Fiona didn't speak for a long time. But she didn't lunge across the coffee table and rip my throat out either so I patiently awaited her reply.

"When is this pixie soiree?" she asked finally.

"Friday."

"Oh, good grief, Charlotte," she moaned. "That's cutting it a little fine, don't you think?"

"Please, Fiona. I'll do anything," I clasped my hands together, pleading with her, "except give you back your youngest son. I won't do that."

She almost smiled. "Does Adam know you're here?"

"Not yet," I replied, shaking my head. "If it goes well, I might confess."

"And if it doesn't?"

"I'll do what I always do," I said flatly. "I'll lie to protect his feelings. I'll deny ever being here and let him think that I'm okay with the decision he made to cut you off."

"But you're not okay with it?"

"Of course not," I scoffed. "Historically, banishing the evil queen from your fairy tale never ends well."

There was a time when I would've regretted such an obtuse comment but it had long since passed. Sooner or later she was going to have to accept me for who I was. Thanks to my new visa status, I wasn't going anywhere. Perhaps she realised that. Instead of rebuking me, she saw the funny side. She almost smiled.

After keeping me hanging for an eternity, she finally agreed to help me, which freed me up to tell Adam the truth. He wasn't pleased to hear that I'd recruited the queen. He likened it to making a deal with the devil. I found myself defending her because I no longer thought of her as the devil. She was more like an angry mother bear trying to protect her cubs – from a mouse. Ryan, however, was the devil, which was the sole reason I couldn't afford to screw up the fairy tea.

"I need her help, Adam," I told him. "She was actually quite nice to me today."

He looked at me baffled, shaking his head. "Working in conjunction with my mother will not go well for you."

"There's no need for lawyer speak."

He chuckled darkly. "Fine. Hanging out with Mom will be impossible," he amended. "Like nailing Jell-O to a tree."

***

The days leading up to the high tea flew by in a blur of fairy cakes and pink macaroons. Fiona had managed to track down everything I wanted, giving me all the tools I needed to host a perfect event.

I had been summoned to the house early that morning to check the last item on the list, fairy-esque table linen. Fiona was kneeling on the floor amongst a stack of boxes when I arrived. She never looked cold and aloof anymore. Somewhere along the line she'd lost her severity, and managed to become a whole lot prettier in the process.

"Charli," she purred, abandoning the pile of cloth napkins in her lap as she stood up to greet me. "I was just going through the linens. I managed to get pink *and* mauve."

Another bad habit she'd let go of lately was the dumb air kissing. She'd become a hugger.

"That's great," I replied, enduring the awkward embrace.

I scanned the room, feeling a little creeped-out by the grand effort she'd gone to. The shift between us had been so swift that I wasn't entirely sure I could trust it. Something about my expression must have exposed me.

"I've enjoyed doing this with you," she insisted, speaking slowly. "I've never really had the opportunity to plan anything sparkly and pretty." She knelt back down on the floor and began rifling through a box. "It's a theme that never rated highly when my boys were small."

I sat near her and dragged the closest box toward me. "My dad endured years of it. Fairyology was practically my religion." I held off telling her that it still was. All of my good work in convincing her that I was sane would have disappeared in an instant.

She dragged a candy-pink tablecloth out of a box and fanned it across her lap. "I made my bridesmaids wear dresses this colour," she said irrelevantly. "Fashion back then left a lot to be desired." I smiled, giving her enough reassurance to continue her tale. "To make matters worse, I made Jean-Luc wear a powder grey suit, but it made no difference. He was still the most handsome man I'd ever laid eyes on."

I giggled. Jean-Luc was the most handsome man *I'd* ever laid eyes on.

"So it was love at first sight then?"

"It was tremendous." She grinned. "But not always easy. I had a terrible time trying to adjust in the early years."

For a second I considered picking up the nearest box and belting her with it. Her admission proved something I'd known to be true for a while: we were cut from the same average, working class cloth. If anyone should've been welcoming me with open arms and guiding me through my New York life, it should've been her.

"I can relate to that." It was the most diplomatic way I could think to say it.

"I acted abhorrently toward you," she conceded, fiddling with the edge of the cloth on her lap to avoid looking at me. "But you were tougher than I gave you credit for."

I shrugged, trying to shake the growing tension in my chest. "I don't feel like I even have a choice where Adam is concerned. I have no choice but to love him. That's why I'm here. That's the *only* reason I'm still here."

She smiled but still refused to look at me. "I have only ever wanted the very best for my sons. I wanted them to find nice girls with similar lives to their own."

I couldn't help grimacing. As far as I knew, there were no nice girls with lives similar to his. They were all spoiled, entitled bitches. "Like Whitney, you mean?"

She ignored me, continuing as if I hadn't spoken. "I knew Adam had put himself in an impossible quandary. He chose to fall in love with a girl who constantly rebels against the fabulous opportunity she's been gifted."

"All I ever wanted out of the deal was Adam," I told her, fighting to keep calm. "Anything beyond that is a curse."

Finally she looked at me. "Why can't you grasp the possibility of what's before you, Charli? I know it takes some getting used to. I came from nothing too."

I frowned, concentrating on not saying anything regretful. "I didn't come from nothing. I have always had plenty."

"But marrying my son guarantees you anything you could ever want."

Things suddenly became a whole lot clearer. Fiona saw marrying Jean-Luc as a windfall. Her initial aversion to me hadn't even been personal. Any girl who managed to crack the Décarie circle would have been considered a threat, especially if she'd arrived with empty pockets. Proving good intentions was impossible from the beginning. Adam's Jell-O analogy came to mind.

"Don't you see?" I asked, frustrated. "I love Adam in spite of that, not because of it."

She shook her head as confusion set in. "Most girls would be thrilled by it. He's the perfect package."

I almost felt sorry for her. She just wasn't getting it. "Money doesn't thrill me. The way he looks at me when he thinks I'm not watching thrills me. And as for being the perfect package, Adam is definitely not perfect." She sucked in a sharp breath, outraged because I'd dared to find fault in one of her flawless boys. I elaborated quickly before she had a chance to speak. "He is not perfect, Fiona. He's very selfish with his time. He can be horribly impatient and sometimes he drives me nuts. But I love him. That's it."

"You're a very fortunate girl then," she mumbled.

"Can I ask you something?" I busied myself folding napkins to dull the chagrin in case she said no.

"Of course."

"What did you bring to the table when you got married?"

Her pretty face crumpled as bewilderment set in. "I don't understand your question."

"Well, if handsome Jean-Luc was prince charming because he brought you wealth and good standing, what was in it for him?" I asked. "You're adamant that you had nothing."

Fiona deliberated for a long time, absently picking at a loose thread on the tablecloth in her hands. "I have no idea."

"Perhaps you should ask him," I suggested. "He might surprise you. There was a reason he chose you."

She laughed lightly, taking no offense. "I might do that. Do you know why Adam chose you?"

"I have a few ideas," I hinted, unwilling to introduce her to merits of hanging out in La La land.

The conversation was a welcome change. I had no idea if the shift between us was permanent, but anything that made life easier was worth the chance.

***

With help from Fiona, encouragement from Adam and an overwhelming desire to prove Ryan wrong, I managed to pull Billet-doux's inaugural fairy high tea together. It was a completely full house thanks to Ivy and her pageant posse. Every little princess in the city was now sitting at impeccably decorated fairy tables at Billet-doux. The little girls feasted on every fairy delicacy imaginable for two solid hours, racking up Ryan's profits to stellar levels.

"I'm very impressed, Tink," he whispered, sidling up beside me as I watched over the crowded front of house from the podium.

"Me too." I grinned. "It's going great."

Obviously he hadn't seen Fabergé wipe her chocolate coated hands along the white upholstered chair she was sitting on – or the little girl who threw up in the potted Ficus tree near the door.

"The bar sales alone make it worthwhile."

I studied the room a bit closer. Every woman there seemed to have a glass in her hand. Maybe alcohol is a necessary evil when you're the parent of a wannabe fairy. By rights, Alex should've been a drunk.

Adam's manic schedule meant he couldn't be there to see how things turned out. Being disappointed about it was fruitless. I was almost used to it.

Bente made a five-minute cameo but ducked out before the sugar hit could affect the already buzzing fairies. Her quick exit might also have had something to do with Ryan's less than contrite attitude toward her. She didn't have to mention how crushing it was that he acted as if nothing had happened between them. It was painfully obvious. The only one who didn't get it was him.

"Do you know if your mother is coming?" I asked, trying to sound casual.

"She's been and gone. She told me to tell you that it all looked amazing and she'd see you later." I was shocked by her humility. If there was a moment that she deserved to be basking in her brilliance that would've been it. "What is it with you two lately?" he asked. "One minute you're mortal enemies and the next you're bonding over sparkles."

I looked at him from the corner of my eye, smirking. "That's exactly what happened. We share a mutual love of sparkles and your brother."

The real answer was actually much more complex. Spending time together meant getting to know each other. Once she finally figured out that I wanted nothing other than Adam, she stopped trying to bury the hatchet in my back.

"Well, whatever the reason, I think it was a smart move."

"I couldn't have pulled this off without her," I admitted.

"Don't sell yourself short."

"You did," I accused.

"A little bit," he conceded, pinching his thumb and forefinger together.

"Say you're sorry, then."

Ryan cleared his throat. "I'm not sorry," he maintained, nudging me in the side. "But I did underestimate you."

"Don't worry about it. I get that a lot."

"Are you sure you want to do this full time, Charli?"

My reply came quickly. "Absolutely not." Ryan laughed darkly as if he'd known it all along. "But I could do it once in a while."

"How do you think Adam will take that news?"

"What does it have to do with Adam?"

"Well, this whole debacle of signing Billet-doux over to you was designed to occupy you. Obviously it failed."

"That wasn't kind."

"I'm just calling it like I see it, Fairy Pants. It's painful to watch." I turned and stared at him for a long time, trying to work out his motive for being so nasty. "You're his most prized possession, his caged little bird. I wonder if he's worked out that he's losing you."

I felt a flutter of panic as I considered the possibility that he was seeing something I'd missed. I knew I wasn't the most content I'd ever been, but I was hanging in there.

"I'm right here. And I'm going to see it through because I love him, which is something you weren't brave enough to do."

A confused frown swept his forehead while he tried to figure out what I was talking about. He got there quickly. "You're talking about Bente?" I nodded. "You just don't get it. Why do you think I let her go?"

"Because you're an idiot."

He shook his head. "How could Bente and I ever work out, Charli? She'd be just as miserable in my world as you are in Adam's. I couldn't do it to her. I wish my brother had shown you the same consideration."

"Why are you being so awful?"

"Like I said, I'm calling it as I see it."

I didn't like the way he was seeing it. There was far more in play than Ryan's disgruntlement at having to share Billet-doux with me, and I was in no mood to deal with it.

34. Peace

I hadn't expected New York summers to be so glorious. Sunny July days made for fantastic beach weather, which was ironic considering I was stuck in Manhattan.

Adam was busier than ever, succeeding in his quest to become the most diligent law student to ever hit Columbia University, which left me in the unenviable position of trying to kill time without injuring my happy ever after. In order to do that, I'd had to tweak my attitude.

Calling a truce with the purple circle was a necessary evil. Occasionally dealing with them wasn't too toxic to my soul. It usually just resulted in fake niceties, false smiles and an overwhelming urge to shower afterwards.

Apparently, the best way to prove that I was with Adam for the long haul was to actually stick around for the long haul. Six months into my New York life, Parker realised it. Even Kinsey eventually realised it. The only one still holding out for my demise was Whitney, who retained the opinion that I was nothing more than a home-wrecking whore. Other than electric shock therapy or filing for divorce, nothing was going to change her mind. I'd long since given up the fight.

Seraphina and I had become unlikely friends. We had next to nothing in common, but she was great company and nowhere near as dreary as the rest of her purple circle teammates. I was surprised to learn that she had a creative streak. She was a student at an elite design school, a gig as prestigious as any Ivy League college.

I had to admit defeat when it came to appreciating her talent, though. I tried to appear enthusiastic as we sat in a coffee shop, poring over her latest portfolio of designs. But to me, yellow denim and pink tulle didn't seem like such a great combination.

"These are great," I lied encouragingly.

"They'll look better in the flesh," she replied, snapping the folder shut. "I'm going to find some girls to model them and have my very first photo shoot."

"Well, that's exciting."

"I was hoping you'd see it that way," she replied, shifting agitatedly in her seat. "I was hoping you'd shoot it for me."

"Who are you going to get to model for you?"

A lot depended on her answer. I had vast experience when it came to photographing amateur pageant princesses, a task Ivy still called on me to do on a regular basis. But I'd never photographed anyone experienced enough to recognise that *I* was a complete amateur.

She shrugged her shoulders. "Probably Whitney and Kinsey."

"I would *love* to shoot Whitney and Kinsey."

"Great," she enthused, ignoring the double entendre. "I'll let you know when I'm ready."

I had no qualms about helping Sera out, especially if it involved taking pictures. Photography was the one thing that had kept me sane and grounded over the months. My portfolio had become so huge that I found myself changing the pictures on the walls at Billet-doux every few days. Some sold and some made their way into the back storeroom, which had now become too crowded to walk around in.

Other than occasional fairy high teas, decorating the walls with pictures was practically my only contribution to Billet-doux, which pleased Ryan no end. I played by the rules and attended every meeting he summoned me to, which usually consisted of him pretending to ask for my input or threatening to send my pictures to the bottom of the Hudson if I didn't clear out the storeroom.

I'd given up trying to rebel against the life I'd stumbled into. I just took solace in the fact that it was temporary. I didn't hate living in Manhattan, but as the months slipped by the prospect of leaving was something I began to look forward to more each day.

***

No matter how hectic Adam's schedule was, Sundays were always reserved for the two of us. We usually headed out for a late breakfast and took the rest of the day as it came. That particular morning, we ended up at a café in Central Park, sitting at an outside table eating chocolate croissants. The sun was warm but the smile on the face of the boy sitting opposite me was warmer.

"Why are you looking at me like that?" I asked, a little unnerved.

"I can't help it. You're incredibly beautiful."

"Had you forgotten?" I teased. "It's been a while since you've seen me."

Adam saw through the lightly veiled dig. His grip on my hand tightened as he brought my fingers to his lips. "I'm doing my best, Charli," he defended. "School is crazy right now, the workload is huge."

"I know," I mumbled, feeling a little guilty for even mentioning it. "But I miss you when you're not around." Sometimes I missed him even when he was around. Quiet nights in that were sabotaged by hours of extra studying made it feel like we were both working toward a law degree.

A long walk always remedied the sins of spending too much time apart during the week and eating croissants for breakfast. Plenty of people milled around, enjoying their lazy Sunday morning. Occasionally we'd step to the side to make room for joggers or people walking faster than us, but it still didn't seem crowded. Central Park was one of the few places in New York that never felt congested to me. The winding paths, trees and rolling lawns had been my saviours more than once.

Adam favoured the walking route to the Conservatory Water over all others. The pull for him was the model sailing boats that were in abundance when the weather was fine. That day was no different. His attention drifted to an impressive yacht being manoeuvred around the lake by a small boy. The boy's father constantly tried giving him instruction, but short of wrestling it away, he had no chance of getting hold of the remote control.

"The sails aren't rigged properly," whispered Adam from the corner of his mouth. "It could go much faster."

I looked at the father trying to win the war against his boy – who giggled maniacally like an evil professor every time he lurched for the controls. "I don't think either of them are worried about the lack of speed," I joked, whispering the words into the sleeve of his shirt.

"She is beautiful, though, right?" he asked, gawking at the model sloop as if she were some long lost lover.

I took a closer look at the little blue boat bobbing on the lake. "It looks like *La Coccinelle,*" I said.

"She does," he agreed, glancing at me as he smiled.

I suddenly felt a little ache for home. Memories of Adam working on the rundown old boat he had lovingly restored in Gabrielle's shed flooded my head. It reminded me of how much had changed since then… and how much had stayed the same. I was a little older, a fraction wiser and still madly in love with the boy with the cerulean eyes.

"Adam, when we leave here, where will we go?"

He slipped his arm around my waist and pulled me closer, making my forward stride reminiscent of a drunk being accompanied home.

"I don't know," he replied, sounding totally uninterested. "I thought you'd have it all figured out."

"We could go home for a while, to the Cove." It was the very first time I'd mentioned going back to Australia. It might have been the first time I'd even thought about it.

"Of all the places I thought you'd want to go, I wasn't expecting it to be there."

"Do you hate the idea?"

Tightening his hold, he pulled me in impossibly closer. "I don't hate any of your ideas."

Sometimes I wondered if ambiguity was a skill taught at Columbia. If so, he was undoubtedly head of the class. Talking about our plans beyond the end of law school wasn't one of Adam's favourite topics, and he avoided it like a pro.

He was slightly tormented by the fact that I hadn't found my niche in New York. It no longer bothered me. Once broken down, the reason why was a simple one: I just didn't belong. And Adam hated being reminded of it. And making plans beyond life in New York was the biggest reminder of all.

I stopped walking, forcing him to a stop. "Eventually we're going to have to talk about this."

"For now, I'd rather you just find your place here and settle in," he replied, either missing or ignoring my ire. "Life happens while you're making other plans."

"You're seriously going to rip off John Lennon quotes to lecture me?"

He replied slowly, trying to mask his amusement. "No, Charlotte. I'm merely suggesting that you do what you used to do best and live in the moment."

I pulled free and began walking away. I should've known he wouldn't follow. Adam never followed. When it came to enduring my hissy fits, he was the master. In order to continue the conversation, I had to stop and turn back. "Do you want to know what else John Lennon said?" I asked, stamping back toward him.

"Well, he was the one who urged us all to give peace a chance." He flashed me a lazy half-dimpled smile, which was his most crippling form of warfare. "Maybe you should give it a try."

"You're an idiot," I accused. "Which is ironic, because he also said that behind every idiot is a great woman. That would be me."

He reached out to me the second my rant was over, kissed the corner of my mouth and dipped me so far backward my hair brushed the ground. "I've always known that to be true."

"Good," I huffed, clinging to him. "As long as you know."

He swiftly righted me. "I'm not a complete idiot."

It was an almost-argument we'd had a hundred times before, and the outcome was never any different. I was left making plans in my own head, biding my time until I'd mention it again.

***

Adam had been right about one thing. My modus operandi of living in the moment had waned over time. I put it down to a lack of inspiration, but the quirk wasn't entirely lost. Somehow I'd managed to transfer a little of my craziness to my mother-in-law.

Spending time with the queen once she'd given up the quest to oust me from her kingdom was harder than avoiding her when she hated me. To preserve my sanity, I made sure our bonding sessions were structured events. Keeping her away from ritzy boutiques and introducing her to markets and vintage thrift shops brought out a whole new side of her. When I could get Fiona out of her Manhattan headspace, she could be an extraordinarily interesting person, especially when talking about her pre Jean-Luc life.

She'd once told me that her first job was as an usherette at a cinema. "They used to issue us with gorgeous black silk stockings as part of the uniform. They were much better quality than I could have afforded. I literally worked for stockings," she remembered. She giggled then, totally unabashed by the revelation.

I loved how far we'd come. Not everyone welcomed the change, though. Ryan was constantly accusing me of bringing out the worst in her, especially on days when she'd decide to return to her roots and introduce her family to pieces of her heritage. That day's lesson in tradition came via her decision to singlehandedly cook Ryan's birthday dinner. Both of her sons had been dreading it since she first mentioned it. Now that they were sitting in her lounge room, minutes away from actually eating her home cooked meal, they looked positively terrified.

I'd grown up eating abominable meals cooked by Alex. She'd have to be a truly terrible chef to top his efforts. "I'm sure it won't be that bad," I insisted, unsure of which brother needed the most reassuring.

"The woman hasn't cooked a meal in twenty years," said Ryan bleakly. "There's a reason why."

"You're both being babies."

Adam shook his head. "He's not exaggerating, Charli."

Ryan interjected. "I didn't even bring a date. I couldn't think of anyone I disliked enough."

The glass doors began to slide open and I shushed them, fearing it was their mother. Jean-Luc skulked into the room, completing the trio of sullen, frightened men. Grandma Nellie shuffled in behind him carrying the cutest little brown dog I'd ever seen.

"Has your mother come to her senses yet?" Nellie asked, directing her question at her grandsons.

They both answered in unison. "No."

She lowered the pup to the floor and he scurried up onto the couch and sat beside me.

"I didn't know you had a dog, Nellie," I said, patting the furry mutt.

"I don't, dear," she replied. "I borrowed him."

I frowned, confused. Ryan started laughing, which set his father off. Adam shook his head, showing no sign of catching the joke I'd missed.

"His name is Chester," explained Nellie. "My neighbour Bruce said he likes scraps. I imagine there will be a lot of scraps tonight."

I thought they were all being most unfair, but even I couldn't help giggling when they all erupted. The only thing that killed the humour was Fiona walking into the room. "Darlings," she crooned, walking toward us all with her arms outstretched. I stood up first.

She hugged me much too tightly, made an insincere comment about my hair looking pretty and turned her attention to Ryan, who stood up and hugged her as if he had no choice. "Happy birthday, son."

"Thank you Mom," he replied. "Dinner smells wonderful."

He was clearly lying. I could smell something rather acrid, reminding me of the time Mitchell set fire to the handle of a frying pan.

"It's roast beef," she said proudly. "Cooked entirely by my own fair hand."

"Great," he replied, drawing out the word.

In what looked like an attempt to rescue his brother, Adam stood and approached her. "I'm sure it will be amazing," he said, leaning down to kiss her.

"Thank you darling," she purred, pinching his cheek. "You're such a good boy."

"Why is he the good one?" complained Ryan. "I said it smelled wonderful. All you got out of him was a half-hearted amazing."

Nellie's chortle had a strange effect on Chester. He let out a gravelly little bark which made Fiona jump. "What on earth is that?" she asked, horrified by the little brown fur ball that had set up home on her couch.

"Moral support," replied Adam, setting off the laughter again.

***

Chester's talents as a garbage disposal were almost wasted. The Décarie men managed to down most of their meal without too much of a performance. Nellie flat-out refused to eat what she didn't like and settled for an endless glass of whiskey and a few roasted potatoes before calling it quits and going home. I wondered how upset her neighbour Bruce was going to be when he found out she'd forgotten to take Chester with her.

I thought it was the best meal I'd had since I'd left home. The stodgy, hearty roast dinner threw me right back to my childhood when I'd gatecrashed family dinners at my best friend Nicole's house. It left me feeling a little nostalgic and wishing I'd worn looser fitting clothes. The queen wasn't a bad cook. She was a homely English cook whose talents were entirely wasted on her too French American family.

"We have dessert," announced Fiona, standing up. "I made that too."

Adam let out a low groan and I ground my foot on top of his. Everyone else sitting at the table looked as unimpressed as he sounded.

Chester and I were the only ones looking forward to dessert. Adam didn't have a sweet tooth. A man who hates chocolate is no authority when it comes to judging desserts. I was practically an expert, which is why disappointment pinned me to my chair the minute Fiona re-entered the room with Ryan's homemade birthday cake.

It was so lopsided that everyone tilted their heads to look at it. Worse than that, it was covered in a thick, lumpy layer of marzipan icing. I detest marzipan.

"Not stomping on my foot now are you, Coccinelle?" whispered Adam. I shook my head but said nothing.

"It's a pound cake with almond icing," announced Fiona. She drove a candle into the top of the cake, which seemed to require the same effort as hammering a nail into concrete.

"Fabulous, my darling," praised Jean-Luc in a convincing tone that only an attorney could accomplish. I secretly hoped the whole cake would combust when she lit the candle. Ryan didn't exactly jump to his feet to blow it out. I imagine he was hoping for the same thing.

"*Faites un désir*!" Fiona said urgently.

I leaned across to whisper to Adam. "Did she just tell him not to eat it because it's poisonous?"

"No. She told him to make a wish."

"Oh, that's too bad."

I was surprised to see Ryan's thoughtful expression when he stood up. He was actually debating how to spend his wish.

"Don't over-think it, Ryan. Just believe it. *À cœur vaillant rien d'impossible*," I told him. Every person at the table glared at me as if I'd just cursed them. Fearing I'd botched the pronunciation, I translated quickly. "Nothing is impossible for a willing heart."

"Charli! You've been holding out on us," Fiona accused, beaming. "We thought you didn't speak French."

I shook my head, feeling embarrassment burn my cheeks. "I don't."

Adam gave my hand a secret squeeze under the table. "She only knows the important words."

"Make your wish, Ryan," I mumbled, chagrined by my big mouth.

"I did. But the cake is still here."

Adam laughed. The only thing that saved him from the queen's wrath was the fact that everyone else cackled too.

"You will eat it. And you will enjoy it," she commanded, waving a knife at us, instantly proving why she was the queen.

The evening didn't last much past dessert. There was a fair chance that everyone was feeling as ill as I was. Once I could feel the sticky lump of cake I'd hidden in my napkin and stuffed in my pocket seeping onto my leg, I knew it was time to get out of there. Adam suggested that we escort Chester back to Nellie's apartment. No one protested, least of all Chester, who seemed grateful to get into the cool night air.

"He suits you, Charlotte," teased Adam. I stopped for the umpteenth time so Chester could sniff at an invisible spot on the pavement. "Maybe we should get a dog."

"We have enough trouble looking after ourselves, don't you think?"

"I think we'd do fine. We should definitely get a dog."

"Adam, no dog," I said seriously. The last thing I wanted was to lay down roots. Getting attached to a dog that we weren't going to be able to take with us when we left was a dumb idea.

He draped his arm around my shoulder and we began walking again, giving Chester no choice but to follow or be choked. "Alright, no dog."

"Promise me," I demanded, tugging on the side of his shirt. "No surprise puppies."

Adam laughed blackly. "Okay, Charli. No puppies."

35. Proof

Dim Whit and Kinsey obviously didn't need much time to mull over Seraphina's offer of modelling for her. She called me just a few days after first mentioning it to let me know they'd accepted.

"Great," I told her. "Just work out the details and get back to me."

I abruptly ended the call, something I was getting quite good at. Ryan taught me the skill, but it was Adam who had mastered the art. He could do it without coming across as a total jerk. Ryan couldn't order coffee without sounding like a jerk.

Some New York perks were awesome, like fresh baked pretzels, cannoli and cutting boring phone calls short. Others took some getting used to. I didn't consider acquiring the ability to run in high heels particularly awesome, but somewhere along the line I'd learned how to do it. The fact that I actually owned a dozen pair of heels to run in crushed the bohemianism right out of me.

It was a frightening transition to make. Every single day, at least once, I'd try to send Charlotte Décarie and her Louboutin heels packing and bring Charli Blake to the forefront. My plans for that day included Adam, but I knew it would be a hard sell. Convincing him to ditch classes and hang out with me was a feat I'd never once accomplished.

I cornered him in the kitchen while he was going through his morning routine of packing his bag. "Adam, I have a proposition for you," I began, trying to pique his curiosity.

He glanced at me but didn't stop shoving books into his bag. "Charlotte, I'm listening."

"I have a fairy high tea today. I think you should come."

Adam had never seen a fairy tea in action. In fact, I couldn't think of a single time that he'd been to Billet-doux in the six months since he'd signed it over to me.

"I don't think I can make it." He didn't even sound regretful.

"What if I told you I absolutely needed you there? Life or death, needed you there?"

He clipped his bag shut and looked straight at me, deliberating for a few seconds before answering. "A life or death fairy emergency?"

I replied in a deadly seriously tone. "Exactly."

He took the few steps needed to reach me, took my face in his hands and softly kissed my lips. "Okay, I'll come."

His hold on my face didn't waver as I leaned back to look at him.

"Promise?"

"I promise." The smile that ghosted across his face was only half believable. "I should be there by three."

I nodded and his hands moved with me. "Don't let me down." He smiled more sincerely and leaned forward to kiss me again. That was as close to a guarantee as I was going to get. He was out the door five minutes later and I was left with a terrible sinking feeling his promise was already as good as broken.

***

Summer had brought on a whole new wave of fairy toddlers with mothers who were looking for any excuse to down champagne at two in the afternoon. I still loved seeing Billet-doux all gussied up like a fairy den, but it was an exhausting process. I always staggered home at the end of the day feeling like I'd spent the afternoon hanging out at a childcare centre.

That day was no different, and my exhaustion was compounded by the fact that Boy Wonder blew off our three o'clock rendezvous. I wasn't surprised, so I shouldn't have been upset about it, but walking into the empty apartment highlighted the fact that I seemed to be coming a distant second to everything else he had going on.

I didn't hear Adam eventually walk in. I was in the shower scrubbing the glitter out of my hair, thanks to an overzealous four year-old who'd whacked me over the head with her wand while casting a spell.

He slunk into the bathroom. The foggy shower screen did nothing to diminish his guilty expression. "I know you're probably furious with me right now," he began. "But I have a good reason for missing the high tea."

"I'm not sure I want to hear it." His excuses were usually perfectly legitimate and study related. And somehow, they always left me feeling as if I was being punished.

"I'm not going to explain it to you," he told me. The fogged-up screen didn't hide his bright smile either. "If you give me a chance, I'll show it to you."

"Please tell me it's not a puppy," I pleaded. "I said no dog."

His laugh echoed around the bathroom. "It's not a puppy. I promised I wouldn't get a puppy."

I turned off the taps and stepped out of the shower. He handed me a towel, but in a childish move, I dragged my own towel off the rail and left him hanging.

"You also promised you'd show up today," I reminded him, wrapping myself in the towel. A sheepish grin swept his perfect face and I felt compelled to chastise him for it. "That sexy little smile thing you have going on isn't always going to work for you, Adam."

He grabbed a fistful of my towel and pulled me in close. "Is it working now?"

"Sadly, yes," I conceded, linking my arms around his neck.

***

As hard as I tried to appear indifferent, I was intrigued by whatever it was that he had planned. It was obviously going to be an overnight jaunt. He'd packed a bag while I was getting dressed.

"What kind of hotel makes you bring your own pillows?" I asked, watching him stuff our pillows into the now bulging bag.

"I never said we were going to a hotel."

I raised my eyebrows. "Are we hanging out in La La land tonight, Adam?"

He kissed my forehead. "You'll have to wait and see."

It had been a long time since we'd had some quality time alone together.

Both our phones were intentionally left on the kitchen bench, which was another reason to be feeling blissful. I was back in the Adam-and-Charli headspace – right until he ordered the cab we were in to stop outside his parents' building.

"We're going to your parents'?" I asked, crushed.

"Technically, I suppose," he replied vaguely, thrusting some money at the driver.

I slid out of the cab and thanked the driver, because Adam didn't. He took my hand and kept a tight grip as we walked into the foyer.

"I'm sure your mum has pillows, Adam," I grumbled, dragging my feet as he led us to the elevator.

"We're not going there, Charlotte. We're going to the roof."

"Why? What's up there?"

"Proof."

"Proof of what?"

He smiled so brilliantly that I folded my arms to stop myself reaching out to grab him. "If you could be anywhere right now, where would you be?"

I barely had to think about it. "On a board, paddling so far out to sea that I can't see the shore anymore, just to prove that I can still do it."

"So if we were generalising, you'd be at the beach?"

I shook my head. "Not just any beach, a rough beach with thundering waves. A winter beach."

The elevator doors opened and we stepped out into a small foyer that I'd never been in before. I had no idea what was on the roof level of the Décarie building, but I imagined it had undergone some changes that afternoon.

"Where are you taking me, Adam?"

"I'm taking you home," he said, quietly. "If only for one night."

My heart began to hammer as I considered what might be behind the heavy steel door leading out to the roof. "What will it prove?"

He hitched the heavy bag he was carrying higher onto his shoulder and took my face in his free hand.

"It will prove to you that I know you. Even on the days when you've forgotten who you are." I felt hot tears prick my eyes. His thumb brushed the first tear away as it rolled down my cheek. "I've been busy lately, Charli, but not oblivious."

I'd never once told him about the Charli versus Charlotte battle that raged within me. Knowing that he was aware of it brought utter relief. I just needed to figure out which version of me he preferred.

Adam took a key from his pocket and unlocked the door. It took a hard shove from him to open it, but the effort was instantly worth it. It was nothing like the roof of Jean-Luc's office building. It looked like any other well-maintained patio garden with big potted plants, a few chairs and a big daybed. The difference was that this garden was fifteen stories above street level.

Looking out of place and swamped by the urban setting was a little dome tent, a staged scene that I was familiar with. Adam was a stickler for details. It was a trait inherited from his mother. When teamed with the need for perfection that he'd inherited from his father, it became a dangerous combination. It was as if he'd packed up every prop from the night we'd spent camping in Gabrielle's backyard in Pipers Cove more than two years ago and dropped it on the Manhattan rooftop.

I walked over to the little tent. "How did you manage this?"

He joined two extension cords together, making the string of Christmas lights flash to life. "Well, Mrs Brown shares the same fondness for trashy Christmas decorations as Gabi," he said, smiling as I looked back at him. "She lent them to me."

"Is there a slide show tonight?" I asked, glancing around for a screen.

"Not tonight. I think I've managed something even better."

"Really?" I asked gleefully. "What is it?"

He walked past the tent to the far corner of the roof. "Come and see for yourself," he coaxed, waving me over.

I had no idea what he was hiding underneath the blue tarp. Thankfully, it was far too big and still to be a puppy.

Adam ripped the tarp away.

I took one look at the inflatable pool and began to laugh and cry at the same time.

"I know it's not quite as good as the ocean, but considering we don't even have a bath at home, I figured you'd be impressed."

I threw my arms around his neck and stretched as high as I could to kiss him. Connecting just under his ear was the best I could do. "You have no idea," I mumbled between tears and frantic kisses.

My feet left the ground as he walked us back toward the tent. "I have one more surprise," he announced, lowering me enough that I was standing on my own two feet again. "We have the tent and the ocean, but we still have the Manhattan traffic."

I hadn't heard it until he mentioned it. The sound of cars and the occasional siren in the distance wasn't exactly raining on my Pipers Cove parade. He pointed to four small black boxes set up around the perimeter of our campsite, half way between the tent and the edge of the rooftop.

"What are they?" I asked.

He walked to one of the boxes. The low light made it impossible to see what he was doing but a second later the unmistakable sound of the ocean drowned out the dull traffic noise coming from the street below us. "They're speakers. I had Gabrielle record a few hours of the waves below her cottage."

The lump in my throat was impossible to swallow away. It was perfect. I didn't need to see the ocean. Just the sound of it thundered through to my very core.

My voice sounded strange as I tried to speak. "This is exactly why you're mine."

The darkness did nothing to dull the intensity of his bright eyes. He ambled toward me and as soon as I was within reach, took me in his arms. "What happens now?" he breathed.

I took his face in my hands, inching his head back so I could see him properly.

"We go swimming."

His face fell forward and he breathed out a long sigh into my shoulder. It wasn't the gesture of an irate man. It was a scheming manoeuvre. His hands slipped around me, expertly unzipping my dress. He slipped the thin straps off my shoulders and I shimmied out of it. Something about the manoeuvre practically liquefied his cerulean eyes.

Letting out an appreciative low groan, Adam snaked his arm around my waist and drew me in close, whispering in my ear. "And this is a prime example of why you're mine."

***

The comfortable July weather was a world away from our first campout. It made slipping into the cool water absolutely heavenly. It wasn't much deeper than a bathtub, but when I lay down and closed my eyes I could almost make believe I was somewhere else. The wandering hands of the boy beside me ensured that wherever the place I was dreaming of was, he was with me. An immeasurable amount of time passed before I even contemplated getting out of the water.

"Your fingers are shrivelling," said Adam putting his palm against mine. "We need to get you out before you wither away."

"Like an Asrai fairy."

Changing his grip, he fettered my wrist with his hand and pulled my body against his. "I am dying to know about Asrai fairies, Charlotte," he whispered, far too dramatically to be believable.

"Well, your mother would be thrilled to know that they are English, and extraordinarily beautiful," I began. "They live in really deep water and only surface once every hundred years or so to gaze at the moon. But they're fragile little beings. If they're captured or exposed to sunlight, they fade into a pool of water."

"Why would anyone want to capture them?" asked Adam, setting my insides on fire by murmuring the words against my shoulder.

"Because they're so beautiful that any man who sees one instantly wants to capture her."

"There's not much point if she turns into a puddle a few seconds later," he teased.

"That's not the worst of it," I said bleakly. "The Asrai doesn't go quietly. She leaves her mark. They say any man who touches one develops a nasty cold spot on his skin that can never again be warmed to match the rest of his body."

He leaned back, gazing at me. "Thank God you're not an Asrai."

"I know, right? I would've been liquefied years ago," I said, sweeping the water off the side of his face with the back of my hand.

"And I would have frozen to death."

I pressed my naked body up against his, raising the water temperature to boiling point. "I would've made it worth your while."

Adam stared at me with an intensity that I hadn't felt in a long time. "You're so beautiful. I love your stories."

I grinned impishly. "You study law, I study lore. No big deal."

"Can we get out of here now, please?" he asked, planting a lingering kiss on my chest.

"Are you cold?"

"No Charli." His voice was low. "I just want to get you into the tent and have my way with you."

***

Our little rooftop hotel was supposed to offer a late checkout, but I was woken early by the sound of the steel door opening and muffled voices.

"Who is that?" I asked, shaking Adam awake.

"Oh, great," he groaned, suddenly alert. "It's the old man from downstairs. I can't believe he still does his Tai Chi classes up here, especially considering he has eight hundred acres of parkland across the street."

Adam sat up and lurched for the zip on the door, taking the blanket with him. "Good morning Mr Locke," he called, lowering the zip just low enough to poke his head out.

I strained to hear the reply. "Young man, you are well aware of the rules pertaining to playing on the roof."

Playing on the roof? That was a weird way of putting it.

"Yes sir," replied Adam, super politely.

"You boys know better than to impede on our Tai Chi group. It's been a longstanding arrangement for many years."

"Yes sir," he repeated. "I guess I assumed the rules might have relaxed over time."

"Do you play up here often, Adam?" I whispered, giggling.

He ducked his head back in the tent. "We used to play up here all the time as kids. He's talking like it was yesterday."

"Is your brother in there with you?" asked Mr Locke, making me laugh louder.

Adam shushed me and poked his head back out of the tent. "My brother is twenty-five years old now, Mr Locke. He hasn't been up here in a while."

It was definitely time to leave, but getting off the roof wasn't going to be painless. Even the most liberal-minded Tai Chi student was probably going to have a problem with us walking around butt naked to collect our clothes from the other side of the roof.

"I've sent for your mother," warned Mr Locke in a voice best suited to chiding a ten year-old.

"Oh no, not my mother," replied Adam slowly, turning back to wink at me. We were about to find ourselves in a very awkward situation, but I found something about the whole ordeal hilarious. Adam did too. He zipped up the tent and fell back down beside me, laughing like a demon.

"So, what do we do now?" I asked, in between maniacal giggles of my own. He fanned the blanket across both of us and answered my question by tracing a long line up my thigh with his fingertips.

As tempting as his silent proposition was, I heard the steel door open again and knew we were out of time. I brushed his hand away and pointed toward the door of the tent.

"Adam," hissed Fiona, too annoyed to whisper discreetly.

I was relieved I couldn't see her through the thin wall of the tent. I was even more relieved that she couldn't see us.

"Ma, can you please pick up our clothes? They're over near the pool."

"Oh, good grief," she muttered. "You brought a pool up here."

I watched her shadow slip past the tent and return a few seconds later with an armful of clothing. She pulled down the zip on the door and tossed them inside.

We got dressed in record time, but we needn't have rushed. The Tai Chi group was totally engrossed in the moves being demonstrated by the surprisingly agile old Mr Locke. They paid us no attention as we skulked toward the door.

The Décarie penthouse was only one level below the roof. It didn't give Fiona much time to chastise her son, but she gave it her best shot anyway. "I much preferred being called to the roof when my sons' unruly game of cops and robbers was interfering with the Tai Chi class."

"Mom, that was fifteen years ago."

"Mr Locke has a very long memory," she grumbled. "Mostly thanks to your brother."

"What did Ryan do?" I asked.

Adam grinned and wiggled his eyebrows at me through the mirror, earning in a stiff elbow to the ribs from his mother. "He lassoed him and tied him up," he replied, rubbing his wounded side. "That's why we have strict rules about playing on the roof."

"You weren't blameless, Adam," Fiona scolded. I burst into a fit of giggles, vexing her even more. "Never, ever again," she warned, alternating her pointed finger between the two of us. "It's taken him well over a decade to get over your last escapade. God only knows how long it'll be before he forgets about this one."

I couldn't have cared less. I hoped that night was something I'd remember forever. I stared through the mirrored door at the perfect boy with bedroom hair and wicked grin. He'd managed the impossible. In a few short hours he'd taken me all the way home.

36. House Of Cards

The Euphoria of visiting La La land lasted only as long as the weekend. It was business as usual on Monday morning. Adam made his early morning dash for the door and I was home alone. For a change, my day was not without purpose. It was the day of Seraphina's fashion shoot.

Seraphina ended up deciding against an outside setting. She managed to con Ryan into letting her do it at Nellie's, while it was closed between lunch and dinner service.

"Did Ryan charge you rent?"

Sera gave her trademark demure giggle. "No. He's okay, if you catch him on a good day."

I went about setting up my equipment while Sera started sweeping through the hangers of clothes she'd brought with her.

"Sera, how far did you wheel that thing?" I asked, pointing at the mobile clothes rack.

"I didn't. I had it delivered."

Of course. Every single thing in New York could be delivered for a price - including bunches of brightly coloured balloons and a smoke machine, as it turned out. The props she'd arranged shouldn't really have shocked me. Any girl who designed outfits that combined tutus and striped socks was a little on the quirky side. Seraphina Sawyer clearly had an anime character living in her brain.

"Too much?" she asked, pointing to the massive bunch of balloons she was grasping. "I don't want it to be too much."

I shook my head. "It's your vision. Let's go with it."

"Go with what?" asked Kinsey, bustling through the front door of the restaurant.

"Sera's vision," I told her, turning my attention back to my camera. "It's all about the vision."

"I hope *you* have good vision," barked Kinsey, pointing to the camera in my hand. "I don't want you to make us look bad."

Yellow tulle and striped socks were going to make her look bad. But I saw no need to burst her bubble. "I know what I'm doing, Kinsey."

"I'm so excited," squeaked Sera, checking the time on her watch. "Where's Whitney? She's supposed to be here by now."

"I'm good to go," announced Kinsey. "We can start without her."

Unless she was planning on attending a Japanese comic book convention, I couldn't think of a single place she was good to go to. All I could do was try not to look too alarmed at the sight of the featherweight Kinsey in the heavyweight studded green mini dress.

It was almost a relief when Whitney finally turned up. Kinsey's vapid personality somehow showed up on every single picture I'd taken.

"Sorry I'm so late. Something came up." She spoke only to Sera and Kinsey, ignoring me completely. "Where do you want me?" Antarctica sprang to mind, but I kept my mouth shut. Sera thrust a pile of clothes at her and ordered her to get changed.

Just when I thought the atmosphere had reached fever pitch, Parker strutted through the door. "It's a closed set, Parker," said Seraphina flatly. "You should go."

He walked toward us, smiling as if she hadn't spoken. "I'll stay out of the way," he pledged. "Kinsey wanted me to come down and check it out. I promised I would."

That was the first time I'd ever been jealous of Kinsey Ballantyne. I struggled to get Adam to give up half an hour for me even on his slowest day.

"Just let him stay," I muttered, endorsing the romantic gesture.

"Fine," yielded Sera. "But keep out of the way."

"That shouldn't be difficult." He pointed to the mass of balloons near the foot of the mezzanine stairs. "Are they latex?"

"They're Mylar," replied Sera. "Just for you."

Kinsey waltzed back into the room, caught sight of Parker and practically threw herself at him, squealing like an excited kid. It gave me chance to ask Sera why he was so concerned about the circus-like props.

"He's allergic to latex," she whispered, rolling her eyes. "He gets all puffy and comes out in welts. I've seen it happen a couple of times."

I couldn't help giggling. "So, how does someone with a latex allergy practice safe sex?" It was my very first thought. Perhaps I should've been embarrassed by that.

"I think any form of sex with Parker would be unsafe, don't you?"

I looked across at the couple canoodling near the nontoxic balloons, and shuddered. I had to agree.

Parker actually did as he was told and faded into the background when Whitney reappeared. I had to admit, Whitney was easier to deal with than Kinsey. She managed to ditch the morose expression long enough for me to take a few hundred pictures, and never once called me on the fact that I was a complete novice when it came to fashion photography. If she had, I might have been forced to call Seraphina on being a complete amateur when it came to fashion design. Expecting someone to photograph well while wearing a purple PVC jacket was a big ask.

I was glad when they finally ran out of outfits. I was even happier to find out that Sera had hired people to come in and pack up her anime-circus-cartoon-themed set. It was a whirlwind of activity for a few minutes while people stormed the restaurant and cleared everything out. "I guess that's a wrap," said Sera, brushing her hands together.

"I'll get these edited tonight," I said, waving my camera at her. "You should have them tomorrow."

She lurched forward, hugging me tightly. "I can't thank you enough."

I took a step back, smiling at her. "You haven't seen the pictures yet."

"I have every faith in your abilities," she told me. "I could've hired a professional but you came highly recommended."

A huge penny dropped.

"By Adam?" I said his name a little too indignantly for a girl who claimed to love him with her whole heart. "He asked you to get me to shoot this for you, didn't he?"

She shrugged, but there was nothing casual about her expression. It was the look of someone who'd let a major cat out of the bag. "He just wanted you to be busy. Please don't be upset with him," she begged, grabbing my wrist. "I would've asked you anyway. As soon as I saw your Billet-doux pictures I knew you'd be perfect for this."

I nodded. "I'm not upset with him." That was a lie. I was very upset with him. It was another attempt by him to occupy me.

Seraphina and Kinsey didn't hang around a minute longer than they needed to. I declined their offer of sharing a cab, deciding to hang back and straighten up the tables. I wasn't worried about leaving the place to Ryan's standards, but leaving it for Bente to sort out seemed mighty unfair. Parker and Whitney slipped out with the clean-up crew without saying goodbye. If I'd given a damn, I might have been miffed.

Sliding the tables back into place took no time at all, so I thought I'd kill a few more minutes by setting them. It was the first time I'd noticed how creepy Nellie's was when it was empty. The silence amplified the clinking of the cutlery as I carried it to the first table. I dumped it down, overcome by a sudden urge to turn around.

It would have been fitting to see the ghost of Nellie standing there – except Nellie was alive and well and spending the day tormenting her canasta club buddies, just as she did every Friday afternoon.

There was no one standing behind me but I could definitely hear people talking. I followed the sound of the voices.

By the time I'd reached the kitchen, I was practically in stealth mode. I managed to open the kitchen doors without making a sound, but it was a hollow victory. The kitchen was as deserted and the talking stopped. For a quick minute I wondered if it was all in my head, then noticed that the cloakroom door was shut. I could have walked away, content that no one was looting the kitchen, but curiosity got the better of me.

I ferociously pushed open the cloakroom door, preparing to catch a thief or a ghost. What I caught was much worse.

I sucked in a sharp breath and quickly spun around, trying to erase the horribly compromising position I'd just caught Whitney and Parker in from my psyche.

"Er, excuse me."

Neither of them acknowledged me, but the sound of scurrying to gather clothing led me to believe they were as mortified as I was. I blindly reached behind for the door handle, pulled the door shut and bolted back to the front of house. I couldn't even leave because I needed to lock up the restaurant. I contemplated just locking them in and leaving them to it, but Parker sashaying into the room put an end to that thought. I struggled to look at him but he acted as if nothing out of the ordinary had just happened.

"Charli, I know it looks bad but we're all adults, right?" he asked smoothly. I nodded, fearful of what I might say if I answered. "I hope this doesn't go any further. I'd hate for people to get hurt."

I continued nodding, unsure of what else to do. There was an underlying menace to his tone that I hadn't heard before. "I'll let you out," I mumbled, rushing to unlock the door for him.

I stood holding the door open for an eternity. Like the pompous, arrogant dick that he was, he sauntered slowly to the door. On his way out, he took it upon himself to lean forward and kiss me as he said goodbye. I practically pushed him out the door, bolted it shut and reached for the nearest napkin to wipe my face, disgusted by the thought of how many different people had contributed to the DNA on my cheek.

I was still scrubbing and cursing him out when Whitney appeared. I had no idea how this was going to play out. I didn't know whether to mention it or pretend I hadn't seen anything.

"I'd really appreciate it if you didn't tell anyone about this," she said shakily.

I stared at her for a long time, trying to figure out what to say. It was clearly a gesture that made her uncomfortable. She burst into tears, and inexplicably I rushed to comfort her. "Oh, don't cry," I pleaded, loosely hugging her. "I won't tell anyone."

"You must think I'm disgraceful," she said woefully.

Releasing her, I took a step back. "Yeah, but in fairness, I formed that opinion long before I knew you were screwing Parker."

My honest answer had the desired effect and she punched out a sharp laugh. The humour was fleeting, though. She buried face in her hands and began sobbing again. I really didn't know what to do about it. I had no choice but to wait for her to compose herself.

"I don't even know why I do it anymore," she muttered finally.

"So it's been going on for a while?"

"Years." I tried not to appear shocked, but the look she gave me implied it was the exact reaction she was aiming for. "Yes. Even when I was with Adam."

The guilt I'd always felt all but dissipated. She could hardly take the moral high ground when she'd been screwing the lord of creepiness the whole time. I pulled out the nearest chair and sat down. Whitney remained standing. I couldn't fathom her confession. Parker was lecherous, sleazy and average looking at best. Adam was, well, Adam.

"Why on earth would you go there, Whitney? And with Parker, of all people?"

"Being with Adam was no picnic, Charli."

"I know that better than anyone, but nothing on earth could make me stray in Parker's direction," I replied, shuddering.

"It really doesn't have anything to do with Parker," she said, shaking her head. "I just wanted a little bit of attention. That's how it started, anyway. I don't know why I still do it."

"But you could do so much better than him. You could have anyone you wanted." It was a stupid, thoughtless thing to say. She scowled at me and I instantly looked away.

"I've never had the one I wanted," she replied sourly. "Adam was never mine. He's been yours all along. And I hate you for it."

"Surely hating Adam would be more appropriate."

She smiled, albeit uneasily. "Well, he is emotionally deficient."

Annoyed, I jumped to his defence. "Deficient or not, how do you think he'd feel if he found out that you were sleeping with his so-called best friend while you were together?"

"Come on, Charli. Adam is no saint."

"Did he cheat on you?"

"Only with you, as far as I know."

"So, you *did* know about me?"

"Of course I knew about you!"

"So why did you stay with him?"

She shrugged. "It served a purpose. I like being envied."

I didn't even try making sense of her comment. I'd wasted far too much time believing she was heartbroken over the loss of Adam. Love clearly had nothing to do with it.

"Do you want to be with Parker?" I had no idea why I was even asking.

"God, no." She screwed up her tearstained face as if the whole idea was repulsive. "I use him, just like he uses me."

"And what about Kinsey? She's supposed to be your best friend."

"Sometimes I think she deserves it," she replied, completely unrepentant.

"You're all mad," I muttered, shaking my head. "Completely and utterly morally broke."

Whitney finally pulled out the chair opposite me and sat. I didn't want the conversation to continue. As far as I was concerned, the more distance I kept from their empire of dirt, the better. I stood and gathered my gear, preparing to leave.

Whitney stood too. "Please don't tell Adam about this."

I knew she wasn't trying to preserve his feelings. She was intent on making sure he retained the title of villain. Whitney could hardly play the victim otherwise.

"I said I wouldn't." Her look of surprise annoyed me. "But make sure you know that when this house of cards finally falls, it wasn't me who betrayed you."

Whitney slung her bag over her shoulder and heaved out a long sigh. "I'll keep it in mind."

If I could have figured out a way of telling Adam everything I knew without ratting on Whitney, I would've done it. I owed her nothing, but I felt a strange sympathy toward her. What I wasn't feeling was a skerrick of understanding toward Parker. It was hard to comprehend the superiority that the purple circle seemed to think they had over the world. To me, they were all completely soulless.

It was even harder to comprehend why Adam felt any sort of kinship toward them. Maybe I'd ask him about it one day when we were far, far away and they'd become nothing more than people he used to know.

37. Rule Change

My idea of lunch in the park included a blanket and a couple of poorly wrapped sandwiches. Fiona Décarie's idea was a little different. I accepted her invitation on the assumption that no matter what over-the-top spin she put on it, a picnic could only ever be a casual affair.

I was wrong. She turned up at our door so early that Adam hadn't even left yet. The reason for the early visit was purely strategic: she was armed with a cache of summer dresses for me to try on.

"Isn't this a little much?" I asked, not even trying to disguise my annoyance. "I'm perfectly capable of dressing myself."

"I know you are, darling," she soothed, thrusting a blue floral number at me. "But today is important. A lot of important people will be there and I want to show you off."

Sometimes I longed for the days when the woman detested the air I breathed. But then she'd do something ridiculous that would turn into something endearing, like trying to dress me but remembering that I liked vintage dresses.

"I thought you said it was just lunch in the park," I complained, taking the hanger from her.

"It is, darling. Just you, me and a few hundred other ladies supporting the Sunkiss Foundation's annual luncheon."

"You should go, Charli," cajoled Adam from the kitchen. "It's for charity."

"Of course she's going," said Fiona. "All she has to do is pick a dress."

Adam walked over. "I like the red one," he whispered in my ear. "I'll show you how much when I get home tonight."

I went with the red dress, teamed it with a cute pair of Ferragamo sandals that I felt guilty for owning, and let the queen twist my hair into an unoriginal but impeccably neat bun.

Looking pretty didn't guarantee a pretty afternoon. I knew as soon as we arrived that there was the potential for a great deal of ugliness. Fiona might have finally accepted me into the fold, but to the rest of her social set I was still a novelty. There was no escaping the fact that one of the most eligible bachelors in the history of trust fund scions had chosen to do the unthinkable. And I was the unthinkable.

"Stop fidgeting," whispered Fiona. "You look beautiful."

Why did no one ever tell me I looked confident, intelligent or poised?

I stood on the terrace of the restaurant, looking down at the tables set up on the lawn, wondering how the day was going to play out. The purple circle girls were there in all their fashionista glory. Sera spotted me and gave a friendly wave. Kinsey saw me too – and turned her back. Nothing about the gesture surprised me. At least it was honest. She tolerated me because she had no choice.

What was shocking was Whitney's reaction. Not only did she wave but she grabbed the elbow of the woman she was with and started climbing the steps toward us.

"Who is Whitney with?" I hissed at Fiona, needing an answer before they reached us.

She handed me a champagne flute. "Celia, her mother," she said, smiling artificially in Celia's direction before leaning in to whisper to me. "And that, darling, is a prime example of why you should never wear leopard print."

I let out a long and unsteady breath, by which time Whitney and her leopard-clad mother were in front of us.

"Charli," purred Whitney. "I'd like you to meet my mother. Mother, this is Charli, Adam's wife."

I shook her hand but had lost the ability to speak.

"Charmed, I'm sure," crooned Celia. I doubted she was charmed by me. I also doubted that anyone had used that greeting since the mid fifties.

Fiona stepped in, leaning forward to kiss leopard-woman's cheeks. "Bygones, Celia. My son is extraordinarily happy."

"And why wouldn't he be?" asked Whitney. "Charli's lovely."

Whitney had never paid me a compliment before. Whitney had never been even remotely pleasant to me before. The reason for it left me feeling a little queasy. I had serious dirt on Whitney Vaughn, and every single interaction from here on was going to be an exercise in fakery.

Even Fiona saw through it. The second they were out of earshot, she whispered, "What do you have on Whitney?" and handed me a second glass of champagne.

"What makes you think I have something on her?"

She linked her arm through mine and we walked down the steps. "She loathes you, Charli."

"Well, thank you, little Miss Sunshine."

She stopped walking, forcing me to a halt. "Oh, you poor mite," she cooed, tucking a wisp of hair behind my ear. "All you want to do is to fit in."

The queen and I had spent a lot of time together over the past few months. How could she have me pegged so wrong? How did she not know that fitting in with her lunatics was the furthest thing from my mind?

"All I want is Adam," I replied sternly. "All I've ever wanted is Adam. And as soon as he's done with school, we're out of here." Her bewildered expression led me to believe it was the first she'd heard of it. I would have elaborated, but a woman wearing a giant floppy straw hat appeared out of nowhere and muscled in between us.

"Fifi," she crooned, nearly knocking Fiona's glass out of her hand with her hat. I hadn't heard anyone refer to her as Fifi before. It sounded ridiculous, but everything about the pushy woman was a little silly. Her flowy silk handkerchief dress was the exact same shade of red as her fingernails, lips and shoes.

"How are you, Joy?" asked Fiona.

"I'm fabulous, sweetie." She quickly turned to me and I ducked to avoid her hat. "You must be Charli. Adam has told me so much about you."

I couldn't imagine Adam willingly telling this woman anything. I had to know the connection. "How do you know my husband?" I never, *ever* referred to Adam as my husband. The word was trite and inadequate. Using it was a weird territorial display that made me feel like a total sellout.

"Joy is a realtor, Charli," interjected Fiona. "We do a lot of business together."

"The best in town," crowed Joy, unabashedly singing her own praises. "And I'm working hard for you." I stepped back as she pointed at me, fighting the urge to douse her in champagne.

"Adam mentioned that you'll be looking for a new home soon. I have a few gorgeous listings in the village at the moment." she said in a condescending childlike voice. "We'll find you the perfect little nest."

What the hell was she talking about? I didn't want a nest in Greenwich Village. I wanted to fly the nest as soon as humanly possible. Something about my expression alarmed Fiona. She took my glass and set it on the table behind us, hooked her arm through mine and excused us both from the conversation. Joy let us go only after thrusting her business card at me.

We walked a long way, well past the tables and out on to the open lawn area.

"What was that all about?" I asked.

"Charli, it makes perfect sense for you both to find a home of your own."

"We don't want a home."

"It's not practical to live at Gabrielle's forever."

"No, it's not. But it's temporary. After he sits the bar exam, we're out of here. That's always been the plan."

"I don't understand, Charli." That made two of us. We seemed to be having two different conversations. "Adam has accepted a judicial clerkship. He's not going anywhere."

"No." I practically whimpered the word. "We're leaving New York."

She put both hands on my shoulders, shaking me as she spoke. "He's worked incredibly hard for this. What would be the point in getting his degree if he didn't put it to use?"

"Ryan did."

Her hands slipped back to her sides. "Ryan never wanted to study law. He'd be the first to tell you that he did it only to please his father. But Adam is different, Charli. It's all he's ever wanted."

I shook my head, trying to clear my brain. "We're not supposed to be here."

"Stop this, Charli." There was desperation in her tone and she resorted to shaking me again. "Pull yourself together. Your life is here. End of story."

I had a million questions, none of which she could answer. I wanted to know if his plans had changed or if staying in New York had been his intention all along. Neither scenario was pretty, but there was only one I could live with.

Devastation, hot sun and champagne were a deadly mix. I didn't recognise the point where I consumed one glass too many; all I knew was that somewhere between the main course and dessert, I developed a bad headache and an overwhelming urge to go to sleep. I managed to escape by telling Fiona I was in danger of becoming drunk and belligerent.

"What does that entail?" she asked, humouring me.

"Dancing naked on tables, usually," I replied, checking the sturdiness of the nearest table by rocking it.

She called her driver and demanded he pick me up straight away.

***

For once, arriving home to an empty house didn't bother me. After painstakingly pulling two dozen bobby pins out of my hair, I tumbled into bed to sleep off the headache.

I didn't hear Adam come in. The first I knew he was home was when he laid down beside me. "Hey," he greeted me softly, wrapping his arms around me.

I blinked spastically, trying to focus on his face. "What time is it?"

"A little after seven."

I tried to sit up but felt a little woozy. "Whoa," I muttered, lying back down.

"Are you sick?" he asked, moving his hand to my forehead.

"Not really," I croaked, closing my eyes. "Don't feel sorry for me. It's self inflicted."

He laughed softly. "Well, I'm glad you had a good time."

"It wasn't a good time, Adam. I was drowning my sorrows." I opened my eyes just in time to see his expression turn serious. "I met your realtor, Joy. You'll be happy to know she's working hard for us. I guess I'm going to need a bigger house to rattle around in by myself while you're out being a law clerk extraordinaire."

His body tensed. "I was going to tell you."

"So our entire plan is busted?" I asked, giving no hint of the devastation I was feeling.

"I just need to be here a while longer, Charlotte. It's an opportunity I can't pass up," he said, giving me a chaste kiss as if that fixed everything.

"How long have you known?"

Everything hinged on his answer. He was either good, studious Adam who'd received the offer out of the blue or manipulative, purple circle Adam who'd planned it all along.

"Not long." I studied his blue eyes closely, detecting no hint of dishonesty. "Do you want to know the best part?"

I was still looking for the mildly okay part. "Sure."

"It was absolutely nothing to do with my father. It was based purely on my own merits," he said proudly.

I trailed my fingertips down his face, settling on the deep dimple in his right cheek.

"When were you going to tell me?"

The hollow in his cheek disappeared as his smile faded. "Just as soon as I could figure out how."

The problem I faced was twofold. Firstly, I really didn't want to stay in New York a day longer than necessary. Secondly, I didn't want to live anywhere without him. I sighed, resigned to the fact that I had no choice but to accept that our travel plans had been put back a while.

"It'll be okay," I replied optimistically. "A few more months here won't make any difference."

He turned his head, looking at me strangely. I got the impression he was on the very edge of telling me something dreadful.

"Do you know how much I love you?" It wasn't such a strange question considering his next sentence. "It's going to be a little longer than a few months."

"How much longer?" He didn't answer, which was a very bad sign. Ignoring the wooziness, I sat upright, preparing to escape the room. It was a reaction he was all too familiar with. He swooped his arm around my waist, drawing me back to him.

"Just hear me out," he whispered in my ear from behind. "Please."

I didn't say a single word as he told me the ins and outs of the position he'd been offered. By the time he got to the part about it chewing up at least another year of our lives after law school, there was no point speaking at all. Something deep inside me snapped and gave way. Our travel plans weren't delayed. They were dead. I felt my whole body relax against his as I surrendered.

"It's everything I've worked toward."

I was outwardly silent. Inside I was screaming at him. I twisted in his arms, wanting to see his face. His dark blue eyes bored into mine, silently willing me to tell him that everything was fine. I nodded, giving him the false impression that all was golden.

"I'll give you whatever you need, Charli," he promised. I couldn't think of a single thing he could offer that would make me feel any less ripped off.

Nothing came out when I first tried to speak. I cleared my throat and tried again. "All I've ever wanted is you. You should know that by now."

He leaned forward and kissed me. "I'm right here." And he'd made it painfully apparent that he wasn't going anywhere any time soon. "Please tell me you're okay with this."

A normal girl would have asked for time to consider her options. But I wasn't a normal girl. I was the girl who loved him to the point of desperation. I *needed* him, which was the very affliction my father had warned me against.

I studied his worried expression closely. "I have to be okay with it."

"I need you," he whispered.

I nodded, semi-satisfied that the desperation was at least mutual.

"I'm not going anywhere, Adam," I murmured, hoping I sounded as crushed as I felt.

***

I staggered out into the kitchen the next morning, enticed by the aroma of freshly brewed coffee. As much as I detested the taste, I adored the smell. Adam had already left; the only hint that he'd been here was his mug in the sink. I was actually relieved.

My mood brightened considerably when I received an unexpected visit from Bente. I hadn't seen much of her lately, but it wasn't necessarily a bad thing. Bente was in a good place. She'd made good on her promise of never giving Ryan a chance to stomp on her heart again, and to Bente the best way of moving forward was doing it with someone else. That someone was a guy called Lucas, an art student by day and the lead singer of a heavy metal band at night. If her objective had been to find Ryan's polar opposite, she'd well and truly succeeded. Lucas had inky long black hair and a scruffy goatee, and always looked as if his clothes needed a good scrub. But he adored Bente, and for that reason alone Lucas was good.

"Is your frog here?" she asked as I opened the door.

"No," I replied. "He only comes home to eat and sleep."

She barged past me, straight for the couch. "Awesome."

"Please, Bente, do come in," I said, closing the door and sweeping my hand through the air.

"Thanks. Don't mind if I do."

At first, the chatter was light and nonsensical, just the way I liked it. But within a few minutes she became fidgety and I began to feel the same unease that I'd felt the night before, just before Adam ripped my travel plans to shreds.

"What's going on?" I asked. "I get the feeling you're about to tell me something huge."

"Very perceptive, Kemosabe. I do have something to tell you."

I tried to think ahead, imagining every possibility. But if I'd had a million years of thinking time, I wouldn't have anticipated her next sentence.

"I'm leaving town with Lucas." I stared at her like an imbecile. She rushed out an explanation in short fractured sentences. "I've finished my degree and done nothing with it. Lucas is going on tour. He asked me to go. I said yes. I'm so freaking happy!"

"Lucas is going on tour?"

I considered Lucas's band to be mediocre at best. Adam and I once suffered through a live club performance, at Bente's request. Adam got a migraine and I came close to dying from smoke inhalation. Other than that, it was unmemorable.

"They're even getting paid for it." Her body stiffened as she battled to contain herself.

Bente was my sidekick, my one constant in the Manhattan madness. The events of the day before only compounded the problems I faced without her. Even though she was sitting right beside me, the loneliness was already setting in.

"When do you leave?"

"Tonight. I didn't want to drag it out in case I changed my mind."

I nodded, understanding completely. In my experience, getting out of Dodge was best done quickly. "I am so jealous," I said, pouting a little.

She laughed. "It won't be forever. Besides, you'll be out of here soon enough. Then I'll be the one missing you."

I shook my head. "Nope. There's no need to hurry back. I'm going to be here for years. I'll probably have a really bad attitude and a drinking problem, but I'll be here."

I tried hard to sound indifferent but Bente saw through me. She demanded I tell her everything, which was probably a mistake.

"I knew it!" she said squinting her eyes and pointing at me. "He's a dick."

"He's not a dick," I defended. "I can't ask him to pass up an opportunity like this. He's worked too hard."

"What about your dreams, Charli? Haven't you given up enough for him?"

I tried to turn it around in the hopes of making her understand. "Put yourself in his shoes for a minute."

"I couldn't afford his shoes."

"What if the New York Times offered you your dream job? Would you still go on the road with Lucas, or would you stay here? And if you made the decision to stay, would you want him to stay with you?"

She didn't hesitate. "I'd stay and he'd go in a heartbeat."

I smirked. "Well, that's true love at its finest."

"At least it's true," she said bluntly. "Which is more than can be said for the life you're living at the moment."

I knew Bente wasn't trying to be brutal. She was trying to be honest. Unfortunately, it was the same thing. "I love him." It was all I could think of to put forward to justify my decision to stick it out in New York.

She granted me a tiny smile that wasn't the least bit reassuring. "And the frog loves you, Charli. He's just not very good at it."

38. Poison Ivy League

Losing Bente hurt my heart in ways that Adam couldn't understand, so I kept it to myself, along with a hundred other grievances that had begun to weigh me down. Resentment is a brutal beast, but for some reason we both chose to ignore it as it crept in.

The love I felt for Adam was complete and resolute. I just couldn't live it the way I wanted to, and I blamed him. I'd grown to hate the way I loved Adam Décarie. His resentment stemmed from frustration. He loved his New York life, and it killed him knowing that no matter how hard he tried, I just wasn't happy there. I no longer knew what he saw when he looked at me – and it was terrifying.

To make matters worse, winter had reared its ugly head again. Along with the abominable weather came an endless round of inane Christmas parties, the latest being Parker and Kinsey's ridiculously decadent event.

Parker's family, like Whitney's, were hoteliers, which meant he had access to the grand ballroom of their hotel for no other reason than to show off. To remind everyone how fabulous they both were, they gathered a hundred of their closest friends and packed them into the function room. I couldn't even claim to know a hundred people.

Even Adam looked as if he wished he were anywhere but here. "Are we having fun yet?" he whispered.

I hadn't decided. There was something wickedly amusing about being in the company of the poison ivy league, knowing that there was major treachery and betrayal bubbling just below the surface. It was a façade that Parker and Whitney maintained well. Whitney had even brought a date, a cute guy called Nate who seemed as excited to be there as Adam. But Nate had a role to play. He was on the receiving end of flirty looks and handsies under the table whenever Whitney felt the urge to get under Parker's skin. Parker responded by groping Kinsey. It was a repellent display.

"How did I not see this before?" I asked, trading glances between the two biggest wretches I had ever known. They both glared at me and I smirked back.

"See what?" asked Adam, oblivious.

I picked up my napkin and fanned it across my lap. "These napkins are the exact same shade of green as Kinsey's dress."

Adam looked at me as if I'd lost my mind. Whitney and Parker relaxed as if they'd just been granted a stay of execution, and Kinsey giggled. "Oh, someone noticed!"

"Of course I noticed, Kins," I purred. "I notice *everything*."

My snaky comment, and several others that followed, made for an uncomfortable dinner. I eventually excused myself from the table on the pretence of needing fresh air.

"Do you want me to come?" asked Adam hopefully, as I stood up.

I shook my head, smiling. "No. You stay."

I slipped out of the ballroom, made my way across the lobby and into the lounge area. I sat on one of the winged chairs near the fire and breathed easily for the first time all night – right until Parker appeared in front of me.

"Are you going to hide out here all night, Charli?"

"I might."

"That's not very sociable of you."

"Yeah, well, I'm not a very sociable kind of girl."

A disgusting, smug look crossed his face. "I guess that's understandable, all things considered."

I couldn't help but ask him what he meant. Parker sighed heavily, reached for the nearest chair and dragged it closer to mine. I tried to appear apathetic as he sat beside me by keeping my focus on the open fire. What I really wanted to do was push him into it.

"Adam is my best friend," he began. "We talk about everything."

"Oh good," I muttered. "So you've told him that you're screwing Whitney?"

He chuckled blackly but ignored my question. "He talks about you a lot. You're such a tortured soul, Charli. It's pathetic really. Did you really think he'd leave New York? I warned you months ago that he'd never follow through with your absurd plan."

"Plans change."

He shook his head, then reached across and touching a wisp of my hair. I slapped his hand away.

"Charli, Adam's plans have never changed."

"He didn't know that he was going to be offered a clerkship," I defended.

Parker gave a condescending laugh. "No one gets *offered* an clerkship, sweetheart. He applied for it, just like a thousand other law students did. He got it because he maintains near perfect grades."

My heart dropped. I had only one question for him. "When was he accepted?"

Parker shrugged his shoulders. "At least a year ago."

Things finally fell into place. Lingering doubts about Adam's intentions of leaving New York had been a constant drone in my head for months. And now I knew why. When he'd stood beside me at the altar and promised that we'd leave New York after two years, he'd already accepted a position that would keep us there. The subject of where we'd travel to when we left had never been his favourite topic: in fact, it usually made him squirm. That was obviously when the dishonesty weighed heaviest on him.

Despite my best efforts to stop them, tears rolled down my cheeks. Parker took it as an opportunity to move closer to me.

I was too distraught to protest as he draped one arm around my shoulder.

"I'm here for you, Charli," he declared, leaning closer to whisper the words.

"Like you're there for Whitney?" I mumbled, suddenly nauseated by his very existence.

"If you want me to be." I shuddered but he ignored it. Harvey Parker made my skin crawl. "Maybe you just need an escape for a while. We could go upstairs."

Maybe he was right. Maybe I did need an escape.

"And you think soulless sex is the solution?" I asked, dabbing my eyes with my fingertips, trying not to smudge my makeup.

"It has some therapeutic qualities," he replied, breathing the words into my hair.

"I wouldn't know."

It wasn't a dark world I'd ever ventured into. I tended to hang out in La La land where love conquered everything and lies covered all.

"You should give it a try," he urged, moving his free hand to my knee.

"Parker, I think you should buy me a drink first."

He was on his feet before I'd even finished speaking, and judging by the speed with which he took off to the bar, I only had a minute to make my next move.

I delved into my purse and grabbed a condom – something I never thought I'd need in Parker's presence. I was going to use his latex allergy to teach him a lesson. I discreetly took it out of the foil wrapper, held it between my palms and feverishly rubbed my hands together. When I spotted him weaving through tables with a couple of lethal-looking drinks in his hand, I dropped it back in my purse.

"For you, Madame," he crooned, in the lamest French accent I'd ever heard.

He set the glasses on the table beside me and sat back down, even closer than before. My heart was almost belting through my chest. If my plan failed, there was a fair chance I was going to be in a whole world of trouble.

Parker's hand moved back to my knee and I made my counter-move, covering his hand with both of mine and kneading his fingers, praying that there was enough latex on them to work. I endured his stupid dirty talk and heavy breathing until I saw the first hint of discomfort take hold. As soon as I saw him scratch his hand, I pulled away. I wanted to see him squirm, not die. I stood and grabbed my bag, preparing to make a run for it if I needed to.

"What's the matter?" he asked in a buttery voice that had always been powerless over me. "I thought we were getting to know each other."

"I already know you, Parker," I said gravely. "And just being in the same room as someone who's prepared to sleep with his best friend's wife makes me want to throw up."

"What if Adam thought you'd made the first move? I could tell him that, you know."

The douche was actually threatening me. He was also scratching his hand with a little more ferocity than before so I let it slide. "Do what you need to do, Parker," I encouraged. "I know I'm going to."

My intention was to return to the party, but I didn't make it that far. The entire purple circle stood at the doors leading into the ballroom. Even before I got there I knew the conversation was heavy. Seraphina was comforting Kinsey, who was sobbing uncontrollably. Jeremy stood in front of Adam as if he was holding him back. Whitney stood alone in the corner, looking calmer than any of them. Deciphering what had happened took no time at all. The house of cards had finally fallen, and judging by the relaxed look on Whitney's face, she was the one who'd blown it down. She'd finally come clean about her affair with Parker.

As soon as I was close enough, I asked a stupid question. "What's going on?"

It was Kinsey who blurted out a reply. If I hadn't already known the answer, her jumbled words would have made no sense. I linked my arm through Adam's, but he was so worked up he didn't seem to notice I was touching him. I wasn't sure who would wear the brunt of his fury - until Parker foolishly appeared.

Adam lurched forward, grabbed a fistful of his shirt and pinned him against the wall. Kinsey let out a scream and Seraphina worked hard to calm her down. Jeremy attempted to separate them, but Adam refused to let go. I had never seen him so infuriated. Parker raised his hands in a motion of surrender and that was when I noticed the angry red welts.

"How could you?" hissed Adam through gritted teeth.

Adam released him with a hard shove. Confident that the confrontation was over, Jeremy took a step back.

It would've been an opportune time for Parker to walk away, but he didn't. Foolishly, he answered Adam's question. "You should've been taking care of business, Adam. I'm only too happy to keep picking up your slack. Your wife is in need of a little TLC too."

Even Jeremy, the peacemaker, couldn't make sense of his audacity. He did nothing as Adam drew back his fist and punched Parker square in the face. Kinsey screamed again and Sera quickly led her away.

Adam stood over Parker. "If you get up, I'll smash you again."

"Enough," ordered Jeremy, putting his hand on Adam's chest and pushing him back.

I looked back at Whitney for the first time. She bestowed the tiniest smile on me and I wondered if her confession had had the desired effect. One thing was certain. After that night, nothing would ever be the same.

The rest of the partygoers continued revelling in the ballroom, oblivious of the drama outside the door. But we were done. Adam took my hand and led us across the foyer to the cloakroom. "We'll get our coats and then we're out of here," he muttered, seemingly to himself.

It took a few minutes for the attendant to find them and the delay was beginning to annoy him. Our coats appeared at the same time that Kinsey came barrelling across the foyer, calling Adam's name.

He turned to face her. "I won't touch him again, Kinsey," he promised.

"No, no," she said, panicked. "He's had a reaction to something. He needs to go to the hospital."

I looked past Kinsey and saw Parker listlessly walking across the foyer toward us. It was hard to tell what was hurting him more – his angry welted hands or his bloody swollen nose. Adam turned his attention back to me. "I have to take him to hospital," he said, sounding totally inconvenienced. "Take a cab home and I'll be there as soon as I can."

I was thrilled to be going home. My intention was to make a quick getaway but hailing a cab was harder than expected.

"I have a driver," said Whitney, appearing from somewhere behind me. "You're welcome to share a ride with me."

I pulled my coat tighter around my body, trying to protect myself from the bitter cold - and perhaps a bitter Whitney.

"What happened to Nate?"

She shrugged her shoulders. "I guess he just wasn't that into me."

"What made you finally come clean, Whit?" I asked, too curious not to know. "Did your conscience finally get the better of you?"

She looked to the pavement. "I saw him talking to you. It made me realise what a tool he really is. His spiel hasn't changed much."

"He is a tool," I agreed, shuddering.

"You made his hands welt, didn't you?"

"Possibly."

"I wish I'd thought to do that."

"You deserve better than him, Whitney," I said, sucking the humour right out of the conversation. "Don't settle for less than you're worth."

"I won't do it again," she promised, holding her hand to her heart.

"Me neither."

"Regrets, Charli?"

I shrugged my shoulders. "None."

I wasn't lying. I regretted nothing, but had finally realised that I'd reached the end of my rope. The desperate need to have Adam in my life had finally given way to self-preservation. My sanity would give out if I continued with the Manhattan madness that had become my life. I didn't end up sharing a ride home with Whitney. I managed to hail a cab and get the hell out of there.

39. Small Details

I wanted to be awake when Adam arrived home, but zonked out on the couch sometime after two. I probably wouldn't have woken at all if he hadn't made such a racket on the way in. He dropped his keys on the floor, bent down to pick them up, and managed to take a dining chair with him. Boy Wonder was drunk. In fact, Boy Wonder was blind rotten smashed. This was a first. I had no idea how to handle him.

"Charlotte." He staggered back a few steps, steadying himself by leaning against the wall.

I made no attempt to get off the couch. "Adam."

He paused. "The chairs fell down."

"I know, I saw. Why don't you sit down?"

It took a long few seconds for him to process my instructions before he pushed himself off the wall, stumbled toward me and fell in a heap at my feet, resting his elbows on my knees.

"I love you so much," he slurred.

I ran my hands through his messy hair, looking into his tired blue eyes. He looked like a man with the weight of the world on his shoulders. "I love you too. Where have you been?"

"Out. Getting drunk."

"By yourself?"

"No big deal," he muttered. "I'm probably going to be spending a lot of time alone from here on in."

"Did you take Parker to the hospital?"

"Yeah. They're keeping him overnight."

I felt slightly bad. I'd done some pretty low things in the past but that was the first time I'd ever inflicted actual physical injury on someone.

"So he's okay?"

"He'll live. Besides, I think his broken nose hurts more than his allergies."

I put my hand under his chin and lifted his head, forcing him to look at me. "You broke his nose?"

A lazy grin swept his face. "You broke his hands."

"He told you that?"

"He told me *everything*," he replied. "Do you know everything, Charlotte?"

His question formed a dangerous line of conversation. In a few short hours, Adam's entire social circle had imploded. And I suspected he knew that our relationship had almost gone down with it. It wasn't a conversation I wanted to have with him while he was plastered, so I censored my reply.

"I know about Parker and Whitney."

He huffed out a sharp laugh. "You knew that? Wow. How'd I miss it for so long then?"

I wasn't about to explain. There was a scar on my brain where I'd burned the memory from my psyche. Thankfully, Mr Oblivious wasn't thinking clearly enough to realise I hadn't answered him. I leaned down and kissed the top of his head. "I'm sorry they betrayed you like that."

Better than anyone, I knew the pain of finding out your friend is a treacherous jerk. It hurt almost as much as finding out I was married to one.

"I probably deserved it," he conceded. "I'm just like them. They lie, cheat and manipulate to get what they want. I do the same thing to you. But you know that now, right? Parker told you."

"I would've worked it out sooner or later, Adam. I'm not giving Parker any credit for spelling it out for me."

"I'm sorry he hit on you," he said, veering off-subject.

"I dealt with it," I replied, surprised that Parker really had told him everything.

He laughed blackly. "Yes. I suppose inflicting anaphylaxis is dealing with it."

I couldn't find the humour. If he had been sober, I doubt he would have either. Ending the conversation seemed like a good idea. I grabbed his hand and tried pulling him to his feet.

"Let's go to bed. I'm tired."

Adam yanked me down into his lap. "Tired of loving me?"

I linked one arm around his neck. "No one ever gets tired of loving someone, Adam. They just get tired of waiting and being disappointed and getting hurt."

"I can't give you what you need," he said bleakly. "I've known that from the very beginning. I was never going to leave here. I belong in New York. I want to finish my degree and practise law. I've been dragging you along for the ride, trying to change your mind about wanting to leave. I tried my hardest to make you happy so you'd stay here with me."

I absolutely believed he thought he'd given it his best shot. In hindsight, everything from stargazing on rooftops to gifting me Billet-doux had been tactical. It just wasn't enough for me anymore. "I know. But I'm not going to discuss it while you're drunk."

"We have to. That's why I got drunk. How else was I supposed to work up to telling you all of this?"

I wrestled free of his grip. "Don't do this now. You'll regret it in the morning."

He brought his wrist to his face, squinting as he tried to read it. "It's already morning, and I already have many regrets."

"Stop talking, Adam."

He ignored me. "Maybe you should get drunk too. Then we can reminisce about all the horrible things my mother put you through when you got here. And when that subject runs dry we'll move on to the torture my friends inflicted."

"Don't – "

"No, let me finish. There's plenty more I don't want to talk about. How about all the times I let you down? All the times I refused to see what was going on because that was easier than trying to deal with it. Your time here's been a living hell." He shook his head, speaking with pure regret. "I'm such a selfish bastard. I did nothing to save you from it."

I couldn't argue with the truth. The best I could do was remind him of why I endured it. "I love you, Adam."

He grimaced as if my words had caused him excruciating pain. "You gave up everything for me. Don't do it anymore. I can't give up anything for you."

It was the most honesty I'd seen from him in a long time. I reached for his hand and held it tightly. "I'm sorry for that, Charli."

"I'm sorry too," I replied, dully.

"Why did you put up with it for so long?"

"Because I thought it was temporary. You let me think we were leaving." It was important that I kept calm. He was barely thinking straight. If I overloaded him with anger, there was a chance the conversation would end up in a place we couldn't recover from. "What did you think was going to happen? Did you think you could string me along indefinitely? Show me enough magic every now and then to keep me loved up and happy? You know me better than that, Adam."

He shrugged but at least he had the good sense to look contrite. "I don't know what to tell you, Charli. Love makes you do all sorts of unreasonable things."

It was the same cryptic quip Gabrielle had confounded me with a hundred times, only this time, I understood its meaning perfectly. It was the very reason I'd stuck it out as long as I had, and why he'd duped me into staying.

"You lied to me," I said, dropping my hold on his hand.

"Every. Freaking. Day," he admitted, enunciating every word. "I won't do it any more. I'm exhausted. I know you're leaving me. I know our five minutes are up."

Of everything he'd just confessed to, those last seven words were the ones that wrecked me, especially the blasé way he'd said them. I covered my face with my hands, willing myself not to cry.

"You're okay with that? Do you want me to leave, Adam?"

He pulled my hands from my face, forcing me to look at him. So many emotions crossed his handsome, wasted face that I truly couldn't pre-empt his answer.

"No Charli. I want to rip your fairy wings off on a daily basis to make sure you can't fly away." The frustrated words hitched in his throat, slowing his rant. "I love you. I want you to stay here and be miserable forever so I never have to face life without you. Is that too much to ask?"

He grinned then, extinguishing the cruelty of his words in an instant. "You're a sloppy drunk, Adam Décarie," I admonished, smiling back at him.

The deep dimple in his cheek vanished as quickly as his smile. "Please wish for things to be different," he urged. The alcohol was talking. He was practically begging me to do something that his normally logical brain had trouble believing in. "Cash in your biggest wish and find a way to fix this."

"You can't fix hopeless, Adam."

His head lolled back and he growled in exasperation. "The universe sucks, Charlotte," he said roughly.

"Tonight, she does," I agreed, laughing at his uncharacteristic choice of words.

Fate is a cruel mistress. She let us find each other and fall desperately in love, years before we were supposed to, at a time when neither of us could completely surrender to it. I was beginning to suspect that my father and fate were old friends. Alex had warned me of this outcome long ago, and only now could I concede that he'd been right all along.

"I know that you're going to hate living in New York," he'd told me. "Adam will win out for a while, but eventually you're going to have to decide when to call it quits."

Now was the time. Somewhere along the line, love and happiness had become mutually exclusive. Our five minutes were definitely up.

***

After an unsettled few hours of sleep, I spent the next morning packing, somehow managing to squash my New York life into the one suitcase I'd arrived with a year earlier. The thing I most wanted to pack was sleeping a few feet away from me. Adam was much stiller than usual, but groaned occasionally, leading me to think that a whacking great headache would add to his troubles when he woke up. He finally appeared just before noon, staggering into the lounge half-dressed, sleepy and sexy as hell. If there was supposed to be a moment that I reconsidered leaving, that was it. Staying would require no courage at all. Finding the strength to leave was going to take all that I had.

"You're awake," I mumbled, stating the obvious. "How are you feeling?"

He smiled sheepishly. "Horrible. Close to death."

"Hangovers suck," I said sympathetically. "I'll get you some water."

"I don't need water, Charli." He caught my hand as I passed him, stopping me dead. "The way I'm feeling has nothing to do with a hangover."

"Do you remember much of last night?"

It occurred to me that my recollection was probably a lot stronger than his. The last thing I wanted was to have to fill in blanks for him. I worried that the mutual decision to go our separate ways might not be so mutual in the cold light of day.

"I remember everything," he replied. "I just want to make sure I that I said everything I needed to."

"We talked about everything," I assured, pulling my hand away. "I'm good to go."

I walked into the kitchen on the guise of getting him some water. I held the glass under the running tap, giving myself the distraction I needed so I wouldn't have to look at him. At that moment, nothing about leaving seemed right. Looking at him just confirmed it.

"So I told you about the billet-doux I wrote you?" he finally hinted.

I turned back to face him, ignoring the fact that I'd left the tap running.

"No. You never mentioned it. Can I have it now?"

He shook his head, smiling only slightly. "No, not now. You'll find it when you most need it, but I want you to promise me something."

"Okay."

"When you read it, I want you to look at the deeper meaning. If you take it at face value, you're reading it wrong." He frowned as if he was having trouble deciphering his own words.

"I will look for the deeper meaning," I promised. "It's what I do."

He looked relieved. "I know."

"Is it a drunken billet-doux Adam?" I asked, trying to lighten the conversation. "If you wrote it last night, I'll give you a chance to rewrite it. Drunk billet-douxing is a big no-no."

He turned off the tap, pinning me against the counter in the process. "I'm pretty sure billet-douxing isn't a word, Charlotte," he murmured. "But for the record, no. I wrote it a long time ago."

As curious as I was, I wasn't going to press him for more information. Instead, I imagined how good it was going to feel to find a love letter from him after I'd gone. I put my hands on his chest and sighed pensively. "Saying goodbye is going to suck."

His hands rested on my hips as he pressed himself against me. "We're not going to say goodbye. Never say goodbye, because goodbye means going away, and –"

I cut in, finishing the very familiar quote myself. "Going away means forgetting. That line wasn't actually in *Peter Pan*, Adam. It was in the movie."

He looked guiltily at me. "I haven't had time to read the book. I took a shortcut and managed to catch some of the movie on TV."

The smile I forced was edged with sadness. Our time together in Pipers Cove had been slow and easy, leaving plenty of time for Adam to concentrate on the small details. Our New York life was the complete opposite. It was fast, fuelled by drama and full of far too many shortcuts.

I crushed my lips to his. "I will never forget," I promised, breaking free for only a second.

***

I knew that letting Adam go wasn't going to be a one-time thing. I was going to have to live through it every day, over and over again. For that reason, I was determined to make it as painless as possible. I didn't want him to come with me to the airport. In my mind, that fell into the dragging-out-a-long-goodbye category.

Adam didn't share my misgivings. "We spent the afternoon in bed, Charlotte." He smiled, though it had a rueful tinge to it. "The get-out-of-Dodge-quickly ship sailed hours ago."

He had a point. I relented immediately, and within the hour we were in a cab on our way to JFK airport.

I put absolutely no thought into where I was going until Adam asked me where I was headed. Only then did I begin weighing up my options. One was returning home to Pipers Cove. I had some serious bridges to mend with my father. Over time, my relationship with Alex had buckled. I couldn't pinpoint the moment it became irreparable; all I knew was that the phone calls between us had become few and far between. There was a time that being out of contact would have sent him into a blind panic, but Alex had stopped chasing me, just as I'd begged him to.

He had always considered my marriage to be a mistake of epic proportions, so going home alone was an ordeal I was happy to delay for a while. I decided to go with option two – Mitchell.

I didn't think Adam would want to be privy to that plan, so I purposely kept my answer vague. "I think I'll try and get a flight to Dubai and figure it out from there."

I could see the tension in his jaw as he nodded. My plans from here were on a need-to-know basis. And he no longer needed to know.

By the time we'd reached the airport, booked my ticket and checked my luggage, the pressure of what we were about to do was starting to hit. The end was close and we were both feeling it. I couldn't bear dragging out the agony any longer.

"Well, this is it," I said shakily, lifting my bag off the floor and slinging it over my shoulder. Adam reached for my hands. He stared at me with the intensity that always made me feel as if he was looking beyond my eyes.

I had nothing to lose by questioning him about it. "What do you see when you look at me that way?"

He looked away and I tilted my head, chasing his eyes.

"The same thing I always see."

I feared what that meant. A million possibilities ran through my mind. "Which is?" My voice was tiny.

He leaned down so close that his words hummed against my mouth. "Our happy ending."

I arched my back, buying some distance between us as I tried to make sense of his answer. "It didn't happen, Adam. I was wrong."

His head moved infinitesimally but he spoke with strength. "You weren't wrong about us. Don't leave here thinking I'm not the one for you, Charli. I am. I just haven't proven it yet."

The burning feeling of wanting to kiss him to death pulsed through me. Perhaps noticing the danger he was in, he put me out of my misery by leaning forward and pressing his lips to mine.

It wasn't just a kiss. There was an underlying promise to it - one day he'd find me again, and things would be different.

We weren't giving up. We were just letting go for a while.

***

The three hours I spent in the airport at Dubai while waiting for my connecting flight to Cape Town weren't good. It gave me time alone to think. Grief was inevitable, but I was never going to get through it if I couldn't get over it. I'd been there before and it wasn't something I could endure indefinitely. It was a feeling of heaviness, as if my chest had been encased in concrete and my heart was trying to smash its way back in. Now seemed like the perfect time to find the billet-doux Adam had promised me. Ignoring the stares of passers-by, I upended the contents of my bag onto the floor of the departure lounge, hoping he'd hidden it there. I checked every pocket, and when the last one came up empty, I spiralled to the point of tears.

Out of sight, out of mind was the motto I quickly adopted, starting with the biggest reminder of all. I roughly twisted my wedding ring off my finger, preparing to hide it away in my bag with the other fragments of my New York life. It was the first time I'd taken it off since the day he'd given it to me, and I was struck by how bare my finger felt without it. I rolled the band between my thumb and forefinger, contemplating putting it back on my finger on the grounds that I'd given up enough for one day. Then I noticed something I'd never seen before. The inside of the ring was engraved.

I squinted to read the tiny script: *I will love you always, wherever you are.*

I'd found my billet-doux.

A normal girl would've been devastated at the realisation that Adam had written that message less than a week after marrying me, and would've been cut to the quick by his prediction of failure. But I wasn't normal. I instantly found the deeper meaning, just as he'd made me promise to do.

It didn't matter that he knew I would eventually leave. His resolve to stay in New York made that inevitable, whether we lasted a week, a year or a decade. What mattered was that just as he knew we'd end, no matter how ugly or hurtful it might've been, he was certain he'd still love me long after I was gone.

Printed in Great Britain
by Amazon.co.uk, Ltd.,
Marston Gate.